W9-ACQ-842

Twelve Trains to Babylon

ALSO BY ALFRED CONNABLE

The Tigers of Tammany:
The Men Who Ran New York (with E. Silverfarb)

Twelve Trains to Babylon

ALFRED CONNABLE

MacGibbon & Kee   London

Granada Publishing Limited
First published in Great Britain 1972 by MacGibbon & Kee Ltd
3 Upper James Street London W1R 4BP

ISBN 0 261 10017 3

Printed in Great Britain by Fletcher & Son Ltd,
Norwich

To Roma

How many miles to Babylon?
Threescore miles and ten.
Can I get there by candlelight?
Yes, and back again.

Twelve Trains to Babylon

1.

"Are you there?"

Someone was pounding on the steel door of my loft. It thundered into the rainstorm of a dream.

Waking, I was startled. I had not dreamed in years.

"It's Sugar Red!" For a backslapper of accomplished nonchalance, his tone was peculiarly urgent. "There's a letter!"

"I'll be down for it."

The alarm clock rang as his footsteps receded. He knew my policy. Although I trusted Sugar Red, no one but Joe Hull, my doorman, was allowed past that airtight door.

I shaved, dressed for work, and went downstairs. Joe was asleep, sprawled across my street doorway. I kicked the soles of his shoes. He jumped up immediately.

"Someone came up," I said.

"I heard him."

"What do you think I pay you for?"

"Only Sugar Red, that's who it was."

I watched Sugar Red through the window. He was making the morning bottle count. Sugar Red was a hulking man, constantly perspiring. He had bought out the bar and grill on the first floor of my building about two months after my arrival. Very quickly he became celebrated for his free drinks and fast-energy wine cakes, and for the huge freckles that congregated on one side of his face.

"Do better, will you, Joe?" I said.

"I need breakfast."

"Come on."

Sugar Red looked up as we came in the door. He took the letter from the cash register and placed it in my hand.

"Expecting bad news?" he said. "You look worried."

"Give Joe a coffee and wine cake."

He was guessing. As I read the letter, I knew that my face told him nothing.

> *There are twelve trains to Babylon.*
> *The first leaves tonight.*
>   S

"You've never had mail so early in the morning." Sugar Red frowned sympathetically.

"I have some business today."

Joe laid his head down on the bar and fell back to sleep.

"This is the first time it's come special delivery, only reason I asked," Sugar Red said.

"Would you mind just tending to our coffee?"

As usual, I was required to ponder the letter's implications. That was Steingut's way, his special, invaluable talent. He was always the master of deception through obscurity. I ranked it second only to my own method of deception through trust.

"You know I don't pry." Sugar Red put down the coffee. "I was concerned."

"I appreciate it."

Trust in people. And if you cannot, do not let them know. You cannot survive without the pretense of trust. So I have gone unarmed, rarely startled by a bell or footfall, refusing to hide my eyes behind dark glass, keeping the faith in the morning mail.

Sugar Red resumed the bottle count. Joe's snores were interrupted briefly each time he sniffed the coffee sitting before him. I congratulated myself. It was my skill that had ensured the safety of this familiar moment. How simple it would have been to continue to rent a box at the post office or even, with only a little danger, to have installed my own mailbox. But when Sugar Red offered, I gladly consented to have my mail addressed care of Fisher's Tavern. By placing such trust in Sugar Red and his customers, I worked to engender trust in me, which from close neighbors is imperative.

The mail came from Steingut three, four, sometimes five days a week. It was a manila envelope with no return address. Inside would be a note or cash or nothing. The money averaged about five hundred dollars a week, but this included expenses. If I was not valued as highly as before, at least they kept me alive. During those five years, I had no complaints. The Bowery was a tolerable haven. I had moved there to be alone.

"Not too bad last night," Sugar Red said. "They lifted two bourbons and a gin."

"You should watch the boys more carefully."

"Oh, no. I was put on this earth to help them." He was a devout Catholic. Over the cash register he had posted these words: "Judge thy day by loss, not gain; not by wine drunk but by wine poured forth."

I overpaid him and walked to the subway. On Fridays I traveled crosstown to Penn Station. If I did not make it Friday, Torre expected me Sunday. That was the safeguard.

The doors strained to seal us in. They reached toward each other, twice bumped apart, and then slid gently together. Our heads bobbed in unison as we were hurtled through the tunnel. In the center, most populous car of the subway, the crowd and I read the morning news in silence.

At Penn Station I stepped off and plunged into the angry bustle of inbound commuters, close-shaved and spotless, throttled by neckties in constipated little knots. I made myself an integral part of their rush hour. We hurried by a newsstand. My eyes were caught by the covers of skin magazines. Zuckerman Enterprises. I looked away quickly from the death masks, the plastic teeth clenched tightly in wretched grins.

I stopped at the Long Island schedule racks. It was early, an awkward wait reading the paper. While twenty minutes crept by, the crowd surged forward, fingers jabbing past me like daggers in a sideshow, spearing Hicksvilles and Bay Shores, Freeports and Great Necks.

The time arrived. We had used nearly all of the racks over the years, routinely, counting across the rows by fives and sixes alternately. This time my heart was racing as I counted. I did not know why. My silent count ended at Babylon. We had never used that rack before. I pulled out a schedule and ran the edge of my palm down to the twelfth train: 10:39 A.M.

Something was wrong. I trusted that feeling, for I had a perfect record of success. I worked up from the bottom and reached the 6:59 P.M. Perhaps. I circled the time, replaced the schedule in the back of the rack, and pocketed a second schedule for future reference. As I did so, I noticed a heavyset man in a seersucker suit leaning against a pillar, smiling at me.

It occurred to me that he might be Torre, but I thought better of it. Torre was too skilled to stand in the open. That much I knew, if little else. I did not know who Torre was, man, woman, or child, what he was wearing or carrying, from where he was coming, to where he was going, or what I was truly saying to him. I might even be destroying him. Or there was always the chance that he was destroying me. There was no way of knowing such things. I was no longer in a position to know the import of my actions.

Suddenly I was seized by the temptation to find a seat and watch for Torre. I did not fear a slipup. We had never failed to connect. I simply wanted to see him, to know that he existed, that Torre was flesh and blood.

But how would I know him? Hundreds would reach into that rack for schedules. If I stood close enough to observe which one pulled out the schedule in the back, it would be small reward for great risk. At the most I would feel enjoyment of something that should merely be an assumption unseen. It was foolish even to think about it.

I checked my watch. In two hours Jenny would be awake. I had not seen her for a month. That was the problem — the dreaming, the unsureness, wanting to see the contact. A month without a woman. I would lose myself in Jenny and banish all doubts.

6

"What do you do?" Jenny asked.

"You promised."

This was no dream. Jenny was saying things I could not control. She was lying on her side in that faded green smock, her eyes laughing at me.

"Why do you play a game with me?" she said. But it was she who was playing the game, withholding herself until she had discovered me. "Time is too precious," she said. "Life is too short for that."

"How would you know?" Not yet thirty. A runaway from Harrisburg. Starved for love and importance. She turned away from me and lay face down, dangling a leg off the side of the sleeping couch, wiggling her toes as if she were testing the water off the dock. Somewhere in the room a fly was buzzing around, grating on my nerves. I reached out to touch Jenny's back. My nails caught on dried clay. What fury did she pour into her work that the clay would reach her back? I pushed up the smock and watched her back move with her breathing. It could have been any girl's back. I wanted her, but it could just as easily not have been her.

She slid off the couch and padded over to the icebox in search of orange juice.

"Do you know something?" she said. "I don't think I'm in the mood."

"It's been a month."

"Not for me."

"I'm not interested in that," I said. "I couldn't care less."

"You're not concentrating on me," Jenny said. "You're off somewhere."

Of course it was true, it was always true. It was true the first night, eight months before. Why did she only now sense it? I was not giving her the pretense of attention. That was all she asked, and why should that have been so difficult? She pressed a glass of orange juice into my hand and quickly walked away. I could not help laughing as she slipped off the smock and threw it in the hamper.

7

"That should help my concentration," I said. She was not amused.

"I mean, look," she said, tending to her hairpins mechanically, "it's, like, you just squeeze me into your busy schedule. Not even me. Just the topic. Fornication with a dandy little sculptress. Whether it's one hour or three hours, believe me, it seems like five minutes. All the time you have one hand clutching your shoes."

She was coming around to that question again. It had been stupid of me in the first place to extract from her the promise not to ask. But there were only two women I could afford to seek out: Tina who knew everything about me and Jenny who was too naïve to know anything. The first had proved too dangerous and the second was difficult to find and hold. I should not have made her promise. It was all wrong. It would have been easier to reply with something dull and unconfirmable. A salesman, perhaps. But I was determined to keep her, and this required mystery. I had little else to offer.

"I need you, Jenny," I said with some discomfort, for it was true.

As she crawled back under the sheet, I felt a tightening within me, a knot of pain and foolish desire. There was something appealingly helpless and pathetic about Jenny, her hands and breasts as delicate as a child's.

"I suppose I'm being silly," she said.

"No. You're not." Jenny was right. For that reason I felt sure that eventually I would have to give her up. Whatever it was she wanted, she would get it. Even to be a great sculptress, though I didn't think much of her work. She had done everything for it — run away from home, waited on tables to pay for classes, resisted the lures of theatrical agents. There were several who frequented that restaurant purely to see her. It was when she doused the most persistent one with the soupe du jour that I was first intrigued enough to risk conversation with her beyond "medium rare." The flashing green eyes did it for me, as well as the firm spine and the good aim.

"I don't think you're silly. I think you're wonderful." It embarrassed me to use such flattery in the service of lust. I had encouraged her again. She came to life and propped herself up on an elbow. Her eyes were shining with innocence.

"You understand, don't you?" she said. "I never thought I could give myself to anyone. But I can and it's terrible. I do love you."

Her mouth signaled more desperation than love. Her tongue felt molten, as if she would burn my dreams, devour my secret. For a moment I was almost frightened by that kiss. Just as I was about to pull away, she lay back, kicking her legs in the air like an infant asking to be held and comforted.

Then, at the worst possible moment, she twisted away.

"Now tell me!" she squealed.

"What, for God's sake!"

"What you do!"

Poor, helpless girl. The little bitch. She hadn't meant a word of it. And I deserved it.

"Afterward," I said.

"Suit yourself." She reached out savagely, without a trace of tenderness, rushing, a desecration of love that would lead to my confession, when she would have me. As we pressed together, I felt a searing pinch.

"You're a desert today," I said.

"Try, darling." She was punishing me. It had never happened before.

"Let's wait," I said.

"Oh no you don't!" She pushed hard, controlling the pace, until all feeling was squeezed out of me.

When I opened my eyes, Jenny was sitting up, filing her nails, celebrating my humiliation.

"I work for an organization," I said.

"How dull. What kind?"

"Chain letters."

"You're kidding!"

"Nobody gets very rich on it."

"Oh, my," she mocked. "Are you very important in it? You must be."

"We're all important."

She lay back, smiling. "And what do you do, darling?"

I could not renege on the bargain.

"I receive the letter. He sends one letter to me and a different letter to the next man. I work out the information and pass it on. The next man puts the two things together and passes something on to another man. It's like a game."

"Mm, poor darling." She laid her head on my chest. "And don't you ever see any people in your work?"

"Sometimes. Different people. I meet them, but I never see them again. Lately, it's just been the letters."

"How long does this chain go on?"

"I don't know. There may be six men, sixty, six hundred."

"I really don't understand."

"That's all there is to it. And that's my end of the bargain, Jenny."

In victory she was soft and moist, writhing like a kitten, oblivious to the fact that she knew more than she should. Poor, ignorant girl. She came in a flash.

"Where have you been?" Thaddeus said as I sat down. "I'm hungry." His fingers were racing through a thick, yellowed volume of braille.

"I was delayed by a girl."

He snorted and continued reading. I ordered our beef and ale. On bad days it was my custom to lunch at McSorley's with Thaddeus. I had met him there five years before, shortly after I moved to the Bowery. He was always there. I did not know who he was but I liked him. He was my one superstition. Others had priests, rabbis, psychiatrists, wives, gurus, oracles, or even friends. The chief value of Thaddeus was that he could not see. Jenny knew too many of the wrong things, the visual things.

"It was like making love in a grave," I persisted, hoping the metaphor would catch his interest.

"I said I was hungry."

"You should try women," I said.

"Does it help? I can't remember."

"It makes one feel even hungrier."

"You always cheer me up," Thaddeus said.

"I feel today like there is nothing inside me, as if my flesh were stretched over a drum. It makes me afraid."

"How was the girl?"

"She has lovely legs. She —" The ales arrived. The waiter looked at me curiously, I thought. Thaddeus quickly downed his mugful. I ordered another.

"And the girl?" Thaddeus said. He continued to read but he was breathing a little harder.

"She does her best," I said.

"Good Christ. You never trust me with the details."

He drank the second ale.

"Well, it isn't love you need," he said.

"No," I said. "It's that I have no love to give. I can't fill up this emptiness. What's missing is me. There is no me."

"That's what interests me," Thaddeus said. "That's why I let you buy my lunch."

He tore into the beef the minute it was set before him. After a few immense swallows, he wiped his mouth, the customary signal that he was preparing to pontificate.

"Do you know what is the supreme triumph of woman?" Thaddeus licked his lips and piled more beef into his mouth, gobbling as he talked. "Presenting herself as a gift to someone strange and ungrateful. Like you. That's the most selfless act of life." A slice of beef nearly fell off his fork into the sawdust on the floor. He secured it nimbly. "Or it can be the most selfish. Maybe you got yourself a selfish one. I know the type. Cool and naked on a blood-hot summer morning while I sat here starving. Disgusting. She disgusts me. You're beginning to disgust me."

He laughed smugly as he sensed my eyes on him.

"Of course," he said, "it's been obvious to me for some time that your life is a joke. But as with other jokes, I suppose it must be taken seriously. After all, there's little enough to it. Birth, illusion, marriage, disillusionment, betrayal, death. I have never heard the slightest evidence from you that you were born or that you had any illusions. You were never married. You can't be disillusioned. So all that's left for you are the last two. That's another reason why I let you buy my lunch."

I ordered him another ale.

"Do you know what the difference is between you and me?" Thaddeus said. "I am perfectly content to sit here on my peaceful cloud and listen to the world creaking on its axis. But you have to be in there mixing with it. Only from the periphery, mind you. You're not really in it and you're not really out of it. That's the danger. That's why you're frightened now." He dropped his napkin on the table. "All right, I've had my lunch. Now get the hell out of here."

By three o'clock the boys who could afford it had begun staggering into Fisher's Tavern. When Sugar Red was behind the bar, he would set them up for one if they pledged to buy a second. His assistants were less charitable. As I came in from McSorley's, the boys were awaiting his return, watching a television program called *To Tell the Truth*. The naïveté of its panelists amazed me, but I enjoyed it nonetheless. There were three contestants pretending to the same identity. The panel tried to guess which was the real person. This was obvious from the outset simply by the manner in which the contestants pronounced the name. Something lurked in the eyes, on the lips, in the voices, to reveal the two liars. Would they be more careful, I wondered, if their lives depended on it?

"He's back!"

A grateful chorus rose as Sugar Red rushed in the door. He worked his way through the crowd, slapping backs, patting shoulders, squeezing biceps. For each of the boys there was a special, knowledgeable greeting.

"Set 'em up!" he ordered. A beloved philanthropist, Sugar Red. And an enterprising man. He worked two jobs, I had no doubt of that, but he never complained about the rise in the welfare rolls. No one knew or really cared what the other business was that caused him occasional streaks of irregular hours at the bar. But about Sugar Red's past there was considerable speculation among the customers. It was said by some that he was once a whaler out of Newfoundland. That tale can no longer be believed. My concern was only that he kept my mail behind the bar and imposed no obligations.

"Anything come later in the mail?" I asked when he reached me.

"That was it," he said. "Hope it wasn't bad news from home."

"No, nothing."

"Hey, whaddya think of that?"

A shapely contestant was fixed in the television eye. The boys went wild.

"Look at that cow!"

"Bend over, baby!"

The noises of the farm were deafening. I turned off my hearing and found myself still dwelling on the letter. For some reason, I was actually excited by this assignment. Perhaps it was only because I knew so little. "There are twelve trains to Babylon. The first . . ." I should have been told more. Never had I been given so little to act upon. Either something was wrong somewhere or they were trusting too much to my ingenuity.

Until that Friday, I had considered each letter from Steingut as the sole piece of knowledge for the day. The day, circumscribed by one image, existed alone, without past or future. Nothing else had real meaning or function, even if I dared remember or foretell. I would know only one thing. Although even of that I could not be positive, I knew I must bet my life on it.

Everything changed with this message. That feeling was strange to confront. I felt certain, with no clear reason for certainty, that it would involve many days, ahead of me and perhaps behind me.

I stared into the mirror behind the bar, seeking a clue. But all I saw, to my great relief, was a face quite dead, devoid of expression, and better yet, not appearing to mask any life of the barest interest. No tension to provoke curiosity. Not an avocado asking to be peeled. A face twice transformed without a trace of scar tissue.

The skin pale, smooth, close-shaved, like the commuters'. The blond hair of an American, a Swede, a Briton, a German. The eyes brown, bright, at times too intense for safety. But I am constantly aware of this and can dull them at will. The figure trim but not taut, its stance suggesting neither activity nor indolence. Not tall nor too short — five feet, ten inches — unobtrusive in the crowd, a being that can appear and vanish without detection. The clothes drab, undistinguished, indistinguishable. I stared through the eyes of the crowd, into the mirror and from the mirror. I could be anyone, anything. Nobody. Nothing.

But now the eyes had become piercing. If I should make such an error along the street, strangers would surely speak to me. Perhaps only about the weather, but that would be too much. I would have to look at them or they would take notice. Worse, I would have to speak to them. And this, though I have flattened every intonation, is still the most dangerous game of all. Talk of the weather leads to talk of the day's events, personal feelings, life itself. The longer the conversation, the more difficult it is to extricate oneself without leaving an impression. One's leavetaking must not seem abrupt, yet it must be swift and irrevocable. A bus, an appointment, things of the instant are necessary. And these cannot always be manufactured with ease.

For this reason, it is necessary to dull the eyes even in the relative privacy of a tavern mirror. The habit of introspection, even if only occasionally indulged, leaves its traces throughout the working day. While it is essential to see oneself, it must always be through the eyes of the crowd. Thus I was disturbed to discover myself that afternoon, staring not at the man in the mirror but at me. It was through my own eyes that I was staring, as if I were looking within me.

"There are twelve trains to Babylon." The words seemed familiar. Vaguely, I sensed that somewhere, years ago, I had either read them or heard them spoken. But I could not understand my impatience to know more. Knowing more, I could only feel more. More of the sick feeling as I stared into my own eyes. I must have known that this one was more important than anything before. There was no other explanation for being afraid. I did not know fear of failure because I had never failed.

"Here you go, friend."

Sugar Red's face eclipsed mine in the mirror. He was looking at me with concern but he did not intrude. He set down a vodka. The clink of the glass scattered my fears. It was foolish to dwell on the message. Perhaps, as with letters between anxious lovers, I was searching for meanings that weren't there.

The laughter and shouts in the bar restored my senses. Yet when I looked around, I felt as if I were seeing through new eyes. Fisher's Tavern. McSorley's. My loft, Jenny's room, Penn Station, the library, the airports. Little by little the world had shrunk to these peculiar settings. They had become my stage, where I could assume the being of another person. And by so doing, without knowing the precise chain of events, I was certain that I was helping even more millions of people than before. Yes, that was the key: actually to be another person. Far better than the fakery of actors or prime ministers. This was right on the line. Thaddeus was wrong. It was I, not he, who had found the way. To be a part and apart. I was sure that Thaddeus was wrong.

I went upstairs and showered. But the dread did not wash away. "Where is the 6:59 to Babylon?" I heard myself say. For sanity's sake, it is important to speak alone, but never to oneself, always to the ear of the crowd. "Where is the train?" I asked the bathroom mirror, and instantly I felt the warmth of pleasure. I studied my eyes, the expression of my mouth, as I spoke the words. Nothing was shown. Friendliness, curiosity, worry, none of these. Only the casual quest for passingly useful information. "Where is the 6:59 to Babylon?"

In the voice there is no accent of any kind, a point of workmanship in which I take special pride. It is the speech of no region, no background, no occupation or concern. Which has also disturbed me at times. It does not sound real. Yet I know that it can never be remembered nor, at the time, is it worth remarking.

At the time. And this is important. The crowd is less attuned to the details of attitude than one would naturally assume. It knows nothing of the painstaking craft that created the voice, the costume, the manner. But while it is not aware of successful minutiae, it will subliminally note the smallest error. This discovery cannot take place at the time or survival is out of the question. But later it might be pieced together and the crowd will remember. That, too, could be the end.

There is always the possibility, moreover, that you may confuse the contact with the crowd. Such mistakes have been known to happen. It is usually the fault of someone who is not taking the risks. The penalty must be paid by those on the scene, for public disclosure renders them immediately worthless. I had never questioned that principle. You do not seek justice on this earth without tolerating the injustice of the search. When that injustice comes your way, it is best to reflect on others. Who knows what you have done to them, in one second, without knowing it?

"Hey! Get out of here!"

It was Joe Hull's voice. I walked to the open window and looked down on the street. The weekend invasion had begun. Two A-Trainers, sleek and brutal pickpockets in dark glasses, down on the subway for a night of easy prey, were poking umbrellas into the ribs of an old boy in a nearby doorway, sounding the depth of his sleep. Joe advanced on them, waving his arms, and they moved further down the sidewalk.

Across the street a busload of tourists was pouring into Sammy's Bowery Follies. An Ivy League couple separated from the group and strolled toward the corner, observing the boys with fascination. A paddy wagon pulled up to the curb near them. The police began to clear the sidewalk for the tourists, slapping the feet of sleepers with nightsticks. Only three of the boys, without money or identification, were hauled off for a night in the Tombs. Most had already panhandled enough for a safe night in the flophouse next door, or would risk being rolled in the Men's Shelter.

Joe knew a good mark. As the paddy wagon moved off, he crossed the street to accost the Ivy League couple. He returned to his post with new riches. A heavyset man, who was clearly neither tourist nor A-Trainer, was waiting for him. He began to question Joe. My suspicion was confirmed that this was not a lucky day. The two men disappeared into the doorway below. I heard them clomping up the long, steep stairway to my loft. Joe knocked on the door. For several minutes I did not answer. But Joe knew I was there. I could not appear to betray his trust.

"Gentleman to see you," Joe said as I opened the door. He left quickly and the man walked in, quite comfortably at home. He wore a blue-and-white striped seersucker suit. His black shoes were shined to glass. He had a peculiar little grin and an unconvincing twinkle in his gray eyes. It did not take long to read his face.

This was the first time Joe had slipped. Normally, he had an excellent eye.

"May I sit down?" the stranger asked, sitting before I replied.

"Your calling card, please."

"Mansfield." He offered his credentials. A Treasury Man. I smiled as hospitably as possible.

"I keep the counterfeit machine in the bathroom," I said.

He sat smiling at me, as if he knew me quite well, an old friend come to call.

"I hate to bother you with this," he said, "but do you happen to know a man by the name of Emil Zuckerman?"

"Never heard of him."

"What about a man called Steingut?"

"No."

"Torre?"

"I'm afraid, Mr. Mansfield, you have confused me with someone else."

"Katrina Athenasios?"

"No."

"You don't know Tina Athenasios?"

"Was that her name? I knew a girl named Tina many years ago but not very well."

"What about Thaddeus Jones?"

"Yes. A friend I have lunch with."

"And Sugar Red Fisher?"

"Oh, yes, the bartender downstairs."

"You see," Mansfield said, the little grin still stuck on his face, "I know quite a bit about you."

"Are you sure it's me you want to talk to?"

He reached into his pocket, watching me closely. I made certain that my eyes did not follow his motion. He removed his hand. There was nothing in it.

"What were you doing at the Long Island Railroad this morning?" he said.

"Oh, that," I said. "I'm thinking of going away this weekend. What were you doing there?"

"To Babylon?" This time something did come out of his pocket. It was the schedule.

Or was it another schedule? I reached for it, making a supreme effort to keep my hand steady.

"Yes, this is it," I said. "To Babylon." My heart was pounding. I turned the page. There was no pencil mark around the 6:59. The man was whistling in the dark. He had nothing.

"What line are you in, Jon?"

"You ask a great many questions."

"Golly, gee." Mansfield's grin widened. "I forgot to advise you of your rights."

"Am I under arrest?"

"No."

"Then go right ahead," I said. "I know my rights. I have nothing of interest to hide."

"Do you want to come with me, or shall we talk here?"

"I'm kind of a homebody," I said. "Maybe I'm waiting for a telephone call."

"Where's the phone?"

"And maybe I'm not."

"Why is that?"

"What?"

"That you have no phone?"

"No need."

"Wouldn't it be useful in your business?"

He lit a slim cigar, puffing and admiring it, relishing minutes as if he had time to burn.

"Tell me," he said, "what is your profession that you're so afraid to have a phone that might be tapped?"

"I just live here. Like the others."

Slowly and very casually, he reached inside his coat and produced a revolver which he proceeded to aim directly at my eyes. It seemed somewhat melodramatic. But I could not hold back the perspiration from my forehead.

"Has this ever happened to you?" he said.

"No." I was surprised at the hoarse sound of my voice.

"Do you know how simple it is to pull a trigger?"

"No."

He planted the cigar in his mouth and pulled a quarter from his pocket, tossed it in the air, and caught it quite skillfully on the back of his hand.

"Sorry," he said, replacing the revolver in his shoulder holster. "I don't know what came over me."

He stood up and walked to the door.

"I'll be around," he said.

For those first few moments I was more puzzled than frightened.

How much did he really know? Why did he tip his hand before he knew enough? If he knew anything at all about me, he should know that once I was aware, it was impossible to follow me.

And then the fear struck: Zuckerman. He had begun with Zuckerman. That would trace me back nine years. Tina. I had not seen her in five years. Torre. Steingut. Mansfield knew a good deal. Too little to make his case, but enough to be dangerous. Not he himself. Far worse than that, there was a peril which he could not realize. I had now acquired a shadow and the others would know it. Somehow, through no fault of my own, I had become the weak link in the chain, endangering all the others. There would be no room for sentiment. Gratitude for my service, appreciation of my talent, were no longer relevant. I was in an instant wholly expendable.

I stood at the window and looked down. Mansfield was questioning Sugar Red in front of the tavern. Sugar Red was saying very little. He kept nodding and looking up. He seemed somehow sympathetic about it all. A strange and terrible feeling came over me that I had been murdered in my sleep and solicitous relatives were whispering in the next room, making preparations for the funeral. Suddenly, for the first time, I wanted to live.

2.

Zuckerman was my first contact. I met him on the day I came in. Or, more precisely, the morning after. For me the delay was the best part of it.

He was living that summer in a bark-shingled house on the Great South Beach. Or so I had been told in advance. It would be perched on a sand dune, they said, toward the eastern end of Fire Island, encircled by scrub pine and bayberry, without benefit of electricity, telephone, or ferry service. On the map the island appeared as a sandbar supporting a number of communities which declined in population as they stretched further east from the city. Beyond the easternmost squatters' shacks and fishermen's huts, in the widest, most secluded section of the island, was Zuckerman. I admired his courage, vacationing on an island with no certain escape route. Or perhaps it was only a fine intelligence that gave him no cause to fear.

The captain was concerned that we could not see the house. When he lowered the binoculars, I saw trouble coming from the nervous way he tugged at the visor on his stained blue hat.

"I can't let you off," he said at last.

"But you must," I said. "It has to be there."

"Too risky," he said.

"Don't worry," I said. "I'll find him."

It took great persuasion to convince him. He, of course, underestimated my abilities. All I required was a description and I could find a man on an island. And the description I had was not likely to be duplicated: six feet three, massive shoulders, totally bald, chain smoker, most likely attired in baggy corduroy trousers and bright-striped jersey, and best of all, constantly guarded by a dwarf wielding a bicycle chain. The captain laughed when I imparted this improbable description. He agreed I could not miss.

We arrived in broad daylight when the Coast Guard would be least alert for us. Our Stars and Stripes were flying high. Two airplanes nosed in our direction as we came within the limit. One was obviously an inexperienced student, the other a Reserve jet on a weekend spree. Both dipped their wings and we gaily waved back. About an hour after they passed, I stripped off my fisherman's gear, shook hands with everyone, and pushed off in the rubber raft. When I looked back, the trawler had already turned tail and the captain had gone below, leaving me alone on the sea.

From two miles out, I could see the length of the island under the brilliant August sun. The surf was running low and hundreds of dots were visible in the water near the shore. Approaching closer, I saw through my binoculars the water towers of several communities, big homes along the dunes, and then perhaps fifty bathers off an area marked on my map as Davis Park. Americans. Children, young couples, elderly shell-seekers, came into view. I started to paddle further east to avoid the crowd. But then the joy of the moment struck me. Suppose I were simply to swim in and join them? There they were, in pure contentment, peacefully frolicking in the sea, dozing in the sand, the very people I was assigned to save. Why should I not be part of them?

I dumped the binoculars and two canteens, deflated the raft, and knifed it into shreds, jamming the wads of rubber into the pockets of my shorts. This gave me some buoyancy but the swim was longer than I had expected. A cramp seized my right thigh. I rubbed it out with little trouble. I flipped over on my back and stared up at the sun. It was the same sun that had burned through the clouds in Italy, roasted the acropoli of Greece, blazed down white-hot in Turkey. The same! A miracle, perhaps, that the world and all its inhabitants were bound together so tightly by that common sight of energy and origin. I felt a sudden exhilaration and began swimming swiftly again. The mood was shattered by an earsplitting whistle.

Standing atop a white tower on the shore, a slim young man in a blue swimsuit was waving at me in a frenzy. It was my first moment of terror over here. My God! I thought I knew America, but did I know enough? The customs, the nuances, the complexities of language, the contemporary assumptions, could change from month to month. There were basic elements to belonging which were not noticed unless lacked. Like the young man on the tower. Who was he? What was he? What did he want with me? I laughed, chiefly at myself for the odd feat of recovering composure while dog-paddling in the Atlantic. He was a lifeguard, of course. A harmless philanthropist concerned only for my safety. I waved to him, perhaps a little too eagerly, seeking to communicate that I was coming in. Amazingly, he sat down abruptly and turned his attention to a group of children wading near the shore. I had succeeded in my first confrontation with the world's most puzzling people.

About fifty yards off shore I dove underwater, came up for air, and dove again, this time gliding close by the thrashing thighs and feet of the more daring swimmers. Ascending to the surface once more, I saw that the surf which appeared so low from far out was in fact quite high, blocking my view of the beach with each powerful charge. I turned again on my back and imagined myself a piece of driftwood, swept straight across from the coast of Portugal, soon to be deposited on a gay and innocent shoreline. The game amused me. I, the helpless, inanimate traveler, had only to lie there, moved by each rolling swell another few feet toward this unknown country. In the identity of driftwood I found for those moments a kind of purity. The strength of the sea pushed me back and forth, while I, impotent and uncomplaining, lay there comfortably without need of decision, without hope or fear, without mission.

The sounds of laughter and the crashing surf intruded on my game. I turned over and found myself atop a giant wave. Too late to recover, I was hurled down to the bottom, jerked over, and dragged back by the angry undercurrent. I let myself go limp and glided up to the surface, only to see above me another huge, curling breaker preparing to fall on my head. I stood up on the sand and dove into the wave, surfacing through the gentle sea beyond the breaking point. Quickly, I glanced up at the lifeguard tower. Was there anything strange about my actions? Was this the way they did it here? Once, long ago, I made contact with a Russian posing as a Polish clerk by observing the way he fingered his cigarette, and with another by the rhythm of his arms swinging in time with his feet. What about swimming? But no. The lifeguard and the crowd were completely uninterested in my cavorting. I had become one of them.

The next wave thrust me forward for the final push. I skimmed along on its power, scraping my chest on the sandy bottom, until I came to rest at the edge of the shore. After the long journey, the sudden stop was a pleasant shock. I stared at my fellow Americans. The waves washed in behind me, cooling my aching legs. The driftwood had arrived.

It was all so absurd, I felt like dancing, singing, laughing, shouting with the crowd. What would I say to them? "Hello, friends! Here I am! From out of the sea, come to save your souls!" But I was too exhausted even to stand up. I lay there numbly, watching two children building a castle of sand.

My attention was distracted by a pair of deeply tanned legs only a few feet in front of me. What foolishness! I rubbed my eyes and shook the water from my ears. I looked again and saw skintight white shorts, then a loose gold pullover. Long coils of coal-black hair, a chin quite broad and prominent, a smile of half-amusement, a large, Grecian nose. Clouded eyes, not really seeing me, yet staring directly at me. She was very young. I must have seen five thousand sunsets she had missed. Why was she staring at me? Who was she? Mother Earth. I had crawled out of the sea into the arms of Mother Earth, who was only a child. I remember everything about that first sight of Tina. How foolish that day was.

"Katrina!"

The voice was sharp, worried, gruffly affectionate. I surmised that it belonged to the short, dumpy figure moving toward us along the moonlit beach.

"Oh my God," Tina said. "Mrs. Poulakidas still thinks I'm a child."

"Your mother?" I asked.

"Our neighbor in town. Mother drags her everywhere."

Mrs. Poulakidas arrived, huffing and wheezing.

"Did you not hear me, Katrina?"

"I heard you."

"Your poor mother is worried."

"I'll bet. She's off in the dunes with that maitre d'." Tina laughed, easily and lightly, but there was something strange beneath, a razor's edge of bitterness.

Mrs. Poulakidas did not laugh. "Who is he?" she said, as if my credentials as a rapist were established, but nothing else.

Tina turned toward me helplessly.

"Pellston," I said. "Ralph Pellston."

"What have you been doing with Katrina all day?"

"Stop it, Mrs. P.!" Tina cried out, embarrassed at this exposé of her sheltered existence.

"Katrina, you will come with me this minute," Mrs. P. commanded.

"No."

"What did you say?"

"I said no."

"You've done this to her!" Mrs. P. wagged an accusing forefinger inches from my nose. "Who are you? I do not remember ever seeing you here."

"This is my first time," I said.

"Your occupation, please."

"Salesman."

"Of what?"

"The product wouldn't interest you."

"Mrs. P., I will not allow this interrogation," Tina cut in, to my relief. "Please go back to the cottage. Tell Mother, when she returns, that I will be home before midnight."

Mrs. P., muttering dark Greek curses, looked after us as we walked off. I suspected that this was not the first time she had played this game and lost. I was correct.

"She's never been the same since I lost my virginity at fifteen," Tina said matter-of-factly.

We walked very slowly, our rhythm attuned to the surf and the breeze in the sea grass.

"You're clever," Tina said. "I didn't even notice you hadn't told me your name."

"Why would that be clever?"

"There's some reason you didn't want me to know it."

"You didn't tell me yours. Tina is not Katrina."

"Katrina Athenasios." She sighed. "Wouldn't you be unhappy about a name like that?"

"I like it."

"It's not me. Your name doesn't sound like you, either. And you don't strike me as a salesman. And I also don't believe that you haven't been out here before."

"Why?"

"You seem so at home."

"I meant to ask you," I said quickly. "Does your mother know you're out?" It was my first American Remark. I was proud of myself.

"She's used to it," Tina said. "Mrs. P. has taken it upon herself to reclaim my soul. Poor dear. It's too late."

I started to reach for her hand. Something prevented me. Would it be so strange after all those hours? Wasn't that the custom?

"What do you do, Tina?"

"Just finished college."

"Nonsense."

"I'm twenty. And don't bother telling me how beautiful I am. I won't believe you."

"You're too young to lie about your age already."

"Is that the impression you get? That I lie?"

26

"I'm not sure."

"Well, I don't. But why do people think I do?"

"I have the impression you're hiding something," I said, purely to divert her attention from any suspicions about me, and it worked.

"That's right," she said. "And I don't know what it is. I don't lie. Not at all. But I don't tell the truth either. Usually, I say what's farthest from my mind. Do you think I'm strange?"

"A little."

"Of course I am. I've got demons inside me and I don't know what they are. They make me lose control. Sometimes I talk too much, sometimes I won't talk at all, and sometimes I don't . . ."

"What?"

"Finish sentences."

It was low tide. The sand was firm under our toes. I watched it pass beneath us as we walked.

"You hardly ever begin any," Tina said. "I suppose that's what intrigues me."

"What am I supposed to say? You don't want me to tell you you're beautiful."

"But aren't you going to anyway? Everyone does. It comes with the proposition."

"No."

She kicked at the sand. "Damn me. Why do I say these things?"

"I'll bite. Why?"

"Because I want you to tell me."

"That you're beautiful?"

"Yes."

"It's too obvious."

"Then you recognize my face," she said.

"No."

"Of course not, why should you? When did you last see the cover of *Seventeen*? It really doesn't matter. I won't believe I'm beautiful until I make the cover of *Vogue*."

"What's *Vogue*?"

"Are you joking?"

It was my first error.

"Yes, I'm joking," I said.

"Can you believe it?" Tina said. "I really want that. I'm serious. I need it to believe what everybody says. And why should I care? Do you know what I truly am? At heart? An ugly little poet, that's what I am. But only one man knows. My English professor. And how do I know he doesn't have a lech for me?"

"It must be a problem," I said.

"Do you think he does?"

"He might."

"Well, I decided that modeling was the path of easiest resistance. You don't have to question your talent. And the money is there, too. Do you have any other suggestions? Would I make a good prostitute?"

"Stay with the modeling."

"What's that supposed to mean? I think I'd probably be a wonderful prostitute. If you're going to be sad, why not give yourself something to be sad about? I'm not happy with the modeling. I could do it for another twenty years, but then what? Where am I then?"

"That's a long time away."

"Maybe I won't last. I get terrible depressions. Sometimes I think I'm a candidate for the nuthouse. Or maybe I'll end up a dope addict. Wouldn't that be ridiculous, getting needlemarks all over my pretty little ass? Go ahead, tell me I'm pretty."

"There's no need."

"Tell me anyway."

"You are beautiful, Tina."

"In what way?" She laughed, and this time I did reach for her hand. Our fingers interlaced tightly as if we had walked this way, and held each other this way, since childhood.

"Your toes," I said. "I like the way they bounce off the sand."

"What about my eyes? My hair? My nose?"

Peculiar. Were they all like this? I had heard strange things about American girls, but I had never walked the beach with one, felt her fingers gripping mine, listened to her pleas for flattery. Was this the right approach? Not to win her, but to win acceptance of me as an American.

Enough of this. I was too uncertain of the conventions to continue. I turned toward the sea and pulled her along. We walked out until it reached up to our knees. Above us was, I suspected, an astronomer's paradise. A clear, black hemisphere dotted by millions of stars and planets. Tina caught her breath as a shooting star raced across our view, down to the sea.

"Stars do not die in peace," she whispered.

"No. And neither will this earth."

It was not necessary to talk any more. From that moment. Now it seems like a foolish fairy tale. Yet that was exactly the way it was with Tina. What an odd feeling it was that night to ask for her telephone number in the city. I felt I should have known it by heart. And when I left her at the edge of Davis Park, I did not have to promise to call.

The sun came blazing out of the sea. I had fallen asleep on the dune. It was a startling awakening. I immediately set out walking east. The strange surroundings had not taken me aback. I was startled at myself, that there was no surprise at being here. I felt I already belonged here.

It would, of course, be disturbing to Zuckerman that I was arriving so late. He was a magazine publisher, probably obsessive on the matter of deadlines. But I would tell him the truth. And after all, what right had he to assume that after forty-three days of travel, I would arrive precisely on the appointed day? Secretly, he was probably intrigued by me, perhaps even fearful of me, living his life of ease on the beach, envying me for the terrors I had survived.

Zuckerman and Crackjaw were standing high on a dune. The wind was up and Zuckerman cut an imposing figure up there, with his great eagle face, his flapping corduroy trousers, the muscular dwarf at his side. From a distance they struck me as more effeminate than menacing. I hoped that I would not be stranded with them on this island. I was anxious to see the city, to settle in the crowd, to begin my work.

It occurred to me that a diabolical opposition could have concocted this bizarre scene of a pseudo-Zuckerman and a pseudo-Crackjaw. But even if they had gone to such lengths, it would not have succeeded. I knew absolutely nothing about the operation, and would know nothing but what I was told. Nor would anything be learned from me about other places and other times. That was the invulnerable beauty of it.

I continued trudging along, making deep imprints in the wet sand, pretending to ignore my hosts, for it was clearly their risk to make the contact. If they were any good at all, they would find a subterfuge to read the palm of my hand.

"Hello there!" Zuckerman's voice was booming but pleasant.

I waved at them and continued on my way. Crackjaw slid down the dune and waddled toward me. He carried the bicycle chain playfully, like a big toy.

"Hi," Crackjaw said.

"Hi yourself." I seemed to impress him with such mastery of colloquial nonchalance. Or perhaps it was simply the lack of accent.

Crackjaw had a warm smile and an intelligent look to him. I felt slightly foolish to have imagined him as the monstrous assistant to the mad doctor.

"Say, I wonder," he said, "which way is it to Davis Park? We seem to have lost our bearings."

They were the correct words. But it remained for him to initiate the exchange.

"The way I figure it," Crackjaw said, "this way is west." He turned over his right hand to reveal an ink drawing of a compass in the palm with the arrow pointing east.

"Yes, I believe you're right," I said. I waited for him to make the move.

Crackjaw smiled. "What's that you're hiding, some kind of shell?" He turned over my left hand. The drawings were identical. He laughed and waved to Zuckerman, who instantly came running down the dune. They both seemed genuinely glad to see me. I liked them.

"Welcome, my friend," Emil Zuckerman said.

We shook hands warmly and began walking east along the shore. Zuckerman talked incessantly, a little overexcitedly, as if, with me in tow, the atmosphere was heady. It was all pleasantries, no questions, not a word about my trip or what lay ahead, but a torrent of words about the tides, the stars, the shifting sand, the changing face of the island he loved. Crackjaw struggled to keep pace with us, occasionally glancing up at my face with curiosity, then shifting his eyes behind us, scanning the long stretch of empty sand.

It must have been a mile before Zuckerman asked me the first question, and it was as I had anticipated. "You're a little late, aren't you, Jon? We were up all night watching for you." But he made it a pleasant inquiry, with more concern for me than anything else.

"Sorry," I said, surprised at my apology. "I met a girl down there."

"Good," Zuckerman said to my amazement, and they both laughed good-naturedly. "Then you've already received your naturalization."

The two men turned in toward the dune and began climbing backward, kicking sand into their footprints. I followed their procedure. From the crest of the dune, I could see that the island was quite wide at this point. Beyond the hollows of the inland dunes, I caught a glimpse of a rabbit scurrying into a thick growth of pine trees. Further beyond, a lonely marshland was crossed by a boardwalk leading to a protected cove, and beyond that was Great South Bay, its waters sparkling in the sunlight.

"That's Long Island," Zuckerman said, pointing to the farthest shore.

"I know."

He swung his arm toward a blue cabin cruiser in the cove.

"That's Crackjaw's boat. You know all about that, too, I suppose." He sounded disappointed.

"No," I said. It seemed to cheer him up.

"And over there is the house." I followed his gesture but saw nothing. They watched my face with amusement. We walked perhaps forty yards along the backside of the dune and were practically on the front porch before I saw it. The house was not, as I had been told in bad translation, bark-shingled, nor was it perched on the dune. It was made entirely of driftwood, a marvelous creation which blended with the sand.

"Built it myself," Zuckerman said. "Crackjaw and me. Everything here came in from the sea. Like you, my friend."

I smiled, for Zuckerman could not know of the game I had played in which I, like the walls of his house, had floated in helplessly on the waves.

"Used to have a radio here," he said, opening the screen door, "but they asked me to give it up. Too dangerous these days."

I wondered how far they really trusted Zuckerman. They gave me no reason to believe their faith was infinite. Perhaps it was a measure of their failing confidence that I had been sent in.

Inside the cottage was a tiny living room with crude driftwood furniture, two bedrooms, a kitchen with an old gas refrigerator and a pump over the sink. Zuckerman motioned me to a chair and seated himself at a wobbly table beneath a hanging kerosene lamp. Crackjaw disappeared into a bedroom. He emerged a few minutes later, grunting and cursing, dragging a duffel bag along the floor.

"Your stuff," Zuckerman said. I opened the duffel and was disappointed to find only worn workclothes, toilet articles, sheets and towels.

"Were you expecting a tuxedo?" Crackjaw said.

"Don't worry," Zuckerman assured me. "You will have money for clothes." He tossed over a clipped wad of bills. "One thousand in tens and twenties. The rest will arrive in the mail once or twice a week. Keep it with you. No bank account. I don't want your signature anywhere."

He surprised me with his efficient tone, this strange giant of a man who wandered the sands in search of driftwood. Perhaps, after all, he was more effective than they thought. I began to trust him.

I went outside and showered under the water tank warmed by the sun. I noticed for the first time that there was dried blood on my wrist. The metal band on my watch had scraped off skin, probably when I rode the last wave onto the beach. I had not felt the pain. It was a good watch, my father's watch, which had survived far more than water and sand. I realized at that moment how much it meant to me. I should not have brought it over here. It was only a small flaw in costume but, nonetheless, a risky gesture to sentiment.

When I returned inside, Zuckerman and Crackjaw were seated at the table, running magnifying glasses over contact sheets of photographs. Occasionally, Crackjaw would nod his head gleefully, whereupon Zuckerman would make marks with a red grease pencil.

"You'll have to pardon us," Zuckerman said. "I have three magazines going to press Monday, two more on Tuesday. Crackjaw must transport these to the city within the hour. Over there is some excellent Jamaican rum. We're out of ice."

I sat down in my towel and watched them work. The rum was terrible. It was black and warm. Still, the hour was pleasant enough. Zuckerman and Crackjaw labored over the photographs while I loafed, listening to the distant pounding of the surf, remembering the walk along the beach with Tina. I would like America.

"These two, both of these," Crackjaw said. Zuckerman appeared to rely on the dwarf's judgment. Perhaps he saw him as typical of his readership. When Crackjaw leered, Zuckerman knew he had connected.

Crackjaw threw one sheet into the wastebasket and began another. "Here. This one."

"The waist is too slim, but I will accept," Zuckerman said. "Find me another with a fat waist."

"Yeah, yeah." Crackjaw glided the glass over another column of the sheet. "Here, you see? The tongue out, too."

Zuckerman marked the picture and they continued. For all the interest they showed in me, I might as well have still been floating on the sea.

"Not one in the whole damned issue cupping her headlights," Zuckerman said with righteous irritation. I found it difficult to conceal my amusement at these two adults, genus *Americanus*, poring over the images of unclad females with purely professional ardor. The whole scene was quite insane. What was I doing there? I chuckled to myself and swallowed another dose of the awful rum.

"One on the haunches now," Zuckerman said. "No, too low. She's on her elbows and knees. Find me one with her feet crossed behind her." He looked up and caught my smile. "I know it must puzzle you," he said, rapping his knuckles on a photograph as he launched into his first lesson in anthropology. "What we have here is an entire culture screwing Mother. That's why you'll find it so easy to work here. They're hare-brained. Read my skin mags and you'll have the whole thing in a nutshell. It's like a national gang bang. Look at these."

He threw a sheet of photographs at me. None of the girls appeared to be especially attractive, but perhaps I was not yet culturally acclimated.

"Crackjaw's harlots," Zuckerman said. "He calls the tune. Do you know what fate awaits these paper dolls?" I shook my head, egging him on. "Why, my good man, they will be thumbed and fingered, attacked in every aperture, screwed in every pore, soaked in the juices and grunts of church-going, spouse-kissing, car-tinkering husbands. I have their number. I follow the styles of each deformity as they come in. Right now it's udders, haunches, paunches. Blood and milk. Rubens. Something to pinch. Everything fat and round from lips to hips to lobes to knees. That's how we acquire a solid commercial grip on the phallus of this happy nation." He searched my eyes, apparently disappointed that there were no questions from the class. "Our readers, your new compatriots, are essentially dead. I offer them life in suspended animation. No one is more alive than these ladies. Look at their eyes, the movement of their lips, the breathing of their nostrils. They are alive, I say, and so they will remain until the Good Lord calls them for the final photograph."

Zuckerman was now beginning to appear more as advertised. Grotesque. Perhaps insane. I would be happy to get out of there.

Crackjaw left hurriedly, a bulging file of carefully selected deformities squeezed tightly under his arm. We watched him run down the boardwalk to the blue cruiser. As the boat roared out across the bay, Zuckerman, without a word, handed me a flight bag. I transferred from the duffel bag a few of my new possessions, such as they were.

"There is a reason why you are not going with him," Zuckerman said. "I do not want you seen with any one of us, at any time, now or in the future. You will go over on the regular ferry from Davis Park. Take the train in from Patchogue. At Penn Station board a Seventh Avenue subway to Fourteenth Street. Here is your apartment lease."

"Is that all?"

"The rest will be done by mail."

"There is no one I'm to know? No one to look for?"

"Sometimes. There will be onetime contacts, usually at the airport. But not our regular men. Your mail will come from Steingut. You will never see him. Your regular messages will go to Torre. Steingut will write you the procedure."

"And what will I be doing?"

"We'll see. A few pickups, a few drops. We'll see."

"This is not what I expected. I have been well trained. I have specialties."

"I know."

"This is not the way I operate," I said. "I always know more."

"This is the way I operate. This is how we've survived."

It was a matter-of-fact conversation with no bitterness on his part or mine. I was in no position to object. I respected Zuckerman for his caution at this point. Perhaps later he would come to know my value.

He was standing on the dune as I left. We exchanged waves and I began the walk west. When I looked back a few minutes later,

Zuckerman was still watching after me. He waved again. He seemed to be troubled about something. I did not make it my business. For all his oddity, he seemed somehow a very brave man.

It was five years later that Steingut wrote, somewhat obliquely, that Zuckerman had died on cigarettes and rum under the Fire Island sun. At the time, I believed it. Now it occurred to me that perhaps Zuckerman had been a weak link in the chain. He had been discarded and the chain welded together again. Somehow, after all these years, Mansfield had found another weakness. Like Zuckerman, I could disappear and the chain would re-form with no notice of my absence. It did not seem real. I would not be needed by the others. Who, then, would take notice? No one. I would not be needed by any living thing.

The blare of trumpets and saxophones roared over from Sammy's, all but drowning out the off-key vocalist. Mansfield had stationed himself over there in the shadows of an adjacent doorway. He did not seem too proficient at his chosen profession. I saw him first from the window and again the instant I stepped onto the sidewalk. It was unpleasant being out on a Friday night, but I was determined to draw him off. Joe Hull was waiting for me at the door. He was not surprised when I refused to let him spend the night on the floor inside. He knew he had failed to smell a policeman, and it was right that I should punish him for being an errant child. There was no time now to chastise him properly nor to inquire of Sugar Red what had transpired in his conversation with Mansfield. I would lure Mansfield, shake him, return to pack, and disappear in the city. If I could drop Mansfield immediately, perhaps they would believe that he knew nothing.

He followed me onto the D-Train, blissfully ignorant that I was aware of his every move. At Fourth Street, I walked up two flights and took the A-Train to Columbus Circle. Mansfield was still with me. I climbed the subway stairs out to the park, slowly, to keep suspicion sleeping, then crossed against the light to the Coliseum. A bus came along and Mansfield hesitated in the middle of the street. For a moment the bus blocked me from his view. It was all that was necessary.

The unmarked green doorway to the Coliseum parking garage was thirty feet in front of me. I sprinted for it, swung it open and bounded down the stairs. The attendant on the first level looked young and sharp. I continued down to the second level and invaded a black Z-license rented car, the closest to the stairs. There was no key in the ignition. Crouched low in the front seat, I peered through the steering wheel at the attendant's booth. He was counting cash with intense concentration. I opened the door and moved out, keeping low. Suddenly Mansfield appeared at the bottom of the stairway, wearing his ominous little grin. Not the imbecile I had thought. I jumped back into the black car and lay huddled on the floor, holding my breath.

Mansfield's footsteps echoed in the underground chamber. As he passed near the car, I saw his profile clearly. He stopped and leaned against the car door, pulled out a cigar and lit it. There was an eternal moment of reflection before he turned and moved away slowly toward the attendant's booth. I judged from the sounds that he stopped there to question him. Then there were four feet circling the cars, traveling at a great rate from one to another. If they did it methodically, they were sure to find me. I slipped out the door on the protected side and rolled under the car. Just in time. Shiny black shoes appeared. The back door opened and closed. The shoes walked by.

I crawled under the next car, a station wagon. Grease was soaking into my trousers. I reached up for the door handle. It was locked. Then to my horror, I saw hands and knees dropping to the cement floor in the next row. The snake. He had figured it out again. I crawled to the rear of the wagon and clutched the handle on the tailgate. It gave. In an instant I was inside, covered with filth, drenched in perspiration. I lay there trying to catch my breath. The footsteps seemed to be moving away. But it was still too great a risk to go out again, or even to rise and glance through the window. Mansfield knew I was in that garage. He must have seen the street door swing closed the last inch. Only a fraction of a second off. No, he was not an imbecile. He could be spotted. He was not used to being followed. But how he could follow! He gambled that I would choose the lower level, and he won. He could not afford to relinquish his bet now. Too much pride. I was beginning to know Mansfield.

The wagon had bucket seats and a floor shift. I raised my head very slightly and looked through to the front without hope of encouragement. Ridiculous! An absent-minded driver. I had found by chance what might have taken hours by method. The key was in the ignition.

Footsteps were moving toward me. Had he seen me? There was everything to lose there. He would find me eventually. I leaped into the front seat, turned the key and sent the car squealing into reverse, hard into a pillar. As I ground the gears into low, the engine sputtered. I hit the floor with the pedal, the car shuddered and then shot forward down the aisle. The attendant was blocking the way. It took two turns to reverse myself and then I was traveling down a longer aisle toward the ramp. The young attendant from the upper level appeared at the end. I turned into another aisle and he pursued me. With the route to the ramp blocked, I drove in circles around the garage, hoping to draw them away from the exit. As I came around the third time, I saw Mansfield standing dead center, palms held out, smiling.

It was really only then that the thought of killing Mansfield first occurred to me. Why should I spend my days and nights eluding him? Why was I expendable rather than Mansfield? He was the weak link, not I. With Mansfield gone, I would be restored to my value, perhaps even to greater value for having removed the threat to everyone. Yes, I could do it without feeling a thing. A scratch on the bumper of someone else's car. As the car neared him, I saw the smile freeze on his face.

He jumped to the left. No! To my surprise, I did not swerve to hit him. No, I could not. Surely, he was not the only one who had seen the dossier. They knew where he was, what he was after. If I killed him, they would all be after me. They would no longer wait to build the case. No, I had not yet killed here. They would not force me to do it.

The attendants both saw Mansfield's narrow escape. This time, as I closed in on the ramp, they leaped out of the way, one to each side. Racing up the incline, I saw a policeman at the top, trying to wave me down. I felt a soft thud as he flew off the fender. It could not have hurt him much. Now it remained to beat Mansfield back to the Bowery.

At the corner of Houston and MacDougal, the steering wheel began to pull. I turned into a vacant lot next to a church. It was a flat. I did not want to attract the attention of police by running, yet that risk seemed better than arriving to find Mansfield at the door of my loft. I ran, first at a jog, then faster, finally with the greatest burst of speed I could muster. Coming around the corner, I saw Joe Hull stretched out cold across the doorway. I jumped over him and climbed the stairs. It took three minutes to pack. I had kept no papers worth burning. I left my suits. I forgot my watch.

From the window I saw Sugar Red stepping out to the curb. But no Mansfield. I took the stairs down fast, nearly tripping over Joe Hull as I reached the sidewalk.

"Rent the place, I'll be in touch," I shouted to the astonished Sugar Red, but at that moment a car came screeching up to the curb. It was too late to run.

"Hey!" Mansfield yelled through the car window.

I halted.

"I thought I'd come in now to answer your questions," I said calmly.

"That's better."

He leaned over to open the door and I slid in. As his hands returned to the steering wheel, I slammed my hand into his neck with a force that painfully bent back my thumb. Mansfield slumped down. I reached for the handle on the driver's door and shoved him into the street. A beer truck braked to a stop. Fine. They would have to pick him up.

Minutes later, I was traveling over the Brooklyn Bridge in a car clearly and unfortunately labeled U.S. Government Interagency

Pool. As I turned onto Schermerhorn Street, only then did it strike me. Steingut. Tomorrow's mail. They will have it.

The telephone kept spitting back my dime. It must have been five maddening minutes before I connected.

"Jenny, I'm in a jam."

"Bring it over. I've got some peanut butter."

"This is serious."

"Since when were you ever serious?"

"Jenny, I want to come and live with you."

There was an excruciatingly long pause.

"My, how could I be so lucky?" Jenny said. "I thought I was just an alternate selection of the snatch-of-the-month club."

"Will you say yes? I'm being honest with you. I could have just arrived and gradually extended my stay."

"Yes, Jon," she said, in surprising earnest. "I say yes."

Tina came to me in the dream. We were sitting in a car by a waterfall. It was raining and we were bogged down in the mud.

When the storm passed, I could not move the wheels. We walked silently in the sun, speaking with our clasped fingers. Tina sat down on the riverbank across from the waterfall, her eyes closed against the sunlight, between her breasts a locket suspended from a gold chain. She opened the locket and I saw the picture. It was a boy of thirteen, lean and blond, with intense brown eyes. He seemed to be some kind of foreigner.

"I have to go now," Tina said suddenly. "And so do you."

"Why?"

"Because they're after me." She was not frightened.

"Who is after you, Tina?"

"It is time, Jon. You will be late."

She vanished. I felt a breeze at my back. I knew it was the contact. I was late and he blamed Tina. I did not fear anything he could do to me. I feared looking at him. I did not want to see his eyes.

But when I turned, I saw nothing. It was not a relief. I knew that somewhere the contact's eyes were waiting for me.

Suppose it were a woman? The thought amused me. Perhaps I could alter the signals, make an obscene gesture, watch her eyes become human. That would be something, to see rage in the eyes of a contact. To see anything.

Then I saw it in the corner of my eye. He was standing with his back toward me, gazing off at the waterfall. He was wearing a white turban with a train schedule on the back. I tapped him on the shoulder. He turned. I looked into his face and screamed.

It was not a face. It was nothing. No eyes, no mouth, no skin. I covered my eyes, hoping he could not find me. When I peeked through my fingers, I saw an enormous, pulsating eye growing between his shoulders.

The eye rolled down the front of his suit and wheeled after me. It was gaining momentum as I neared the river. I stopped at the edge where Tina had sat in the sun. My mind took charge, all fear left me, and I remembered my assignment. I turned to face the eye, holding up the palm of my hand. Something was written there in ink. "Look!" I shouted. "When is the next train to Babylon?"

I awoke, holding Jenny's hand.

Late Saturday morning I drove the car back over and dumped it at the Fulton Fish Market. As I walked to the subway, I wondered if I should see Tina. Perhaps she really was in danger, unknowing, and I should warn her.

Ridiculous. A dream. The only danger would come from my seeing her. I had avoided that for five years and I could do it forever. Women are inside. They do not exist apart. There was a time when I thought constantly of Tina. But in time she disappeared and was replaced. She had only been an illusion. I had never loved a woman. Nor had anyone, but at least I admitted that I had only loved a dream and I pretended each woman was that dream. If Tina had returned inside me, I could purge her with Jenny.

The only safe harbor was Jenny's. Mansfield had not mentioned her name. There was time to sort things out. She would be at the restaurant until midnight. I took the subway back to Brooklyn Heights.

When I called from Jenny's, Sugar Red answered. I was lucky.

"I want to explain about last night," I said.

"Listen," he said, "all I know is this guy comes up and starts asking all kinds of questions about you. I don't tell him a thing. Your trouble is your business."

"I need a favor, Sugar."

"Name it. You're a good customer, you've been damn nice to the boys. I owe you one."

"Good. Is there any mail today?"

"The usual. One letter. It's in the cash register. That same fuzz was in here an hour ago asking about your mail. He's still in the neighborhood."

Thank God for Sugar Red.

"I really appreciate all this, Sugar," I said. "I'll make up for the commotion. I'll make all of this up to you."

"Where are you?"

"I can't tell you. But I have to find a way to get that mail."

"There's no money in it," he said.

"What do you mean?"

"Look, I got eyes. It's too flat. Just a letter."

"Sugar, there's never —"

"Don't bull, man. I can feel when there's a wad in there. That's your business, I don't ask questions. I guard it for you like a bank. So tell me your forwarding address."

"They must have a tap on your line," I said.

"You think so?"

"Anyway, I can't have mail coming here."

"Well, we'll work something out," Sugar Red said. "Call me tonight." He clicked off abruptly. I sensed that Mansfield was back.

I narrowed my problems to three, which was comforting: getting the mail; regaining Steingut's trust, if it was lost; and if it was not lost, carrying out my assignments without being shadowed. At first consideration, the last bothered me the most. I had prided myself on being unobtrusive. Now, with Mansfield around, I had to be invisible.

Jenny returned before midnight. She was early. I was in the midst of dialing Sugar Red again. Jenny's eyes were glowing. I hung up.

"Can you imagine what it's like?" she said. "I mean, can you possibly imagine how I feel at the end of such a crummy day, coming home and knowing all the way that you'll be here?"

"I go through it every night."

"You just wouldn't appreciate yourself." She flung her arms open wide, and then dropped them. "One thing," she said. "I don't want you here unless you honest to Jesus love me."

"I love you," I said, and it was true. There are kinds and shades of love, and I felt something for Jenny.

"Be truthful," Jenny said. "I'm being truthful. Do you know what's been happening these last eight months? At times I tried to forget you. Sometimes I'd think I could. Then you'd come back and I'd know I couldn't. I haven't enjoyed that. And I'm getting damn sick of crying. Last night as I lay in bed, I had this awful feeling that I'd really lost you this time. When the phone rang, I didn't dare hope. But it was you. It was almost magical."

"I've hurt you a great deal, Jenny. I don't mean to."

"Oh, I forgive you, don't worry. But only because I love you, not because you haven't been a rat."

If my love was pity, it seemed a strong enough affection for this little gypsy. She was the only friend to whom I could turn at the worst moment in my life. She asked me no questions that night. Jenny was truly a wonderful girl. I did mean it. Somebody would be lucky to have her.

When she had fallen asleep, I called Sugar Red. We agreed to meet at Saint Patrick's the next morning.

"Are you Catholic?" Sugar Red asked as I slipped into the pew. "No."

"Then why'd you cross yourself?"

"Protective coloring."

"Here."

He handed me the envelope. I knelt with him in prayer.

"Holy Mary, full of grace, what about tomorrow?" Sugar Red said.

"Fruit of thy womb, I don't know. I'll have to call."

As I moved to go, I felt his hand on my arm.

"Be careful, Jon," Sugar Red said.

I had forgotten the key. Jenny answered my knock. She was in a flowered apron, very frilly for her.

"Hello there," I said. "I just dropped in from church."

"But who are you? And what do you want?"

We held each other more tightly than usual. Her bare feet left the floor.

"How much do you weigh now?"

"A hundred and nineteen."

"Good God!"

"Too much?"

"That's a very fancy smock."

"Oh, this little thing?" She fingered the apron. "No, no. It's for cooking!" She rushed over and opened the oven, anxious to impress me with her fit of domesticity. A magnificent bird was sizzling in a pan.

"Tell me," Jenny said, busying herself with spoon and baster. "What do you look like?"

"I have no memory," I replied in my best Peter Lorre accent. "My face has been altered so many times by ze knife."

She did not laugh.

It was then that I saw it. In the alcove, under the skylight, was a white pedestal. On it she had been modeling a bust. It was a lean face, a boy of about thirteen. He seemed to be some kind of foreigner.

As Jenny turned toward me from the stove, I feigned ignorance of my discovery.

"To answer your questions, madam." I bowed low. "My name is Jon and I am here to save the world."

"Don't lie to me," she said in that new, serious tone of hers. "You mustn't anymore. Who were you calling when I came home last night?"

"Whom."

"All right, I won't ask."

"I was dialing for the time."

"We'll always doubt each other until we're sharing the same bed every, every, every night," Jenny said.

"Maybe even then."

"Have I ever told you about this fantastic moment I've been waiting for?" she said. "Listen. It's New Year's Eve. And who should I be with but the one, true, and only. I mean, like, the prince. Right at the stroke of midnight, right at the stroke, I'll come out of myself like never in history."

"That will be quite an explosion."

"Will you be here New Year's Eve, Jon?"

"Come here, Jenny. Let's not talk about it."

We smelled dinner burning about an hour later. The new message from Steingut was still in my pocket.

Not until after Jenny had left on Monday morning could I bring myself to open the envelope. My worst fear was another trip to Penn Station or to the airport. I could not afford to be out in the open. As it turned out, that should have been the least of my fears.

I will be sending your mail to the girl's place.
S

Everything in vain.

They knew. The weak link. Mansfield. My escape. Jenny. That was the worst part. I had placed her in danger.

With only a word, I could straighten it all out, I was sure of that. But how could I get a message to Steingut? I had never tried to reach him before. Was the chain vertical or horizontal? Suppose

I passed the word to Torre that everything was in order, that I had shaken the shadow of Mansfield, that Jenny knew nothing. What could he do? Pass it to the next man. And who was he? What did he do? Would the message ultimately reach Steingut? No. It was impossible. There was no way to reach Steingut.

Next to the envelope in my pocket I found a plastic bookmark. I laughed aloud. Sugar Red must have slipped it into my pocket in church. It was a garish color portrait of Jesus of Nazareth, a bright orange flame burning in the middle of his halo. On the back it said: "Prayer in Trials." Sugar Red was a thoughtful man.

"To be said in great affliction, or when one seems to be deprived of all visible help, and for cases despaired of." I could not stop laughing as I read further: "Most holy Apostle, St. Jude, faithful servant and friend of Jesus, the name of the traitor who delivered thy beloved Master into the hands of His enemies has caused thee to be forgotten by many, but the Church honors and invokes thee universally as the patron of hopeless causes . . ." That was all I needed, Judas on my side.

I watched the smoke curl up to the skylight as the envelope burned in a glass ashtray. I tossed the bookmark into the blaze. The plastic began to melt into black goo, emitting a sharp odor. The flame was almost hypnotic. As the heat encroached on the sickly green robe of Jesus, I spoke softly, as if to an old friend, "Rabbi, I appreciate it, really I do. You and Sugar Red. But so far as I know, this is the only time around. I must proceed on that assumption. It is now to die or to live, that simple. I still have the freedom to choose between the two." The fire died. The ashtray cooled and cracked down the middle. I picked it up like a guilty husband discovering his cigar ash on the rug. Dearly beloved, we are gathered together here in the sight of God and in the face of this ashtray. Jenny the housekeeper, who could forget about the oven after one pat on the fanny. If any man can show just cause why they may not lawfully be joined together, let him now speak, or else hereafter forever hold his peace. Should I hide the ashtray? As ye will answer at the dreadful Day of Judgment when the se-crets of all hearts shall be disclosed, that if either of you know any impediment, or should I just show it to her? What excuse could I concoct? I wouldn't have to. She would never notice.

This time I packed slowly. I did not want to leave her.

But to stay might kill her. She would think me cruel when she returned. Or many hours later. I would not leave a note. There was nothing to say. Not until that night would she realize that I was gone. Not for a week, perhaps a month, would she know that I would never come back. Love her, comfort her, honor, and keep her in sickness and in health, and forsaking all others, keep thee only unto her, so long as ye both shall live. Yes, strangely, I felt I might have.

He was standing across the street. As I looked out the window, he smiled and waved. I opened Jenny's door and stepped into the hall. The fire escape was in front, but perhaps there was a back way. Where was the route to the roof? Before I found it, he was halfway up the stairs, the revolver pointed quite accurately at my head. "Freeze!" he yelled. For a flatfoot, Mansfield was always very quick.

3.

"No, sir, no chances this time," Mansfield said. "You get back in there."

"Where?" I stared at him. Blankly, I hoped.

"Jenny O'Leary's," he said.

"Who?"

He kicked at the door but it would not budge.

"I don't live here," I said. "I don't have a key to any of these doors."

Mansfield opened the door with a passkey and pushed me inside.

"I know she's not here," he said.

"Who?"

He turned on that awful little smile.

"Really, now, Mansfield," I said, "if you think you have some sort of case, arrest me. I haven't time for games." I smiled. It proved the best method for destroying his smile.

"Do you know what you've done," he said, "in addition to everything else? In the space of just one hour Friday night. Attempted murder of a police officer. You're lucky at that. Only two broken ribs. Theft of two cars, one a government vehicle. Assault and battery on a federal officer. That's all I need."

"It's all you have."

He rubbed his neck thoughtfully.

"It wasn't kind of you to thumb me like that." His voice was almost pleasant. I agreed with him. "But I'm going to be kind to you, Ivan," he said.

"Ivan?"

"Or is it Giovanni? Or Jean? Juan? Yohan? Johan, single

n, double *n*? John with an *h*, without? I forget." He wrenched from his inside pocket an impressive packet of documents.

"This time," I said, "I think I will call my lawyer." I made a move toward the telephone.

"As if you have one," Mansfield said. "Now, you listen to me very carefully. Born in Utrecht. Father Dutch, mother Indonesian. Forty-three years old. We have your birth certificate. Also Italian citizenship papers. Two passports, British and Belgian. I'm sure you have more. How am I doing?"

"Not well at all." I walked to the window. If Jenny should return, I would have considerably more to explain than a broken ashtray. "Mansfield, I'm not blaming you, understand. Some bureaucrat has given you the wrong dossier. I am as American as huckleberry pie."

"Apple."

"Don't I look American to you?"

"Yes."

"I speak American, I dress American, I think American. For heaven's sake, man, that's exactly what I am."

No, the stoical pose would not do with Mansfield. A different game was required. Clearly, he had no intention of arresting me. He was trying to feel out some sort of bargain with me.

"This dossier is correct," he said flatly.

"No. To begin with, I am forty-two. You are all wrong about that. There is an important distinction between forty-three and forty-two. You have robbed me of an entire year of life. At the age of forty-three, Mozart had been dead for eight years, not seven."

"I won't argue," Mansfield said. "But Utrecht is right."

"Wrong again. Baltimore. I don't often bring that up. It embarrasses me. But I'm stuck with it. I am a citizen of the arsenal of democracy, the leader of the free world, have always been and shall always be. If you really would like to see my genuine birth certificate or any other conceivable document, I will be happy to make arrangements."

"I've seen them."

"Then let's dispense with this conversation. I have to go now."

He waved me back with the revolver.

"They're well done," he said. "Very well done. Believe me, I have a great deal of respect for you. I don't think you realize that. That's why I'm not holding this against you." He massaged his neck.

"What do you want?"

"Simple," he said. "I want you to bring him in."

"Who?"

"The one at the top."

"You can't mean it. Tricky Dick himself?"

He was not smiling.

"I want Torre, I want Steingut, and I want whoever is over them."

"Those names again," I complained. "And suppose I had the vaguest notion of what you were talking about. What have you to exchange?"

"Your life."

"Hardly seems a fair bargain. Might I just have thirty pieces of silver?" But I was listening. I did not exactly cherish Mansfield but I was tempted to believe him. He would probably deliver.

"Unfortunately," Mansfield said, "you only have ten seconds to decide." I heard the click of metal in his hand. "That's just an arbitrary figure, of course."

But he meant it. Not that he would kill me on the spot. There would be a democratic trial and a whole smorgasbord of libertarian blessings before I was whisked to Sugar Red's celestial paradise.

"Mansfield," I said, "much as I have faith in your professional ethics, I would like to establish some conditions."

"I'll listen," he said. He put away the revolver, lit a cigar, and sat down next to the door.

"You pushed me into this strange room," I said, "with your usual boyish charm. I have no idea who lives here. Suppose that the occupant of this apartment were to walk in at this moment. I assure you that he or she would be completely bewildered by our conversation. I don't want this person touched."

"That's fair."

"Second, I really can't fathom what it is that you are asking me to do. I have never heard of the names you mention. Your entire game escapes me. But suppose that I were to gain an inkling and that I did not disappoint you. That would be a terrible thing, wouldn't it? Not just for those individuals, but for a cause. It is a cause, and I am quite serious, to which I am committed."

"You're joking."

"Not a bit."

"You're not the type," Mansfield said.

"Oh? What type am I?"

"You're in it for the money like the rest of them."

"I wish it were that simple."

"So what is it you're asking?"

"I would need far more than my life to carry on."

"How much?"

"Not money," I said. "My freedom. To go anywhere."

"I can arrange that," he said.

"Third and last. What you ask will take time."

"You have a week."

I caught my breath. Did he realize how little I knew? Perhaps even less than he knew? I would have to begin with Steingut and work from there. How would I find him? Where would I even begin to find him?

"That's not much time," I said.

"I know."

"You can't know! I'm the only one who knows how much time this would take, and I tell you it's not enough!"

"It's all you've got."

"Then you'll have to meet another condition."

"Go ahead."

"Don't shadow me."

"I can't meet that," Mansfield said.

"It's off. If these people are not creatures of your imagination, which I suspect they are, they certainly know about you. I couldn't move an inch while you lurked about with that silly-looking smile on your face."

Mansfield fiddled idly with the documents. He was not sensitive enough to be hurt by insult. He was thinking hard. Finally, he pulled a quarter from his pocket and flipped it.

"You win," he said, and stood up.

I sighed a little too loudly.

"But remember this," Mansfield said. "You have one week. Wednesday morning, two days from now, I want a progress report. Call me. Here's my card. Next Monday, if you haven't brought him in, I pick you up. And allow me to guarantee something to you: I'll find you. No matter where you go, how far, with what identity, I'll find you."

Somehow I did not doubt him at that moment. He was not as skillful as I, but he seemed more determined.

I watched through the window as he climbed into his car. He drove away fast.

The car did not return. Mansfield was true to his word.

"You're late," Thaddeus said.

"How would you know?"

He had already ordered enough beef and ale to feed the First Army.

"Do you suppose," he said, "I have nothing better to do than wait around McSorley's half the day for someone to pick up the bill?"

"Yes."

I sat quietly while he snorted, chewed, and guzzled. At length, he lifted his napkin and wiped his lips.

"You're a dead man," he said.

"Thanks."

"That's why you're not talking today. But I hear you." He snapped his fingers for another ale. There were eight empty mugs on the table. "I hear a dead man crying to me silently. I hear your lifeblood trickling out right at this moment. And I say this in sympathy, friend, because I'm probably the only one who will send flowers."

"Yes." I touched Thaddeus' hand. It was cold. "It's become like a dream, Thaddeus. There was a time when I wondered what I was doing here. I'm beginning to know it now and it's not real."

"Of course it isn't." He downed the ninth ale. "Look at this room. You think I can't see it? I'm like you. There's no difference between where I've been and where I am now. This room is everywhere. Over there." He raised his mug toward a dark corner. "Fearful, isn't it? In my mind's eye I can see it in every detail. Shadows from the past. Shadows moving through time and terror. The shadow of a reckoning yet to come. And now the shadow of a dead man."

I moved in my seat and the sunlight hit the corner. Thaddeus nodded as if he had seen.

"Don't worry," he said. "This room is safe. That's why you come here, isn't it? Not to have lunch with a dirty old man. You come here like a bleeding animal hiding in the shadows. Because shadows are darker than blood."

Her voice sounded hoarse from crying.

"Jenny, I had to call. To explain."

"Funny, but I can't seem to find your bag," she said. "Maybe it's in some closet I don't know about. Or maybe I'm asleep and this is just a nightmare. I'm going to wake up any minute."

"I have that same feeling, Jenny. It's like a dream."

She started to cry.

"I could actually murder you," she said. "I really found that out today. I have murder in my heart."

"Look!" Through the glass door of the booth I saw the orange sunset. "Look out the window, Jenny. It's a beautiful sun."

"I see it. And why aren't you here to share it with me? It just looks to me like the sun is dying."

"You sound like a jealous wife." I tried a chuckle.

"I am, Jon," she said. "I am your wife. That's the way I feel."

"I don't expect you to understand, Jenny, but I need a week. Just one week, then I'll be back. We'll talk about it then, very seriously."

"No, I just don't trust you anymore."

53

"If you ever believed in me, now is the time, Jenny. I need your love to be there all the time. I never thought I'd hear myself saying such a ridiculous thing. But I don't want to leave you."

"You already have, Jon. Goodbye." She hung up.

I opened the door and looked again at the sunset. She was right. It was a dying sun. Zuckerman had probably watched that sun over the bay the day he died. It was the sunset that Tina and I were watching when we knew for the first time that it could not last. First Zuckerman. Then Tina. And Thaddeus, who looked at me through sightless eyes as if I were already a corpse. Now Jenny, too, was gone from me. Well, isn't that the truth? We are all alone. Better to know it.

Once, in Amsterdam, I dreamed that eels were slithering through the streets. I awoke sweating profusely, and yet the night before, my father and I had drunk fine wine that plugged the pores. It was my first trip to the city. I must have been twelve. Those were good days. We laughed a great deal, as I recall. No, I was not always alone. But the eels were in the streets.

They came the next night. We were awakened by the sounds. To me it was exciting, like a circus come to town. I ran outside in my bare feet and lifted my eyes above the havoc in the streets. Thousands of fluffy white circles were floating in the black sky. "It must be a visitation from another planet," my father said.

My uncle told us later how polite they were. They knocked on the door of his pillbox and waited patiently. Someone bade them enter. They opened the door very softly and fired. We visited him at the hospital and were impressed that he received the finest medical treatment until the end. From then on, it was an orderly, disciplined occupation. When the truck finally came to the house, it was only part of a system. They allowed my father to fetch his cloak and mittens, for it was a cold day. He gave me the watch and put his hand on my shoulder. One of them started to take me. The corporal stopped him and gave me a piece of candy.

My grandmother sent for me from Brugge. The girls wore earrings and trailed behind the nuns. One gave me a lace handkerchief she had made herself. I thought she was trying to sell it to me. I could not understand Flemish. When I reached into my pocket for a franc, she blushed and ran off.

Bergère was then a young instructor who worked afternoons in my grandmother's garden. Each day after school I would follow behind him with the wheelbarrow, listening to his dreams. The world would someday be free, he said. All would share in the fruits of that freedom. But the road to justice would be bloody.

He brought me books which I read late into the night and hid under my pillow. Their righteousness sent chills down my spine. I began to believe. I was no longer an orphan.

One afternoon Bergère failed to appear for work. There was a note in the wheelbarrow. It said simply: "Are you ready?"

The first snow of the winter fell that evening. I pulled on my boots and made my way along the Duke's canal to the house where Bergère lived. A man whom I recognized from the bakery stood outside the door, slapping his arms against the cold. He led me into the cellar. Bergère was sitting in the center of a group of seven men, all of whom were familiar to me. One was a teller at the bank. He was stacking hand grenades in a suitcase.

"Sit down," Bergère said. "You will listen to everything and say nothing."

His tone was no different with me than with the others. The men treated him with such deference that I quickly realized Bergère was not just one of them. He was not a poor schoolteacher who daydreamed in the garden. He was the leader, certainly for Brugge and perhaps for an entire district.

When they had finished their planning and left one by one, I confronted Bergère with my surprise at his importance.

"For Belgium," he said quietly, "I am only third in command."

"For all Belgium?"

"Of course. And before it is over, I will be first. But that is nothing. I see a day when all Europe will be linked together. A brotherhood. And perhaps even, in our lifetime, we will reach across the sea."

I understood very little of what he said and I believed it all.

Grandmother died that winter and I went to live with Bergère. It was a time not of sorrow but of relief. They would have come for her sooner or later. Her luck could not have lasted.

I began my work. Bergère would send me with the messages. Sometimes he would let me carry the suitcase. Its weight varied but it was always quite heavy. I would never see the results. But when from my bed I heard explosions in the night, I smiled.

When April came, the work stopped. Weeks went by before, one morning at breakfast, I dared ask Bergère why.

"It is not for you to question," he said.

"Have I done anything wrong?"

"No," he said. "It is not you. Someone here is not to be trusted. We have lost too many men. We are finished here."

He did not tell me what that meant until school was out for the year. Then he announced suddenly that we would be leaving at dawn the next day. Just like that. We would go to Brussels. From there I would be driven to Amsterdam. He would stay in Brussels.

I started to protest.

"You are a soldier now," Bergère said. "You will go where you can be most useful."

That night I walked along the canal for the last time. I reached into my pocket and found a franc. I threw it into the canal and watched it sink. They said it would bring luck in love.

Stupid! The rain caught me by surprise. I stopped along Sixth Avenue to buy an umbrella. I was not sure where I was going. It would be pointless to call Jenny again. I could not tell her why I had called before. She would think me heartless.

Well, it would be child's play to open that mailbox. I did not really need her key. But could I afford to risk drawing them back there? Not Mansfield. He would hold to his word. It was my own side that concerned me. Someone, perhaps Steingut himself, was keeping track of me. And once I returned there, could I leave without seeing Jenny? Could I stand at the bottom of those stairs, knowing she was up there crying, without going up to comfort her? I was becoming a foolish, sentimental old man. How ridiculous to think of Jenny as a wife! She was my daughter. I felt protective toward her. It was a good feeling. But there was little I could do about it.

Yet I knew that Steingut rarely failed to have something in the Monday mail. Perhaps, once again, he knew I was on the move and he had sent it to the Bowery. I descended underground. There was no one following me. In the subway car I glanced at each face. Not one was a shadow.

I walked through the doorway of Fisher's Tavern as if I had never been away.

"On the house," Sugar Red said, returning my nonchalance.

A beefy, short-legged tourist waddled in from the rain. He plumped down on the next stool like a hippopotamus and was immediately spotted. A small conference over seniority rights ensued in the back of the room. Then the largest of the bums sat himself down on the other side of the stranger.

"Pardon me, sir," he opened, "I wonder if you might help me out."

The tourist turned to me as if we were roommates in the class struggle.

"He's broke," I said.

"I'm broke, too," the tourist said.

"Then show him your wallet." I said.

"I will not."

"Are you lying to him?"

The boys laughed feebly.

"I'm not lying," the tourist said. He opened his wallet. It was empty.

"I think you're holding," I said. "You're hiding your money."

"Suppose I were? What about you? Show your wallet."

"I don't have to. I belong here."

"Look," he said, with a slight whine, "I've got some money, sure. But just enough for a few drinks. I came down here for a good time, is there anything wrong with that?"

"All right, let's everybody stop bothering my customer," Sugar Red barked.

I walked behind the bar where Sugar Red was mixing a grasshopper for the tourist.

"Any mail today?" I asked quietly. My voice shook just a little. "No."

So there was no alternative. I would have to return to Jenny's.

The bum was still pestering. Passing them on the way to the door, I laid a hand on the tourist's shoulder.

"Why don't you just give him a cigarette?"

The man looked up at me, searched my face, and then smiled, nodding his thanks.

As I stepped out into the rain, an emaciated little man came staggering by, dressed only in his underpants. He was lugging a large jug. He tripped over the foot of Joe Hull, who was asleep in my old doorway, and lurched against the door. Joe awoke with a curse. First he saw me. Then he saw the man. Immediately, his fist shot out toward the man's stomach. I was amused. It seemed to be the shadow boxing I had seen so much of on the street, where one drunken blow was landed out of every fifty.

But I knew, too, that Joe stayed scrupulously sober during the day. Joe was a businessman. He did not begin drinking until well toward midnight, when he had a fistful of dollars. No, this was no joke. He was pounding this man in dead earnest. He held him by the shoulder with one hand and smashed a fist into his jaw. The man did not fight back. He was holding on to his jug. He fell down on his knees. Joe picked him up.

"Stop it, Joe!" I yelled.

But Joe was in a fury now. It was clearly not the man that bothered him nor his lost sleep. He was enraged at himself for having failed me and admitted Mansfield. He was trying to impress upon me that whenever I returned, Joe Hull would be the trustworthy guardian of my door and earn his keep. I watched as he hit the man in the stomach three times. I felt the pain but I continued watching, as if I were helpless to stop it. The man slumped down for the last time. Joe turned to me and held out the palm of his hand. He expected me to pay him for his hazardous duty.

"You shouldn't have done that, Joe." I gave him a dollar. "That man wasn't bothering you or me or anyone else."

"I know him. He's no good."

"I'm giving you this because I haven't been around lately. But I am not paying you for what you did, is that clear?"

Joe put the dollar in his pocket and walked away. The man seemed to be unconscious. The rain was washing the sidewalk clean. Perhaps the police would come along and give him some rest in the Tombs. I had to get to Brooklyn. There was no time to indulge pity toward a stranger.

As I walked toward the subway, I heard a voice crying weakly. "Help."

The man in the underpants had turned over on his side. He was staring up at the rain. I hurried on. Someone would see him. There were people walking by who could hear him.

"Help!" The voice was more insistent now. I stood on the corner looking back. Bums, tourists, students, salesmen, at least twenty people passed by, glanced at him, and continued on, giving him a wide berth.

I went back. He reached up his hand toward me. His eyes were hollow and dark. The flesh barely covered his ribs. He was still clinging tightly to the jug. I pulled him up. His fingers were clammy. He stood there unsteadily, looking at me from far off somewhere. A smile began to form on his lips.

"I appreciate that," he said. "You're very kind."

I walked away as fast as I could.

What would Thaddeus have said? Was I still on the periphery? "I belong here." But I was no longer playing the part convincingly. I could not leave the tourist without a piece of helpful advice. I could not pass by an old wreck on the pavement without offering my hand. How many such corpses had I seen down there in the past five years? Hundreds. They had expected nothing of me, I gave them nothing.

Something smelled. I looked down. My palm was smeared with blood.

"There are twelve trains to Babylon."

Yes, I was growing certain, the words were familiar. I had not heard them spoken. I had read them years ago. Had I carried out the mission they implied? It seemed absurd that all they would ask of me was to pass it on to Torre.

I watched Jenny's window from a doorway across the street, exactly where Mansfield had stood; not a good place, not if Mansfield had chosen it. Perhaps I wanted her to see me. I would have to go up then. I stood there, feeling a little like a forlorn puppy dog, the rain dripping on my shoes from the umbrella. Jenny's curtains were drawn. The lights were out. I checked my wrist and remembered I had forgotten to retrieve my watch from the loft. She must have been at the restaurant. The sky was black. There was a soft rumbling of thunder.

I ran across the street and jimmied open the mailbox. There was the familiar manila envelope with no return address. I jammed it into my pocket and raced through the rain to the subway.

"Step back, please!" the loudspeaker blared. "Train coming in."

I slit open the envelope. It was empty.

Loudspeakers blared out the names of groups present in the audience. The visitors from Napoli, men of the United States Army in Austria, pilgrims from Spain. As the names were called, great shouts resounded. What would be my category? What language would they use?

I had come, like all the others, merely to see what made Eugenio Pacelli infallible and supreme. I was swept through the Bronze Doors by a bevy of plump dark women in mantillas. The Swiss Guards reached for my pass. I had none. "Viva Papa," I said. They let me through.

He was borne into the room, smiling broadly, one arm gracefully swooping down to answer as many of the waiting hands as he could without losing dignity. Once on the throne, he ran through the roll call again, and so I received no blessing for myself. But anxious to conform, I held up the lace handkerchief the little Belgian girl had given me fourteen years before.

In the Vatican treasury I saw gems the size of my hand and enough pure gold to feed every Italian peasant for a lifetime.

It was foolish the way I clutched that empty envelope in my pocket, as if somehow, magically, a message would appear. There had been times before when Steingut had sent nothing. It was routine. It meant simply that the last move had succeeded and I should await further instructions. Could that be all there was to it? Was there nothing more for me to do? Torre had fed my Babylon schedule into the chain, and the links had stretched to that goal of which he and I, and possibly even Steingut, were unaware. Yet there I was, opening and closing my hand in my pocket, crushing the envelope and then smoothing it out, perplexed and fearful as I stood in the subway car sandwiched between two squat Italian ladies in flowered dresses. I had descended again to the underground with no mission, no destination, only to keep moving, away from Jenny. No, I could not see her now. Suppose she asked me once more, before she would take me back: "What do you do, Jon?" What would I answer this time? "I don't know"? That would be it. "Jenny, I don't know anymore what the hell I'm doing, and nobody can tell me!"

The crowd was pouring in, dripping wet. It seemed impossible that the car could hold as many rainsoaked bodies as it did, yet at each stop more shoved and sloshed into the crush. By Times Square we were a boxcar en route to the extermination camp. By Fifty-ninth Street we were a mass grave. I grasped the strap with one hand and the envelope with the other. The noise was deafening, the odors overpowering, and there was nothing to see.

My eyes focused on my own hand holding the strap. The blood was still there. It was darker now, dried and crusty. The hand of one of the Italian ladies was riveted to the lower part of the strap. I glanced at her quickly. She was staring at my hand with a look of disgust. I moved my other hand to the strap and hid the stain in my pocket, groping for my handkerchief. I had to wet it thoroughly with saliva before the blood would come off. The Italian lady watched curiously. The handkerchief was thin and faded from many washings. It was not abrasive enough to do a thorough job.

I smiled at the Italian lady. "It was blessed by the Pope," I said. She thought I was insane.

"You see all the submachine guns?" My host was pointing at the guards on the palace steps. "Very impressive, eh? But there is good reason. We need the monarchy."

"We?" I said.

"They."

We climbed into his car and sped out of Brussels along an exceedingly bumpy road.

"This road cost a lot of money." Garneau shook his head in exasperation.

I was barely listening to him. I was thinking ahead.

"There is no capital investment here," he said. "Just luxuries. The franc is worthless." Apparently he was convinced that I had never been in Belgium. It was a good operation.

"I don't like the Germans," Garneau said, turning to scrutinize my face. "What about you?"

"Mm."

"And the Dutch I cannot tolerate. Almost as bad as the French." He was watching me very closely.

"Which are you?" he asked. There was a sickly grin on his face.

I did not say a word from that moment until we reached Antwerp. I was taken in to see Bergère immediately.

"It was a long drive," I said. "Garneau is not a pleasant companion."

"Tell me something new." Bergère motioned me to a chair.

"I don't trust him," I said.

Bergère was angry, but I felt very little to fear in him. "He does his work," he said. "We are all aware of his weaknesses."

"I wonder."

"I have no intention of letting him go." That was obvious, it wasn't necessary for him to say it. Yet it was important for Bergère at the outset of the briefing to establish that he was in command. After all, he had been my mentor. I did not object further. It would be my last day in Europe.

He laid a set of blueprints on his desk. I gave them a quick study.

"You're not familiar with the ship," he said.

"How could I be?"

"Have you any idea what you're to do?"

"No."

"Then what information do you have?"

"I know only that once this is over, I go to America."

"Yes." He sighed. I was surprised that he so poorly concealed his relief to be rid of me. It was not my fault that he viewed me as a threat. The rumor that I might replace him had not originated with me. In fact, I had always looked upon Bergère as a very competent administrator. Those who were promoting me did not fool me with their flattery. They hated Bergère and had tried to use me for their own game.

"I'm looking forward to America," I said.

Bergère looked at me as if I were some kind of odd specimen in the laboratory.

"How is your strength?" he asked with a trace of condescension.

"Fine."

"Lungs?"

"Excellent."

"How old are you now?"

"Thirty-three."

"A little old for this."

"We'll see."

He picked up the telephone receiver and dialed.

"Martinez. Jon is here. Can you radio Zuckerman to expect?" He reached into a drawer for his pipe. "You did stop sending to him? That's wise. I'll write, then. There's time."

Bergère listened in silence and then hung up abruptly.

"They're sending the Commander to photograph the hull, keel, propellers, everything," he said. "You are to protect the ship."

"Is that all?"

"No. If he slips through, no offense, please, but just if he happens to, the camera must not go back."

"Fine. Anything else?"

"Of course. The Commander must not go back either."

I took a deep breath. They would not trust me on this. I had evaded such assignments through every conceivable ruse. They would not believe me again.

"That is not my specialty," I said.

"Oh, but it's every man's specialty," Bergère said softly. "And I am sending you precisely because you do not think it is yours."

I stood up and paced the floor, aware of his eyes. Long before, I had learned to live with their means. But I did not have to practice them.

"Tell me about it," I said.

"Good." He thought he had convinced me, but he was wrong. At least he was not yet right. "They are fifty-five miles out to sea." Bergère checked his watch. "That gives you sufficient sleep before they arrive. But it gives us no time in the morning. You will begin at five o'clock. Therefore, you will listen to me carefully now. There will be no second chance."

I leaned against the wall and watched him. He was a peculiar fellow, freakishly tall, with long, sad features. He had aged in an odd way since the war, not by wrinkles or loss of hair but by growing thinner and sadder, as if the flesh were slowly peeling off him. He would die already a cadaver.

"Our information is that the Commander will dive down in one of the locks," Bergère said almost in a whisper. I heard the words but it was difficult to concentrate. I was wondering if I would sleep that night. "We are not sure which one. Probably the Badouin. Or we may be entirely wrong. He may drop down when they are still on the river. Whichever is safest for him. But we do know one thing. He is very thorough. He will need time. He will still be with it when it comes into the harbor. Therefore, you will wait in the harbor. We are taking no chances of your being seen by his people, just as he is taking no chances with us."

"If you don't mind, Bergère," I interrupted.

"Certainly." He looked up from his papers, irritated.

"The Commander will be missed by a great many people. He is kind of a hero."

"Is that what's bothering you?" Bergère said disdainfully. "That he is a hero?"

"I'm concerned only that he is known to the public," I said. "It's really not my concern. I'll be gone. It's you who should worry. Unless you care to be revealed as a public figure also."

"That's right," Bergère said. "It's really not your concern."

"I would suggest you think that over," I said.

"It is a policy matter."

"When I am down there under the harbor, it is policy that I will be making."

"I hope," Bergère said, "it is policy you will be carrying out precisely as instructed. If you do, no one will ever know what happened to the Commander."

"Someone will know."

"Not the press. Not the public about which you profess such deep concern. They will never know that two men went down there. All they will know is that one man came up. A dead man."

"I don't understand."

"Which is why I ask you to listen with your mouth closed." Bergère lit his pipe for an extraordinary length of time. He was enjoying my curiosity. I had not displayed it to him often. I sat down. His sudden smile informed me that the major problem of this discussion had been how to make me return to my seat without stooping to a direct order. "In a few days' time," he said, still applying the match to the pipe bowl, "the public will know that a decapitated corpse has washed ashore. We alone will know it is the Commander. The British will not be so sure. Oh, now I'm interesting you? Then perhaps you will appreciate the felicity of this plan, because it is my own. We protect the ship, we rid ourselves of the Commander, and I rid — that is to say, you are presumed to be dead."

I could not admit a second time that I did not understand. Bergère pushed over a thick envelope.

"To memorize and destroy," he said. "In addition, I should warn you that sometime after you are down tomorrow, we shall arrange for the British to know about it. The following day, we shall leak word of our consternation about your death. And here is the nicest part. We shall make them believe that we have the Commander."

It was, I had to concede, a fine project. If I succeeded, I was off to America, out of Bergère's hair. If I failed, I would be dead, either at the hands of the Commander or Bergère. The ingenuity of the scheme convinced me that Bergère had at last attained brilliance in order to evict me from his sphere. Clearly, he was jealous of me, but I saw now that he had no reason to be.

"What about afterward?" I asked him.

"It's all in there." He waved a finger at the envelope. "You will cease all contact. Once in America, you will follow the instructions of Emil Zuckerman. You will be entirely in his hands."

He arose to indicate that I had taken enough of his valuable time.

"Goodbye, Bergère," I said. Our handshake was none too warm.

"Goodbye, Jon."

I started out.

"You know," Bergère said, "I really envy you. They say that America is a most pleasant assignment."

My hands are so pale now. But in nightmares I have seen them through the glass, brown and strong, disconnected from my body, reaching through green silence toward the rope which moves further and further away, until suddenly I am alone. I see the churning of the propellers in the distance. I swim until the rope comes into view again. At last I reach it, pull on it, pulling him toward the hull. The silence is shattered by the whine of the ship, the sound of my breath, the rumbling of waterdrops in the tube.

He tried to free himself. For an instant I thought to give him his freedom. My fist unclenched and the knife dropped out of my hand. I reached down for it but it was gone. He had not seen. He was thrashing about in panic. He could not untangle the rope from his feet. How must he feel! A man too old for the job. A father. A mother's son. He might have been my friend, but then, what would happen to me if I loved mankind that little? I could not fail Bergère. The Commander would do the same to me, perhaps worse. We were caught in this trap together.

I gritted my teeth until pain shot up a nerve into my ear. I pulled the rope toward the churning waters. He fought for life. The propeller sliced into his neck.

One train after another. I changed from local to express and back again, automatically, without thinking. There was nothing to do but keep moving. What were all the others doing? Did it truly matter whether they stepped off at Seventy-second Street or Ninety-sixth Street? Suppose, just this one night, they walked out one stop too soon. Who would notice?

But then something was pulling me toward the exit. My journey was at an end, I did not know why or where. The sign said 168th Street but it seemed to mean nothing to me. I came up into the air and breathed deeply. The rain had thinned to a sprinkle, falling gently on the pavement, the crowd, the flowers in the cart on the corner. Freshly watered flowers. It seemed a perfect time to buy them. The vendor smiled at me as if he knew me from long ago.

I studied his face until he shrugged and turned his back. Of course I knew him! That was why I was there. It was the dream. I had to warn her, to save her.

Yet as I stepped into the telephone booth, I already knew that it was quite the opposite. I wanted her to save me.

"I'm at the subway entrance on the corner," I said.

She clicked off without a word.

Two minutes later she came running down the block. Waiting on the corner for the light to change, she stood strangely, her head arched over to let the rain wash down on her bare arms and legs.

Her hair was drenched, strands jutting out in all directions. I crossed over and put the tulips in her hands. She raised my hand to her cheek and I felt the moisture of her tears mingled with the raindrops.

It had been five years. Tina and I walked silently in the rain, speaking with our clasped fingers, but this time we were not sure what we were saying.

4.

I slumped into the old scratchy armchair, hiked my feet up onto the familiar leather ottoman, and watched Tina hug the scarecrow. The sleeves of my suit coat within the raincoat were draped around her neck. It was ridiculous. She ignored me and emptied the pockets on the coffee table before hanging the whole bundle in the closet. Each object she fondled as if I were gone and these mementos were all that remained of me. Once again I felt I was looking out at the aftermath through the eyes of my corpse.

Tina crumpled the empty envelope from Steingut and dropped it in the wastebasket.

"My, aren't we rich these days!" She was poking into my wallet like a hausfrau on payday. "And do you still keep two fifties inside your belt?"

"I haven't changed."

"What's this, Jon?" It was another plastic bookmark slipped into my pocket by the incorrigible mystic, Sugar Red.

"Religious sentiments from a bartender in my building," I said. "He should have been a pickpocket. You wouldn't do badly yourself, lady."

Tina poured us some ouzo and went to the kitchen for water. When she returned, she sat on my knee and read the turquoise bookmark. My instant thought was that she was heavier than Jenny. It swiftly converted to the notion that Jenny was too light. After five years, I could no longer share such trivial dialectics with Tina. It was uncomfortable hiding from her.

"Nothing religious about this," she said. " 'December. Birthstone: Turquoise. Flower: Narcissus.' That's you, Jon."

"Thanks."

" 'Great energy. Expecting everyone else to be as honest, they are often the victims of designing sharpies. Aggressive. Progressive. Command success. Not vindictive.' "

"Is it Capricorn or Sagittarius?"

"Either one, I guess. 'Secretive as to their own private affairs. Careful and methodical in work. They can follow their inspirations with confidence, and for this reason are impatient when others try to instruct them how to proceed.' Oh, this is very good, Jon. 'The men are inclined to allow their business to outweigh their domestic duties, although there is no lack of love in their basic natures. Failure rarely comes to persons born in December, but when it does, they fight very bravely.' Well, I think he is a remarkable bartender. May I keep it?"

"Why not?" I held her shoulders tightly. It was difficult to believe that it was Tina and not the dream.

"Jon," she said, with the same half smile I first saw at the water's edge, "what's my birthstone, what's my flower?"

"You're testing."

"Do you remember?"

"It's April," I said. "April Fool's Day." Tina hugged me as I knew she would, then jumped to her feet and picked a tulip from the vase.

"I really don't know what the April flower is," she said. "My flower is the yellow tulip. A man walked up to me on the corner twenty minutes ago and gave me some yellow tulips. A strange man who once came in from the sea. He used to bring me yellow tulips every week."

I stretched my arms toward her from the chair. "You were the only one, Tina."

She smiled, a wise and sad little smile I had not seen before. "Greedy, wasn't I, to want everything," she said. "Every little piece to the puzzle."

She did not come back to me. I lowered my arms in surprise. Our desires were a complete mystery to each other. Stupid. How could I expect, after five years, that she would be the same? She was still young. Last April Fool's Day could only have been her twenty-ninth birthday. But the lines marring her forehead were strangers to me. Her arms were oddly pocked by time. That much of my thoughts she must have read.

"Well, Jon, why?"

"I wanted to see you, that's all."

"Why now?" But she knew the answer. "You're on the run, aren't you?"

"Yes."

" 'Careful and methodical in work.' You're here on duty."

"I need help, Tina. You're the only one who knows me."

The telephone rang. She started for it and then stopped. It rang again.

"I have an appointment," she said.

"Then answer it."

There were three more rings.

"It can wait," she said.

I picked up the receiver. "Hello."

There was a click and the line went dead.

"Very friendly," I said. "I'm sorry if I've frightened away some panting admirer."

"I told you it can wait."

"Oh, but I'm so careful and methodical. And so are you, Tina. That's why I find it hard to understand such a careless investigation of my pockets."

"What do you mean?"

"This, Tina." I scooped up the railroad schedule from the table-top. "And this." She had placed beneath it the message from Steingut about twelve trains to Babylon.

"What is it?" she said.

"It came from an envelope like the one you threw away."

"Jon, I don't want to know what's in that envelope."

"That one was empty. You do recognize those envelopes I used to receive, Tina?"

"Yes, I remember."

"Then go ahead. Read the message. Maybe you can figure it out."

"I don't want to know any more."

"You used to be so curious."

"I don't want to know!"

"Then I'll tell you. It says, 'There are twelve trains to Babylon. The first leaves tonight.' And Tina, for once in my life I don't know what the message means."

"I can't help you."

"You have to. Because, you see, I think it's locked away somewhere. It's something I don't want to remember. Didn't I ever mention it to you, Tina? The twelve trains to Babylon?"

"No. It means nothing to me."

"Tina, we're talking about my life. There's a man who can take my life. He has it all in a file. He even knows your name."

"Who is he?"

"Mansfield. Do you know him? Did he ever question you about me?"

"No."

"Somehow he found out too much. I have to find Steingut."

"No, Jon!"

"There's no choice."

"Please stop this."

"Who else is there but you? Think, Tina! I don't know where to begin. What would you do in my place? How would you find Steingut?"

"Dammit, Jon, I can't tell you! I don't know what I'd do. Don't you think I'd help you if I could? God, what a fool I was! I was so excited when you called. I couldn't wait to see you. I thought you wanted me."

"I do."

"Then no more questions, baby. No more questions."

She brushed by me into the bedroom. I was uncertain whether to follow her or to leave that instant, before it began all over again, just as before, a love that turned in on itself and destroyed its addicts.

As her skirt fell to the floor, I saw blue veins pressing to break through the flesh of her thighs. She freed her breasts. Once I had joked about apples in Eden. Now they were soft teardrops. Her nipples had swollen as if she had been suckling an infant. She sat down on the bed, her back to the doorway. I disliked myself for that microscopic inspection. I was seeking out every blemish, hoping she would be tarnished beyond desire.

I wondered if it were possible to forget the present, to begin at the first moment on the rim of the ocean and this time change the ending. On the beach that night we had been the only two on earth, watching stars fall at the beginning of time. Was it too late to control our own time machine? No one could hurt us together. Not Steingut or Mansfield, not all the schedules and letters and empty envelopes. We could make our escape that night. What was she doing? With whose lives was hers entangled? None of it could matter. We could live on an island in the Aegean, run naked on the beach, eat fruit from the trees, fish in the surf, make love under a moon so bright it would blind all intruders. I smiled at the seizure of middle-aged romanticism. Yet was it so impossible?

I stared at her back. She raised her hands behind her head and pushed the stem of the yellow tulip into her hair.

"Tina!" I said. "Please don't move! Stay as you are."

My father and my mother were blissful from beginning to end. He went to great pains to reassure me about that. It was important to him that he establish it over and over again, and perhaps even more important to me. There were three things that he never tired of telling me. One was how he had taught me my right hand from my left, north from south, and east from west. I had begun left-handed with my spoon and he punished me for it. "Now try it again," he said. "This is your right hand. At the moment it is also your west hand." Thereafter, the sense of left and right, east and west, was obsessively acute. The second lesson was how to judge distances. That was a specialty of his. It was our favorite game. I learned to tell a kilometer by superimposing on the landscape the length of our block. Later it proved useful.

And he never tired of telling me about his first meeting with my mother. I must have heard the story literally hundreds of times, even when my ears were too young for it. I never believed it entirely, but by the time I was ten or eleven I was beginning to understand it and it embarrassed me. Yet I could not let on. He would sit gazing into the fire, puffing on his long pipe, weaving the tale as if for the first time, and I would fidget in my chair, sometimes suppressing a giggle, wondering why he was telling me and whether he knew he had told me before. I have a feeling that he even whispered it to me in the cradle. He did not want me to forget it. He wanted to assure me. Over and over again.

It would begin, each time, as a great joke on himself. He would chuckle about how he, the renowned professor of anthropology, was famed for his detachment in observing each culture. But in one moment he lost that quality of intellect and (here he would chuckle again) became an even greater anthropologist. It was on the second expedition far north of Bengkulu.

"The others had gone back to camp, lazy loafers," he would say, and the words were always the same. "They were keeping office hours out there in the jungle. Nine to five with an hour out for lunch. But you will never discover anything, never do anything significant in life, if you live by the clock." At that point, enigmatically, he would wind his watch and turn toward me with a stern look. Each time I would nod my pledge to live my life as he wished. Then he would resume.

"They went back east for lunch. I walked west. Toward a village we had never seen. I came upon a stream. It was wide and fast and clear blue. Strangely, it was the colors that held my eye first. I will tell you why that was strange in a minute." (It was as if I had forgotten that Laertes kills Hamlet in the last act.) "The noonday sun was shining directly on the stream. The jungle on either side was deep green, all but one tree, with bright yellow leaves, that reached out over the stream and cast a shade on the girl's back. Now you see why it was strange I noticed the colors first. There was a girl sitting in the stream bathing herself. And, son, she was the loveliest girl I had ever seen. The water, sparkling in the sun, rushed over her legs as if to carry her off with the current. But she was strongly planted, like a graceful tree, her roots dug into the sand, her limbs swaying in the breeze. She held her arms, beautiful brown, above her head as she burrowed a crimson blossom into her thick hair. Thick it was," he said, as if I had not fully appreciated a nuance, "not soft and fluffy, but long and black, streaming out behind her in the water. The strength in that body! She was large-boned, her buttocks a wide pillow on the sand. Her breast — for I could view but one from my vantage point — full and low. I could not see her face at all. It seemed to me quite possible that it might be ugly. Or it might be beautiful." He always relit his pipe at that moment, savoring it until my fidgeting grew audible. "Well, as time passed, the sun dried her shoulders and her back. I knew that soon she would be running back to the village. As she moved to face the sun, she saw me. And in an instant she was gone."

There he ended the story. I always thought it peculiar that he should end it with my mother gone. In fact, that was only the beginning. He bought her in marriage and they went back to Utrecht together. She was, I learned from others, gay and charming, quick to learn, anxious to please. My father never mentioned the year they had together in Utrecht. And I never did learn whether she was, as that first day he feared, ugly, or as he hoped, a beauty. I never saw a photograph. They told me that I looked very much like my father but I had my mother's eyes.

My father sought constantly to assure me, even before I needed assurance, that I had nothing to do with her death. She was vulnerable to the diseases of civilization, he said. There was nothing that could have been done. Whenever he was angry at me for trouble in school or a fight on the street, he would raise his hand to strike me and then stop. Then he would hold me very close to him and tell me that he could never be angry at me and that I had not killed his bride, though I knew that at the moment of my birth her heart stopped beating. We would sit down and he would tell me the jungle story, with a gentle, faraway look in his eyes, and I would pretend I had never heard it before. It was many years before I vaguely sensed that I was searching for the vision I had killed.

Tina sat motionless on the bed. I stood staring at her back, wondering what thoughts at that moment she, too, could not share. Then she lay her head down, reaching back for me, her hair streaming down to the floor. I knelt by the bed and kissed the tulip and touched her hair. "Thick." I smiled at the ghost of the old man by the fire. "Not soft and fluffy, but thick."

Her eyes were closed tightly. She was smiling as if she had won a game. I touched her cheeks, neck, shoulders, all still soft. But for the lines on her forehead and the marks on her arms, no angle or rise or fall was a surprise, everything had been explored and memorized long ago.

Five years of longing were poured into those hours. And it seemed like years later when I saw that my hand was shaking as I reached over to feel if she was still there.

"How are you, Jon?"

"Tired. Forty-five minutes' sleep in two nights. Half-an-hour Saturday night. Fifteen minutes last night."

"Why?" she said.

"Dreams. The dreams keep me awake." I turned my head toward her on the pillow. "And you, Tina. How have you been?"

She stared silently at the ceiling. I wondered if we were still together.

"I dreamed of you by a waterfall, Tina."

"What happened?"

"I was wrong. It was all wrong to let you go."

"No." She kissed my cheek. "I don't blame you. I know it was for my sake."

She turned away from me. We were silent again. Neither of us wanted to talk about the sunset that day, or any other day.

"We could escape, Tina. To an island."

She pressed a finger to my lips.

"Are you still tired, Jon?"

"Mm."

"Then shh, baby. Let's talk about it when we wake up." Her voice sounded very far away.

Sometime after midnight I reached over. She was gone. Her hair on the pillow had turned to paper.

Jon dearest,

Forgive me for not waking you but I cannot speak these things.

My baby, in all this time, each day you have been my first thought. I have missed you so, but I cannot share all I want to. There are parts of your life and mine that can never be joined together. I have a son now. So simple.

I have left to keep that appointment. I need him.

I cannot change things. I have a feeling of fear about us, much more than before. If we parted to save each other from danger then, we have even greater reason now. My feeling is that this time we would kill each other.

I cannot come back here to you. If you like, we can meet at the library at noon. But I beg you, Jon, no questions! And please, if you come, this must be the last time.

Toujours,
Tina

I, I, I, I, I. Selfless Tina, long-suffering American Girl.

"No questions!" No questions? Dear Tina: Do you know that you could make a fortune writing for Zuckerman's old pulp magazines? Why not call your column 'Toujours, Tina'? Millions would hang breathlessly on your every cliché. Better yet, they would believe you. Unlike me. With renewed affection for your evasive talents, Jamais, Jon.

No questions! Tina had not hurt me with her melodrama, as she flattered herself. She had puzzled and angered me. As I walked up the library steps, I felt like feeding her to the stone lions.

It was not the news that infuriated me. I had heard worse confessions in my life. And why should I care? She did not belong to me. Yes, it had been pleasant, much more than pleasant, reliving a memory. I was an idiot, lost in desire, even to consider an island with Tina. Why did I think that she could have saved me? How could I have been so stupid as to move back from the present, away from Jenny, only because Tina knew more about me than Jenny? Sweet Jenny.

What infuriated me was Tina's tone. It was all so maternal and condescending. And transparent. With all her denials, Tina was saying that she needed me. She was asking me to save her. I was in no position to save anyone.

But as I entered the library, I was not looking for Tina. I had already pulled out a tray of index cards and begun flipping through before I realized. It was not time for Torre's pickup! It was Tuesday. The clock showed two minutes past twelve. Monday at eleven should be the time. Yesterday! Where had I been? The envelope from Steingut. It was empty. Torre must also have received an empty envelope. He would not have come.

I shoved the tray back in. No, it was not here that Tina and I used to meet. It was at the Donnell Library. I was losing my grip, to confuse times and places, Torre and Tina. Three minutes past noon. Would she still be there?

I raced out the door and down the steps, across Forty-second Street, up Fifth Avenue. Damn! Eleven blocks north. With luck, I could be there by seven minutes, eight minutes past. The visibility of speed. The crowd was looking at me now, but I didn't care. Would she wait? Or had she held me to noon, or five past, and then left?

The book guard at the Donnell door was startled as I rushed past. I stood by the elevator and worked to slow my breathing. Of course the Donnell. Why had we chosen a library? Perhaps it originally came to mind from the Torre pickups. I had selected it when we discovered that her home was being watched during those last months. Once a week we would meet there and then go to the hotel room, until even that seemed unsafe, too great a risk for too small a fraction of each other. Yes, the third floor. The reference room. In the far corner, southeast, near the microfilms, she used to sit facing the door. And she was there.

"Hello, Tina!" Heads turned as I approached her.

"Shh!" She was furious at my indiscretion.

"Sorry." But it was not impulsive. I meant to chide her out of her damned self-pity. I knew she would try to have our farewell there to protect herself from speaking too much.

"Please," Tina whispered, "just tell me that you agree with me, and then go."

"I can't hear you!"

She looked around at the crowd, more in embarrassment than fear.

"All right," she said. "But not to my place. And not to a hotel room."

"Of course not."

We walked north toward the park.

"A son!" I whistled in appreciation. "Where was he last night?"

Tina was hurt. She must have expected me to arrive clutching her letter, well stained with tears, and confess I had just taken an overdose of Seconal.

"Next door with Mrs. Poulakidas," she said.

"That's a relief. At least you're not married."

She smiled at last, playing the game.

"But you wrote me there would be no questions," I said. "You just answered a question."

She reached out for my hand. I ignored the gesture. It was not a game. We walked into the park.

"Do you want to tell me about it?"

"No," she said.

We sat on a rock watching two teen-agers paw each other clumsily. The girl opened her eyes and saw us over the boy's shoulder. They moved behind a tree.

"Well, that was a night," I said. "Never quite like that before."

"No. Never."

Useless. It should have been abandoned in her apartment, or perhaps even on the street. When I gave her the tulips, I should have walked away. Now we could only sit there wondering who would finally have the courage to stand up and go, who would stay to watch the other disappear. What words to say? There were no more words.

"Do you remember the first true thing I said to you, Jon?" Tina had solved it. To end it at the beginning.

"Yes. We were watching a shooting star, and you said something about stars not dying in peace."

"I wrote a poem about that."

"Did you bring it along?" We laughed. That was all that was left to do.

"It's somewhere," Tina said. "I may have lost it."

"I hope it was more truthful than the letter." We laughed again but not much.

"It was," Tina said. "But the letter was almost truthful."

I decided that it would be me. I would be the one to go.

I moved my foot from the rock to the ground. But I could not stand up.

"And do you remember, Jon, what you said when you left me five years ago?"

"No."

"That there is no good way to end a love. You were right. It's just as true now. This is not a good way."

"Tina!" I gripped her shoulders.

What did I want to say? Let's try, try again? The last illusion, a pathetic burst of life before death. I tightened my grip and felt her wince. Something in her manner, the sudden, sharp pulling away, trying to conceal the pain, made my fingers grope for a sensitive spot. I pushed up the right sleeve of her dress. Her skin bore an ugly black bruise.

"I didn't do that!" I said, more to myself than Tina. I was angry as a cuckold.

"No, Jon, it wasn't you." And she was on her feet, running from the park, expecting, I knew, that I would come dashing after her with "Who? Who, Tina? I'll kill him! I'll save you, Tina!"

But I sat very still on the rock with my hand over my eyes, listening to her fading footsteps, the coo of a hungry pigeon, the rhythmic groans of the young couple behind the tree. I did not even watch her go.

5.

Jenny! Her anger would be cooled. Just another of her passing fits. Jenny had never stayed angry.

It was a game of subway badminton and I was the shuttlecock. I laughed at the blackness whirling by. So that was the game they were playing with me. They had forced me to search for a home.

I had gone to save Tina and instead begged for help. I had left Jenny, thinking to save her, and that, too, was to save me. How could I possibly endanger Jenny now? Steingut already believed I was living with her. He had sent the empty envelope there. Mansfield would not return to Jenny's. He had given me his word. On condition: tomorrow's progress report.

Progress. It was enough just staying alive. The working conditions have not been the best, Mansfield. I need a headquarters, a cook, a warm cheek close by on the pillow. I know, don't say it. It is not like me. "Careful and methodical." For five years a life of austerity in the loft. I have not needed anyone. It is laughable, inconceivable, that I would pursue a mission by shuttling back and forth between two women. You do not cover the sudden shape of fear. That is not in your documents. It is useless information.

From Tina to Jenny. Not to an island, no. Just to ease the pain. For tonight, tomorrow night, to kill the dreams, to survive this week. Blindly and overwhelmingly, I needed Jenny with the soft, fluffy hair red as the dawn, the breathtaking legs, the little hands and breasts, the tiny pearls in her ears. And no questions. This time, afraid to lose me, she would have no questions. She knew nothing and I would tell her nothing. It was right, I could do it easily. There are kinds and shades of love. The greatest passions never last. Funny Jenny O'Leary with the dirty bare feet, the green eyes that flickered from sadness to joy, filled my thoughts with warmth and affection. I smiled at the comfort of the feeling. Even her sadness made me happy. As I walked up out of the subway into the Brooklyn twilight, I felt foolishly young and light-hearted. The weight of Tina had been lifted from me.

It took a dozen loud knocks before the door opened slowly. One look at me and she moved to slam it shut. I jammed my foot inside.

"Fuller brushes, madam."

"I'm not home."

"Ouch!"

She jumped hard on my foot and shoved the door closed as I retreated.

"Jenny O'Leary," I whispered through the crack, hopping on my good foot. "What's wrong with you? You're acting like a school-girl."

I knew that would work. There was an angry silence. Then I heard her scuffling around, cleaning up fast.

This time the door swung wide open and she stepped aside to admit me. She was wearing a bathrobe and a sly, triumphant smile. She clasped her hands and bowed like a geisha girl.

It was quite a scene. The boy on the bed was frantically pulling up his pants. He was frightened to death.

As I entered the room, Jenny closed the door behind me.

"All right, Douglas," she said. "Hit him."

The boy was far more concerned with covering himself. He looked to be about eighteen or nineteen, handsome, probably loaded with charm and bon mots under other circumstances.

"Look, I'm sorry," he said.

The lid flew off Jenny's rage when she saw that he was talking not to her but to me.

"Like this, Douglas!" She reared back and belted me in the stomach.

The blow was easily absorbed. My laughter only heightened her frustration.

"Look at that!" she screamed. "Like a pillow! Last year you were hard as a rock. You're positively middle-aged!"

Douglas scrambled for safety as I threw Jenny on the bed, pinned her down and spanked her.

"Hit him, Douglas!" Jenny squirmed vainly to free herself.

"Look, I had no idea." Douglas was barely avoiding a stammer. "If I had known this . . ."

"Douglas! Hit him!" Each time she issued the order, I increased the velocity of the spanking. "Douglas! Don't you hear me? All right then. All right for you. Hit him, Jon!"

I released her and looked over at Douglas. He raised his fists in perfect boxing form.

"You're making a real mistake," he said. "She didn't tell me she was married."

"C'mon!" Jenny said. "Somebody hit somebody!"

"Why don't we just talk this over?" Douglas said.

"All right," I agreed.

"Douglas, this man is not my husband!" Jenny shrieked. "Don't believe him! He lies constantly. Lies and cheats, robs and kills, breaks his word, sneaks out on people."

"Is this true?" Douglas said.

"Yes, I do all those things."

"I mean, you're not her husband?"

"Oh, now, you can't really believe Jenny when she gets hysterical like this. Why, it was just yesterday, Douglas — it is Douglas, isn't it? — just yesterday she admitted to me on the telephone that she was a very jealous wife."

The pillow struck me squarely in the face. Jenny's aim had always been remarkable. She bought books about Zen archers. Next came the cracked ashtray, a near miss. As I came up from my knees, I saw her lift from the pedestal the clay bust of the boy in the dream. It flew directly at my chest. I caught it and was sent reeling back against the door.

"Now you're going too far," I said. "You wouldn't want to destroy your greatest work of art."

Douglas stood watching like a tennis spectator, his head whipping back and forth.

"You're right," Jenny said. "It does need improvement, doesn't it?" As I held the clay head in my hands, she went to work on it furiously. "The mouth. Too boyish. It should look like this. Tight and sinister and ugly. And the ears are too small." She stretched the ears to giant size. "Always listening, listening, listening, but never feeling a damn thing. And the nose." She smashed it in. "Like a punch-drunk plug-ugly. Now, this side of the face is one face." She pushed in a cheek with the flat of her hand. "And this side is another. No, that's wrong. It should be at least three-faced. Possibly four. And the eyes. They're all wrong. I think I'll just start over." She gouged out the clay eyes and threw them on the floor.

I stared at the head in my hands. The more I looked at it, the more fearful I became. Funny little Jenny had done it now. She was sobbing in exhaustion. It subsided as she saw my face.

We stood there, the three of us, Jenny and I together for the first time, Douglas not sure whether to leave nor how to leave. He put a tentative hand on her shoulder, not to comfort her but to reach her.

"Don't touch her!" I said. His hand jerked back.

I put the clay head on a chair. The room was silent as I left.

Joe Hull barred the doorway.

"You can't go up there," he said.

I glared at him until he dropped his eyes.

"That's a new game, isn't it, Joe? Charging me to cross my own threshold."

"It's not yours. There are new people up there."

"Well, well."

I looked at him with contempt. It was not difficult for Joe to sense contempt, even when it wasn't there.

"Do you know why I left here Friday night, Joe?" He shifted his feet uncomfortably. "Because you guessed wrong. That was a cop you let in. Or maybe you guessed right. How much did he pay you?"

"Five bucks."

"That's what I've always admired about you, Joe, your candor."

"So he gave me five bucks. How much have you been giving me?'" He spat on the pavement. "Not enough for a man to live decently."

I moved but not fast enough. He jumped inside the hallway.

"You're not coming up here," he said. "You don't belong here."

"What are they paying you, Joe?"

"It's not what they've paid me, it's the feeling I have. They're going to be good to me."

"Well, I'll tell you, Joe, there's no point in ending our friendship with a fist fight, is there? Why don't we be reasonable about this? I have nowhere else to stay tonight. I thought I did, but I was wrong. Now, why don't both of us go up there and we'll see if they'll let us stay in the back room."

Joe pulled out a ten-dollar bill.

"See?" he said. "You see it? That's what kind of people they are."

"You're not trying to take me, are you?"

He was silent.

"I've supported you pretty well, Joe, and I'm not sure why I should top ten dollars simply to enter my own home. I still have stuff up there. And I have a key right here. So I'm giving you a chance to be reasonable."

Joe snarled. It was an animal sound he had never before thrown at me, the one reserved for uninvited guests.

"You know what I'm going to do?" he said. "I'm going to show you what the bum's rush feels like."

As he came at me, I lifted my knee into his groin. I was surprised at how quickly he collapsed. Halfway up the stairs, I looked down and saw him still crumpled.

"That's a present for you, Joe," I said. "From the old man you beat to the pavement."

The key would not turn in the lock. I twisted it back and forth. Something was wrong. I jerked it hard. It broke off in the lock.

The door opened from the inside. The man was dressed in old

fatigues, about thirty, a closed, nervous face, thin lips almost concealed by a handlebar moustache.

"You must be the new tenant," I said cheerfully.

He appraised me up and down until his eyes came to rest on the broken key in my hand. Then he turned to inspect the lock. The tip of the key was imbedded too deeply to see.

"Now you've done it," he said with quiet exasperation.

"I'm sorry about that. Do you have a hairpin?"

He regarded me coldly and stepped back inside the room. A girl in paint-specked wheat jeans was sanding the floor. When she looked up, I saw that behind her long blond hair she was hiding a remarkably ugly face.

"What are you, some kind of jewel thief?" the man said, trying to maintain calm in front of the girl.

"Righto. Just flew in from Cannes."

"What's your name?" he demanded.

"Perkins. Chester Perkins."

"Well, I'm Alec Brooks. I am now the lawful tenant here. And you are out twenty-five dollars, Mr. Perkins, for that new lock you just ruined. I'll take it now."

"Awfully good to know you, Alec." I reached for his hand. He did not move. "Oh, I'm sorry, I thought you knew. I have been the tenant here for the past five years."

"The bartender said this place was for rent and I signed the lease this afternoon. Now, will you kindly get out?"

"Oh, the bartender is right, of course. What I was going to ask you, Alec — but you haven't introduced me to the young lady."

He clenched his fists and stepped toward me.

"I'm here for a watch, Alec. I really would appreciate its return. It's very valuable."

"Let him have it," the girl said. "He looks human."

"Thank you," I said.

"Stay out of this, Sandra," Alec said. "Two weeks we're married and already you're on top of me. How do we know it's his watch?"

"I'll pay you fifty dollars for it," I said.

Alec looked at me with a new interest.

"What'd you say your name was?"

"Perkins. Chester Perkins."

"What's the J for?"

"J?"

"Inside one of the suits you left."

"Awfully nice of you not to sell them. That's my Uncle Jack. Poor chap died and left me all his suits but one. The one he's moldering away in."

"You're lucky I didn't throw that junk out of here," Alec said.

"Those are very good suits."

"Dull."

"Oh, yes, Uncle Jack was a very dull man. So where's the watch?"

"Where's the fifty?"

"Alec!" the girl said. "Is this any way for a social worker to act?"

"This fellow is not disadvantaged," Alec said.

"I think it's terrible," Sandra said.

"Well, I'll be taking my clothes now." I went to the closet. My suits were hanging in a plastic bag. It was very thoughtful of them.

"Perkins," Alec said. "Here it is."

He reached to the top of an orange crate and missed. The watch fell to the floor.

"Sorry," he said.

I picked it up. The crystal was broken.

"That's all right," I said.

"Forget the money," Alec said. "That squares us for the lock."

On the way out, I spotted near the door a bottle perched on an upside down barrel.

"That wouldn't be ouzo, would it?"

Alec did not reply.

"I wonder if I might have a drop, just to celebrate our meeting."

"It's very expensive," Alec said.

Sandra walked over and handed me the bottle.

"Here," she said.

"Thank you, lady."

"I'll get some water," Sandra said.

"No, I'll just have a drop." I took a sip and put down the bottle. Alec looked relieved. "I used to go around with a Greek girl," I said. "Lovely girl. Not as lovely as you, my dear, but then, what can you expect from Greeks? I had to leave her, though. She threatened to poke out my eyes with her nipples. Doesn't that call for a toast?"

Sandra giggled. Alec was gaping. Before I realized it, I had poured half the bottle down my throat.

"Yes, you're the second young couple I've seen tonight. The other girl was a sculptor. Never sanded a floor in her life. Amazing how some people miss the finer things. It's good to have Alec around to separate those things out. Specialization of labor and all that. But the second girl, you see, I went straight to see her after I returned from that last little caper on the Riviera. 'Chester,' she said, 'How good to see you.' Then she gouged out my eyes and threw them on the floor."

Alec and Sandra were both smiling now, anxious to establish that they could not be put on. They tried to think of something to say but, fortunately, they were at a loss.

"Well," I said, "I think it's only appropriate that the next toast should go to the sculptress lady, don't you?"

Alec's hand moved to stop me but his fingers ended up nervously in his mouth.

"Just a drop," I assured him. "I know it's expensive for you, Alec, and I do appreciate it. Believe me. But I thought I should introduce you to the code of the Bowery. Sharing is the byword here. Generosity, honor, justice, and all that. You see, this toast to the sculptress lady might be very important, because I think I love her very much." I raised the bottle. "I think, mind you. Can't ever be sure, can we?" They watched wide-eyed as I drained the bottle dry.

"Thanks for your hospitality," I said, giving each a personal, individual smile.

I threw the bottle against the wall. It smashed nicely into a thousand little bits.

Sugar Red was waiting for me the next morning at Fisher's.

"I hear you went upstairs last night," he said.

"I didn't know you'd rented it, Sugar. After all, the body isn't cold."

"You moved, didn't you?"

"Yes, I've moved."

"Where to?"

"I'm not sure."

"Well, you should have come in for the mail."

"I'm in no hurry."

"Funny. You're usually anxious for it."

He served up a wine cake and a scalding hot cup of coffee. I watched him mix his special medicinal aperitif, known to his customers as a Late Dawn.

"Where the hell you sleep?" he said.

"Hotel. Somewhere."

"First time I've ever seen you with a hangover."

"I lost yesterday. A whole day out of my life."

Sugar Red tossed an envelope on the bar. I could not understand the contents. Why now? Steingut knew I had no current need of money. Was it to say I was still valued? Or a bribe not to turn evidence. How could he know about Mansfield's offer? Inside the envelope were ten crisp fifty-dollar bills. I slipped eight of them into my wallet plus the two rumpled fifties from my belt, which I replaced with new ones.

"I'm not used to being drunk," I said to Sugar Red. "It's against my code."

"I know."

"It was a bad feeling. I demand sobriety."

Sugar Red looked at me strangely. A prematurely balding young man walked in and sat down on a barstool.

"I don't serve junkies," Sugar Red said.

"Man, I kicked it," the young man said. "I got no use for drugs."

I laid one of the bills on the bar.

"Give him breakfast," I said.

The man turned toward me angrily.

"Don't tell me you can't throw it off," he said.

"I'm not telling you anything. I'm buying you breakfast. I've never seen you before."

"Sugar Red knows me."

"I don't know him," Sugar Red said.

"I squared up," the man said.

"I believe you," I said.

"And I know oldtime junkies — fifteen, twenty years — squared up, too," he continued as I tried to drink my coffee. "There's no such thing. There's no animal can get you down. You can't say I can't get it off my back 'cause, man, there's no such thing."

Sugar Red slammed down a wine cake and orange juice in front of the stranger.

"You're no person, dig?" the man said. "You're no person if you're a junkie. You got nothing, no identity, nothing to hang onto. I know, man."

"How'd you do it?" I asked without interest.

"I locked up. The old man locked me up and I screamed it out. And all the time pounding those walls and biting my lips. There's no reason you can't. You gotta cold turkey yourself."

"What's your name?" I said.

"Gonzalo."

"Well, Gonzalo, I've never had that problem."

"You can do it." He would not be stopped. "You think it's just kicks. But one morning you'll wake up and wonder, when was it I got hooked? Think of all you missed. Think of all the cats you got to avoid. Avoid, Jack, because you're ashamed. Ashamed like you got nothing to live for."

Sugar Red fairly threw a plate of fried eggs at Gonzalo.

"Eat," he said. "My friend is buying for you. He doesn't need a lecture. He may look hungover but he doesn't have your problem."

I got up to leave. Sugar Red handed me my change. $48.13. I gave it to Gonzalo.

"Buy a few drinks," I said. "You don't look happy this way."

Wednesday! Mansfield had asked for a progress report. What would I tell him? I had lunch with Thaddeus after you left. He said I am a dead man. That's thanks to you. Jenny hung up on me. Again thanks to you. Thought about my father being taken away by the flatfoots. Like you. Turned Good Samaritan for a tourist and a bum. Jimmied Jenny's mailbox for an empty envelope. Remembered I did a nice job on the Commander. You asked about Katrina Athenasios. Bumped into her. A few ins and outs, nothing to report. Jenny threw my eyes on the floor. Some creep moved into my loft. Just received five hundred dollars from Steingut while having breakfast with a junkie. How's that for progress?

MA 0–3 — what was the rest of the number? I fished through my wallet for his card. There it was. Lee Mansfield. I dialed. The booth was sweltering but I kept the door tightly closed.

"Customs Enforcement."

"Mr. Mansfield, please."

"Who's calling?"

"A friend."

"May I have your name, please?"

"Just tell him Jon is calling."

He came on immediately.

"Where are you, Jon?"

"How are you, Lee baby?"

"Don't get cute. Look, I've kept my word. I don't know where you are. What can you report?"

"Nothing. I'm working on it."

"You have five more days."

"I have to go."

"Wait a minute, Jon. Have you heard from Steingut?"

"No."

"Nothing at all?"

"Nothing."

"No mail?"

"When I get what I want, I'll let you know. I have to go."

"One more question, Jon." Why was he so persistent? "Do you have any leads at all? I know it's tough, but I wonder if . . ." On and on he went. For Mansfield, it was a very long question. Slowly, the danger grew clear. He was keeping me on the telephone. He was stalling me. Mansfield was tracing the call.

I traveled more than twenty blocks to make the second call. As it turned out, it was not really necessary. The call took all of five seconds.

"Hello, Jenny."

"Come over."

We lay on our sides, strangers, loving from a distance. I was thinking of that moment the night before with the boy and the clay bust when we were together. But now, alone, it was difficult to be together.

"You're wonderful, Tina," I said.

The feather touch vanished. I felt terrible. There was nothing I could do, no way to repair the damage. Jenny was sitting up, her knees pulled up to her chin, a little in shock but still Jenny.

"I'd like to say, 'The same to you, Douglas,'" she said. "But I have to say: who is she?"

"Someone I knew. I'm sorry."

Jenny turned her back to me. I knew she was not crying. She was thinking. And whatever dismal thoughts she had, she would overcome them. I rested my hand on her shoulder. She did not turn back. But she did not pull away.

"What happened to Douglas?" I said.

"Somehow I don't think he'll be back." She thought about that one until, despite her best efforts, her shoulders began shaking with laughter. Then we were both laughing, uncontrollably, simply at being together and unafraid for the moment.

"You're great, Jenny."

"Yeah. That's me."

"I missed you. Just this short time, I really missed you."

"Did you feel what I felt last night?" Jenny said. "Like, it was just us in this room?"

"Like now," I said.

"No, not like now." She swung her feet to the floor and reached over for her clothes on the chair. "What is it that's standing between us, Jon?"

"Nothing permanent." I looked at my naked wrist. "My watch is broken. Where you going?"

"To work, of course. I'm late."

"Don't go, Jenny."

"Sorry. I'd listen if you were the landlord." She searched the room for her shoes.

"I want to be."

"What are you talking about?"

"I'm going to pay your rent."

"Sweet Jesus, I've heard that one before." The shoes were under the couch.

"Jenny, listen to me. I want to support you. No obligations."

"You mean, like a kept woman?" She giggled at the prospect. "But why?"

"Because I want to stay with you for a long time, as long as I can. There's something I have to do. I'll be coming and going. I can't have you worrying about me and I don't want to worry about you. It's your choice."

"That's a hell of a choice."

"I know. It's not fair."

"Are you going to be thinking about her all the time?"

"Who?"

"The one you mentioned."

"That's all over now."

"Well, I suppose if you were with her now, you'd be thinking about me." She stood there in a quandary, wringing her blouse like a handkerchief. "That's really the way it is with you, isn't it?" she said. "United we fall, divided we stand." She paced back and forth. "A kept woman! Who would have ever thought?"

"It's your choice."

"You mean, I'd never have to go back to that crummy restaurant?"

"That's right."

She kicked off her shoes.

"Now what do I do?" she said. "I've never been a kept woman before."

"You take a nap," I said. "You look like you were up half the night making fancy explanations to Douglas."

"Yes, that's the obligation." She lay down beside me and I stroked her back. "I have to look like Madame Pompadour all the time. Next thing it'll be facials."

"I'm going to make a telephone call now, Jenny, and you aren't going to ask me anything about it. We're going to have a kind of truce in this household."

"Go ahead, who cares? Jenny is a kept woman."

I reached over for the telephone and lay back. This was the life.

"Any mail?"

"I gave it to you," Sugar Red said.

"That was yesterday's."

"Wait a minute. I'll look." Jenny watched my foot bouncing nervously during the wait. "No. Nothing here," Sugar Red said.

"You're certain the mail's come in?"

"It's all here. Nothing for you. Were you expecting something?"

"Thanks."

Of course not. Why should I expect mail every day?

But I needed word from Steingut. I had nothing to go on.

"I won't ask you about that phone call," Jenny said.

"They were going to send the mail here," I said, "but somehow they know I left. How would they know that? They sent money there. And now there's nothing."

"Jon, what do you do?"

"Oh, my God."

"I promised not to ask you about the phone call. I didn't even ask why you broke into my mailbox. Who else would be crazy enough to break into my mailbox, I figured. And the crack in the ashtray. Didn't think I'd notice? But I distinctly did not say this time I wouldn't ask you what you do."

"I told you."

"Chain letters, shmain letters."

"All right, then. I wind electric clocks."

"Where do you come from, Jon?"

"Baltimore. I told you that last year."

"I still don't believe you."

"Must I fill out an application for half this bed? It's only a sleeping couch."

"You don't have an accent."

"What does a Baltimore accent sound like? H. L. Mencken?"

"You have a strange way of talking. It's, like, each syllable is a word, each word is a sentence. As if you had learned each word, how to say it well. As if you had learned some kind of actor's part."

"You're sharp, Jenny. I talk different ways to different people. Peculiar, isn't it? That's the way I think, too."

It was the first honest thing I had said to her. Honesty always worked with Jenny. She held out her arms.

"What does a kept woman do now?" she said.

"I told you. You go to sleep, which is what you want to do."

"What a selfless master I have! How did you know I'd rather do that?"

"Because your master has to leave. He has a lunch appointment."

"You rat."

"I'll be home for dinner."

As I dressed, I heard a familiar buzzing.

"You've still got that fly in your room," I said. "Our room."

But Jenny was asleep. I watched her lying there. She was smiling. However little I had given her, I had made her happy for this day. Smiling in her sleep. I was home at last.

"Dinner at seven," I said, double-locking the door behind me.

"Tch, tch. Drinking again," I chided Thaddeus.

"I am never drunk," he said. "And you're late again."

"You are drunk," I said. "It's I who am never drunk. Except last night."

He ignored that. He wasn't interested.

"I am never drunk," he said. "Take it back."

"I'm sorry."

"That shows how you're slipping over the margin these days. False accusations. Character assassination. A dozen ales is all I've had."

"I said I'm sorry."

"Long ago, I carefully worked out this regime. To avoid all hangovers and major mishaps. Daily maintenance of a nineteen-hour ale haze. Nothing extreme. Scheduled dosage. Numbs the fingertips very slightly. Not enough to interfere with my reading. Keeps the old bladder kicking. Through this method I have become invulnerable. Especially to slanderous remarks like that."

"I agree, of course. It was I who was drunk last night."

"A dozen ales is all I've had. That's perhaps one too many for this time of day. It's all your fault. Don't you carry a watch?"

"Somebody broke it," I said. "It's my father's watch."

Thaddeus pulled from his pocket an odd-looking timepiece.

"Almost one o'clock," he said. "My watch never stops. Sensual time. Sixteenth century. The highest dot is noon. Nearly an hour late. I've had my lunch. You may pay the bill and leave."

"I think I might marry the girl," I said quickly.

"Contracts! Get me an ale. There's distrust in contracts. Marriage, social security, life insurance, installment plans, divorces, wills, death certificates, burial plots, no trust. Trust people, I say. Glass houses. A rolling stone. An apple a day. And tell me this: how do ants bury their dead?"

"You're the one with the answers." I signaled for another ale.

"The answer is a question," Thaddeus said. "The only question that matters now: why does the snow melt in April, in spite of the sheep?"

"You don't need that ale."

"In spite of the sheep, do you understand? In spite of the sheep!"

He tossed down the ale and wiped his mouth on his sleeve. Then he carefully cleaned the sleeve with his napkin.

"See those girls in the corner?" he said.

"Those aren't girls."

"There's not supposed to be any women in McSorley's. Lately you keep bringing them in all the time."

"Not me," I said. "Women's Liberation."

"Those are visions I don't need. I'd rather have shadows than visions in that corner. But you're insensitive, that's your trouble. Talking about someone I don't know, don't want to know. I won't notarize any contracts."

"Do you need any money, Thaddeus?"

"You see? You're not sure. You're making out your will already. But at the same time, you're trying to stay alive. Make up your mind. Certainly, if you plan on dying, leave me your money. See if I care."

"So long, Thaddeus."

But he looked worried. Thaddeus was not noted for his coherency, but neither was he a man of nonsense. It was never difficult to know when he was troubled. I waited for him to settle down. He sensed that I was still standing there. He tapped his fingers excitedly on the table.

"Someone was asking questions," he said at last.

"When?"

"Around noon. I thought for a minute it might be you when he first walked over here. Questions, all kinds of questions."

I surveyed the room. No one was there but the regulars.

"What did you tell him?"

"Everything I knew. He asked me if I were acquainted with a man named Jon. I asked him how do ants bury their dead. He asked me if you were coming over today. I asked him why the snow melted in April, in spite of the sheep. He asked me if I knew where you were. That one made me lose my temper. I told him it was the last stem of grain to sever the tergum of the dromedary, and I would be damned if I would give him any more helpful information."

I squeezed Thaddeus' arm affectionately. He pulled away.

"Don't get sentimental," he said. "It's not friendship. It's all these lunches you've provided to buy my silence."

"Did the man say where he was going, Thaddeus? Was he going to look for me?"

"Didn't say. Left rather hurriedly. To get away from me, I pride myself."

"Thanks."

I turned to go.

"You never asked me his name," Thaddeus said.

"I assume he didn't give it."

"Wrong."

"I already know," I said. "It was a man named Mansfield."

"No."

Thaddeus smiled, a rare feat for him. For hundreds of luncheons I had been free to take or leave his ruminations. Now, at last, he knew he was the indispensable man in possession of a hard fact.

"All right, Thaddeus, who was he?"

"Well, now, I really don't know. But he said his name was Torre."

To work. The crowd was moving fast and purposefully up the avenue, returning from lunch to work; there were things to be done and we were all a little late. Our Jennys were at home with their dust mops, thinking of diapers and maternity gowns. America. I still longed to like it.

Bergère must have predicted that. "They say that America is a most pleasant assignment." It would make every humiliation bearable. Nine years! And still they had not used my talents. I had long since passed beyond hope and disappointment. Bergère knew it would happen in time. He had envied me, hated me, feared that I threatened his job. Another year and I might have toppled him, or so he thought. What to do? Kill me? He tried his best. He thought I could not kill and he knew the Commander could. But catch Bergère in a miscalculation? Never. The safeguard was perfect: off to America. In my excitement I was blind to the fact that he was sending me into oblivion.

It must have been a full year before I realized that new orders would never come. By then I hardly cared. What if I were reduced to being a link in the chain? I was the strongest link, of that I was certain. The names of those who took chances for glory were household words. How much, in the end, had they given to a new world of justice? They had endangered us all. Each time I read of an arrest in the paper, I was tempted to despise them as weaklings, but I could not. They had done as well as they could. It was easy for them to fail. They were leading false lives. Only through error could they lose the burdens of anonymity. I had the advantage, for I had spent most of my life underground. I knew its lessons. Torre and Steingut knew, too. There can be no star system in the underground. The largest and the smallest roles must be accepted without question.

Moving with the crowd, I smiled at such remembrances in one preparing to betray duty. Mansfield was turning my life into a joke. The iron pretense of principle had softened on the Bowery, little by little, or Mansfield could not have put a hole in it. Bergère was right after all. I had embraced this demeaning walk-on in exchange for the pleasures of America. And he would still be right if I had not chosen to banish all pleasures when I left Tina's bed for the Bowery.

Now I was moving back into America, even further than before, surrounded by the marvels of the wonderful square world. Our women were at home and we were hurrying back to work, not too late but just late enough, all of us fearful of the boss's wrath, wanting to knife the boss. But unlike the crowd, I had Mansfield's bargain to make that worth my while.

So Torre was trying to reach me. He knew only one thing, from some unpredictable twist in the grapevine: I often had lunch at McSorley's with a blind man. That was all he knew. But it was enough. Whatever the message, it had to be vital for him to take such a risk, giving his name to Thaddeus, depending on a stranger to pass it on. It could only be outside the operation. He could not wait. There was no mail from Steingut. Torre wanted me to know something fast. Did he want to help me? How could he know?

Mansfield had reached him! No one had touched me before. If Mansfield could do it, he could find Torre.

Yes, it would have to be that for Torre to take the risk. He was too intelligent to leave a note for me with Thaddeus or drop the name of a meeting place. He gave only the name, which meant nothing to Thaddeus. Torre was counting on me to find him. It would have to be one of the regular spots. How would we know each other? We had no descriptions, no passwords, no signals. Surely, he did not expect me to leave word with Thaddeus. He could not return there. He would go to one of the four places. It could be the library index files. It could be Kennedy or La Guardia, where twice a month I would meet a onetime contact, take the baggage, and leave it in a locker for Torre. That was a clean system. We had lost one or two contacts, but never the baggage. And I had always left empty-handed. Or it could be Penn Station, where I was heading, walking up Eighth Avenue, hurrying back to work with the crowd. It was the last place I had contacted Torre. It was also the most dangerous. Mansfield had spotted me there. Had he seen Torre, too?

No, it was too risky. As I walked through the long underground passage, past the train gates, I knew it was wrong. Doubtless, Mansfield's men were swarming all over the place. I looked straight ahead and continued on quickly toward the subway. The library would be it. I could not even glance to see if I had attracted a shadow. It would just have to be fast and complicated: the A-Train to Fourth Street, down two flights, D-Train back up to Forty-second Street. Going uptown, I walked through the cars toward the front of the train and looked back. No one had followed me.

I fingered through the index cards in the library for nearly an hour. It was too long. The only chance of alerting Torre to my presence was exactly the same as alerting the crowd. I had to be conspicuous, even suspicious. It would not work. The airports would be worse. I was not fool enough to court suspicion with Customs men breathing down my neck. The next move would have to be Torre's. Most likely, his thoughts were running in the same channel. He had made his move. He could take no more risks. He did not know what to do. He would wait, as I would wait, for the next letter from Steingut. Then we would meet.

Returning to the subway, I stopped at a newsstand for the afternoon paper. My eyes wandered to a laundry line of magazines seized by clothes pins across the front of the stall. The attendant was watching me, chewing his gum, wondering if I would be a paying customer. It was the cover of one magazine that held a special fascination. In the center of the rope was *Phantasy*, mighty flagship of the old Zuckerman line. A blood-red headline shouted: *Lady Godiva of the Drag Strip*. It was laughable. The girl on the cover wore crimson boots, somewhat sinister goggles, and a massive blond wig which splashed down strategically, rendering the illusion of nudity. She looked strangely familiar. Wigged and painted, she was barely recognizable. Perhaps I was wrong. It might be a look-alike.

I looked again. There could really be no question about it. It was Tina.

According to the masthead, Zuckerman Enterprises had become Phantasmagoria, Inc. I found it housed respectably on Madison Avenue in the Fifties, sharing a top floor with an operatic agent and a textbook publisher. The sitting room was dustless, Danish, foam rubber, Japanese silkscreens, and a receptionist who believed she was pretty.

"I'd like to see the editor-in-chief immediately," I said. "I'm Lieutenant Feegan, Homicide."

Her eyes widened. She did not ask for credentials. In under two minutes, I was ushered into the over-dressed office of a Mr. Philip Flake.

"How may I assist you, Lieutenant?" He stood politely behind a ridiculously huge desk.

I threw the magazine down in front of him.

"Do you know this woman?" I said.

He scarcely glanced at the cover.

"Yes. The pied piperess. What is she wanted for?"

"Why do you call her that, Mr. Flake?"

"Well, she has quite a following. People even write letters to her. That's rare in this field."

"Do you know who she is?"

"The pied piperess, that's all I know. Leading a parade of mesmerized scroti." He chuckled diffidently.

"You sound like Zuckerman," I said.

"You knew him? My, yes, I trained directly with Mr. Zuckerman. Oh, that was a great loss to the profession. There was no one like him. It's not as easy as you might think." He flipped through the pages of the magazine. "Mr. Zuckerman taught me precisely how to put together this little picnic basket of psychedelicious snacks." He looked up for some sign of appreciation. "I'm a bit like a mortician, you know, palpating all these paper corpses. Not at all dissimilar to your line, is it, Lieutenant?" Flake came around from behind the desk, waving the magazine. "Have a look-see. You notice something? It's the expression that counts. That's what distinguishes Phantasmagoria, Incorporated, from the cheap merchants of filth. These are true actresses. It's not easy, I assure you, to find someone who can leer convincingly from the bowels of a heart-shaped bathtub." He returned the magazine, opened to a page in which he had apparently invested pride.

"Sit down, Mr. Flake."

He was startled into compliance.

"You will excuse my rush, Mr. Flake, but I've already had this lecture, years ago from the late master. What I want now, and all I want, is information on this woman." I carefully folded the magazine and slipped it in my pocket. Flake watched, concerned, as if I were wrapping finger-marked evidence in a handkerchief.

"Is she involved in something?" he said.

"I'll ask the questions."

He buzzed for his secretary. I studied him. He seemed extremely uncomfortable. But who would not be, under interrogation by a police officer? Still, I did not warm to Flake. Cold eyes, pasty complexion, hollow cheeks, minimal lower lip, heavily padded shoulders. He was authentic, no question about that. This was his business. He did not look capable of leading a double life. Zuckerman would not have trusted him beyond this enterprise. No, Flake was not living in my world. Thank God.

"Margaret!" Flake shrieked into the intercom.

"Sir?"

"Who is the dish on the cover?"

"Of what, sir?"

"The current *Phantasy*."

I reached over and clicked off the intercom.

"Mr. Flake, that's not necessary at all. You must know who she is."

Flake reddened. It was an unpleasant sight.

"Why do you assume I know, Lieutenant?"

"All that mail she gets, Mr. Flake."

Flake's secretary knocked and entered.

"Mr. Flake, sir," she said, "that's Miss Athenasios again."

"That will be all, Margaret."

He nervously tapped a gold fountain pen on the desk.

"Katrina Athenasios?" I said.

"Yes." He lowered his eyes.

"Why were you so hesitant to give me her name, Mr. Flake?"

"It's not generally our policy."

"But that's not the reason, is it?"

"It's a difficult name to pronounce."

"Try again, Mr. Flake."

"The pied piperess. She always photographs a little pied. Look at her eyes."

I did not look. This was unreal. It was totally unlike Tina, everything about it.

"How long has she been modeling for your magazines?" I asked.

"A number of years," Flake replied. "Originally, as I recall, she was a discovery of Mr. Zuckerman's."

I did not want to hear more. Suddenly, I needed air. I walked to the door.

"Should I not use her anymore, Lieutenant?" Flake said with a cooperative whine. "I have no idea what she may be mixed up in."

"Just don't mention my visit," I said. "You can use her for anything you want. Whatever she's mixed up in, it needn't affect your business. It might affect mine. But that's the lot of a public servant, isn't it, Mr. Flake?"

There were candles on the table and four bottles of champagne in the icebox. Jenny had an icebox, not a refrigerator. She took great pride in carrying home blocks of ice split into quarters by the corner delicatessen man, who appreciated her eccentricities.

"You look devastated, dear," she said. "Hard day at the office?"

"Now, then," I said, with a quick peck to the cheek, "this suit to the cleaners. The right pocket needs sewing and take off that silly J on the inside of the coat. I'll put the laundry in the hamper. No starch. This watch to the jeweler. It's a good watch. Waterproof, dustproof, but apparently not shockproof. Seems to be broken. And by the way, I'm a stickler for a punctual breakfast. Noon sharp."

I smothered her reply.

"Stop that," Jenny said. "We'll wake the children."

She had cooked a magnificent paella. The shrimp was fresh from Fulton Street.

"There's no rabbit," I said.

"Interesting you should have noticed, señor. Tomorrow it will be Yorkshire pudding. Friday night, lox and bagels. On Saturday, Irish stew, smorgasbord, Welsh rarebit, Chateaubriand, caviar. For Sunday dinner, Polish sausages, ravioli, goulash, Swiss cheese, moussaka, shishkebab, moo goo gai pan, sacred cow curry —"

"Don't forget hamburger, the national dish of Baltimore."

"I'll find out, Jon. Don't underestimate me."

"Has it ever occurred to you that I might be a superbly assimilated Eskimo?"

We rubbed noses and fed each other champagne until the candles burned out.

"Jon." She had that deadly earnest tone again. "Don't you think we have something?"

"Yes."

"And it deserves our courage."

"Really a delicious dinner." I got up and retreated to the alcove. The head on the pedestal had been smoothed back into a round ball of clay. She had either abandoned it or was starting all over again. I rolled it in my hands like a huge snowball.

"What's your plan for this, Jenny?"

She clamped the lid on the remnants of the paella and marched the pot to the icebox.

"My plan is to save the leftovers for tomorrow." She was pouting. It was, to me, a very attractive pout. She knew that. It made her all the more angry.

"You're furious with me," I said.

"I'm going for a walk on the promenade."

"May I come with you?"

"No."

She moved toward the door, a little hesitantly. I did not stop her.

"Do you know why I'm angry?" Jenny said.

"I think so."

"Well, if my anger has any strength, it's because I love you, damn it." With a dramatic flourish, she slammed the door behind her.

I should not have smiled, even behind her back. I did appreciate Jenny. The more she labored to be accepted as something other than a child, the more she made me smile. She had a right to be angry. I was condescending when I had no right to be. I knew how she felt. It was the way Tina had treated me. And, I now saw, it was for the same reason: to protect a secret. Yet I wanted Jenny. I wanted to share everything I could with her. I could not blame her if that was not enough.

She was leaning on the promenade railing, gazing across at the skyline. I stood for a moment about ten feet away before edging over and putting my arm around her. The wind from the harbor was cold. I watched it blow through her hair. She was sniffling from the breeze but she was not crying. Her face was very firm and brave.

"You didn't have to come," she said, without looking at me. "I wanted to be alone."

"It's no good being alone."

I pulled her closer.

"All that champagne, Jenny. Let's go home."

She met my eyes and at last she smiled. At that moment I realized, quite soberly and hardheartedly, that nothing in the world, no cause or reward, was as precious to me as Jenny's smile.

A little Dutch boy was skating on a pond with his mother. It was windy and bitterly cold. He did more falling than skating. Each time he fell, his mother helped him up and they continued on a few more feet, hand in hand. I could not see the mother's face but she seemed to be dark-skinned. The boy was somehow very strange-looking.

On the edge of the pond an old man in a cloak had built himself a fire. He sat before it, rubbing his mittens together, smoking his pipe and staring at the blazing sticks. He seemed to be a captain or a fisherman. He had cut a large hole in the ice, perhaps in the hope that the fish were biting. The boy and his mother skated toward the old man. The boy fell down but this time the mother did not stop to help him up. She went skating across the ice and fell through the hole into the water.

The boy tried to crawl toward his mother but the ice was too smooth. His knees kept slipping backward. He cried but the man did not hear him. The man was talking with three very stern-looking soldiers. They wore black coats and strange armbands. They kept pointing at the man's nose. The man looked over at the boy, waved at him, and walked off with the soldiers.

I heard the boy crying and I wanted to comfort him. He was so small and helpless. I skated over to him and tried to pick him up. At close range, he did not look like a boy at all. His eyes were closed and he was bent into a little ball. He looked something like

107

an embryonic reptile. I looked at his face. He had no features. His head was a smooth gray ball. I touched it. It felt like clay.

In terror I skated away. I forgot all about the plight of the little boy. I forgot his mother, drowning in the pond. I kept skating around and around the pond until suddenly I noticed people staring down from above. I was not on a pond, it was Rockefeller Center. I was skating with Tina. But my eyes were on the crowd above. There was one face that loomed larger than the others. It was a man standing apart from the crowd, staring directly at me. His face grew larger and larger as if I were seeing him through a zoom lens.

It was Mansfield. He smiled and nodded as if we had a secret I would understand. Then his face began to shrink. Eventually it disappeared entirely. I looked at Tina to see if she had noticed. It was impossible to tell. Her eyes were far off. She looked beautiful. It seemed that the crowd was there to watch her. She did not skate very well but I was proud to be with her.

It began to snow, softly. Big, gentle flakes, spaced far apart, were caught in the lamplight. The crowd drifted away. Tina wiggled her fingers into mittens and pulled a golden hood up over her hair. Then she donned a pair of enormous goggles. I asked her to take them off. I told her I wanted to see her eyes. She laughed at me.

I skated away from her, circling around and around the rink until I saw that she was gone, the crowd was gone, everyone was gone, except a girl sitting alone in the middle of the rink, tying the laces on her skates. I stopped to help her. She seemed afraid of me. She asked me where I came from. I told her that I was a professional skater from the Netherlands. She was pouting a bit, and that's when I saw it was Jenny. I told her that I specialized in thin ice. She smiled then. They turned on a waltz. I asked her to dance.

It was like floating through the air. Everything we did was effortless and flawless, every turn, dip, and whirl. We were all-powerful, unbeatable, gods on ice, gliding through space and time together and forever. We leaped up to the plaza, out to Fifth Avenue, down to the Battery, across the harbor and over the ocean, hand in hand, laughing at the magical ease and speed of our journey, all the way to the Zuyder Zee.

We were still skating when I woke before dawn and felt Jenny next to me. I was surprised, as that first dawn on the beach, that I felt so fine. There was a slight buzz from the champagne. But more than that, there was an astonishing feeling of well-being, the omnipotence of the dream. Nothing could harm me. And I would allow nothing to harm Jenny. We were invincible.

Today I would begin the search. I knew I would not fail. It was impossible for me to fail. I would find the Man. Not because I was threatened, but because I wanted to succeed. It was a challenge without at that moment a trace of fear. It would be no more difficult than skating across to the Zuyder Zee.

I kissed Jenny's hand very softly. She did not awaken. What was she dreaming? Why was she smiling? Was she racing by my side across a frozen sea? She would not remember. For Jenny, each day held too much excitement to remember sleep. No, my love for Jenny was not pity after all. It was envy. I envied her joy. I wanted all of it. But what could I give her in return? I fell back into sleep, smiling with Jenny, holding her hand, feeling her cheek close by on the pillow, vowing that someday I would give her everything. It would not be an island but whole continents and seas, sounds and colors, textures and sensations beyond dreaming, moons and suns and sons.

6.

"I really dreaded this moment," Jenny said. "But thank Gawd you don't read the newspaper at breakfast."

In fact, at that moment I was wondering how I could slip out for a *Times* without a lengthy discussion about the tendency of eggs to grow cold.

"I mean," Jenny said, "I don't intend to sit here every morning staring at That Cosmopolitan Girl on the back-page ad."

She giggled nervously at the sound of teeth biting into overdone toast.

Thursday. Why was I dawdling so? I was like a suburban husband savoring the waning minutes before the 8:07.

"What did you dream last night?" I said.

"I don't know." Jenny frowned, and then her eyes lit up. "Do you realize that's the first question you've ever asked me?"

"Sorry."

"I mean, really asked me. Fantastic. Next thing you'll be caring what I do today."

"I do care about that." But, in truth, I was thinking only of what lay ahead for me.

"None of your business," she said. "I'm a kept woman now and I'll do what I like."

We sipped our coffee leisurely. No, I was not anxious to go. Why leave my castle to grope in the void? Daylight had blunted the illusion of supreme confidence. But the dread was gone. It was no longer a matter of whether, only overwhelming questions of how.

"Do you work weekends?" Jenny said.

"This weekend, yes."

"The better for our cupboard, I suppose. I assume you'll get time and a half, doubletime, golden time, extra-hazardous, etcetera."

"Very possibly."

"Do you belong to a union?"

"I'm not sure."

I telephoned Sugar Red while Jenny washed the dishes. She pretended not to listen.

"Do you know what time it is?" Sugar Red said.

"Have no idea."

"It's not even ten o'clock. Since when would there be mail so early?"

"Last Friday."

"That was special delivery."

"It feels later," I said.

"I just got here," Sugar Red said. "Four hours sleep on account of you."

"What do you mean?"

"Joe Hull. He closed the place up last night. Couldn't get him out till four o'clock. You must have crossed him somehow. He was badmouthing you."

"Joe doesn't drink much."

"He's been drinking and he's been talking. He owes me eight bucks from last night. The new tenants stopped paying him. Joe's taking it hard. Might have to go out and work for a living. Those sonsobitch tenants, they never come in here, not one dime of business."

"What's Joe been saying about me?"

"Your money. Where does it come from? You've got mysterious ways, coming and going at odd hours. He thinks you're a shylock or in the numbers."

"That's ridiculous, you know that."

"Look, I don't know anything. You've always paid your bills, you've been good to the boys. I don't want to know anything more about a man. I don't like Joe running you down."

"Joe's bitter, that's all."

"Where are you now?" Sugar Red asked.

"I'm at work."

"Well, why don't you at least have a talk with Joe? He's living over at the Shelter now."

"I'm busy today."

"It's for your own good. Straighten him out."

"Sugar, you stick to those plastic sermons."

But I knew, as I slammed down the receiver, that Sugar Red was right. He seemed concerned, of all things, with a benefactor upholding his reputation on the Bowery. I was worried that Joe Hull might be endangering my life.

I pulled on a frayed shirt, slipped my tie in a pocket, mussed my hair, and took a swig of sherry, pouring a small puddle into my cupped palms and splashing it on my face. Jenny looked up from the dish pan.

"Is that your usual shaving lotion?"

"Not shaving today. Doing a bit part in a film on the Bowery."

"You might keep the little woman posted a day in advance."

"Didn't I mention it last night?"

"This is part of the chain letter business, I suppose."

"Sort of."

"You're lying, Jon," Jenny said. "And like every decent, God-fearing wife, I'll get used to living with a liar."

I gave her a breadwinner's hug and raced out to catch the subway to work.

A burly welfare guard was stationed in front of the Shelter. He seemed to be waiting for someone.

"Come here, bum," he said.

I looked behind me. There was no one close by. For some reason I panicked. I wanted to turn, run, forget all about Joe Hull. Why? That damned question had been plaguing me for a week, ever since Steingut's message about twelve trains to Babylon, after every move and every word. Why did I do that? Why did I say that? Surprise had entered my life, less from others than from myself. I could no longer depend upon my own calculations. I would hear my own voice, between gulps of ouzo with the new tenants or ale with Thaddeus, and it was not what I had planned to say at all. I would ride a subway, destination unknown, one day toward Tina, the next day toward Jenny, and yet I had not prescribed it. I was being pulled this way and that by a stranger within me, or perhaps by someone I knew long ago and had forgotten. A bum! I had become the sloppiest of technicians. Already, at the first assault, I had not remembered my role. Of course he was talking to me! Why did I look around? How could I be insulted when nobody knew me?

"I said come here, bum!" He took a menacing step toward me.

"I'm sorry, I'm hard of hearing."

"Nobody goes in or out of here this morning," he said. "We've got enough trouble."

"I'm just looking for a friend."

"Yeah, maybe you can cut his throat and sell his bridgework."

The guard's eyes drifted away from me, down the street toward Second Avenue.

"What are you waiting for, sir?" I adopted a friendly, respectful tone.

"You see that window up there?"

I followed his gesture to the third floor of a tenement across the street.

"There's a big fat hooker gets up about now," he said. "Walks around half naked. It's always the bottom half." He bared his teeth in something approaching a grin. But he was not looking at the window. He kept glancing down the street, anxiously.

"I have every right to go in here, sir," I said. "I'm trying to locate my cousin."

"Thought you said a friend."

"We're friendly."

"Is this him?"

He showed me a wrinkled Social Security card. 089–22–9278. Joseph V. Hull.

"Yes," I said.

"I was joking."

"I'm not," I said. "That's my cousin's card."

The guard cast another glance down the street, then wheeled and disappeared into the Shelter. He returned with another man, short and bespectacled.

"You are Joseph Hull's cousin?" the second man said.

"Yessir."

"Come with me."

I followed them inside into a small office. There was something on the couch. The guard lifted an old, torn sheet.

Joe Hull looked like he was having a bad dream. His mouth was twisted in horror, his eyes were staring straight ahead in shock, his hands were curled stiffly into claws. A leg dangled off the couch, limp and battered. His scalp was specked with purple. From beneath his right eye down to his neckbone there was a wide, circular area of red pulp.

"Yessir," I said. "It's him."

"Are they here yet, Ernie?" the man with the glasses asked.

"I'll have a look," the guard said, and he left.

I looked quickly around the room. There was a window with a drawn shade. One other door, probably a closet. The situation was not good.

"I'm Dr. Bernardi," the man said. "We did everything we could. There was no need for an ambulance."

"You can imagine this comes as a great shock," I said. "I'm an educated man, Notre Dame '48, just down on my luck, but I think I've got something going now. I wanted Joe to be in on it. I came here to —"

"Save it for the police," Dr. Bernardi said.

"You see, I heard that Joe was living here, and I just happened to come over."

No, I was not as sloppy as I had thought. My instinct had been right: to run when I saw the guard on the street. I had been exactly right. But it was so hard now to know which impulses to follow. I could no longer trust myself.

"When did it happen?"

"Six o'clock this morning," Dr. Bernardi said. "The police wouldn't let me call for the ice wagon. Leave everything as it is, they said. But I couldn't leave the poor fellow lying there at the bottom of the stairs. And what do they do? It's five hours now and they're still not here. Inhuman. They don't think these are people down here. I feel it should be handled like every other emergency investigation. I want you to know that."

I nodded appreciatively. "I hear he'd been drinking lately," I said. "Must have lost his balance."

"Pushed," Bernardi said. "And for nothing. He has two bucks on him. Pushed to his death by some maniac. How can we protect them? There aren't enough guards. The A-Trainers can slip in. A man goes to sleep in here and he may never wake up."

"You did your best," I said. "Thank you. I'll be going now."

Dr. Bernardi was first to the door.

"Just a formality, you understand," he said. "I know how you must feel. But they'll have some questions for you."

I returned to the couch. "Poor Joe," I said, and held his hand for the doctor's benefit. There was a time when I forced myself to live with this. Life was relatively tidy then. People threatened your safety, they disappeared, the threat was removed. I did not like it but I knew its purpose. At least there was some meaning in their deaths. Each disappearance was a building block in the structure. But what meaning was there to this? I dropped the hand and it swung limply. Joe was an innocent. He had been lonely, unhappy, worthless to everyone. Perhaps there really was a cousin somewhere. He wouldn't care.

Bernardi's black bag was resting on a corner of the desk. I moved slowly, taking care not to arouse his reflexes.

"You'd better sit down," he said.

"I noticed this bag," I said. "I wonder if you might have some kind of tranquilizer in there. I'm rather upset about all this."

"Sit down, please," Bernardi said.

As he crossed to the desk, I backed toward the wall and felt behind me for the windowsill.

"If there is any trouble, I am responsible," Bernardi said.

"There won't be any trouble, Doctor." I sat down on the windowsill. He opened the bag. My fingers glided up the glass, behind the shade, to the window lock. It was no problem. But would there be bars outside?

Footsteps sounded in the hallway. I heard Ernie the guard's voice: "In here. We got a cousin of his. Look him over good. Some sort of strange bum."

As the shade flipped and spun loudly, Bernardi's head jerked up from the bag. I leaped onto the sill. There were no bars. But the damned window would not give!

"What are you doing?" Bernardi said.

It opened a second too late. I was losing too many of these. It was the same second that had tipped Mansfield to the green door at the Coliseum. Just as I succeeded in pulling up the window, they came in the door.

It was not a long jump but I made it too hastily, turning my ankle slightly, not a serious mishap, a small handicap to speed. I began to run without looking. And then I saw I had nowhere to go. I was running around a cement yard, boxed in by barbed wire, a brick wall, a locked gate, and the side of the Shelter. The only possible opening was a basement door leading back into the Shelter. As I started for it, I looked up to see a policeman leaning out of the open window with his revolver drawn.

The shot sailed well over my head, smashing into the windshield of a parked car. Stumbling through the basement doorway, I vowed to write to the Commissioner. I had not heard a warning. It was clear that stealth was out, I would have to rely on whatever speed remained, to catch them off balance, make my way past them by surprise. There was the risk of death, but if I hid in the basement it would be more than a risk. And so I charged, blindly, having no idea what lay behind each door, depending only on others' fear being greater than mine, finally reaching a stairway up to a kitchen, then storming through a swinging door into a huge neon-lit room where the boys were playing checkers, and out the exit least suspected, the way I had come in, the street entrance to the Shelter.

Two buildings down the block, I raced inside and up the stairs to the roof. The fire escapes were in the rear. My mind was clear. I was breathing regularly. It was exhilarating, being hunted again. I had never been trapped. That confidence could not be shaken. Mansfield had failed, like all the others, that night in the Coliseum. These, too, would fail. There could be no more than two policemen plus the unarmed Ernie. They would not bother with reinforcements, not to find the vaguely suspected killer of an old bum. They would go through the motions of the hunt.

From the rooftop I watched them disperse: one next door, one across the street, Bernardi down to the corner, Ernie into my building. Would he be stupid enough to try the basement first? I stood next to the roof door. He was not that stupid, but he was stupid. My punch struck his neck just as he stepped through the doorway. He crumpled in the awesome way peculiar to large men.

It could not be the fire escape. They would be watching the rear of the buildings. I had to risk the stairs. Descending, my feet moving faster than I had expected, I ran a comb through my hair and knotted the tie. On the bottom step I saw Tina's face. The magazine must have fallen out of my pocket on the way up. I folded it, slipped it into my pocket, and moved out the door.

A police car tore in from Second Avenue, dome light flashing but no siren. I was wrong. They would have their justice for Joe. As the car passed me on its way up the block to the Shelter, I began walking briskly toward the Avenue, feeling in my feet the temptation to speed, slowing them with a stern reprimand from that corner of my brain still controlled by experience.

Coming out of the building on the corner, Bernardi saw me. I halted immediately and allowed him to block the sidewalk.

"It wasn't me, Dr. Bernardi," I said. "I ask you to trust me. I have a record and they won't believe me. This is my last chance. I've straightened up. If a bum can't have a second chance, what hope is there for mankind? I didn't lay a hand on you back there. I beg you not to deliver me to my death."

He stared at me for what must have seemed an eternity to him. It did not seem so to me. I knew my man. As he walked back toward the Shelter alone, eyes on the sidewalk, shoulders sagging in defeat, I composed a short postscript of tribute to Dr. Bernardi for my letter to the Commissioner.

Thereafter, it was a comfortable, inconspicuous stroll down Second Avenue, through the neighborhood shopping crowd, past the dairy restaurants to Houston Street, and west to Fisher's Tavern.

Sugar Red had the mail. What a relief to hear from Steingut at last! I was no longer in the void.

> JFK–LBJ Intl
> *So, Jon, there is no Shelter for pigeons*
> S

Tina and Zuckerman. It was incredible. I pulled the folded magazine from my pocket and stared at the cover. What kind of a joke was this? How many of Zuckerman's worlds had she entered? Did she already know him when I met her on the beach? Impossible. It had to be a coincidence. She must have started doing this for a lark, to mock herself and that ridiculous ambition to make the cover of *Vogue*. That would be like Tina. But it could be the other Tina, the one she always refused to let me know, who could not accept the smallest compliment, who could never believe that anyone loved her. It was possible that I would never know. I could not call her again. She would tell me nothing. Flake would be no help. He knew nothing. Was the answer locked in Zuckerman's coffin? How could I possibly —

"The least you can do for me is buckle your seat belt," Nathan P. Silver said. His voice was a shade more pleasant than the picture on the license. "This is a favor, taking you to the airport. There's nothing in it for me. I could make twenty bucks on short hops in half the time. I'm not asking for a big tip, I'm just explaining to you. I wouldn't have even stopped for you if you'd had a suitcase. What are you, a pilot? Fasten your seat belts, fasten your seat belts! It's a small courtesy. You owe me that much. I paid good money for these belts. Put them in myself for the safety of my passengers. I'm not asking you to wear a shoulder harness like me. Just the seat belt. And to hell with your safety anyway. I don't want you flying into my head. Would that be fair? I take all the precautions and then get all the lumps. You look like you just got a shave and a haircut. It was a bad job. He nicked you."

He was studying me in the mirror with unabashed curiosity.

"If you don't put on your seat belt, I'm going to stop this cab," Nathan P. Silver said as we turned onto the Brooklyn Bridge.

"I'm sorry," I said, with a thick accent of no particular origin. "Not so good, the English."

"Seat belt!" He turned and pointed.

"Ah!"

I smiled and complied. He shook his head in disdain.

"That's an amazing thing," he said, "I could swear you're a native New Yorker. Queens maybe. I have a knack for faces. Now, you're a man who doesn't look European. Or maybe some kind of actor who doesn't want to look European. You could be half this, half that. That's important. Speaking frankly, I'm an expert on this whole thing about faces, people you know, people you don't know. Who are they? People you work with, even. Who are friends and who are enemies?"

My ruse with the accent had failed. Nathan P. Silver intended to pursue conversation relentlessly whether or not I uttered one word. I stared down from the bridge at the heights of Brooklyn where Jenny had stood the night before, where she had smiled, and where I thought I had learned something about priorities. Yet there I was, propelled not by Jenny but by Steingut, in a taxi heading toward the airport, away from Jenny and home.

"War. What do you think of war?" Nathan P. Silver said.

I shrugged helplessly and smiled into the mirror.

"Peace is what we need," Nathan P. Silver said. "You agree with me, I can tell from your face. Everything is there. It's in the face. Opinions. Occupations. That's my specialty. You are some kind of businessman. Some kind of strange business, I don't know. War is a natural condition, you know what that is? Human nature.

We kill our own kind without mercy and without cause. But! Listen to this: what is the only creature on earth that can control and direct its passions? I'm a pacifist. You know what that is?"

I should introduce him to Thaddeus. Let Nathan P. Silver buy Thaddeus lunch. They could exchange lectures and I would not have to listen to either of them anymore. Or, better yet, kill him. That would certainly make for a quieter trip. I chuckled inadvertently.

"Go ahead and laugh," Nathan P. Silver said. "Do you think I enjoy a one-sided conversation? I'm a lonely person, and I admit it."

As I had anticipated and tried to prevent with silence, the life story of Nathan P. Silver commenced. I did not laugh again, but I could almost feel the quieting knife slip into his back. It was a strange thought, slaughtering an innocent for the sake of temporary peace and quiet. That, after all, was the way Joe Hull had died. And who would miss Nathan P. Silver? Mrs. Silver and all the little Silvers. "I warned Nathan not to talk so much," she would sob. At the funeral they would be more charitable: "He was a good man, lonely, generous, peace-loving, unsuspecting . . ." The vision began to intrude on reality. I was surprised to see my hand actually reach toward the bobbing head in front of me.

Not again! The palm was smeared with blood. I could not believe it. It could not be my hand, it was detached from me, a part of the crowd. Even if I were looking out at myself —

". . . so it wasn't planned. I just naturally fell into it. It was easy in those days. Now it's not so good. Not safe, you know what that is? You take your life into your hands. You never know what kind of nut you're going to pick up. My theory goes that the best protection is to keep talking. Keeps up your confidence, throws them off guard. After a while it becomes habit. Of course, the money is not great. Just last Friday, I think it was, I began at six in the morning and didn't get through . . ."

He was no longer glancing at the mirror. He was staring straight ahead, intent on himself. No, he could not have seen Joe Hull's blood, no more than the Italian lady on the subway truly saw the blood of the old bum with the jug. I reached into my pocket. Damn, I had thrown the handkerchief in Jenny's hamper. Wasn't there another? No. I had washed it and spread it on the mirror each night, without thinking, forgetting until the other day that it came from the little Belgian girl. How many such things had I done through the years, without the slightest memory of how they began? I examined my palm closely. Ridiculous. There was no blood on it, not a speck.

What came from my pocket was not the handkerchief but the note from Steingut.

> JFK–LBJ Intl
> So, Jon, there is no Shelter for pigeons
> S

Instantly, I felt the same dull kick in my stomach as when I had read the message at Fisher's Tavern, a sledgehammer striking full force while I lay anesthetized on the operating table.

It was a warning, of course. Joe Hull had been killed for the minor purpose of silencing a loudmouth, and for the major purpose of vivid illustration to prevent my defection. It was to prove that Steingut knew about Mansfield, to present me with a faceless terror, the certain knowledge that I was under scrutiny.

But it was also a second chance. That was why the warning came with the mission. Back to work and all would be forgiven. They were trusting to my instinct for survival. The warning was only the last five words. "LBJ" was the one clue they would give on the contact at JFK airport. "So, Jon" was an incoming from San Juan after three o'clock, the unscrambled "there." The contact always varied but the rest was familiar. It was the 3:45 Pan Am, which I met four or five times a year. I had learned not to puzzle over the contact clue. It would be self-evident. Steingut knew his business.

The puzzle was "Intl." Why there? That was the International Arrivals building, an arena that Torre and I knew well from other flights. Our system there was a beautiful one, no problem. But why was this flight, a domestic flight from San Juan, not arriving as usual at the Pan Am terminal?

". . . it's from driving a cab for so many years, talking to all the experts. I am proud to say I have developed something close to genuine humanity. That takes work, my friend. Every one of us is prone to bigotry, hatred, greed, envy, suspicion. That's a fact. It came to me last spring when I picked up an old priest in East Harlem, and we got to talking in a friendly way, just like you and me, about abortion, which should not be a religious quarrel. Call it by its rightful name. Aborticide. It's murder, pure and simple. Starvation, napalm, it's all the same. Reverence for life. And Schweitzer was a Gentile, a great Gentile. I picked up a botanist, you know what that is? He was going out to Astoria, I think, a very long ride, but I remember only one thing he said: when you pick a flower, it screams. That's true. He was a scientist with all the equipment. So it was no longer enough for me to be vegetarian and a pacifist. I began to worry about the vegetables. Vegetables are like people. They get angry and scared. Even the simplest form of stink cabbage. Or cauliflower! That night I got home, my wife had cauliflower on the table. She had boiled it alive! All the time the cauliflower was screaming, she couldn't hear it. Not attuned, you see? I wanted to hit her. But I couldn't because I'm a pacifist. It was a hell of a fix."

We were passing the Narrows. On the other side a Norwegian freighter was steaming out from Staten Island toward the open sea. I longed to be standing on that bow, my face in the cold wind, leaving this land behind me. Would Jenny be at my side? The wish was foolish. To be aboard that freighter, or a luxury steamship courtesy of Mansfield, was not a schoolboy's dream. It could happen within hours. For I had the plan.

I would follow the routine: make the contact, take the luggage, place it in the locker. But this time I would wait for Torre. With this mission, Steingut had linked Torre and me together at the very moment when we had both despaired of finding each other. In this one detail the omniscient Steingut had failed. He knew that I would try to find Torre. But he did not know that Torre was looking for me.

As we passed Coney Island and began curving around Jamaica Bay, Nathan P. Silver's droning confessions were no longer a part of my world. I was trying only to picture Torre. Why had I wondered if he were man, woman, or child? I saw him now as a very small man, able to dart in and out of the crowd, perhaps dapper, with a little moustache and spats, quick eyes, canine, nose quivering at the approach of danger. I began to tear up Steingut's letter and changed my mind.

Occasional patches of fog swirled low along the highway as we approached the baffling array of airport signs. It was comforting to hear the whine of jets queuing up for takeoff. The ceiling was still high enough to permit traffic. But it appeared to be closing. How much time had elapsed? Damn. I hoped Jenny had taken the watch to the jeweler. She had probably forgotten.

". . . putting the safety belts in the cab. People thought I was nutty to do it, but I have respect for human life. There's more carnage on the highways than on the battlefields. The statistics —"

"What time is it?" I said.

His shoulders jerked forward. He shot a startled glance into the mirror, surprised, it seemed, that there was a passenger in his taxi.

"Three thirty-five," he said glumly. "I thought you didn't speak English."

"The time, it is always important." I thickened the accent.

"Fog's getting bad," he said before lapsing into silence. I had offended him by daring to interject the mundane. I felt a little sorry about that. But we were too early. The plane had been reported on time. I did not want to wander around the lobby until it arrived. It was best to be there a minute late and put the burden on the contact.

My hope was that Nathan P. Silver would resume his autobiography and get lost. There was no such luck. I had insulted him. He was now completely focused on following the blue "2" signs direct to the terminal.

"Stop here," I said.

He slowed the taxi but did not stop.

"I thought you wanted International Arrivals," he said.

"Yes. I will walk from here."

"It's no trouble."

"I will walk from here."

"No trouble turning off the meter if you need the extra dime."

"Please stop this taxi."

"I can take you right to the door."

"This is fine, thank you. I will leave here."

He pulled over on the roadway between the Fountain of Liberty and Our Lady of the Skies chapel. I placed in his palm fifty dollars for the little Silvers, and stepped out of the taxi.

"Wait a minute," he said. "I can't change this."

I gave him a final shrug and my baffled foreign tourist smile. He stared at the bill, unsure whether to feel grateful or guilty. I patted his shoulder and he drove off.

Gulls were circling above the chapel. They dropped down with a sudden gust of wind, then rose again at the sound of a jet taking off. The noise from the runways was earsplitting. I could not see the jets. They were landing and leaving somewhere out there in the fog. The gulls began to glide toward the bay. I followed beneath them slowly. If I paced it correctly, it would be a five-minute walk with sufficient time to wash my hands. I climbed up the ramp, rising above the fountain. A swarm of starlings fluttered into the airspace abandoned by the gulls. At least they were staying below the fog and would not get sucked into the jets of my friend's airplane.

Inside the terminal, a man stood too casually by the door of the men's room. I decided to forgo washing my hands. Uniforms are one thing, plainclothes another. I have two customs at the airport. When there is a policeman in uniform and my normal course is past him, I pass very near to him, practically brush against him, rather than circle around. The trick is more for me than for the crowd. I lose suspicion of myself and build confidence in my ordinary appearance as an unremarkable passenger. Secondly, I ask for the gate number at the desk. It does not matter that it is posted. Again, one must place trust to engender trust. Only then is invisibility assured. It is the untrusting contact, too sure of himself and his destination to ask questions, who is always visible and in danger. One should rarely speak a declarative sentence to the crowd. One should ask of them what is already known.

"No, not at a gate," the young lady said. I did not like the color of her hair. It had dried too much in the sun, blood red, not fiery like Jenny's but gory. If a bloodied hand stroked her hair, it would be invisible. "You may wait downstairs near the baggage claim, if you wish, sir. This flight must come through Customs. You may see arriving passengers through the glass at Customs Inspection East."

"Thank you very much."

Customs for a San Juan flight! Somebody had tipped. Customs was always handled in Puerto Rico. So that was why the plane and I were both sent to this terminal. Somebody had tipped and Steingut knew about it. Suddenly they were double-checking at this end. The contact might never get through.

I stood on the balcony and looked through the glass down into the huge pit. Across from me, six cheerful collegians, pleasantly drunk, were unfurling a banner to greet a returning friend: HARVEY LIVES! They were all laughing, but beneath us Harvey and his fellow tourists were grumbling impatiently at the inspectors opening suitcases. All were incensed but one man, who sat patiently, very patiently, at the end of the luggage ramp, awaiting his turn.

He had gray hair, a high forehead, shaggy eyebrows, mean eyes, big ears, brown coat, blue pants, tan shoes, an enormous silver ring, and, what Steingut knew would mark him for me, a Texan Stetson pushed back on his head.

But I had spotted him immediately for the same reasons that others might. Alone among the passengers, he did not complain about the Customs check. Not once did he glance up at the greeters behind the glass. He had not a trace of suntan, no straw bags or hats or the least evidence of a happy return from a Caribbean vacation. It was a very sloppy operation.

My heart leaped as he opened a brown trunk for the inspector. The search was quite thorough. Amazingly, he passed. But was I expected to meet such a conspicuous character and lug off a trunk? The contacts, I had noticed, were getting worse as the years went by. They used to be smooth, probably European, well trained in all details. For some time now, they had appeared to be all Americans, a little vicious-looking, men that the jury would hang before the evidence was in.

I walked downstairs and waited a good sixty feet from the Customs door. No doubt he was already under surveillance. He had waved off a porter with all the subtlety of a tobacco auctioneer. From the look of him, he had probably told the porter that the trunk was too valuable to entrust, and, in case anyone was interested, it contained documents, and, if you'd really like to know, here's a list of them right here, what am I offered?

He came through the door. He lowered the trunk to the floor as if he were resting for a moment. He seemed to be staring directly at me. Did the idiot actually think that I would approach him two feet away from Customs? I turned away and moved across the lobby and through the door leading to the taxi stand outside. I would give him two minutes and then return. But suddenly, there he was. The fool was standing next to me on the curb, the trunk handle gripped tightly in his hand. This was murder. What was he doing? I could not get it back for Torre without attracting attention. I would have to take a taxi and circle back to leave it. The taxi queue was shortening fast. The gray-haired man put the trunk down as he saw an empty taxi approaching. I reached down quickly, grasped the handle and started toward the taxi.

"Hey!" The damn fool was yelling at me!

What was his problem? Were there code words to exchange? I had not received them. The driver took the trunk and threw it in back. I opened the rear door.

"Hey, you!" The man came hurrying up to the taxi. "Where you going with my trunk?"

If those were the code words, then this organization had plummeted to the bottom.

"Now, you lookee here," the man said. "I'm going to call that cop over there."

The taxi driver stood between us, not sure which was the guilty party. He finally decided to hide in the driver's seat. At that moment, a man came through the terminal door and stepped toward the next taxi. He was an ordinary figure, about my height, a bit stouter. He was carrying a gray suitcase. I did not study his face. My eyes froze on the only distinguishing feature about him: a ludicrously large Stetson.

"A fine country this is getting to be," I said to my taxi driver. "You help a man carry a big trunk like that and he accuses you of being a thief. Now, you get right into this taxi, sir, and enjoy yourself. I'm Jud Mitchell, community relations representative of the New York Board of Trade. I want you to enjoy your stay here." I shook the hand of the gray-haired man. He gaped at me in bewilderment. "Wonderful to see you, sir," I said, pushing him into the taxi. "You read about crime in our streets, I know, but I hope you will also keep in mind the unusual hospitality of our great city." The taxi roared off. I was certain that driver and passenger would not lack for conversation.

Wrong! The wrong man. That, too, for the first time. Like the radiance of Jenny's smile, it had never happened before. Yes, I had always known the danger. The contact may turn out to be the crowd. Whose fault was that? Steingut's. Were they trying to do me in? No, it was not Steingut, it was I who was sloppy. I was losing my touch. I should have known at first glance that he was not the man. Instead, I jumped: no suntan, no straw, no impatience. Would a contact be that bad? He was only a salesman. But I was too jumpy to see it until I turned and saw the second Stetson come walking through the door.

As the next taxi pulled up, I sauntered over to the contact. He looked straight ahead at the taxi. Had he seen what happened? Of course. But he did not know me. He was only a link in the chain. Nonetheless, it would be best to acknowledge the mistake so that he would not report it, acknowledge it fast before I began to draw an audience.

The gray suitcase was sitting next to him on the curb.

"That was a close one," I said, reaching down to pick it up.

"Yes," he said. He stepped into the taxi.

I looked down at the suitcase. It bore clear gold initials: LBJ.

Back inside the terminal, I headed for the lockers. Normally, I would use one of the 270's in the right bank, close to the Customs door. If it did not inspire complete trust, at least it was above casual suspicion. But I could no longer be certain, after my blunder, of being without shadows. I moved to the bank left of the escalator and placed the suitcase in locker 209. There was a second reason for that choice. Nearby, a row of comfortable chairs sat against the wall. This time I would wait for Torre.

It was 4:07 by the clock. The man by the men's room door had left. No doubt he was nothing. If in my distracted state I could mistake the crowd for the contact, it was not beyond me to mistake it for the police. I wondered if it required the same kind of unerring confidence to turn traitor as it did to carry out a mission flawlessly. I hoped not. I had no way of knowing. It was a new position for me. I was uncertain what talents were in order. Perhaps I could succeed only if I lost my ability to read faces. Apparently, that was already the case. Or perhaps someone like Nathan P. Silver, with his exuberant self-delusion in that department, would be a better choice for the job.

There was a man in the third stall. I washed my hands and watched the mirror for signs of progress. Black loafers showed under the folds of gray pants. An occasional grunt broke the silence. As I turned on the hand drier, I heard the sound of a spinning toilet-paper roll. When he emerged at last, he spent an interminable time washing his hands and face, cleaning his fingernails, and combing his hair. I brushed my coat, fiddled with buttons, and buffed my shoes on the backs of my pant legs until he made his exit. I had won the battle of the meticulous groomers. It took only a few seconds to dash into the stall, place the key to 209 on the floor behind the toilet, and make my way back to the lobby. How absurd are the flywheels by which great enterprises turn. Yet in the nine years I had been performing this deadly serious feat, this was the first time I had allowed myself the luxury of a smile.

4:13 by the clock. Torre would be there before six. That was the deadline, determined solely by the schedule of the janitor. At that time the men's room would be scrubbed and polished, mopped and wiped, all strange objects removed from the gleaming floor. Torre knew the deadline. I sat in a chair near the locker and awaited him, buried in the Wall Street final of the New York *Post*.

5:15. I could not remember a time when I had sat in a public place for an hour. In school, of course. But not since the age of fourteen, when I went to Amsterdam from Brugge, had I been so vulnerable to discovery. I learned in the months thereafter, as a courier, the fastest of them all, that capture lay not in the skills of the enemy but in one's own ineptitude. The imperative was that very avoidance. One kept moving in public. One rested in private. But youth was simple. Our passwords were so purely Dutch that a German guttural invited instant death. Now there were no passwords and the waiting was done in public. This was the way of the quisling.

At 5:42, I saw a janitor step on the escalator. He was early! Or was it a different man? I had never been there at that hour. I watched him rise slowly to the top, this obscure laborer who might hold the key to my life. He was a handsome man, erect, muscular, resigned to his fate. He looked intelligent enough to be a Ph.D. Or perhaps even to be in my place. Did that any longer require intelligence?

Eighteen minutes remained. Seventeen. Sixteen. If Torre was not there, he was in trouble. We were all in trouble.

5:54. A big man with a green Alpine hat shading his eyes came down the stairs next to the escalator and walked directly to locker 209. His gait was light, unnatural, it seemed, as if to mask his size. As he turned the key in the lock, I admired the magnificently precise angle of Torre's hat. It concealed without attracting suspicion. One inch further down it would have drawn attention, one inch up it would have failed to hide his face. I could not see his face at all. In that moment, I was proud once again to be in the organization. Torre was a man of great skill and power. He was not the dapper little dog I had visualized. He looked to be over six feet, broad-shouldered, confident, no furtive glancing or hurrying the job. He stood with his back to me, only fifteen feet away. As he slid the gray suitcase from the locker, I walked over and put my hand lightly on his shoulder.

"Torre!" My whisper was sharp. It must have sounded to him like a resounding shout. Instantly, he wheeled around, keeping his face away from me, knocking out my wind with his elbow. I reached out and seized the suitcase, I did not know why, perhaps because I guessed that Torre would not let go, that I would have him. I was doubled from the pain of his blow, clinging to the suitcase, as his knee barely missed its mark and burned into my thigh. I fell to the floor, carrying the suitcase down with me. Torre hesitated for one second, looking over at the stairway, unsure whether to abandon the suitcase or risk the precious two or three seconds it would take to kick me hard and recover it. Suddenly, he leaped toward the escalator and went racing up the moving stairs, knocking down a passenger whose wide back barred the way to the top. He had panicked. But he was correct. How was he to know that I was Jon?

I pulled myself up from the floor, clutching my throbbing stomach with one hand and the suitcase with the other. The key was in the locker. I fished a quarter from my pocket and retrieved it. Then I was fighting my way through the crowd up the escalator and out the exit to the overhead ramp. I saw Torre running fast into the fog. He disappeared but I could hear his footsteps as I pursued him. He was running straight to the railing overlooking the fountain. There I knew he would face the alternatives of a short run to the left and down a stairway, or around the circling ramp to the right, gradually descending to the level of the fountain. As I reached the railing, I could no longer hear his footsteps. I decided on the stairway.

Once on the ground, I could see no more than ten feet in front of me. I stopped to listen. The fog had closed in, forcing incoming planes to seek other cities and those on the runways to roll back. It was deathly quiet. I could hear only the splash of the fountain water in the reflecting pool. The wind blew the cold spray gently against my face. I circled very slowly around the pool. Could he be in it, floating silently behind the shroud of fog, waiting for me to leave? Not likely. I must have lost him.

Lights came on. I could see faintly into the pool. Obscene jets of water were shooting high into the air. The wind was sculpting eerie forms of fog and spray. Suddenly, a hand gripped my arm.

It was the same shock of discovery that Torre had felt. I spun around, swinging the suitcase in a wide arc. More hands came at me. A knee stabbed my back, rough sleeves tightened around my neck.

"All right, you settle down now." The voice was unfamiliar. "You just come quietly."

7.

Two men sat on the edge of the desk. One had an open, friendly face, curly black hair, the frame of a football tackle. The other was thin, dour, hunched over. I saw at a glance it was the old suspicious-trusting game.

"You have keys to this suitcase?" the suspicious one said. "It has three different locks on it."

"Yes, at home."

"This would take three keys," suspicious said. "Of course, we could just bust it."

"No, I don't approve of that," trusting said. "We'd much prefer your cooperation." He was smiling sympathetically.

"Where do you live?" suspicious snapped.

"Look, I really don't understand what's going on here. May I go home now, please? My wife is waiting dinner."

"You've got a point," trusting said. "Just give my ugly friend here a good explanation and I'll see that you're out of here in two minutes."

"Explanation for what?"

Suspicious was brandishing a small notebook.

"Sometime after four o'clock you put this suitcase in locker number 209."

"Is that a crime?"

"Now, just listen to him a moment," trusting urged me.

"It wouldn't have bothered me," suspicious continued, "except that you sat there for more than an hour, right near that locker, which is a strange way to waste a quarter."

"That's his right, though," trusting said.

"But you were watching that locker," suspicious said. "Looking for someone. And he arrived a little before six. He came down the stairs. This I saw with my own eyes. You walked up and said something to him and he knocked you down. Now, how did he get the key to your locker?"

"That's an interesting point," trusting said. "I think you'd better clear it up so we can all go home."

"I don't know what you're talking about."

"This man ran up the escalator," suspicious said.

"Yes, I saw that myself," trusting said. "He seemed to be in a great hurry."

"And you grabbed that suitcase and took off after him," suspicious said.

"Yes," trusting said. "You see, that's why we're required by regulations to question you. Believe me, I'd rather be home myself. My wife is waiting dinner, too."

Trusting poured a cup of coffee and put it next to me with a pack of cigarettes. He seemed deeply disappointed that I touched neither.

"It's very simple," I said. "What would you do if a man tried to steal your suitcase?"

"Of course," trusting said.

Perfect. They had not picked up on it. They knew nothing. What a relief! They had not seen me with the two Stetsons at the taxi stand.

"But how did he get a key?" suspicious said.

"Must have picked the lock, I don't know."

"Just show us your key and this will all be cleared up," trusting said.

I withdrew the key from my pocket and threw it on the desk. They were clearly surprised, both of them, at my foresight.

"What flight did you come in on?" suspicious persisted, but he was off guard now.

I studied their faces. I would win, yes, I could give a story they could not shake. But at what cost? They had reached their conclusion already, as any fool would. They knew I was lying. Each time I defeated them I would increase their frustration, and their determination to make the case. That would mean time, days in custody I could not afford.

"Or maybe you were waiting to take a plane?" trusting suggested. "Just tell us what you were doing here and we can all go home."

Yes, even with the best of stories, I would be lost. There would be no way to earn Mansfield's promised reprieve. Or I would be killed after my release. Steingut had offered me a last chance with this assignment and with the warning of Joe Hull's death. I would be throwing it away.

"All right, then," suspicious said. He opened a drawer and pulled out a hammer and chisel.

"Oh, we shouldn't do that," trusting said. "Let's give the fellow a chance. He looks honest to me."

"I'm in charge," suspicious said. "You just mind my orders." He laid the suitcase flat on the desk. Did they think I was an amateur? Those locks could be picked in thirty seconds apiece. Did I look like a man fearful enough to fall for dramatic gestures with hammers and chisels?

"Wait a minute," I said.

Suspicious stopped the hammer halfway to impact and looked over at me, beautifully concealing his glee. Trusting's friendly grin was transformed into a broad smile of victory.

"Are you accusing me of something?" I said.

"Certainly not," trusting said.

"Not yet," suspicious said. "But we're going to see what's in this suitcase, whether you open it or I open it."

"I'm not sure that you have the right to open it," I said, "but I do know that I have the right to make a telephone call."

"You're absolutely right," trusting said. "You call your wife to hold dinner." He pushed over a telephone.

I dialed Mansfield. I did not like to do it but it was the only hope.

"Mr. Mansfield is not here at this hour," the switchboard girl said. "I'll switch you to Mr. Gallagher." She clicked off before I could protest.

"Gallagher."

"I'm trying to reach Lee Mansfield."

Trusting and suspicious looked worried.

"He's not here," Gallagher said. "What can I do for you?"

"I need Mansfield. How can I reach him?"

"Who is this?"

"What's his home number? I don't have it with me."

"Try the phone directory," he said.

"It's not listed."

"Listen, give me your name, and I'll try and put him in touch with you. What's this about, anyway?"

"Just the home number, please. I'm in a hurry. This is important."

"I can't give you that."

"This is a matter of the utmost urgency."

"You're a friend, you've got his number, right?"

"I don't have it with me."

"Go get it, then." Gallagher hung up.

It was a little late to tell Mansfield what a poor shop he had at night. Suppose, for example, a pigeon had been calling in who could not talk to Gallagher. Suppose he were trapped at Kennedy Airport by two of Mansfield's naïve colleagues who had no inkling of the arrangement. Just suppose, for example. The whole thing would be blown.

"That's your phone call," suspicious said.

"Do you know Lee Mansfield?" trusting asked.

Yes, it was blown. There was nothing left but to operate on that assumption.

"Now you two listen to me," I said. They were startled by the sudden tone of authority. "You're very smart but you're in the process of ruining the whole case. The name is Crane, Howard Crane, from Washington. Yes, I know Lee Mansfield because I happen to work for Lee Mansfield. I have been taking the risks for you bright fellows who sit around high above cover worrying about your dinner and nowhere near making your case. I'm the one who's making this case. I'm going to make heroes out of you if you don't mess it up. And what you are going to do is very simple. Give me that suitcase and forget you ever saw me. Because if you don't, by the time you roll out of your soft beds tomorrow morning, I will have you on a list in Washington, and the only choice left to you will be just exactly what kind of security risk you want to be. How would you like it? Perverts? Traitors? Or just plain incompetents?"

Trusting was too frightened to open his mouth.

"Your credentials, sir," suspicious said.

"I can't do that."

"Then we have no choice but to hold you."

"Call Mansfield," I said.

"That won't be necessary," suspicious said. "We called him the minute we picked you up. He's on his way out here."

They left me alone in the room for more than an hour. I was certain that Mansfield had arrived and they were reporting to him. Through the window I saw the red and green flicker of wing lights circling overhead. The fog was lifting. I called Jenny. There was no answer.

When Mansfield finally came in, he was not smiling. He looked at me as if I were an errant pupil who had caused his teacher the final exasperation. Without a word, he strode over to the suitcase and ran his fingers over the locks.

"What did you tell them?" he said at last.

"Look, I had no alternative."

"What did you tell them?" It was the first time I had seen him really angry.

"Howard Crane from Washington. I work with you undercover."

"That much they told me. What else?"

"Nothing."

"That was more than enough," Mansfield said. "You've had a brilliant day today. Open this suitcase."

It took longer to pick the locks than I had guessed, perhaps a little under five minutes for the three of them. Mansfield lifted the lid and began rummaging through shirts, socks, underwear, slacks, nothing but clothes.

He picked up a pair of black socks, rolled neatly into a ball, and tossed it to me. I caught it, wondering if I had become a juggler's assistant who had missed the dress rehearsal. Mansfield's customary smile returned as he sensed my puzzlement.

"Didn't they tell you I was on my way out here?" he said.

"Not until I tried to call you."

"At least somebody keeps their mouth shut in this operation."

He walked behind the desk, leaving me standing there holding the damned sock ball. I dropped it on the desk. I have always equated danger with looking foolish.

"Hold on," Mansfield said. "You're not playing the game. I want you to put that behind your back and I'll guess which hand."

"May I leave now? I have business."

"But it's all my business, isn't it?" Mansfield said.

I did not reply.

"Isn't that true?" he said. "Your business is all for me, right?"

"Yes."

"Then you pick up those socks, Jon." I did. "Hold it behind your back. Good. How many guesses do I have?"

"One, obviously."

"That would just about reduce my chances from one hundred percent to fifty percent, wouldn't it?"

His smile was actually beginning to verge on charm. For some reason, Mansfield truly wanted to be my friend, even though I had nearly split his larynx.

"Left hand," he said.

I shifted the pair of socks to my right hand and brought out an empty left.

"You cheated," Mansfield said. "Give me that."

I threw the ball hard at his face. He caught it easily. It was an absurd game but Mansfield was trying to convey something. He was telling me that in our other game he was my match.

"Now for my second guess," he said. "I believe you said I had only one guess, but I never agreed to that. Never assume an agreement unless you have it." He lit one of his little cigars. "My second guess is what's inside these socks."

From the moment I saw Mansfield in my loft, I did not like him. But I had trusted him. Now I was barely beginning to like him, and to distrust him.

"What do you think?" he said. "A microfilm of a draft treaty? Instructions for disarming an intercontinental missile?"

"Listen," I said, "I almost had Torre."

"That's interesting. But let's continue on the main track."

"Will you listen to me, Lee? You wanted a pigeon. I'm telling you that I am going to cooperate. There was a message from Steingut for a pickup here. I waited by the locker for Torre. He was wearing a green hat. A big man. Which is odd. I had imagined him as a small man."

Mansfield was unrolling the socks, feigning boredom with my exploits. He turned one sock inside out. An envelope was taped inside. He ripped it open, inspected it, and handed it to me.

"Do you know what that is?" he said quietly.

"What are you talking about? I said I almost had Torre!"

Mansfield stared at me with blank gray eyes.

"No, I don't believe you do," he said.

I did not recognize the taste. It was not my field.

"Heroin," Mansfield said.

The drizzle was too slight to kill the brilliance of the sunset. Only a few swirls of fog remained. I looked for a rainbow. Then I remembered that I had never seen a rainbow here. The last one was a quarter of a century ago, over Scheveningen. That was a word no German could pronounce.

"Rainy for August," I said.

Mansfield turned onto the parkway, driving slowly. He flicked on the lights and we began moving faster.

"Beautiful sunset," I said.

"Air pollution," Mansfield said. "The air pollution filters it like that."

"Another triumph of industrial democracy."

He was silent. I knew he would break soon and I feared it.

"For tomorrow," I continued, "the paper wants sunshine."

"All right!" His foot stomped on the accelerator and the car jerked forward. "You don't want to talk about it, is that it?"

"About what?"

"That gee-whiz suitcase in the back seat."

"Well, isn't it all obvious? It's a plant. Steingut baited the hook and I swam right to it. Now he's rid of me. Of course, I won't be convicted. I have my defense all planned. After my release, I suppose I'll be shot sooner or later. In the meantime, he's succeeded. I'm in your custody. It's your problem, not mine." I smiled at his discomfort.

"I can't have this going to trial," Mansfield said.

"Naturally."

"It would be very messy, right when I'm moving in."

"Which is why you will let me off at the nearest subway."

"No, I can't."

"But you will. And you will also let me have the suitcase."

"You wouldn't live an hour."

"I have a talent for survival, Lee. I also have something else they want now. They'll have to come to me. And then I'll have them for you. We made a bargain."

"Do you realize what's in that suitcase?" Mansfield said. "Not just in one pair of old socks, but taped inside every other piece of clothing. Do you know what all those little envelopes are worth?"

"It's not my job to know."

Mansfield glanced over at me.

"Three million dollars," he said.

I slumped down in the seat, suddenly exhausted.

"Some plant!" Mansfield said. "This was only the year's big shipment. And it was entrusted to you. It was on the level."

He dropped a thick manila envelope on my lap.

"Read it," he said.

"What is it?"

"Read it."

"Why don't you just pretend I've read it?"

"It's up to you." He snatched it back. "But there's a reason you won't read it. It contains the truth you've been avoiding for a very long time."

"I don't need to know anything from you," I said. "You know less than I do. I've told you too much already. You and I struck a bargain. If you're not willing to keep it, then lock me up. But if you really want to bring in Steingut and Torre, you will let me off with the suitcase."

"Don't listen to me, then. It's your funeral. Literally. I'm a very literal man."

Accidents forced us to a crawl. Mansfield turned on the windshield wipers. He was well aware of my tension. He had decided to outwait me.

"Tell me how it works," I said finally.

"It comes into San Juan, we think by freighter."

"But you don't know."

"No, we don't."

"Ships from where?"

"Probably Istanbul, we're not sure."

"That's it," I said. "You don't know anything."

"Everything, you mean. Do I pretend to?" One hand left the steering wheel to light a cigar. The motion was depressingly steady. "It's a hard trade," he said.

"You could be in the wrong line." I laid a sympathetic hand on his shoulder. "Have you ever thought of running for President?"

"And it's no easier now than twenty years ago," Mansfield continued, flicking away my hand. "But I'm ahead. I'm into them in Puerto Rico. I slipped a good man in there. My best man."

"I trust he's better than me."

"You're first-rate, Jon. I've admired you for years. Don't bother to laugh, you're arrogant enough to know it's true. The question is: are you my man?"

"The man in Puerto Rico, what's his name?"

"What's your name?"

"Oh, but it's all in that big envelope of yours."

"I have seven of your names."

"Is that all?"

Mansfield slid the envelope under the seat, as if such protection would heighten its value in my eyes.

"Surely, you trust me with the name of your man in Puerto Rico," I goaded him. "How about Jones?"

"Smith."

"Thanks. What does he have?"

"Not much," Mansfield said. "Yet. We know it doesn't stay long at the docks. It keeps moving, possibly for weeks, before it reaches the airport. It's a very tight operation. Smith is between two links, same as you. But he's starting to work his way around the chain. This was my first real tip. They trusted him with this suitcase, he's that good. He brought it to the San Juan airport and left it for the passenger. Did you get a good look at him, the one who arrived with it?"

"No."

"We did. In San Juan. Arresting him there would have jeopardized Smith. I decided to bring the plane through Customs and grab the suitcase at this end."

"Brilliant." I gave him a short burst of applause. "He got away."

Mansfield solemnly ignored the jest and pulled a quarter from his pocket.

"That's because of this," he said. "Always keep your options open. Especially when you're winning."

"You couldn't decide."

"My decision was to wait until the last minute before telling my people at Kennedy why I wanted that plane to come through Customs."

"Cold feet."

"Could you measure it any better? Could you predict the effect of an arrest here, on Smith in San Juan? Jump at the first break and you may never get another. So I flipped a coin and changed my mind." He tossed the quarter to me. "Expense account. For the locker."

"Buy yourself a cup of coffee." I dropped it on the floor. "I don't make my choices this way."

"Why not admit you're in the dark, Jon?"

"I know what's happening every minute. You may be interested to know that those two inquisitors were very bad actors. I could see they knew absolutely nothing."

"That's right," Mansfield conceded. "They saw you sitting by the locker."

"May I tell you more?" I expected at least a shrug but I received nothing. "When you changed your mind and began to worry all over again about the man you so coyly call Smith, you couldn't cancel the Customs order and have the plane simply go to the Pan Am terminal. Could you? That would have aroused even more suspicion. Am I correct?" Mansfield's irritated glance sufficed for confirmation. "You, too, are running a tight operation, except for your night line, which I should tell you is a shambles. You had not yet given your men at Kennedy a description of the passenger. So you told the Customs inspectors to proceed with the check but make it routine. It was nicely packed, wasn't it?" Mansfield grunted something incomprehensible. "The problem is, Lee baby, they have Smith anyway because they have lost the suitcase."

"No," he said. "You were right the first time. I was probably too cautious."

"You don't believe that."

"Damn it, I don't flip a coin when a choice can be made. It came up heads to let the suitcase through. Tails was just as right. This is too much junk to go on the market."

"Did Smith open the suitcase? Why don't you answer? Don't you trust me?"

"He couldn't take that chance," Mansfield said. "I wasn't sure of it until you and I opened it."

"But he had the flight number."

"It came to him with the suitcase. That and the locker number he was to leave it in at San Juan airport."

"And then he called you?"

"Yes."

"Did you mention to him your plan to bring the plane through Customs at Kennedy?"

"Of course," he said. "My best man. I talked it over with him."

"From where did he call you?"

"His hotel."

"Through a switchboard?"

"What's your point?" Mansfield drew hard on the cigar. He refused to recognize that it had died.

"When did he call you?" I said.

"Yesterday."

"That's what I thought. Today he's dead."

"Not a chance," Mansfield said. "I worry less about him than about you."

"Shall we bet that quarter? I say they've torn him apart."

"You really think grim, don't you? You're not in touch with Puerto Rico, I know that."

"But why do you think I was at International Arrivals? My message was postmarked yesterday. Steingut knew that the plane had been diverted." I held Steingut's message in front of Mansfield's eyes, placing a finger over the line threatening "pigeons." "Kennedy International," I said.

The right wheels of the car bumped against the curb. I pulled back the piece of paper, tore it into shreds and dropped them in my pocket. Mansfield brought the car under control. He was frowning. I surmised it was less for the safety of his man than for his own stupidity in not questioning why I was at the right terminal. That was exactly the kind of blunder I expected of a coin-flipper, but apparently he did not expect it of himself.

"If they knew," Mansfield said, "they would have sent the suitcase on a different plane."

"Wrong. That would upset an intricate schedule. Have some more free evidence, it won't help you. This is the only plane I meet at Kennedy. Torre depends on my timing and someone else depends on his."

"I don't care," Mansfield said. "They would not have risked this suitcase."

"Don't flatter yourself. Dealing with you is a very small risk. I don't believe for a minute that you flipped a coin. You were rash enough to endanger Smith and wise enough to have second thoughts. I told you your every move. If I can figure you out, Mansfield, they can anticipate you. That's their business. The instant they knew about Smith, they also knew that you had to proceed with care. It gives me great pleasure to nominate Smith's phone call for this year's careless award."

"I'm not worried about him," Mansfield insisted. "You're my headache. You don't know what you're doing."

"Don't be certain. Here." I reached down to the floor to pick up the quarter. "You may need this."

"Will you listen to me for a change? I'm not blaming you. When this broke, it wasn't your fault. They didn't deserve you."

"Oh, come off it."

"It's all in the envelope," he said.

"I'm not listening."

"You came over here for a cause, bright young man of thirty-four."

"Thirty-three."

"Fine." He relit his cigar. "Just ripe for a crucifixion."

"That's typical of your sources," I said. "I guarantee that everything in there is wrong."

I turned to look for the suitcase. It was sitting upright in the far left corner of the back-seat floor, just beyond my reach. It would be impossible, should the opportunity arise in slow traffic, to seize the handle and jump out the door before Mansfield took action. I watched the headlights of the cars behind us.

"Thirty-four, thirty-three, whatever, it may be old for baseball but it's a child in this game," Mansfield said.

The lights were hypnotic. I closed my eyes and shook my head to clear the effect. When I looked again, my suspicion was confirmed. While most of the headlights were either falling behind or moving up to pass us, one car was keeping exact pace with us, slowing and speeding to match the irregular pressure of Mansfield's foot on the accelerator as he talked.

"They knew you were a prodigy," Mansfield said. "All that training, all those missions without a flaw, but beyond that, all that goddamn moral fervor. That was your weakness and they knew it. Obedience born of passion. I understand it, Jon, because you and I are fairly alike. That's why I found you. No one else could have cracked this case."

"Apparently, someone has," I said. "Look in the mirror."

Mansfield lifted his foot off the accelerator. "That's interesting," he said.

"Does it surprise you? The question is who."

He brought the car to a halt and then started up again.

"Can't see," he said. "The headlights stopped when we did. Now they're moving at our speed."

"You'll get used to being followed. It's good for the reflexes."

"Probably a coincidence that they stopped," he said. "You won't rattle me that way. I'm going to say my piece. You tried to fool them just like you've tried to fool me. The fact is, you'd have a nightmare if you swatted a fly."

"Do you know why I came here? Why I had to come to America?"

"No."

"Find out. You could be driving a killer."

He checked the mirror again and then shrugged.

"I'm watching," I said. "They're gone."

"I have no idea why you came," he said. "But I know how long you've been here. I know what you've been doing, and I know that I scare the hell out of you."

"Don't be ridiculous."

"You're beginning to understand what you've been afraid to admit: I know far more about this whole operation than you do. Look at it. I have nothing to give you but help. Yet you're afraid. I can't blame you for hating me. I'm the one who came bearing the truth. That's why you tried to kill me."

"I didn't."

"It was a fair stab. When you drove that car at me in the parking garage, it wasn't my idea of a friendly game. Something changed your mind at the last minute. But you don't flip coins, do you? Not you. You saw me through the windshield. You were aiming straight for me. What stopped you? I jumped, but not far. You could have swerved and hit me. Remember?"

I remembered. I saw Mansfield ahead of me through the windshield. Each time the wipers swept across, his face seemed to grow larger, as in the dream. Yet there was Mansfield sitting beside me, driving the car toward himself. I covered my face with my hands.

"You listen now, Jon." His tone sharpened. "You made my men listen to that fancy story back there. You've done enough talking for today. I know everything you told them. You said they were ruining the case, but all the time you were ruining it. You came very close. I can quarantine those men and save this case. They're good men, even though you don't think much of them. They had no instructions from me on this. They don't need them when a man sitting by a locker pretends to read the paper for one hour and forty-one minutes. The careless award is yours. A man in a green hat tried to steal your suitcase, huh? They listened to you and now you're going to listen to me. You're going to get answers without even asking those questions you've been afraid to ask yourself. Like who killed Zuckerman?"

"Nobody killed him," I said quickly. "He died of smoking and drinking and whoring."

"What did the obituary say?"

"I don't remember."

"Are you always pretending when you read the papers?"

"I tell you, I don't remember! It was four years ago."

"How did he die, Jon?"

"He drowned."

"That's right. So weighted down the divers let him rot. Why did you choose to forget that, Jon?"

"It's not important. He was swimming dead drunk on godawful rum."

"You have that on Steingut's authority?"

I nodded. "He wrote me about it."

"Some authority," Mansfield said. "I think they did it."

"Who?"

"Steingut, one of his men, I don't know who, that's not my end of the case. What's crucial to me is that after Zuckerman's death, this whole operation began to change."

"No," I said. "It's been exactly the same. The letters from Steingut, my work with Torre, nothing has changed in all these years. This is a foolproof network."

"Not quite."

He steered to the far left lane to pass a slow truck. He was brooding. I felt that I was beginning to convince him. It remained only to convince myself.

"You wondered about Zuckerman," Mansfield said. "But you didn't ask any questions. That's how they did it. Step out of your skin a minute. Picture your arrival: young man ablaze with dedication, survived the war, tried to deflower the peace, won an international reputation in underground society. But they put you in your place here. A link in the chain. You never saw the other links."

"I saw Zuckerman once."

"And he was disposed of very neatly. You were sharp on the little dangers, but you were too proud to question the big danger. Someone could take over that chain, someone who wanted it for something else. It could be taken over with every link intact!"

"That's impossible."

"Who does Torre deliver to?" Mansfield barked at me. "You don't know. Who orders Steingut? You don't know. Who is Steingut? An initial on a letter. Who is Torre? A man in a green hat. Or maybe he's two men. You don't know. You don't know anything. Only that you do your work and the money comes in. You think it's a foolproof network. Somebody else thought so, too."

"Who?"

"Who is it that specializes in cement burials at sea? They own it now, every bit of it, including you. It was bad money that bought out Zuckerman Enterprises. They may have been blackmailing him, we're not sure. But they found him and took it step by step: bought into his magazines, put him in debt, killed him, infiltrated his network, and took it over. That's why I was assigned to this. You and I are in the same field, Jon. It's in that suitcase, in every suitcase, briefcase, laundry bag, all the baggage you've been carting around for four years. You pass on a message, you make a drop, a pickup, every assignment you've carried out so goddamn proudly and efficiently has been part of that operation, to get it into the country. Of course you don't want to believe it. You won't read my folder. It's only two weeks old. It took us three years to piece it together. But it's here now, documented. All we need are the names. Real names. You're the one who can do that for me, Jon. You should be giving me everything you can, if only out of honor or anger or whatever you can still feel. They've tricked you and twisted you and corrupted your whole career. You thought you were still working to bring up the downtrodden, tear down the oppressors, cure all the diseases of civilization; that big swollen ego of yours splashing itself all over humanity and asking so little in return. Oh, that's a great part you play. But, man, you are nothing but a high-class pusher."

I did begin to speak then but something was caught in my throat. I waited for it to clear. I could not afford the sound of doubt.

We drove through the tunnel. He stopped for the light at Thirty-fourth Street.

"Will you let me out now?" I said.

"I want you to say something. Just a word. Yes, you see it now. Or no, you don't."

"Neither," I said.

Mansfield turned west and then made a left on Fifth Avenue. I did not know where he was going. From the set of his jaw, it did not look promising.

"Rain's letting up," I said.

"Back to the weather again."

"Ever been to France?"

"First you're a weatherman, now you're a travel agent. But I say you're a garbageman."

"It's beautiful in France this time of year," I said.

Somewhere in France, but where? I was waiting for a man in a museum. He was late and I thought he might be dead. I was watching for his reflection in the glass of a tall case against the wall, but it never came. As I started to leave, I saw the vermeil in the case, delicate pieces, not like the Vatican. There were horses, carriages, footmen, every detail fused in silver and gold. I thought at the time: how many years it must have taken to shape all that beauty! They told me the artisans lost their sight working with it. They went to their graves without eyes. They are dust and the vermeil lives on in that museum.

"Those who lost their sight for the beauty we can admire," I said to Mansfield. "Was it worth it?"

He looked over at me with a rare flash of interest. As we crossed Fourteenth Street, I caught sight of the Washington Arch brightly lit.

"Sure," he said. "I may be on the other side of the omelet, but I'm a great one for breaking a few eggs."

"That's not funny."

"No, it isn't," he said.

I could not give him my own answer. It would have betrayed me. No, it was not worth it. Mansfield had the same answer as everyone I have worked with and everyone I have worked against. But it was his system which gave that value to things. I have worked very hard to destroy it. That is why I have trouble killing. Ten thousand pieces of exquisite vermeil that will endure for centuries are not worth the blinding of the meanest French artisan, no matter how many children he struck and how many women he betrayed. I have tried to follow that principle. It has not been easy.

"It's good work that I've done," I said, regardless of Mansfield's presence. "No one knows my name but I've made a good name with myself. You're not going to take that away from me."

"You and your goddamn corny ego."

He parked on the corner of Ninth Street and Sixth Avenue and sat back in silence. We listened to the Jefferson Market clock strike ten.

"So," Mansfield said after the tenth stroke, "you don't believe me."

"No."

"It's hard, but you will," he said. "For four years, from the day of

Zuckerman's death, you have been a link in the rackets, bleeding the poor, killing the young, torturing God knows how many junkies who couldn't pay off."

"You're wrong."

"What kind of a man are you? Haven't you ever wondered what happens from one link to the next? When you drop a train schedule or a briefcase, don't you even think about the consequences?"

It was the most obvious of his tricks but it reached me. I saw Joe Hull's terror-stricken face.

"Of course I've wondered! What do you think I am? A man was killed on my account this morning. I don't like it but I'm convinced I've done the best job possible. I didn't kill him. I would have given anything to prevent it."

We watched the crowd crossing the street in front of the car, mostly young people with dead faces, walking aimlessly. Mansfield smiled. He had worked every angle. The banderillas were in. I knew it was time for the kill.

"I want to show you something," he said. "Would you believe your own eyes?"

"I've seen what's in the suitcase."

"But you don't believe it."

"This is the first time I've been involved in anything like that," I said. "Something got mixed up in San Juan. It's a mistake."

"How do you know?"

"I know."

"Have you ever looked inside before?"

"I know, that's all."

"Let's go."

He pushed open the car door.

"I'll stay with the suitcase," I said.

"Oh, bring it along, if you like."

He was chuckling sanctimoniously as we crossed the street.

"You had every opportunity to jump out of that car and run," he said. "Or kill me, of course. You've made every excuse not to. But you're still with me because you believe me. So I'm going to reward you with a little treat. I'll give you all the evidence you need to find me what I need."

I followed him under the iron arch and up the steps of the dismal old brick building.

"You don't believe that suitcase?" Mansfield said, opening the door. "It's just a three-million-dollar stone. Now we're in for a few cheap ripples."

From the small, barred windows above, harsh female voices reached out desperately to the night. Across the street, a few passersby stopped to gape and laugh. Most hurried on in embarrassment. "Don't run off, peckerwood, fly up here." "Hey, whitey, I'll do it for anything in pants." "Anything in pants, you kidding? I'll go down for anything alive."

Mansfield took my arm and pulled me along through the door. Inside, he touched a policeman's shoulder and whispered a few words I could not hear. A gate opened before us. We moved down a corridor and into an office. An anemic little woman, her snow-white hair squeezed tightly into a bun, stood up from behind a desk to greet us.

"Oh, yes, Mr. Mansfield. Right away, sir."

We were ushered into another room, bare-floored, lit dimly by a naked bulb. Our hostess left. Mansfield and I sat on a wooden bench cornered in the shadows. He watched the door. I clutched the suitcase on my lap and waited.

Tina came in supported by a matron on either side. When they released her, she fell to her hands and knees, not with pain but with total exhaustion. The sharp slam of the door behind the departing matrons revived her spirits. She crawled quickly toward the door, like an infant discovering the speed of locomotion, pulled herself up by the knob and turned it. The door would not budge. She crashed into it, first with her shoulder and then with her head. She was clawing beneath the door with her fingernails when I jumped up. Mansfield pulled me back to the bench. The noise of our brief scuffle startled her. Her head snapped in our direction. Mansfield pressed down hard on my shoulder, cautioning me to remain seated, as he pushed himself up and moved slowly toward her.

"What seems to be the problem?" he said. His voice was chilling. I would not have recognized it as Mansfield's.

"Please help me," Tina whispered. "They won't give it. I've tried, I can't kick it, I swear. Pretty please. I'll kill myself. For Christ's sake, I'm begging you!"

I ran to her. Mansfield pushed me back against the wall. He pulled some coins from his pocket and threw them on the floor.

"I'm going to save the taxpayers some money," he said, in that same unfamiliar voice. "You pull yourself together, girl, pick up your dime and your subway token. You're free to go now. But I don't ever want to see you here again, you hear?"

"Yessir, I swear!"

"I'm making you a profit, girl," Mansfield said. "This gentleman is going to escort you home. You don't have to make a phone call and you don't have to take a subway and maybe he'll be nice to you." He turned on me. "I expect to hear from you, Jon, before tomorrow is out. Consider tonight your round. Take the suitcase and take her, too. You've got what she wants in there and maybe she's got something you want."

She was stroking his shoes in gratitude, those black shoes always shined to glass. It was a terrible sight. Mansfield's farewell smile was crueler than I would have expected of him. It was a rough game. He had played his best card.

I reached down and helped her up to her feet. When she came up level and her eyes began to focus on my face, she screamed so horribly that it brought the matrons running back.

8.

"I want out of this thing. Now!"

Her laugh was sour. I slapped her, not hard, but with enough sting to bring the tears, enough hurt to make me feel I had to put my arm around her.

The taxi driver glanced quickly into the mirror and then away. It was not his chivalry showing, only his fear of potential thieves.

"Stop here," I said, to his great relief. The corner was well lighted. I looked through the rear window. A black Dodge pulled in slowly and parked behind us. The headlights died. The doors did not open.

I tipped the taxi driver generously, hoping to cleanse his memory. We stepped out. Heat lightning crackled overhead. The rain had stopped. Tina was shivering and perspiring, laughing and sobbing, her knees buckling at each step. As we walked west toward Broadway, I threw my suit coat over her shoulders and held her tightly around the waist. The knuckles on my other hand were drained of blood by a life-or-death grip on the suitcase handle.

The crowd walked past us fast, looking as if they were late, glancing at their watches over and over again. We passed an appliance store. They were standing at the window, staring through the glass at models talking soundlessly to their cars on television screens. We turned up Broadway and they came pouring out of a movie theater, blinking at the lights.

"Get me away from here," Tina said. "It's written all over my face."

"No! I need the crowd and the lights. There was a car following us. I can't deal with them until I find out what you know. Just keep those legs as stiff as you can. And stop rubbing your face! If you won't behave yourself in a taxi, we're going to stay with the lights."

"Always thinking of the other fellow," Tina said.

"It's not you who's about to be shot," I said. "Hang on, I'll find another taxi. And this time keep your mouth shut."

We climbed into the Fifties, still without success. The theater crowd had captured the corners. Every taxi was taken. Tina's sweats were coming in jolting waves. She was making a valiant effort to walk erect. Every few steps she would stagger without warning, and I would haul her in closer. It began to develop a strange rhythm and my reflexes improved. But there was one slip. Near the corner of Fifty-sixth Street, she lurched away. In my haste to grab her I dropped the suitcase. It bounced hard into the gutter. A sailor ran over and picked it up. He appeared ready to sprint. Then he saw Tina. Slowly, he undressed her with his eyes. He winked at me and returned the suitcase. Tina laughed at the fear on my face. But she could not have known.

"The subway won't do," I said, pulling her away from a subway entrance.

"Embarrassed?" Tina whispered. "That's why we left that cab."

"The driver might have turned us in."

"Remember me, Jon?" Her teeth were chattering. She bit down on her lip. I buttoned the coat. "I know you, remember?" she said. "You'd rather be shot than look foolish. You're embarrassed to be seen with me."

"Embarrassed is hardly the word. There's one!" I waved at a taxi letting off an old couple across the street. As my hand left her waist for that instant, Tina nearly fell to the sidewalk. I pulled her in again and tried to act a little tipsy as we approached the taxi.

"Go through the park," I told the driver. "We need some air."

"No!" Tina's voice rose to a shrill pitch. "Amsterdam! Up Amsterdam!"

"Which is it?" the driver asked, unperturbed, as if he had survived such marital disputes many times before.

As I pulled the car door shut, I saw a flash of green in a telephone booth near the corner. The window of the booth held the reflection of the taxi. I credited to my anxious imagination the blurred view of a man in a green hat dialing the telephone.

"Amsterdam!" Tina said.

The driver did not wait for my countermand before starting up. The urgency in Tina's voice carried authority.

I watched the sidewalk faces flashing by. The game had changed. No longer was I merely under suspicion. They knew. Or they would soon know, as soon as they discovered that I had the suitcase. How long would it take Torre to transmit that message through all the links in the chain? Did it mean days, or only hours? There would be the fear, from that night on, that someone out there was no longer just watching me. Someone was stalking me for the kill.

Yet there I was again, just as I had been with Mansfield, driving under someone else's power to an unknown destination. Amsterdam.

"Only mild curiosity," I said to Tina. "Where are we going?"

"Where are we now?" Her eyes were wild.

"Passing Eighty-first," the driver said.

"Stop at the next corner." She dug her fingernails into my arm. "Fifty dollars, Jon. Please."

"No."

The driver pulled over. Before the taxi had come to a stop, Tina was clawing at the door handle. I fought to keep the door closed.

"I need it, Jon."

"No."

"For God's sake, I need it!"

"You'll survive. Let's go to your place."

"Do you want me to get it free?"

It was too desperate to bear. I gave her the money. She pushed open the door and tumbled out of the taxi, landing on her knees. Painfully, she pulled herself up, took two halting steps, and tripped over the curb. I jumped out and knelt beside her. The damage was not severe. She had skinned an elbow and acquired an ugly-looking gash in one knee.

"Take your damn coat," Tina said.

"I'm taking you home."

"Take the coat! He'll wonder."

I pulled off the coat.

"I'll wait for you, Tina. Don't forget that I'm waiting."

She held onto my shoulders and lifted herself up. I was amazed at the explosion of energy that propelled her stumbling down the block. Once again she fell, halfway up a brownstone stoop. She pushed herself up to her feet, steeled herself, and walked slowly and erectly through the door. I watched her without empathy or shame. There was something magnificent about her performance.

"If you don't mind," the driver said over his shoulder.

"I do mind. We'll wait, do you understand? There's ten. I'll triple it before we're through." I felt sorry for him. He was beginning to be frightened. I stood with one foot on the pavement and the other hard up against the suitcase on the taxi floor. Ten minutes went by on the meter, thin little sounds of my life ticking away.

Thirteen minutes. She would not come back. And I could not go in. It would be instant death for a meddling escort carrying that suitcase. If my throat had not been so dry, I might have laughed. It was too beautiful! Tina was up there with the cockroaches, scrounging for one night's watered-down trip from a dirty needle, humiliating herself before some vicious little chiseler. And there, a half-block away, in the suitcase next to my foot, were enough pure dreams to last her into the next century. Hadn't Mansfield told her that I was the master pusher of them all? Didn't she know I had been carrying the stuff all over town for years? Or did she cling, as I, to some grand illusion that Saint Jon was still slaying the dragons of inhumanity.

Eighteen minutes. No, she would not come back. Perhaps she had escaped out the back of the building. The key would be lost. For I now understood Mansfield's brutal message. Tina was the key.

The driver flipped off the meter. I sat down and watched the sidewalk. It was deserted. I turned to look out the back window. There were no green hats or black Dodges or other vengeful figments. Then I saw a quick movement. A pretty white cat trotted into view, hissed at us perfunctorily, and lay down to sleep next to a garbage can. I signaled the driver on.

We were moving out slowly, waiting for a mail truck to pass, when I heard footsteps coming up the block.

"Stop!" I shouted at the driver.

Tina ran into the lamplight. When she saw the taxi, she smiled and slowed to a walk. She was apparently unaware that I had nearly left her behind. I stepped out.

"Thank you for waiting," she said. She kissed me on the cheek.

I put my arm around her. The cold spasms had vanished. Her legs were steady.

"You wanted to go to an island, remember?" she said. "I'm ready now."

We climbed back into the taxi.

"My God, he's back!" Mrs. Poulakidas wailed as I opened the apartment door.

Tina lived on Fort Washington Avenue in the old-law tenement where she was born. True or false? Early in life, I learned to question the accuracy of facts. I was now beginning to doubt their existence.

If Tina was the key, then who was Tina? I knew no one better. Yet nearly everything I knew about her, she had told me.

It was the same rambling railroad apartment where as a precociously ripe teen-ager she had been pampered by her mother, where in the gay years of her early twenties I had shared her bed, and where, two days before this night, I thought I had bidden a second, final farewell to the old scratchy armchair.

An odd place for Tina. I assumed that it held too many memories for her to leave it. Her father had returned to Crete to die. His was a seismic career. During Prohibition he opened three successful restaurants on the East Side. Thereafter, he very slowly went broke. True or false? I never met him. I was given to know by Tina that he had many fine qualities, including his determination

157

to send her to college, but did little to conceal his lechery and was afflicted by sudden fits of brutality.

Tina's mother had operatic aspirations forty years ago. They never materialized. True or false? I did meet her once, about three months before she fled to Arizona with her lover, a very slick and wealthy maitre d'. She doted on her only child. I remember her as quite tall, with remarkable grace and serenity. She did not approve of me. It was after Mrs. Athenasios made her escape and her husband set sail for Crete that I began spending the nights there. Tina was modeling infrequently, still pursued by visions of *Vogue*. It was a ridiculous life goal, but much as she laughed at it she wanted it, desperately, it seemed. I could never understand why. She also stayed up late pounding out stories which were read with relish by her old English professor at Hunter College, but were never sold. The stories were all about a young, very frightened girl who lived her life through daydreams. In one of them, she fell in love with a strange man who came in from the sea.

Mrs. Poulakidas, the widow neighbor, used to bang her broomstick on the wall nightly at eleven sharp to stop the clacking of Tina's typewriter. We would make love until Mrs. Poulakidas had been provided with ample time to fall asleep or fly away on her broomstick, and then Tina would resume typing and I would doze off. I went early to work in those days, for the mail from Steingut arrived first thing in the morning at a box in the Lexington Avenue post office. When Steingut began sending his letters care of Tina, I was certain it would have to be finished. She knew my profession, she knew my whole life, but I did not want her to have the dangerous knowledge of each mission's movements. How did Steingut know I was living there? He seemed to know everything. True. And I did not want to endanger Tina. False.

She began to read extensively in cryptology, hoping to decipher Steingut's language. It was, of course, no use. There was no code, only assumptions natural to the user. Tina would test me, passing me her own messages, in the hope that I would break them and thus provide a clue for Steingut's. I remember only one, but I remember it well: "My love seeks you. It feels like a silent river cutting deeply into the soil. There are dry tears, joyous tears, choking in my heart. I have this weird feeling that I cannot even express to you now. The tears are crystallizing into sparkling walls that keep us inside safe from harm, so that all light is magnified and all the searching rays are filtered. I thank you for loving me, honoring me, and trusting me." I suppose I was affected by that, but when I reached for her, she pushed me away and said it was far from spontaneous, all designed to yield the message "Honing the edge of fate" — and what, Jon, is the system? She smiled devilishly.

It took me a full evening to discover that the key was all the way down to the seventy-second word — "honoring" for "honing" — taking the first three and last three letters of the basic word. And what was the rest of the system? I can't remember. The words themselves disturbed me. I thought at the time it was because I loved her, that there was nothing I wanted to keep from her, and that her curiosity was placing her life in danger. Later I realized that the message informed me that I could not love her enough.

In the weeks that followed, our love became a ritual of theater without climax. She was a great actress, but I knew. She was hiding from me. She knew I had discovered, in that message, that there was an emptiness I could never fill. And I was acting, too, by silence, when I found the joints of marijuana in the toilet and the black tie left by a careless daytime lover. Or were there two, or three? What did it matter? What was I to do, scold her? Strike her? What was I to say? You have a need that can never be satiated. Nonsense! I knew that emptiness. I felt it, too. And she would only shame me with desperate outpourings of gratitude for my love. She was so damned grateful, as if she were not worthy of anyone's love. No, I am not a jealous man. It takes too faint a heart. People are not things to be possessed and hoarded. That is the murderous system I pledged to destroy. The power to own is the power to kill.

Mrs. Poulakidas was ecstatic to see me go. I thought she might organize a block party in celebration. It was all my fault. I had started on the wrong foot with her by letting on that I was a soft goods salesman named Silas Marner. I had forgotten all about Ralph Pellston. Later, her cousin the mailman confided to her that mail was coming to a man living with Tina and that the name was not Silas Marner nor Ralph Pellston but Jon Baruch. Mrs. Poulakidas did not like deceit. Nor did she like soft goods salesmen, loud typewriters, Greek girls flaunting their college degrees, and neighbors practicing nocturnal laughter and fornication. Her respect was reserved for those who arrived punctually at Orthodox services, notably, her cousin the mailman, and formerly, Tina's mother. It was our suspicion during those good years that Mrs. Poulakidas spent her evenings writing long, scathing letters to Mrs. Athenasios about the dire consequences of Tina's living in sin. At any rate, the postcards from Arizona did trickle off. This hurt Tina and undermined us. I tried to assure her, to no avail, that even if her father had felt more lust than love, her mother would always remember her with affection. I also suspected that beneath it all, Mrs. Poulakidas loved Tina very deeply. It was this suspicion that rooted my fondness for Mrs. P., even though I knew she loathed me.

"Look at yourself, Katrina!" Mrs. Poulakidas said.

There was a cry from a back room off the center hallway. It was short-lived.

"Where is he?" Tina said.

"In his bed. But he will not spend the night here under such circumstances. I will not have that," Mrs. Poulakidas said.

Tina tiptoed to the back room.

"You always bring trouble," Mrs. Poulakidas said to me. "Where was she last night?"

"I'm just seeing her home, Mrs. P. She had a slight accident."

"I see that. You pushed her down somewhere. Always drinking, drinking, drinking. Or maybe something worse. I'm not blind. I see you moving in your baggage again."

Tina returned, carrying a small boy on her shoulder. He was asleep.

"You should be ashamed, Katrina!" Mrs. Poulakidas said.

"Shh."

"Where have you been this time? You left him alone with me since yesterday. It's shameful."

"I know you take good care," Tina said.

"I do not leave here until the salesman leaves," Mrs. Poulakidas said. "He will not sleep under this roof with the child. You take your suitcase out of here and leave my Katrina alone!"

"We have something to talk about," Tina said quietly.

"I will not leave the boy here," Mrs. Poulakidas said. "If the salesman stays, the boy sleeps with me." Tina transferred the boy to Mrs. P.'s shoulder.

"What would your mother think of you at this moment, Katrina! If the boy were not asleep, I would slam this door. You are not fit to be a mother!"

"Oh, my," Tina said, as she closed the door behind Mrs. P. She clapped her hands and skipped gaily to the cabinet for the ouzo. But her hand was shaking as she poured. She bit hard on her trembling lip.

"No thanks," I said.

"Please."

I took the glass.

"We don't need water tonight, do we?" Tina said. She smiled and lit a cigarette. I had never seen her smoke before. She paced nervously about the room, holding the glass and the cigarette in one hand, frantically opening drawers and leafing through papers with the other.

"Start talking, Tina," I said, uncomfortable in the depths of the old armchair.

"I'm looking for that poem I wrote. About the night we walked along the beach."

"Don't bother."

Did she actually think she could divert me with such nonsense? It was too late for that, long too late. I would not fall into the whirlpool again. There was a saying in Italy: *Guarda che ti multi in brute acqua!*

Beware of sweet water.

No, Tina was not that foolish. She abandoned the search and seated herself on the hollow leather ottoman. I inspected the gash in her knee. She took a stiff swallow from her glass.

"Talk about what?" she said.

"From the beginning."

"Well, as a young girl I featured myself as something of a free spirit. The best secret I learned at fifteen. And, to tell the truth, I enjoyed it."

"I know all this, Tina."

"But I never fell in love until I met you. Did you know that, too?"

"Yes."

She lifted up the lid of the ottoman and slammed it back down. "What do you want, Jon? There's nothing you don't know."

I pulled the magazine from my pocket and tossed it to her.

"You see what I mean?" Tina said. "You know everything."

"It's not quite *Vogue*," I said.

"But pretty good, don't you think?" She flipped through the pages appreciatively. "I hadn't seen this one yet."

"You knew Zuckerman," I said, pushing for a denial, hoping she would make a liar of Flake.

But for the rustling of the pages, there was silence. I wish it had continued.

"A gifted man, in his own peculiar way," Tina said. "His plan was to steer me to the top as a high-fashion model. It appealed. It shouldn't have but it did. I thought the idea was hilarious." She smashed out her cigarette and lit another one. "I always knew at heart I wouldn't make it. Only the skinnies do." It was not her smoking itself that distressed me, it was the way she did it, the incessant, nervous puffing, as if the words were trapped within her and would not come until deadly fumes smoked them out.

"Wouldn't that be nice!" she said. "Wouldn't it be nice if you had seen me home for something more gallant than a third degree?" She threw the magazine across the room. I went to retrieve it. "Don't say it, Jon. You loved me, I know. That's quite a reward, the past tense. I have a demon inside me and if you had eyes to see, you would know that I'm asking you how to drive it out. I'm asking for your help, for God's sake!"

"You've been helped! You went up to the little man. That was the same appointment you kept when I was here Monday night, am I correct? Now I'm the one who needs help, Tina. I have demons outside. There may be hundreds of them."

Tina smiled at me in such a mysterious and calculated way that I was sure she had decided to close the door on everything painful, just as she had slammed down the ottoman lid. It was, at the same time, a very sad smile of resignation. It transformed her into an old woman, weary beyond pain.

"You're not going to win, Jon."

"I am. If I can measure the odds. That's what I want to know from you. I trusted you most on this earth and you betrayed me. I told you nearly everything. But I neglected one thing. I never asked you to keep my identity a secret. I didn't think I had to ask you that." Tina shook her head vigorously. "Then you tell me everything, Tina. I don't intend to sit here all night listening to Mrs. P. knock on the wall every time I lace into you. You tell me. You owe me that much."

She shook her head, this time slowly, maintaining the same sad smile.

"All right, Tina, you've always had trouble talking. But you still fancy yourself a writer. Exhibit B." I patted my coat pocket. "I have your heartfelt letter." I gave her a pencil and pad. "Write me another. I'll just sit here quietly until the mail arrives."

She stared down at the carpet, nibbling pensively on the eraser. I did not have to wait long. She scribbled something fast and ripped off the top piece of paper. There were only six words: "Get out of here, Jon. Quickly!"

"Is someone coming?" I asked.

She did not look up.

"Or is someone already here?" I was on my feet, running toward the back rooms, before I realized the danger of the search. It would be a trap back there. The fire escapes were in front. I returned to the living room and looked down on the street. No cars were passing, those parked had their lights off, not a single pedestrian was in view. From the stillness of the block came an aura of innocence in which I had no choice but to believe. The only way to question it would be to go down and challenge it.

Tina did not help me close the curtains. She sat silently on the ottoman. I opened the front door and peered into the hallway. It was as deserted as the street below, as the block off Amsterdam, as — What was it she had said when she gave me the glass? "We don't need water tonight, do we?" I fastened the door chain and moved very slowly toward the kitchen.

The door to the kitchen was closed. When I kicked it open, it crashed against a pegboard on the wall, sending spoons and pots clattering to the linoleum. I groped for the light switch. Then I remembered it was above the sink, ten feet into the darkness.

One pot was still quivering on the floor. It made the only sound in the room. I wended my way through the minefield of utensils, my heel flattening a spatula as I reached the light. Mrs. P. had not been idle. The kitchen shone. I locked the window. There were five rooms to go.

With each room, I took fewer precautions. It became increasingly obvious that no one was there: I was still alive. The dining room, stripped of the old china that had filled the glass cabinets, looked as if it had not been used in years. The bathroom was too small for anyone to hide safely.

Tina's bed was tightly made. Mrs. P. had failed only to beat out of the spread the imprint of her vigil. A second bedroom, in which Tina's mother had locked herself on tempestuous nights, was completely bare. The third had been converted into a nursery. A picture book on family life in foreign lands lay on the boy's pillow. The sheets were wet. Next to the bed was a candy-striped bureau. On top of it, in a thick black frame, was a handsome photograph of Emil Zuckerman.

I sensed Tina standing in the doorway behind me.

"What happened to the old china?" I said, closing my eyes against Zuckerman's glare.

I heard heavy breathing. It occurred to me that it might not be Tina's. I turned to face the door.

"Mother sent for it," Tina said. "She's a widow now."

"Yes, that would be important down there in the desert, having the old things around you." I stared at her until she retreated.

"It was an interesting tour," I called after her. "There's no one here, is there?"

I followed her into the living room. She shook her head.

"Why did you let me go through with it, Tina? I suppose you had to see me make a fool of myself."

"I knew you were frightened," she said. "Now I know how much."

"You're wrong."

"You should be frightened, Jon, that's what I'm telling you."

"No, I don't believe so. I jumped too fast. That's been happening to me lately. I misunderstood you, Tina. You told me to leave because you're afraid to talk, not because you're afraid for me. So goodbye."

I walked to the door, bluffing.

"Don't!" she cried. "Damn it, I want you with me. But I don't want you to know me, Jon, I never have."

"You said you wanted help with that demon."

"Not here. Somewhere else. Let's fly out. Tonight."

"The boy."

"We'll take him with us. Please, Jon, it's what you wanted."

"You're hooked, Tina."

"I'm not hooked, damn you, not, not, not hooked!"

She would talk. I moved back in.

"I can't provide that kind of kicks," I said.

"It's not kicks! Don't you understand? It's different with me. This is me now, Jon, why won't you look at me? It's only in my eyes that it shows, everything else is me, can't you understand? If I don't have it, I'm not myself. It restores me to myself. You want that for me, don't you? You gave me the money. What are you worried about? That you'll wake up one morning and find me dead of an overdose? I have a wooden arm, Jon, that won't happen to me."

"Tina, I can't go away now."

"They'll kill you."

"No. I'm not working for them any more."

"That's why they'll kill you. Will you look at me, Jon? We have a second chance, don't let them do it again. They destroyed us. When you moved away to God knows where, it wasn't us, it was them."

"Tina, we had simply fallen out of love."

"No! It was those letters from Steingut."

"You can't change it, Tina, you know the truth."

True or false? She turned away. True. We did not need to say it. When those letters began to arrive at Tina's, we were both relieved. It was the excuse we needed. What a sublime parting of the ways! We pretended to protect each other, when, in fact, we needed that danger to help us break apart.

"Ah, well, it was a beautiful illusion," Tina said. "I thank you for it. And I hate you for it, Jon."

"Let's take it from the night I left you, five years ago."

"Emil called the next day. At that point I had no idea who he was. He asked for you."

"He was lying."

"Of course he was lying, but how was I to know?" She reached for a cigarette and changed her mind. "They were watching you. He was checking to make sure that you and I were really finished. But he didn't say that. He said he had something for you. He asked if he could drop it off that night."

"What was it?"

She pulled up the lid of the ottoman. There was a package inside. It measured only about eight inches square but it felt quite heavy.

"You've never opened it?"

She shook her head.

"I had no idea where to find you," she said.

"Why didn't you give it to me the other night?"

"I fear it, Jon."

"What happened to the old curiosity? You wouldn't look at the message from Steingut in my pocket. You've left this package unopened."

"I don't want to know any more."

The worn string broke loose immediately. Beneath the wrapping was a small metal box with a padlock. The hinges unscrewed easily. As I lifted them off, I glanced over at Tina. She was terrified. What did she expect? A cobra? A tarantula? Still alive after five years?

There was only a card. I turned it over. It was blank. In the box was nothing. Tina's laugh crescendoed to near hysteria. I waited while she calmed herself. I was not going to slap her again, however much she might wish that. I would not be son, father, judge, executioner. She demanded too many parts from me.

"All these years," she said, "I truly feared it."

But, of course, it had to be this. What else could there be but nothing? Everything was slipping through my fingers. Mansfield was right. They had played a game with me. The message from Steingut about trains to Babylon, had I implemented it correctly? I could not be sure. The next message: "I will send your mail to the girl's apartment." A warning to leave Jenny O'Leary, the same as with Tina, five years before. And when the mail arrived: empty, assuring me that I had set events in motion on the trains to Babylon. But what did that mean? How could I be assured? And why did the money arrive when I did not yet need it?

Going to see Tina, had I willed it? I had taken the same subway two years before, to walk the neighborhood, hoping to see her, not daring to enter the building for fear that her name would no longer be on the mailbox. The strange marks on her arms that night, I saw them but she had distracted me. I would have thought further. She had done it deliberately. And then her silence, leaving in the night for a fix, the letter on the pillow, it was almost truthful, she said. The black bruise on her arm, was it from the pusher?

I felt heartless, concerned only for my own skin, as I stared coldly at Tina, looking away each time she winced from her cuts, while she held to the hope that I would be the one to remove the pain. It was not worth the cruelty.

My memory had been sharpened. Cotton, alcohol, and bandages were still far back on the second shelf of the bathroom cabinet. When I returned with them, she smiled and lifted her glass in a victory salute. I did not care. This was for my comfort, not hers. With the smug pity of a savior, I could no longer bear her pain. That had been frail bedrock for love but she was still relying upon it.

She reached inside my pocket for her letter and read it while I swabbed the gash in her knee. I thought of Thaddeus, who had somehow managed to salve my wounds during the Bowery years, without even knowing it. It was possible that he did know. In some odd way, Thaddeus understood. That was a world away from Jenny's smile, but still safe, until Torre invaded it. My search for Torre at the library and then Tina again, the magazine cover — was Flake as guileless as he seemed? Was Tina? "As I recall," he said, "she was a discovery of Mr. Zuckerman's."

Her leg jerked when the alcohol seeped into the cut. I saw the red pulp of Joe Hull's face. "There is no Shelter for pigeons." That was another poor message. The wrong man in the Stetson. Before the trains to Babylon and JFK-LBJ, Steingut had always been meticulous. My hand on Torre's shoulder, his elbow sharp to my ribs, it was so close, but I had touched him, he existed at last, they all existed. They disappeared with Torre into the fog, and with an empty box, but I had seen the photograph of a dead man on the boy's bureau. Each time I doubted Mansfield, I had discovered that he was right. He had tried to fake me into trust, finally by linking Tina with the chain, and he had won. The great interrogator was at her feet, full of shame, tending to her wounds.

"Shall I burn it?" She put down the letter.

"If you like."

She was disappointed, but it was her question, not mine. I stood up from my ministrations and admired the results.

"Zuckerman brought an empty package as an excuse to meet you," I said. "I can't blame him for that."

She smiled at me as if I were an incorrigibly naïve little boy.

"Don't be silly," she said. "Emil interested in girls? Flesh and blood? The only way I could excite him was laid out in a photograph or on a slab in the morgue." She lit a match to the letter and watched it burn. "I never met him till he arrived with this package. I was out there with Mother, sir, like all the nice girls on the beach. He never knew that I was the girl you met that day."

"Then why did he have me watched?"

"He didn't trust you, Jon." Her voice dropped so low I could barely hear the words. "Not from the moment you arrived. 'Too damned cocksure,' he said. Isn't that the worst danger in an underling?"

"That's hard to believe," I said. "Unless Bergère gave him that notion."

"Oh, I think Emil envied you. This was the feeling I had. You contacted him a day late. You trifled with his network to walk the beach with a girl. That was dangerous, certainly. In his position you would have felt the same way."

"Of course I would." The ghost of Zuckerman was beginning to irritate me. "But he was so damned friendly about it. He actually congratulated me on taking so well to America. It was good reason to like him right off."

Tina decided to light the cigarette.

"Let's try out this theory," I said. "Zuckerman didn't trust me because he suspected I was sent over to keep watch on him. I thought that myself at first, something about the way he acted. But it was not true. I never heard from Bergère. So why would Zuckerman have cause to believe it? Because he was up to something that Bergère didn't know about. Whatever it was, it caused his death. He told you about it, Tina. I know from experience it's not you who does most of the talking in bed."

The slap was her best defense. I was relieved to have it back, grateful that she gave it twice the force of mine in the taxi.

"Don't bother to apologize," I said, rubbing my jaw.

"Don't worry! That is really disgusting."

"No worse than bearing his child."

"I think I will get some water after all."

She carried her glass to the kitchen.

"That man who was with me in the detention home, Tina, do you know him?"

I heard an angry blast from the faucet.

"No, I don't," she shouted out.

"He put you there, didn't he?"

"I don't know." She reappeared, nervously drumming her nails on the glass. "The police picked me up here yesterday. I called Mother's lawyer and he promised to look into it. The shyster didn't bother."

"That man knows you. He's on this case. His name is Mansfield. Are you sure you don't know that name?"

"Only from you."

"He is the man I have a bargain with. I can't wait ten years to hear your answers. I have three days."

Finally, I struck real fury.

"Oh, that's wonderful! You make the bargains to save you and I make the bargains to save you. Everything for Jon and nothing for Katrina."

"What's your bargain?"

"I made it, damn you! Emil left me holding it. How could you be so absolutely stupid? I admit I'm weak, I'm on the needle, I'm human, but I have never stooped to being as stupidly selfish as you. I told him nothing about you. And I made him promise me your life."

"He was no danger to me," I said.

"What does it take to kill in your profession? Suspicion is all. He would have done it but for me. I paid for that in installments. I'm still paying." She spat on the magazine. It was very ugly for Tina and she knew it. "High fashion, cover of *Vogue,* do you think I believed it for a minute?"

"Did he introduce you to the man who fixed you?"

"You bet he did, and I'll tell you something else: I liked it! I am still with it, all of it. Just name the worst corruption and I have made it pure, because I deluded myself that everything I did was to protect you. Isn't that the marvelous thing about great causes? You can do any filthy thing and you know you are serving virtue."

I started to speak again but she thought she knew my words.

"Don't try, Jon. 'Oh, poor Tina. All this for me. And look at her now. Zuckerman's gone and she's hooked.'" She was wrong. "You will never convince me, Jon, that you feel shame about anything you've done to me or to anyone else. And you would be all wrong about this. I agree, we have lied to ourselves about protecting each other. I did this, it was my decision, it was for me, and I've enjoyed it, every minute of everything."

It all sounded true: her love for me, her hatred of me, her pride, her self-contempt, her knowing everything and knowing nothing. To make certain was well worth a three-million-dollar bet.

"I won't thank you, Tina. I'm going to ask you one last favor to save my life."

"That's more like you."

"Where can I leave it?"

I picked up the gray suitcase. She took it from me and vanished into the bedroom. I knew she would not hesitate. There was more to it than proving herself. She knew that I would have to return for it. This was our bargain.

She came back, carrying a purse.

"It's under the bed," she said. "Do you want to check it?"

"I trust you. Sit down."

"The money, Jon. I owe you fifty dollars."

"Forget it."

"Will you call me tomorrow?"

"Sit down."

"I need another drink."

"No you don't. I want you clear."

"You don't want me at all. I'm tired."

"I want what you know, Tina. You will not go to sleep, you will not get drunk, you will tell me about you and Emil Zuckerman."

"Will I?"

"He brought you this box the night after I left. Was it then he offered you a job?"

"You're too thoughtful. Did it ever occur to you, during five years, that I had to pay the rent?"

"I left you money."

"Nice. Two weeks later I would have been a secretary. Or just possibly three weeks, allowing for yogurt dinners."

"Sorry."

"I do type ninety-three words a minute, isn't that what you counted on? Believe me, it was more than a pleasure on that bleak night to meet someone who thought I had other attributes."

"You knew that, Tina. You could have done more modeling than you did."

"I'm a sponge, right? I could have, but as long as you were here, why bother, right? Now you sit down. Stop standing over me like a very bad-mannered inquisitor." I sunk into the armchair. "I assure you," she said, rewarding my concession, "this was more fun than anything I had ever done. I went to the studio the next morning, you're damned right. Sensational poses. My best. I never improved on them."

"Was Zuckerman there?"

"No. He called again a week or two later. I told him it had been a ball, but that was enough. I wasn't serious, of course. I wanted to do more, and I knew damn well from the photographer's rapture that I could get a lot more money. But apparently he believed me. That was when he first dropped the hint that your life might depend on my decision to continue. I was goddamn mad at you but not that mad."

"How often did you see him?"

"After the first night? I didn't. Not then. Later in the year, after I'd been going to the studio twice a week for three or four months, he suddenly took to calling me every day, asking to see me here.

But he would always turn the conversation to questions about you."

"Tina, I wonder if you realize who Zuckerman was."

"Certainly. The owner of Zuckerman Enterprises, obviously. And a most intriguing man, not so obviously to you."

"And my first contact here."

"He didn't tell me till much later."

"But he was testing you," I said. "He was trying to find out what you knew about me. That's why he came to see you and why he kept calling you."

"I told him nothing, Jon."

"At first. I believe that. If you had not been secretive, he would never have dared tell you who he was. But it was a full year later that he was killed. I know he had time."

"That's all I have to say, Jon. I'm not lying to you."

"All right, let's back up now, you're doing fine." I was beginning to gain confidence but I knew that flattery was required. "Nine years ago I met a lovely girl on a beach. I told Zuckerman, by way of apology for being late. The identity of my distraction was unknown to him at that time, or so says the lovely girl."

"That's true," Tina said. "He didn't know her. And I'll grant the compliment, too. She wasn't bad-looking."

"She became my one friend in a strange land. Within a year, my pursuit of that friendship came upon good fortune, or so it seemed at the time. Her mother moved out and I moved in. I then had three good years with her."

"Two good and one bad," Tina corrected me.

"What she calls the bad one ensued, coincidentally, after Steingut and presumably others, including Zuckerman, discovered that I was living here. They had me watched, she speculates. And, lo, the day after my departure, who should arrive but my old friend Zuckerman?"

"The end," Tina said. "I liked the beach better."

"Zuckerman, whose time was borrowed, nonetheless had an entire year of life remaining, long hours of which he devoted to prying secrets from the lovely girl. Even without her knowing it, her smallest comments could be pieced together by a skillful man."

"Like you?"

Dead end. She knew me too well.

"Damn it, he had every opportunity. He paid your salary, he fathered your son, he made your drug connections, he no doubt even brought you into the network."

"No."

"Don't try to fool me, Tina. He told you everything about himself, just as I told you everything about me."

"You did not tell me everything, Jon. You never once mentioned the name Zuckerman. You never told me the specifics of what you were doing and neither did Emil."

"Would it surprise you to know that he was playing more than two roles? Tina, I have reason to believe that he transformed the whole operation."

"I don't know that. If you want to know Emil's role, you ask my son. He adored him. There's your surprise. My son has clothes, he has food, he has books, silly little things, aren't they?"

"Yes, I don't question that Zuckerman was generous."

"You do question it and you're wrong."

"The man was deranged."

"A little eccentric, is that so important? Why, Jon, you're as envious as Emil. You could no more be a good father than he could be a good lover."

"Don't you give a damn how he provided? The money was not his."

"He made it."

"Not the way you think, Tina. I learned tonight who the paymasters really are."

"Oh, for heaven's sake, who knows the spots on a dollar? There's no such thing as clean money. Does it make any difference whether my son's shoes are bought by that magazine cover or by a detergent factory where I would type ninety-three words a minute? For Christ's sake."

"It does. Zuckerman was killed by the men who bought his magazines."

She looked away quickly. I watched her reach down to the floor for her purse and place it next to her on the ottoman. She opened it and pulled out a compact.

"How do you know?" she said.

"My concern is whether you know."

"He told me once that the magazines were in trouble, that's all he said." She raised the mirror, powdered her nose and patted her hair.

"Steingut may have helped kill him," I said. "Did Zuckerman ever mention Steingut?"

"You did."

"But did he?"

"Who is she, Jon?"

"Are you telling me that Steingut is a woman?"

"That's not what I mean, as you well know. There is someone, isn't there? All done up in blue jeans and pigtails, I'll bet."

"I want you to answer my question."

"You shouldn't keep her waiting." She snapped the case shut.

"There isn't anybody," I said.

"Oh, yes, there is, it's very plain. You've been treating me like a computer. An untrustworthy one, at that."

"We're not going to begin it all over again, Tina."

But I realized, as I said it, what a perfect move she had made. She had decided exactly where to draw a hard line, and it would take more than flattering words to cross it. Either way, I was in trouble. If I did not respond to her jealousy with real assurances, she would simply refuse to talk further. But if I did, hoping it would lead me to more information, she would help me find the softness under her words, I would show the gratitude she pretended not to covet, and I would be lost in sweet water, the past gliding in to soothe the pain of the search.

"She doesn't care much for glamour, does she?" Tina said. "Would you like me that way, Jon? That's what used to make this your home. Or is it the gloss you like? Don't hesitate to express your preference."

"Please help me, Tina."

"I want to, baby, look at this arm. Nothing, you see? No marks.

Performed with a magical powder puff. Or do you like those marks? Do you like to see under the surface? Now look at this one. The bruise that bothered you the other day, my poor baby with his delicate sensibilities. Did you think I'd had a lover's quarrel? You see how well it's healed? I hate to disappoint you but it was only a fall. I've been trying to kick it, Jon, really trying. And I fall a good deal. Does that interest you?"

"Tomorrow, I do promise to call," I said. "We may still be able to help each other."

"I don't want your help. I don't want to owe you one damn thing." She fumbled in her purse.

"Just the suitcase," I said.

"That's odd." She looked up in mock surprise and then smiled. "I could swear I had a fifty somewhere. Do you accept payment in kind?"

I started to get up as she slipped to her knees but her elbows dug sharply into my legs, pinning the butterfly will to escape. I saw her pupils at close range, huge and lifeless, rolling over me without sight. Her mouth was cool and dead.

"I'm numb, Tina."

"Try to leave."

"I can leave."

"I'll bet you," she whispered.

It could not be the same. This time we would be distant voyeurs, panting with rage, watching and feeling from outside ourselves. We had nothing to give each other anymore.

She was sobbing very softly as I closed the door behind me. There was no way to comfort her. She would cry herself to sleep like a baby.

9.

I was already seated in the last subway car, before I saw that it was empty. My thoughts were still with Tina, wondering if she had fallen asleep. I was not concentrating on safety. It was no time to be away from the crowd, I knew I should have boarded a middle car. But I was too exhausted to move.

Perhaps I was being deliberately careless in celebration. It was a relief to be rid of the suitcase. I knew that Mansfield was using it as bait. Now I was free from it and they could not take it from me. They would have to deal with me to find it. The secret of its whereabouts was my one protection against death.

Yet when the train stopped at 145th Street, I realized how vulnerable I still was. The doors opened with a crash. I held my breath. Who would step in? How many? I was unarmed. That had never bothered me before.

But no one entered. The doors slid closed and the train moved on. Again, at 125th Street, they opened and closed. As the train rolled out of the station, I saw that the platform was empty. I could not decide whether they had all boarded other cars or if no one had been there. In all the tunnels of the underground at three in the morning, was I the only passenger? But for me, the car was as empty as the package from Zuckerman. The entire train might be empty. Was there a driver? For all I knew, the thermonuclear Armageddon had arrived overhead, the city's inhabitants were destroyed, and the only survivor was condemned to ride eternally beneath the rubble on an automated train.

The empty vision weighed heavily on my eyelids. I strained to keep them from falling but the struggle was too great. I patted my

coat. The magazine was still in my inside pocket. Without aware-
ness of passing the borderline, I nodded into sleep.

A blond wig flashed on and off neon-like, assaulting the eye of
my mind. Tina's moonlit face appeared, her eyes hidden behind
goggles. Above her swirled a ghostly scrawl, letters stretching and
rolling obscenely, caressing, breaking apart, a *t* moving through
the circle of a *P*, two *a*'s rubbing gently together and separating, a
y and an *h* slithering toward each other, and then, at a wink from
Tina, they all fell into formation above a motorcycle: *Phantasy*.
Tina climbed on the motorcycle seat and bounced to start the engine, making love to the roar. She was carried up a steep mountain road toward the full moon, riding the wind, fiercely naked, the
long strands of dead hair trailing behind her.

I heard laughter rising and echoing beyond the mountain.
Ahead of Tina on the road a nun was walking hand-in-hand with a
green-haired, red-eyed girl. The girl had lovely legs. The motorcycle crashed into the nun, passing over her, leaving her crushed in
the middle of the road. The laughter faded and I recognized that it
had been mine. The girl bent down, listening for a heartbeat. Tina
reached the top of the mountain, turned the motorcycle around,
and came rolling back down out of the moon, aiming directly for
the girl. The girl looked up fearfully, her eyes changed from red to
green, her hair from green to red, and I saw that it was Jenny. In
the same instant, Tina appeared to recognize her, too. The motorcycle stopped dead and she was frozen into the magazine cover.

The roar of the motorcycle was replaced by the clacking of
wheels on the subway tracks, louder than before, as if I were standing on the platform between the cars. Half in sleep, I dropped my
hand and felt the seat still beneath me. I heard a door slide
closed. The noise from the tracks receded. A door? But the train
was moving. There was no stop between 125th and 59th. Opening
my eyes seemed as impossible as pushing giant boulders up the
mountain road. I did not even try. The sounds of the tracks and
the sliding door, I decided, must have been part of the dream.

Not until I felt the cloth pressing against my mouth, then tightening on my nostrils, strangling me with a sweet, wet stink, did I

realize it was the door between the subway cars that had opened and closed. By then it was too late. I was falling down an endless chute into darkness, my head throbbing and shrinking, and I was certain that I was dead.

"Officer, is there a coffee shop open? Our friend here is dead drunk."

"Around the corner. Down half a block on the right."

"Thanks very much."

We moved around the corner. But we did not stop for coffee. I tried to make out the shadows of the buildings. My eyes would not stay open. I could feel stiff fingers gripping my arms. I could hear every step clearly. There were two men, one on each side. I pulled my right arm free. A fist slammed into my stomach.

"We'd better put him out again," the man on my left said.

"No. He'll be here in a minute."

My arms were jerked painfully behind my back. It felt as if they would tear loose from their sockets. Handcuffs were clamped on my wrists. The pain vanished. A blindfold was tied tightly over my eyes. We stood still. I listened.

We were near a traffic light. In the silence of the night I heard the loud clicks from red to green and back again. I counted a cycle of thirty seconds, then forty-five, then thirty, then forty-five. It did not seem to be a busy intersection, at least at that hour. Cars whizzed by very occasionally, spaced up to two minutes apart. At one point I heard the engine of a motorcycle. I fully expected that Tina would come charging up to save me. Or perhaps to reveal herself as the queen of my captors. But the motorcycle turned a corner at least a block away. Then, from the opposite direction, came the tattoo of a jackhammer. Dot-dot. Dash. Dash. Dot-dot. A utility man piercing the floor of the city. Dot-dot. Dash. Dash. Dot-dot. The rhythm was amazingly consistent, as if the worker had found freedom in the triumph of his style over the hard demands of the pavement.

That was all the information I had. It seemed peculiar that with so many distinct sounds pinpointed on my blind compass, I could not be sure which was north, south, east or west. It was almost a relief when the car stopped for us; they pushed me in, and one of them said, "Let's take him down." They circled a block to reverse direction. We were heading south. Either that, or I was dealing with very intelligent men.

The car came to a halt too many minutes later to count. As we stepped out, we were greeted by blaring music, saxophones, trumpets, a low female voice that reeked of whisky and bad dreams. "Me and my shadow," she was singing, far off-key. In the few seconds before I was pushed through a doorway, I heard heavier traffic, some trucks, and then the door slammed shut. I walked seventeen steps, through another, narrower doorway, and they shoved me into a chair. My hands were cuffed to a leg of the chair. The blindfold was removed. Three men moved quickly to join a fourth behind a blinding strobe light. I tried to decipher the silhouettes. It was futile. I rested my eyes and contemplated my plight. Captured. Twice in one night. Ridiculous. Whose side was it this time? Mine?

"We're going to talk a little, Jon, not too long, because you haven't much time, you're finished." The voice did not belong to either of the two men who had brought me, but it was just as unfamiliar.

"You go to a lot of trouble for a mugging," I said. "Why don't you just take my wallet and let me go home?"

"We're not interested in your wallet."

"Then why me? I was only minding my business, taking the subway home from work." I pulled on the handcuffs. They slid a precious inch up the chair leg, allowing my spine to straighten. "Are you from the company? Listen, I can explain the moonlighting. I have a family to support, fellows, same as you."

"We're interested in your suitcase, Jon."

Naturally. But why were they taking so long, being so polite?

"What is this 'Jon' business? My name is Frank. Frank Miller."

"Let's not waste time." It was a different voice, very rough around the edges.

"You didn't lose that suitcase, did you?" the polite interrogator resumed.

"Look, I have one suitcase to my name. It's home in the closet. If you want it, take it."

"No, Jon, this is a very important suitcase. It does not really belong to you. It belongs to me."

"Who are you?"

"Torre."

I opened my eyes. The rays of the strobe light burned into them.

"You took that suitcase from me," the voice said. "I'd like it back now."

Yes, of course, it was Mansfield's boys up to tricks again, trying to break me.

"I'm afraid you have the wrong man," I said. "Believe me, I don't know you. I don't know anybody named Torre."

There was whispering and then silence, the air crackling with a current of violence. I was not sure whether they might well succeed by force. The minutes passed. I listened. They did not move.

"I suppose," the voice said, "we'll just have to wait here until you tell us where that suitcase is."

"Don't you know?" I said pleasantly, relieved that they had decided on a strategy of nonviolence. "You were following me, weren't you? Why, fellows, if I had a suitcase, you must have seen me go in somewhere with it and come out without it. If I had that suitcase, which I didn't."

"Went in where?"

The pause that followed was uncomfortable for them, but with each passing second, increasingly comforting to me. Slowly and absurdly, it began to dawn: Torre, if he was Torre, was telling the truth. These were not Mansfield's men, they were mine. They had hunted me down in the streets and subways of the night and found me alone in the subway car. The last time Torre had seen me, I had the suitcase. Where had it gone? They were desperate to know. I had already won my bet. Tina was not part of the network. She was safe, the suitcase was safe, I was safe. Whatever steps they took against me, they would not dare destroy my knowledge of the one fact they needed.

"Went in where?" the voice repeated.

Two men had found me. Out of how many? Surely, they could not have been crouched on every corner, could not have scoured every subway. Or could they? How vast was this chain to which I was linked? It had grown in my mind to the size of the city itself, every stranger my enemy. Out there was a force so irresistible that no one, not even I, could escape. If so, my capture was no coincidence. It was as inevitable as the night. These men spoke for hundreds, perhaps thousands. Only four were there: Torre and three who knew him. But this was not the way we worked. We were not supposed to know each other. Was it the same chain?

"You seem to know that we aren't going to kill you," the voice said. "That's good thinking. But you may come to wish it."

I did not need to ponder the threat. There was nothing more to gain.

"All right," I said. "If I do have it, I'll get it to you."

"Let's go." There was movement behind the light.

"Not tonight!" I said. "Tomorrow."

"We want it now!" It was the rough voice again.

"Do you actually think I would lead you to it?" I offered my best incredulous tone. "No. If it exists, it will simply appear."

"Good." Torre's voice was friendly. "Tomorrow you will receive instructions as to where."

"How?"

"A message from Steingut."

It was not the same corner. As they freed my wrists from the handcuffs, I listened for the cycle of changing traffic lights and, in vain, for the sound of a jackhammer. By the time I had untied the blindfold, I had counted the lights at sixty, twenty-five, sixty, and the car was far down the street. I was at the corner of Third Avenue and Forty-second Street, a stone's throw from the *Daily News*. They missed quite a photograph.

For two or three changes of the lights, the street was empty of taxis. Then I saw one with its roof light off, moving east along Forty-second Street. It stopped in front of the newspaper building to discharge a passenger. As I approached, the driver pulled down the sun visor to display an off-duty sign.

"Oh, no!" My hand shot back from the door handle.

"I don't believe it!" Nathan P. Silver said.

I looked up and down the street. There were no other taxis.

"So get in and put on your seat belt," he said. "You wouldn't be going to the Bronx, by any chance? I'm on my way home."

"That's fine," I said.

We drove toward the river.

"The man I just dropped," Nathan P. Silver said, as if our conversation had paused briefly for a twelve-hour interruption, "you'd think he was a reporter, right? He's a janitor. I can tell, you see. Where you going in the Bronx?"

"I'm not going to the Bronx."

"And I could tell you spoke English, you didn't fool me. Not going to the Bronx?" We were already speeding up the East River Drive.

"Keep going," I said. "Drive over the Willis Avenue Bridge to the Bronx."

"I thought you weren't going to the Bronx."

"Keep driving."

He shrugged and continued.

"At first I thought I'd quit for the day," he said, "when I saw you'd given me fifty bucks. Was that a mistake? You can have the change, you know."

"Just follow my instructions and you'll have the other half."

"No kidding? But then, you see, I thought to myself, now, that would be the common thing to do, the first instinct, go out and celebrate, spend it all. A primitive instinct. So what do I do? I end up working overtime so that this will be my biggest day in history. And, you see, it paid off. I meet you again. For another fifty. Luck rides with Nathan P. Silver."

"Nathan, old friend, the other fifty depends upon your following my instructions exactly."

"Shoot."

"You will not ask me any more questions. You will not comment on my appearance, concerning which I am sure you are preparing many well-turned remarks."

"It's true, I was wondering —"

"You will not wonder. You will not talk. You will not tell me any more about yourself. You will not query the strange itinerary I will announce from time to time. The only sounds in this taxi will be simple, direct commands, such as, when you reach the other end of the Willis Avenue Bridge, turn left on Bruckner Boulevard, come back over the Third Avenue Bridge, return down the East River Drive and go over the Brooklyn Bridge. Have you absorbed all that?"

"Yes."

I had hurt his feelings again. It was the only way. He wouldn't talk now if I paid him to. As he followed my instructions, I watched the other cars carefully. No one imitated us. We started back down the Drive. There was no one behind us.

"Very good," I said. "Here it is." I could not smooth his feathers. He grunted and shoved the money in his pocket. Clearly, he valued an attentive audience more than a profitable one. Nathan P. Silver was a good man, whoever he was.

When, at last, we had crossed the Brooklyn Bridge, he began to speak and then stopped.

"Where are we going?" I said. "Is that what you want to know?"

"Yes."

"Montague."

We reached Montague Street. I put my hand on his shoulder.

"Look," I said, "here's another ten. I'm sorry. I'm just very tired."

"Keep it," he said.

I stepped out on the street.

"I know you're in trouble, I can tell," Nathan P. Silver said. "Good luck."

"Thanks, Nathan."

I waited for him to leave. He made some notations on his chart. The taxi did not move. I was not going to let him know my real destination. Like him or not, no one in the city could be trusted on that night.

When he had finally exhausted his stalling tactics, he drove off. I walked over to Schermerhorn Street.

The door was unlocked. Across the room in the alcove, a gooseneck lamp cast the shadow of the clay bust on the wall. The head was hanging down from the skylight in a hangman's noose.

"Very funny," I said.

"I knew you'd appreciate it." Jenny's voice came from deep beneath the sheet on the sleeping-couch.

"For a moment I was frightened," I said.

"Really?"

"Yes. You see, they plan to kill me."

"Don't go paranoid on me. I might puke."

"I told you to keep this door locked." I slipped the police lock into the floor.

"How do you like my new dress?" Jenny said.

"Which one?"

"The white."

"Have I seen it?"

"The one I wore at dinner."

"Dinner?"

"Nine hours ago. You'll find yours in the icebox. I hope it's frozen solid."

"I'm not hungry."

She threw off the sheet.

"On second thought," she said, "that remark is not even worth throwing a pillow."

"And where were you? I called at seven."

"Shopping for dinner. So sorry to be late."

"You have lovely legs, Jenny."

"Jesus!" She turned over and buried her head under the pillow. I sat down on the edge of the couch to unlace my shoes.

"I ran into some trouble, Jenny."

"Oh, dear, what can the matter be, Jonny's so long at the fair."

"I am truly sorry."

"Cooking, cleaners, laundry, took your watch to be fixed. I mean, it's really a fascinating life, being a kept woman. Will you get off my bed now?"

I retreated to a chair. One eye peeked out from under the pillow.

"I don't understand you," Jenny said.

"Yes you do. That's why I'm here."

"But, like, who are you? I mean, if you think the mystery intrigues me, you're wrong. What I like about you is what I know, not what I don't know. And I don't know where you've been tonight."

"Riding the subways."

"That's all?"

"Pretty much."

"Funny. I could swear you look just like a guilty husband."

"Ah, Jenny me girl, the world has plowed us under."

"And don't give me any of your Irish sentimentality. I might puke."

I knelt by her.

"I love you, sweet Jenny, I do."

It must have been the chloroform.

"Phew!" She wrinkled her nose. "When you get there, squeeze the toothpaste at the bottom, not the top."

I dragged myself into the bathroom. Home was not the haven I had anticipated.

"I started to tell you something, Jenny," I shouted over the running water, "but you wouldn't listen to me."

"About their trying to kill you?"

"I thought I'd tell you a little about that. I want to tell you."

"Well, I've guessed, don't you know. This chain letter thing, it never fooled me. You're some kind of gangster. Very nice, as gangsters go, I suppose. And I'm like a moll. Very exciting. I cook fancy dinners for myself."

I stood in the bathroom doorway, debating candor.

"You're dripping toothpaste on my brand new rug," she said. "And your fly is open."

"Do I take out the garbage now or later?"

"So where do you get your money? And what do you do with it, apart from paying cheap rents?"

"Taxi drivers get rich off me. I retired three of them just today. I buy drinks for bums. And then there's this very expensive girl I keep who refuses to wait dinner until five in the morning. Not a good bargain at all."

"How was your part?"

"What's that?"

"The film on the Bowery."

"Oh, yes, well, you see, that was the story I was going to tell you. That's when they were going to kill me. Really a fine story. All about this bum who was pushed down the stairs. I play his cousin. I go to investigate. But I'm a bum myself, you see, and the police don't trust me. They chase me around a bit and I grab a taxi to the airport. That's why it took me so long. I had to go out to the airport."

Jenny was staring at me intently.

"I'll tell you one role I'm not going to play," she said. "The long-suffering little woman. It bores me."

"Just a few more days."

"And then what? It will all be settled in one swell foop? I can't believe that, Jon."

The hanging head was unnerving me. I slipped it out of the noose.

To my horror, I saw in my hands the face I had seen in the mirror at Fisher's Tavern, the face twice transformed without a trace of scar tissue. She had made a perfect likeness. No tension to provoke curiosity. The smooth skin. The eyes that I could dull at will. But she had made them bright, like the eyes in the mirror, too intense for safety.

I lifted the head into the cupboard over the icebox.

"Don't you like my work?" Jenny said.

"Of course I do."

"I suppose it must be hidden away, to be viewed only by my patron."

"Yes. It's too good a likeness."

The instant I crawled into bed, she hopped out and went to the cupboard.

"Please leave it there," I said.

"Why should I?"

"One hanging's enough for tonight."

She placed it on the white pedestal and stood back to admire it.

"It's really good, isn't it?" she said.

"The artist, not the subject."

"That's what I meant."

She lay down beside me.

"How many O'Learys are there, Jenny?"

"Don't bother with the malarkey."

She turned her head to the wall.

"I want to know," I said.

"Four. But my brother never came back. Nantong Valley, Korea, and they made it very clear. Jimmy was not a hero. He had a heart attack. One night I came home from work and I saw my parents sitting in the living room, staring at the television screen. The only thing is, there was nothing on the screen, and they were just staring at it. That's when I decided to leave. It was a cruel thing to do, but I had to."

She drifted away from me, breathing heavily. But I knew that she was not asleep. Her eyes, like mine, were open wide, staring into the dark. She was wondering who we were, and what terror awaited us.

I was walking down a dark street. Along the sidewalk was a giant trough. They were all kneeling before the trough, raising their heads to glance at me as I walked by into the subway entrance.

The car was empty, as before, but the lights were very dim. I kept watch on the doors. This time they would not catch me napping.

The doors opened at 145th Street. My heart beat faster. No one entered.

At 125th Street I heard a distant tapping along the platform outside. It moved steadily closer.

Thaddeus entered the car. He probed the seats with his cane. He knew I was there.

"Soothsayer," I said, "you know I am in your hands."

He sat down opposite me and stared across in silence. It was horrible. I was relieved when, at Fifty-ninth Street, he stood up to go. Yet I blocked the door. He had still not spoken to me.

He raised his cane in the air.

"Beware," Thaddeus said. "Beware the twelve trains to Babylon."

The telephone was ringing. How many times it had rung I did not know. I reached over from the couch and lifted the receiver. I did not speak. There was a click at the other end of the line.

It was dawn. I dressed.

"My God," Jenny said. "One hour's sleep."

"You sleep," I said. "I had a bad dream."

"Sweet Jesus, a tie. What role are you playing today?"

"I don't know yet."

"And will your royal highness be here for dinner tonight?"

"I don't know if I'll be here or not."

"You take up space. I'll know whether you're here or not, I'm clever that way."

"Jenny, I'm leaving the police lock in place. I want you to keep it there. I don't want you to go anywhere today."

"Dare I ask about lunch?"

"I can't make it."

"Might I join you somewhere, your highness?"

"No. I'll be at McSorley's. I'm serious about the lock."

"Are you, now."

"The telephone rang," I said. "It clicked off. I don't know who it was."

"Mother. She calls to see if her little gun moll is sleeping at home."

I put the clay head back in the cupboard. Jenny did not see. I hoped she would accept an action twice taken. It was for her sake. Except for the old days of waitress and customer, we had never been seen together. We had not exchanged photographs. I could not allow all my precaution to be ruined.

"I'll try to be back tonight," I said. "But I want you to wait here for me. If the telephone rings, don't answer. Is that clear?"

"You're crazy."

The sun was rising fast as I walked along the promenade. I was the only one there. Your royal highness, she said. Not the sun but I. So, Mansfield, I am still the center of the universe. Around me revolve the planets Jenny, Tina, Thaddeus, Torre, Steingut; and Joe Hull floating out there forever in space. The sun climbed higher. I walked for the last time into the subway.

The receptionist still thought she was pretty.

"Lieutenant Feegan again," I said.

"Yessir. For Mr. Flake?"

"Exactly."

This time Flake did not snap to attention behind that ridiculous desk.

"I've been trying to call you," he said, swiveling in his chair. "They don't have a Feegan at Homicide."

"Deegan."

"Oh, my mistake."

I sat without invitation. That had been my first lesson in the role from Mansfield.

"Why were you trying to reach me, Mr. Flake?"

"I wanted to apologize for being quite so vague about Miss Athenasios. You understand, we protect our models. It's a matter of ethics with us."

"I see."

"But I am aware of her problem, which I assume is why you came to see me. I am sure, however, that it could bear on no homicide. She is a hophead, I know that, but, you understand, we consider that her business. My business is merchandise, Lieutenant. As a craftsman, mind you, not as a businessman. And, as you saw from the magazine, Miss Athenasios comes across on the printed page as that rarity of rarities, what I like to call a shimmering tower of orgiastic fury."

"Mr. Flake, I am not interested in your profession. I am here to inquire about the relationship between Miss Athenasios and the late Mr. Zuckerman."

"Yes, well, I'm afraid I really don't know much about that."

"I believe you do, Mr. Flake. Perhaps you could start by telling me just what happened to Mr. Zuckerman."

"Well, I always say about Mr. Zuckerman, he didn't go to heaven, he didn't go to hell, he went to expurgatory."

He grinned wisely, expecting me to match the laughter of past audiences. Restraint was not difficult.

"How did he die, Mr. Flake?"

"Sunstroke, I understand. Fell prey to aprication on the beach."

"Our records indicate that he drowned."

"True. That's what the obituaries said."

"Do you doubt them?"

"No," he said. "I believe that he was washed away by the tide."

"Is this a private theory, Mr. Flake?"

"There's no other possibility. Mr. Zuckerman often boasted of his swimming prowess."

"Are you positive you can think of no other explanation?"

"Lieutenant, I trust you are not impugning the sobriety of the dead."

"Not at all. Let me put it this way. Who owns this corporation now?"

"The estate of Mr. Zuckerman."

"How do you know?"

"I don't know, Lieutenant. I must remind you again, I am a craftsman, not a businessman. My duty has been to carry on exactly as Mr. Zuckerman would have had me do. I believe the results speak for themselves."

"You know nothing about the ownership?"

"Very little. As I understand it, Phantasmagoria, Incorporated, is a rather intricate conglomerate, established by Mr. Zuckerman shortly before his death. Its name appears on generous paychecks to myself and my staff. We are well satisfied."

"Then turn to what you do know, Mr. Flake. We know that the relationship between Mr. Zuckerman and Miss Athenasios was a close one."

"Do we?"

He smiled at me quizzically. Dealing with this man, whom I had so easily intimidated before, I was now ill at ease in my role. I wondered what I was doing there. It did not seem to be leading me any closer to Torre and Steingut. My questions struck me as those of an angry lover. Flake could not know that. I was making myself uncomfortable. I pulled the magazine from my pocket and balanced it upright on his desk.

"Mr. Flake," I said, "you print crap. No redeeming social value whatsoever. I may have to close you up."

He looked frightened. I took a thigh-shaped lighter from his desk and set the magazine afire. The flames licked at Tina's knees, curled into blackness long wisps of the blond wig, then her whole body was ablaze, her face shrinking and crumpling. Both of us watched in fascination. Somehow I expected to see pain on that photographed face. But it dissolved with the same static expression of sensual mockery.

Flake cleared his throat, pleased with himself that he had not panicked. He rubbed the burnt spot on his desk with a Kleenex.

"No, Lieutenant," he said slowly, "I don't believe you want to close us up. In fact, I don't believe that you are a police lieutenant. I do believe that you are interested in this girl. I can't give you her telephone number, but we have available for five dollars apiece some rather nice blowups. Ask my secretary for one on your way out."

"You misunderstand my mission, Mr. Flake."

"On the contrary, I completely understand your interest. She's our biggest item. We have her in bed pillows, too. Or, perhaps, the very latest for your couch, a life-sized foam rubber bolster. Or would your wife object?"

"Mrs. Deegan would, indeed."

"Oh, take one. Compliments of the house."

"Good day, Mr. Flake."

But he was already guiding me gently to the door.

"Good day," he said. "And may I advise you of something? No offense, please. But if I were you, I think I'd watch my step."

Black crepe was hanging over the doorway to Fisher's Tavern. A small group of the boys stared in surprise at my stylish arrival in a taxi.

"Who would want to kill poor Joe?" Sugar Red mourned. "He had nothing worth stealing."

"It must have been an A-Trainer," I said.

I ripped open the day's envelope from Steingut.

"What happened over there?" Sugar Red asked.

"I told you. He was dead when I got there."

I resented his questions.

"It's all so crazy lately." Sugar Red shook his head sadly. "Joe's dead. And you, where you staying these days?"

"Sleeping around."

He was right. It was a crazy world where I could no longer trust anyone with my address, not friendly taxi drivers or sympathetic bartenders or blind lunch companions. And I could no longer trust the message from Steingut:

> *Try harder.*
> *Ft Wash*
> *Second train to Babylon*
> *S*

"Where you going?" Sugar Red asked. He was looking at me queerly.

"I don't know."

I felt his eyes following me as I walked up the street.

"You never look at me," Thaddeus said.

"How do you know?"

"I know." He spit out a chunk of onion. "Every time I say something, you look away. Why? Because you'd be looking in the mirror."

"Thaddeus, do you know about the trains to Babylon?"

He stopped munching for a moment, opening and closing his fist on the handle of the ale mug.

"Why?"

"Nothing. Just a dream I had."

"Now you're dreaming about blind men."

"Not blind men. You."

"You're not here to see me. You want to know if I've had any more visitors."

"Yes."

"I haven't. Not since that one called Torre. But I didn't like him. That's my opinion. Oscillation is the only preventative for bryophitic vegetation. That's a lesson."

"I'll go."

"And as you roll away, dwell upon that which I'm dwelling upon: which is it worse to be, a blind black man or a black blind man?"

"Which are you?"

"I'm reaching a decision. I'll know tomorrow by lunchtime. Don't be late."

"I won't."

"Splendid. I've enjoyed browbeating you. I can't afford the vanity of self-degradation. It would take too many ales. Enjoyed, see? Notice the tense. You can't last forever."

I stopped at a telephone booth to call Jenny. There was no answer. She was following instructions. I called Tina. No answer. Replacing the dime in my pocket, I discovered a new plastic bookmark from Sugar Red.

"How firm is your faith? Can it stand up under trial? Through the pages of the Bible, God tells us why evil is permitted, and how this wicked system of things will be removed and a righteous new world ushered in. 'Except a man be born again, he cannot see the kingdom of God' (John 3:3). 'We are all as an unclean thing, and all our righteousnesses are as filthy rags' (Isaiah 64:6). 'The heart is deceitful above all things, and desperately wicked: who can know it?' (Jeremiah 17:9). 'There is a way which seemeth right unto a man, but the end thereof are the ways of death' (Proverbs 14:12). 'Behold, now is the day of salvation' (Corinthians 6:2). God has said it, and it is hard to fight against God."

The girl in the red blazer was, as Tina used to say, straight out of Andy Hardy.

"Car reserved for Mr. Steingut," I said.

She flipped through a pile of forms. How, I wondered, did such wide-eyed, well-scrubbed docility travel the long road from the farm to a car rental agency in the big city? She belonged on a milking stool in a blue pinafore.

"Yes, of course. All taken care of. Your keys, sir."

By the clock at the Triborough Bridge tollbooth, I was running late. The key had to be the Babylon schedule. 1:49 was the second train. "Try harder Ft Wash" was the standard Steingut instruction to pick up the rental car and drive to meet an Eastern shuttle flight from Washington at La Guardia. But he had given no time. It could only be the Babylon schedule, the nearest flight on the half-hour to 1:49. I surmised, too, that this time it was more likely to be a drop than a pickup. They expected the suitcase with me.

Driving fast, I saw the emergency telephone sign pass by. I slowed the car and then sped up again. No, I could not call Mansfield. He would have no qualms about arresting Torre and me together. He could no longer be trusted. If I did not bring in Torre and Steingut myself, patriotic jurors would look upon my memory of Mansfield's "bargain" as a desperate fabrication. I reassured myself that Mansfield was still shy of evidence. If we in the network were now puzzling over our own communications, how could he have broken us?

Ft Wash. I kicked the brake. Tina! Fort Washington Avenue! Steingut once knew that address. Had he changed the signals?

Surely it could not be to tell me they already had the suitcase. He had arranged for the car, assigned me a mission. Suppose, rather, that he had chosen Tina's block as the drop point, counting on me to remember. That would be like him, changing the signals but not the words. Of course. They could not risk the airports. In his newfound ignorance, Steingut was telling me to bring the suitcase to where it was!

I arrived five minutes late by the Babylon schedule and the car radio. There was no one standing in front of the building. A black Dodge was parked across the street, its engine idling. As I approached, it moved away slowly and turned the corner. I stood in the doorway and waited. The Dodge returned. I concluded that it was someone who did not know me, someone who was looking only for a man with a gray suitcase. I went inside. When I reached the second floor hallway, I thought I heard Tina's voice. It was indistinct. I wondered if I were still dreaming. She did not answer her doorbell. I knocked at Mrs. P.'s next door.

"Where is Tina?"

"Who is there?"

"Where is Tina?"

Mrs. P. opened her door to the short length of the chain.

"My God, the salesman! You always bring trouble."

"Where is she?"

"She is with the boy. Hush. It's nap time."

"There is no answer, Mrs. P."

"Because they are asleep. We sleep at this hour in the old country. Go away."

Wrong. It was the standard message. I should have been, at that moment, at La Guardia. My best opportunity was lost. I would have to wait another day for the next message. But they could not afford to wait. They would find me, at Jenny's, at Fisher's, at McSorley's, anywhere.

"Mrs. P., I think something may be wrong. I would appreciate borrowing your key."

"I tell you, go away."

"When I called before, there was no answer," I said. "Something is wrong."

"I see them an hour ago."

"Please give me the key."

"No, mister."

"Please."

"You waste my time."

"Then I will have to break in, Mrs. P."

She unchained her door and pushed past me.

"I look myself," she said. "You stay out here. Damn bumbling salesman, you wake everybody up."

She unlocked Tina's door and walked back to the nursery. I slipped into the bedroom.

"The boy is not here," Mrs. P. shouted out. "I no understand. They go for a walk maybe."

I crouched down and peered beneath Tina's bed. The suitcase was gone.

Behind the old armchair in the living room, the window and the screen were open. I climbed out on the grill in time to see the back door of the black Dodge close. Halfway down the fire escape, I jumped.

Three cars separated us going down the Harlem River Drive, at least a dozen on Second Avenue. Moving around a bend in the Midtown Tunnel, I was desperate enough to swerve into the oncoming lane, trying to regain my view. A thundering oil truck forced me back. Then I saw the Dodge racing into the sunlight at the end of the tunnel. I followed past the tollbooth with the pedal flat. The speedometer rose to seventy, eighty, ninety-two and they were still winning. I was convinced that in the end it would be like this, for all of us, our bodies hurtling forward at ninety-two miles an hour, the final impact snapping our legs, impaling us on the steering shafts, smashing our heads into the windshields.

But Queens blurred into Nassau, and I marveled to discover that I was still alive, defying the end, oblivious to every car but one, still hoping to reach it, even after it had passed out of sight.

Crossing the Suffolk border, I realized that they must have turned off. But I could not go back, I refused to believe that I was chasing Torre into the fog again, that I could drive to the tip of Long Island at higher and higher speeds, and nothing would be achieved. The exit signs flashed by. I scanned the side roads for the car, not willing to concede that I had lost it.

And I was right. Beyond a disabled Volkswagen, near a clump of trees on the side of the highway, a black roof glinted in the sunlight. I stomped the brakes and flew fifty yards before stopping.

It was already apparent, as I backed along the grass, that no one was in the car. I saw in the mirror the green Volkswagen parked far behind it. From a distance it, too, appeared to be empty.

The Dodge had been stripped of license plates and stickers. Not a shred of paper remained in the glove compartment. Under the hood, even the engine number had been filed off.

I combed the floors and came up with nothing. More in anger than purpose, I ripped off the cushion of the front seat. The rewards were burnt matches, paper clips, old pennies. Under the back seat I found an unmarked envelope. I stuffed it in my pocket and walked back to the trunk.

It was not locked. The lid pulled up easily. Standing upright was the gray suitcase. It was splattered with blood. Tina lay next to it, her head dangling by thin slivers of flesh.

I heard a voice cry out.

"No! He's one of us!"

What did I feel! There was no time to feel anything but the hard jolt of metal crashing against the back of my neck, curving around my throat, slicing and strangling, and then, nothing.

I knew I was not in heaven. The nurse was thoroughly plain.

"Here," she said. "This must mean something to you."

She handed me the unmarked envelope. Inside was a weathered piece of paper and a turquoise bookmark. "December. Birthstone: Turquoise. Flower: Narcissus." It was the bookmark from Sugar Red that I had left with Tina. "What's my birthstone, Jon? What's my flower? A man walked up to me on the corner and gave me some yellow tulips. A strange man who once came in from the sea."

The handwriting on the old piece of paper seemed basically familiar, but confused by sudden drops and wavers. I wondered if they reflected fatigue or perhaps alcohol. It did not look like one of Steingut's messages. No, it appeared, though it bore no title, to be some kind of poem, oddly punctuated by slashes.

we walked that night along the shore / stars do not die in peace i said / but in the blazing agony they knew at birth / and so this earth / will go you said / now it has come to pass / under a feverish sun / swollen by the fourth angel's vial / courageous air and sea / that once battled the sun to be / can no longer resist / now in the blinding mist / proud flesh scorched and steaming / bursts into flame / in the awful heat of that passion / that painfully crawled across the ocean's floor / up the sisyphean slope / to seek the soul of peace

At the bottom of the page, in different ink, much smaller letters, but the same handwriting, the words were scrawled: "Jon dearest, I found it. Your Tina."

"It's nice," the nurse said.

"You read it?"

"The police were going to take it away. I thought it might mean something to you. You were in a very bad way."

I reached up to my throat and felt the brace.

"My neck!" I could not move my head.

"It will mend."

"Is it broken?"

"No. Some nasty cuts. Your head should be kept still."

"There was a suitcase," I said.

"Oh, they have everything else, dear, whatever was there. But this, I thought, was special. You knew the young lady, didn't you."

"No."

"You needn't tell me anything. They'll be in to question you shortly."

She moved toward the door.

"The boy," I said. "There was a boy."

"What, dear?"

"Didn't they have a boy with them?"

"I don't know who you mean by 'them.' You were found with the poor girl. Was someone else there?"

"No. No one else."

She must have thought me an ugly customer, thinking of the suitcase before the boy.

As she closed the door behind her, I caught a glimpse of uniforms and holsters in the hallway. She locked the door from the outside.

No, not a bad poem, but Tina could do better. Certainly, it was not worth the frantic search she had made the night before. After all, man had come ashore from the sea not to seek peace but because he developed a kidney. Tina was always too much the romantic for such facts. But more than that, it was a curious style for her, a little disjointed. She had an iron discipline in meter and rhyme.

A strange poem. Unless, of course, it said something more.

Yes. If I could only remember! Those foolish messages she tried out on me. "Honing the edge of fate." "Honing" from "honoring." The seventy-second word. The first three letters and last three letters of the seventy-second word.

I read the poem again, counting carefully down to the sixty-eighth word — *proud;* sixty-ninth — *flesh;* seventieth — *scorched;* seventy-first — *and;* seventy-second — *steaming.*

Steaming. S-t-e-i-n-g

10.

Steingut knows me. I know him. At some point in time, we searched each other's eyes and for that instant wondered, and then forgot.

That feeling returned as I lay helpless, wrapped in the sterile sheets of a hospital bed. I knew Steingut, no doubt had even talked with him, neither of us certain but both suspecting. It was wise at that time not to be aware. Early, I had learned the lesson of the centipede. Bergère taught me to saw logs while looking at the sunset. One day I watched myself and instantly cut my hand. I still bear the scar.

S-t-e-i-n-g- And how did I work it from there?

For how long had she known him? Telling me. She was trying to tell me something. But what was her system? The seventy-second word. Then what?

I could not remember!

"Well, well, land sakes alive."

Mansfield looked as if these were the scenes of hilarity he lived for.

"Shucks, aren't you the lucky fellow just to be breathing."

He seated himself in the visitor's chair and waited with ostentatious patience. My suit coat was draped over his arm.

"Where am I?"

"Suffolk County. Good Samaritan Hospital. You have Blue Cross, I presume."

"Saturday?"

"Still Friday. You were out for less than an hour. Must be your neck is as thick as your head. Hard to tell. I'll recommend an autopsy."

"She's dead, isn't she?"

"Yes, she's dead."

"You share that with me, Mansfield. You brought us together last night."

He looked uncomfortable then.

"It almost worked," he said. "You were a little late, apparently. And then you forgot to look behind you. I'm surprised at you. What did she tell you last night?"

"Nothing."

"That's a waste. What about her message?"

"There was no message."

"A poem, isn't it?"

"I don't know what you're talking about."

"You're hiding it. Is there anything in it?"

"Do you have the whole world working for you, Mansfield? I thought that nurse was doing me a kindness."

"No reason to be nasty. I gave you enough time to study it, didn't I? What have you got?"

"Nothing."

"And what about that piece of plastic? It's in the envelope with the poem."

"Just a bookmark some bartender gave me."

"Another question. Why would a man of your experience leave a corner of an envelope protruding so carelessly from under the pillow?"

"Damn it," I said. "I want everything else returned to me."

"Your clothes are here. The police took car and contents. As I understand it, you are charged with a number of moving violations." He smiled and reached into the inside pocket of my coat. "And this one? 'There are twelve trains to Babylon.' That means nothing, too, I suppose."

"I don't know."

"Then it would seem that you're the one I'm after, Jon."

I pulled the letter from his hand.

"Visiting hours are over," I said.

"You've never been honest with me," Mansfield said.

"I simply don't remember, is that so rare? How much can a man store? I don't carry your files. These things were not important."

"You don't choose to remember, Jon. I'm warning you that you had better start pressing the right buttons."

I lay back and closed my eyes.

"What's your next move?" I said.

"What's yours?"

"To wait here until they get me."

"Oh, they won't try that. Not while I'm around."

"I've had enough," I said.

"Look, Jon, I'm going to get you out of here. We're too close now to abandon it. This time I'm putting a tail on you, day and night."

"No. I'm not interested anymore."

"Our bargain still holds."

"You do what you want. I'm finished."

"Think of Jenny O'Leary."

"Who's that?"

"I'd have to tie her into this, aiding and abetting."

"You don't have a thing there."

"I'd do it," he said. I believed him.

"Do you have it in your files, Mansfield, that I once slashed my hand sawing a log?"

"Small white scar, left hand."

"And how are you on the first time I cut weeds?"

"I'll check."

"They sprouted again and I cut them again and they sprouted again. So I learned. I took them out by the roots. You can't win. Yesterday, a taxi driver told me they scream."

"I think you've got more than an injured neck."

"He's right. They all fight to live. That's where I've been wrong, we've all been wrong, cutting away year after year. It has to happen fast. The system won't rot away. There are too many of you, Mansfield. The world will end in fire. I thought I'd help save it from that."

"All done now?"

"Yes. All done."

He threw the coat at me.

"Let's go."

It was the same rented car. Had he questioned the girl in the red coat? She, or someone there, had taken the order from Steingut. But they gave me back the car and it took a quarter tank of gas before I left the tail stranded pathetically on the expressway with a flat tire. I doubled back and found my way to the police property bureau.

"The personal effects of Miss Katrina Athenasios," I said.

The sergeant in the wire cage, with the jutting jaw and scowling brow of a baboon, did not bother looking up.

"You got a court order?" he said.

"I'm her brother."

"Got a notarized statement?"

"I'm here for the suitcase."

"There's no suitcase."

"A gray suitcase, please. She had some personal things in it."

"I said there's no suitcase."

He glanced up at me. Was my manner too anxious? I turned to go.

"Wait a minute now," he said. "Let's see your identification."

He signaled to a policeman seated near the door reading a magazine.

I was out of breath when I reached the car and saw that the keys were gone.

"In a hurry?"

Mansfield leaned out the window of his government car, jangling the keys.

"I have to get back to the city," I shouted at him. "Now!"

"Sit in here," he said.

The policeman approached, fingers tapping his holster. I decided to obey Mansfield's instruction. He jumped out and disappeared with the policeman into the building. For perhaps ten minutes I sat alone, staring at the keys he had left in the ignition of his car.

Mansfield returned and slid into the driver's seat.

"That was a good choice," he said. "You can use a friend."

He flicked a switch on the dashboard and a siren sounded. It was echoed by a police car which appeared from behind the building and moved out ahead of us. On the first curve we were already lifting wheels.

"I'm taking your word," Mansfield said. "Who are you meeting?"

"Whom."

"What time?"

"As fast as we can get there."

"You were right that I missed my calling," he said as we entered the expressway. "It should have been the Grand Prix."

"Do you call this fast?"

"Wheels in the air, flashbulbs at the finish, smooching starlets, paid endorsements of spark plugs."

The police car was easily a half mile in front of us.

"Have you checked your tires?" I asked him. "Your man forgot."

"Was that it? Chalk up another for Mansfield's marauders. But I knew you'd go to the property bureau. Excuse me." He pressed down on the accelerator and swung over to the far left lane.

Two Nassau patrol cars were waiting at the Suffolk border. We followed the first while the second kept pace close behind us. It was a comfortable life, being a star witness.

"She really told you nothing?" Mansfield said.

"That's right."

"I don't believe you."

"You have to."

"It's no joy," he said, "dealing with a man who has so little education."

He was musing as the city police took up the torch near a construction barricade. Our marathon avoided the major traffic and crossed over the Fifty-ninth Street Bridge. The streets cleared quickly before the sirens until we were trapped in the rush-hour taxi jam on Fifth Avenue.

"Stop here," I said.

"Why?"

"So I can think."

Mansfield pulled over and signaled the police car on.

"You may be right about pushing the buttons," I said.

"Maybe not. I've expected too much of you. I know you're not a college man."

"I was busy."

"That's been my mistake, treating you as a peer," Mansfield said. "I went to St. John's Law."

"Congratulations."

"I can't remember how many years of night school, which is the point: I don't want to remember. The wife hated me for it, my daughters were screaming to see me. Let us also consider an examination question on the right to bear arms. I had crammed the cases, useless information which I knew would not be asked, not by that kindly old professor. He fooled me."

"Do you mind? I'm trying to dope this out."

"Partway through the second hour, there was the question staring at me. I didn't know the answer, didn't know it, hadn't the vaguest idea, couldn't begin to bluff it. That would have been the end for me, a complete blank, all those years wasted. And suddenly two pages on the key case —"

"Appeared in your mind with absolute clarity."

"Yes."

"Suppose," I said, "the question had never been asked. Would your knowledge of the answer have existed?"

"It was asked," he said.

"That's easy."

"But it was fear that forced me to ask it of myself."

"It's further down the street," I said.

He started up the engine and cut out in front of a cursing taxi driver. We were first at the light. The block ahead was clear.

When the light changed, Mansfield shot ahead. The taxi moved up to pass us.

I seized the steering wheel and pulled it hard to the left. The impact bounced the taxi to the curb, dumping the passenger and his newspaper on the floor. I was out the door and racing toward the park before the chorus of horns began. When it did, I looked over my shoulder to see Mansfield cowering beneath the blows of the passenger's rolled-up newspaper, and struggling in vain to break through an angry cordon of taxi drivers.

The horns gradually faded as I ran crosstown through the park, keeping to the paths until I saw the shortcut through the field, then throwing the outfielders into confusion as a fly ball landed near me, terrifying the mothers standing in a row at the swings in the playground, running fast, not in fear but in haste to be there, to reach Amsterdam, to watch the crowd coming home to supper, to find among them the pusher, the man who had hooked Tina and perhaps also killed her.

Whites, blacks, one Chinese, a red turban, a pretty secretary on spindle legs, two girls in Levis, a Wall Street vest, grandmothers and delivery boys, all turned off the corner from Amsterdam, hurrying home to the joys of the night, dinner, Brillo, cigarettes, Johnny Carson, bathrooms, prayers. I was with the crowd, seeing through their eyes, but far from hidden in their midst, as I paced back and forth on the corner, too nervous to affect a ruse, sporting the ridiculous neck brace, my visibility complete. With so much time already borrowed, I no longer considered whether my luck would hold but only how long.

As they came around the corner, I was certain that each one would head for the pusher's brownstone. But none did. All went past or stopped short. Did no one live there? It was five stories tall. Did all its occupants work at night? Were they all on welfare? Watching the passersby, I began to discriminate in my guesswork: not this one, definitely not that one, perhaps this one. Not this one, I said of a chunky little man with a yarmulke, and, naturally, he went in. As did, eventually, a mother with three small children, a bus driver, and a Marine carrying a duffel bag.

I had nearly reached the dangerous decision to enter myself and ring every bell when the door opened from the inside. My man was not going in. He was coming out, descending the steps very slowly, deep in thought, the gray suitcase in his hand. As he reached the bottom step, he glanced toward Amsterdam, then stood still, looking down at the sidewalk. I stepped back, searching for cover. He started walking away from me, toward the park. My foot hit an empty garbage can and the lid fell to the ground. He stopped, looked back, then continued on his way with slow, heavy steps. I was startled by something against my ankle. I looked down. It was the little snow-white cat.

The night shift was beginning. I listened. There it was. Dot-dot. Dash. Dash. Dot-dot. The sound of the rhythmic jackhammer. Not a busy corner, no, not at three in the morning. But now it was bursting with life, the traffic light changing, by my count, one-thousand-one, one-thousand-two, one-thousand-three — thirty seconds for eastbound, forty-five seconds for north. At last. The pieces were beginning to fall into place.

Bergère handed me a thick envelope.

"To memorize and destroy."

"What about afterward?" I said.

"It's all in there." He waved a finger at the envelope. "You will cease all contact. Once in America, you will follow the instructions of Emil Zuckerman. You will be entirely in his hands."

"Goodbye, Bergère," I said.

"Goodbye, Jon."

I started out.

"You know," Bergère said, "I really envy you. They say that America is a most pleasant assignment."

I could not concentrate that night. I lay back on the cot and thought of the Commander, of the voyage, of America. It was an ugly job, and I was far from sure that the reward was not a punishment. What was America? Perhaps an innocent enemy, certainly something to be seen before its destruction. I wanted to know its energy, its vulgarity, its zest for foolishness. Would it seduce me?

Not likely. Its charms were fatal, but they could be savored and regurgitated. I would not grow to hate it, I was too old for hatred. Perhaps pity would come. A mercy killing.

The words were a blur. What more did I need to know? I would be there, in their hands, far from Bergère.

"Zuckerman . . . Great South Beach . . . East of Davis Park . . . The captain will know . . . Rubber raft . . . Coast Guard . . . Secluded, bark-shingled house perched on dune . . . Six feet three, massive shoulders, totally bald, chain-smoker, likely attire: corduroy trousers, bright-striped jersey . . . Bodyguard: dwarf with bicycle chain . . . 'Which way is it to Davis Park? We seem to have lost our bearings' . . . Ink . . . palm . . . compass . . . arrow east . . . He will have clothes, money . . . You are in his hands . . . Emergency instructions . . . If you do not . . ."

Emergencies! There will be no emergencies, Bergère. ". . . If you do not locate Zuckerman, you will report to the embassy immediately . . ." No, Bergère. I know what fate that could bring. If anything does go wrong, I will be free of you. I will report to myself. You will never find me.

Thus did I merely glance through the remainder. Emergencies. I had never bought life insurance, never drawn a will, who would benefit? There was good reason to believe in my indestructibility.

"Messages by local code except new emergency warning linked to name of local headquarters . . . Twelve trains — traitor suspected. First train — traitor identified. Second train — traitor to be liquidated. Memorize and destroy."

I lit a match to the page and watched it crumple and die before I drifted off, thinking of the dawn and the Commander.

Sugar Red was sweeping up when I walked into Fisher's Tavern at two minutes past three in the morning.

"Can you spare one last drink?" I said.

"My God, Jon, what happened?" Poor Sugar. First Joe Hull's death and now my neck in the brace.

"It's not that bad," I said. "I'm alive."

He poured out a vodka on the rocks with a slightly trembling hand. Things in the neighborhood were happening too fast for Sugar Red.

"Where you been?" he asked.

"Walking. Thinking. Join?" I lifted my glass. "It's on me."

"Thanks, no," he said. "I'm in a rush."

"Oh?"

"Didn't you know? I'm through here. Closing down for good."

"I didn't know that."

"It's too much for me." Sugar Red mopped his brow. "People getting killed. And, you know, the clientele's changing. It's going to get worse when Sammy's locks up next month."

"I heard Sammy died."

"That's not it. It's urban renewal. They're tearing down the whole block across the way. There'll be no doorways for the boys to sleep in over there. And no tourists from Sammy's. I like the bums. But I need the tourists, too. And now I'm getting the junkies in here. That's a sad thing and I don't like to be around it."

"The man I bought breakfast for the other day. Gonzalo. He said he knew you."

"That's it. Too many of them coming in."

Sammy's was still going full blast across the street. It was the oldtime music, the kind that used to keep me awake in the loft. Sugar Red finished sweeping and began stacking glasses under the bar.

I dropped a five-dollar bill and three singles on the bar.

"A man shouldn't close his business with unpaid bills," I said. "There's the eight dollars Joe Hull owed. My treat."

Sugar Red stared at the money. He did not touch it.

"I also wanted you to know my appreciation for those bookmarks you've been slipping into my pockets," I said. "Saint Judas and all that. I guess people never get around to thanking each other until it's too late."

He smiled sheepishly, a hand-in-the-cookie-jar smile.

"That's all right," he said. "Hope they did some good."

"Maybe they have." I put the turquoise bookmark on the bartop. "A lady friend kept it for me. She thought it was very perceptive. How did you ever guess that I was born in December?"

"After a few drinks you make a big thing of it."

"Funny. I don't believe I mention things about me like that, Sugar. Especially after a few drinks."

He returned with another vodka.

"I have a good memory for birthdays," he said.

"And you're a thoughtful friend. That's funny, too. I can't recall your ever wishing me a happy birthday."

Sugar Red leaned over the bar. He winked confidentially.

"At our age, friend," he said, "a discreet bartender knows when to leave well enough alone."

"You're right. I've always felt discretion to be your finest virtue, Steingut."

Sugar Red's huge face froze. I knew the shock would not last long. I lunged for his collar and twisted his head down on the bar. What could I have been thinking? That the force of my anger could pump enough adrenalin to hold a man of twice my strength? Just as I was regretting my rashness, his big hand reached my neck and I was forced to follow the power of his twist onto the bar. As I hit flat on my back, I felt something snap under the brace. But there was no pain, no fear of death. I had passed over that border hours before, when I saw Tina. There was only cold rage now, my arm still choking him, my other hand groping frantically under the bar, scattering lemons and glasses and swizzle sticks until my thumb touched the smooth handle of the paring knife.

"You wouldn't," Sugar Red said, feeling the tip hard against his back. "I know for a fact you wouldn't."

"That's where you're wrong, Sugar. You've always underestimated me." I was gasping for air. "She left me a message. It was the name Steingut. She left it in an envelope with this bookmark. You killed Tina but now she's killed you."

And it would have been easy, no consequences, not like the

Commander. I could slip in the knife without emotion, like cutting a dead animal on a plate. It would be noiseless, pitiless, fearless. Fear for me was no longer exhilarating. Sugar Red's death would be a passing incident of my ennui. He knew that. He was, after all, an intelligent man. His hand relaxed its grip on my brace. He gestured high in surrender.

It was I who was trembling then, more afraid of myself than of him, the ice melting on my anger as I tried to keep the point of the knife in tight without breaking the skin, for I knew I would not be able to stop myself once the blood began to flow. I would plunge the knife in to the handle, splashing blood on blood, avenging all the blood that Steingut had spilled; trembling, for I had not expected so quick a triumph, uneasy lest he sense that, too, and squirm away from me. But the knife held. He knew wisely that I would be satisfied with vengeance. What he could lead me to alive seemed at that moment far less important than seeing him die.

The music from Sammy's drifted over, the last set, louder and brassier, trumpets, saxophones, and the poor off-key vocalist still singing "Me and My Shadow."

"Into the back!" His body jerked forward as if he thought I had given that command to the knife. He staggered ahead in front of me, debating my determination but keeping both hands high. I kicked open the narrow door. The gray suitcase was sitting under the chair.

"Down! There!" He was bluffed, mistaking my hysteria for orders that carried the death penalty for disobedience. In those few seconds, unknown to him, I had moved swiftly from casual killer to demon and back to frightened warden, uncertain that I could kill.

Behind a mop was a laundry line. The knots did not satisfy me until he began to groan. I hooked his wrists under the chair to his ankles and slipped a noose around his neck that would tighten with the slightest movement of either foot. His shoulders relaxed as the knife point withdrew.

"Let's have a chat, Sugar, just like last night. This time you can have my chair."

Sugar Red shook his head back and forth very carefully, testing the noose.

"You are going to talk," I said. I pulled out his foot. The noose tightened. He shook his head again and bit down on his lip until a spot of blood appeared.

"I know you are going to talk, Sugar, for a simple reason. You are a coward."

"I don't like loudmouths," he whispered.

"That's your code, isn't it? That's why you killed Joe Hull. It wasn't an A-Trainer, it was you. Wasn't it, Sugar?"

He nodded slowly, enough to convey menace but not enough to confess.

"Now, just where did you get this suitcase?" I said.

"What suitcase?"

"Oh, come now, Sugar, that was my line. You know what suitcase I mean. This!"

I threw the suitcase hard at his chest. It hurt him but he did not make a sound.

"Sugar, why pretend? I saw you carry it out of that brownstone. I know enough to hang you. Save yourself, if you can. I know where you live. I know that Tina came to you when she needed it. I was with her last night when she went in there. And I was brought back to that same corner, wasn't I? Your boys did not succeed by blinding me. I listened. You drove me down here. It all happened right in this room, didn't it?"

He glared at me in silence, his eyes red with pain and loathing.

"Maybe what you need is that light," I said. "Where do you keep it?"

I walked out into the barroom and paced the seventeen steps to the outside door. As I pulled down the shade, I heard a stomping of feet from the back, then a painful grunt. He had used his chance. He could not move in that chair. I poured another vodka, surprised at myself for doing so but enjoying the feel of liquor calming the turmoil inside.

His eyes were closed when I returned. For an instant I thought he was dead. I did not want him dead. That moment of madness had passed. I wanted to know everything. It was sitting in that chair. I found the strobe lamp in a closet and turned it on him. I was relieved when his eyes blinked open.

"Let's hear you talk now," I said. "You'll feel much better. Where did you get this suitcase?"

"Brought to me."

"What?"

"It was brought to me."

"Who brought it?"

He was silent.

"Who brought it? Torre?"

"No."

"But Torre was here last night, wasn't he? He was the one who questioned me."

"No."

"He said his name was Torre."

"That wasn't Torre."

"Then who was it? You were here last night, weren't you?"

"Yes."

"But you said nothing last night. I did not hear your voice."

"Yes."

"You gave me the message about Fort Wash. Was that the airport or was it Tina's apartment?"

"Airport."

"You meant for me to bring this suitcase to La Guardia?"

"Yes."

"But I don't believe you, Sugar. I think you meant Tina's. That must have been quite a surprise for you. You didn't know the suitcase was already there. Not until you arrived there. But, in the end, she outsmarted you. You should have been more careful, cleaning out that car."

"I wasn't there."

"You're lying."

He shook his head and stared hard at me through the glare of the lamp.

"You'll get nowhere with this, Sugar. You can't fool me, you know that. You must have seen a file on me. You know everything about me, right down to my birthdate. Five years ago you came down here to keep an eye on me. Why?"

"They didn't trust you."

"Who is 'they'?" His eyes and mouth closed tightly. "They thought I was the weak link, was that it? Why won't you talk about them? The Federals have all this. They know what I was too trusting to know, that this network was captured. You went along with that. You liquidated Zuckerman and you weren't sure of me. There was too much money riding on the new operation to trust the old ideologues. But you needed me. It was useful to retain an efficient patsy. Would I ever guess that you were a pusher? Of course not. Not my old friend Sugar Red. Business was good, you expanded, you hooked anyone who might cause trouble. You even fathered her child, didn't you? It wasn't Zuckerman, it was you."

His eyes opened in surprise.

"No, I didn't."

"What a sweet fellow you are! Using the one talent I would not suspect because it's my own. I trusted you, Sugar Red. You were the only one I did not suspect. Handing me the letters you had mailed and received. The twelve trains to Babylon. That was your best."

"It wasn't mine."

"You gave it to me."

"It wasn't mine. I passed it on."

"Don't lie to me."

"That's the truth. I don't even know what it means."

"Do you think I believe you? Sweet Sugar, my true friend, with all his religious garbage and his bleeding heart for the bums and junkies. Giving me my orders, watching my every move, and what did you decide? Who is the traitor, Sugar? Who rates the twelve trains?"

"I don't know what you're talking about."

"Then I'll tell you. I am the traitor. You'll have the proof you need very shortly. A friend of mine will be picking you up right here. You are going to pay for Tina's murder."

"I didn't kill her, no."

"Who did?"

"Torre."

"Where is Torre?"

He closed his eyes again. I leaped in front of the light and kicked over the chair.

"Where is he?"

He was choking. I reached down and loosened the noose.

"Sugar, you have only one decision left. You can tell me about Torre and I will leave you here for my friend. Otherwise, I will have to strangle you."

I pressed his foot down under mine and watched the noose tighten again. His skin turned crimson.

"Who is Torre?"

"Man."

"What man?"

"Man." His eyes were bulging.

"Don't jive-talk me, Sugar."

"Man."

"Tell me, Sugar, or I'll kill you! Tell me!"

But, of course, before he said it, I knew. I pushed harder on his foot not to force him to say it but to stop him, stop the doors from opening into the fog, where I would be lost again, so close to discovery, only to have it all slip away. I knew that fear would return and Sugar Red, Steingut, would have won, but I could not stop him. "Mansfield," he said. Me and my shadow.

11.

I was in his office at nine o'clock that morning. He came in smiling ten minutes later, calm as a corpse, accepting my presence without surprise.

"I have a lead, Mansfield," I said.

"So why not tell me about it? Saturdays are always my best days."

He ushered me to another chair inside near his desk. An agent followed us with the morning mail. Mansfield began opening it with elaborate casualness, handing most of the letters back to the agent. I took a deep breath.

"I know who Torre is," I said.

In the midst of slitting an envelope, the letter opener stopped. Mansfield studied me, playing with the opener, rapping his knuckles, hitting his palm.

"That'll be all, Russ," he said.

"No," I said. "I'd like to make a sworn statement."

"I'll be the judge of that," Mansfield said. "If I need it, I'll ask for it."

The agent hesitated at the door. Mansfield waved him out.

"That was a damn stupid thing," he said when the door closed.

"Don't you all work together?"

"I'm talking about your running off yesterday."

"You weren't interested in finding Torre at the airport," I said. "And you don't want to listen now."

"We searched every inch of that airport. I'm listening. What have you got?"

"Torre was there in Penn Station a week ago yesterday, the morning you shadowed me."

"Obviously."

"I didn't get a good look at him then, but I saw him that night. He came up to my loft and threatened me with a revolver. Then I saw him across the street in front of Sammy's. He followed me to Columbus Circle. I got away in a car, back to the loft, but he drove up as I was leaving."

Mansfield loosened his tie. He smiled and worked the customary twinkle into his eyes.

"I had to knock him out," I said, "but he found me the next day in Brooklyn and asked me to make a deal. On Wednesday he went over to McSorley's, trying to find out where I was from a blind man I have lunch with. Thursday I had him at the airport, but he ran off. Strangely enough, he reappeared later and offered to drive me back to the city. He had arranged a surprise for me."

"You're getting your days mixed up. I drove you back."

"I didn't see him again until yesterday afternoon. He came to visit me at the hospital."

"For God's sake, why didn't you tell me that?" He threw down the letter opener and reached for the telephone. "We'll pick him up right away. Where is he?"

"No. I want to bring him in myself. That's the least I can do for you."

Mansfield replaced the receiver in the cradle and swung his chair toward the window, presenting me with the back of his head.

"You sure you can handle it?" he said quietly.

"I already have."

He jumped to his feet and paced around the room, avoiding my eyes.

"Believe me," I said. "Torre is here."

He returned to his desk and sat staring past me with glazed eyes. Very slowly, he brought out a quarter from his pocket and threw it on the desk. I was surprised to find myself feeling a little sorry for him.

My sympathy faded when he flashed his grin again. The coin rolled off the desk.

"You're guessing," Mansfield said.

"No. Sugar Red told me."

I did not wait to watch his reaction. I walked to the outer room and returned to the doorway with the gray suitcase.

"Steingut told me," I said.

Mansfield's face flushed with anger. He pulled the revolver from its holster and laid it on the desk.

"Close the door," he said.

"No thank you. You remember the bargain. I give you Steingut and Torre. You give me my life."

"Where is Steingut now?"

"Safe."

"Where?"

"What about our bargain?" I asked.

"It's still on."

"Tied up in the back at Fisher's," I said without thinking, still clinging to my trust in him.

Mansfield moved swiftly to the door, pushed it shut and locked it. He ran back to the desk and pressed an intercom switch.

"I want someone brought in, Russ. Big man, name of Fisher. He's trussed up in the back room of Fisher's Tavern, on the Bowery near Houston. Knock down the door if you have to. And bring him to me personally."

"Will do."

"Poor Sugar Red," I said. "I assume that's the end of his mortal life."

Mansfield sat down hard in his chair and turned again to the window. I stared at the back of his head. Why did I feel so triumphant? A gentleman's agreement, not even a handshake. I was in his custody. He could kill me now. Attempted escape. It would all be very neat.

"You're right about that," he said. "Sugar Red doesn't have very long. I know him. He'll leave me with no alternative. I won't be able to make him talk. Just lies, like he gave you. He tried well, and so did you. That's why I'm almost sorry to disappoint you."

He swung his chair around to face me.

"I'm not Torre," he said.

He had to be lying. I would not let him destroy the truth like this. It was not just Steingut's truth, it was mine. I had fitted the pieces together even as Sugar Red spoke the name. I had found Steingut and now I had Torre.

"If he hadn't given you a name for Torre, would you have killed him?" Mansfield said.

"Yes. At that moment, yes."

"Obviously, then, he had to give you a name."

"He gave me your name, Mansfield. You are Torre, I will bet my life on that."

It was, of course, quite the opposite. My life now depended on his innocence. For a moment I thought to pull back, to save myself, to convince him that I believed him, that Sugar Red had deceived me.

"What did you ask him?" Mansfield said.

"I asked him who Torre was."

"And he really gave you my name?"

"That's right."

"Tell me his exact words."

" 'Mansfield.' That was enough."

"He said nothing more?"

" 'Man,' he said at first. Three times he said that. But he was choking. He was trying to finish it."

"As I thought." He reached into a bottom drawer and withdrew a sheet of hotel stationery. It was filled with incredibly small, neat handwriting. "Smith's latest report," Mansfield said. "He's better than you thought, isn't he? They didn't kill him."

"When did that come in?"

"Yesterday. He's worked his way up to the man who runs it in Puerto Rico. Read it."

"You are forever handing me these damned things, Mansfield."

"And you are never reading them."

"Of course not. There's no trusting you or your documents."

"Afraid you might believe it?"

I shoved the paper back across the desk. It sailed onto his lap.

"Manley," he said. "A faceless millionaire named Alexander

Manley. He's also the silent partner in this hotel and two others in San Juan. But he lives on the south coast. Smith drove down to look for him. He found only one man who would talk, the village drunk, who by good fortune happens to be a cousin of Manley's chauffeur."

"The village idiot, I believe it. That sounds like your sources. How much did you pay for that fiction, Mansfield?"

"Last week his cousin drove Manley to the San Juan airport. For a New York flight. They left in a hurry. The car was sent back and there has been no word from Manley. The chauffeur has nothing better to do than drink with his cousins."

"So?"

"I propose that Manley is Torre."

"Impossible. I've been working with Torre for nine years."

"But not the same Torre."

"Mansfield, when I write my memoirs, I shall not fail to mention that of all the liars I met, you were the most ridiculous."

"You won't live to write them, Jon, unless you believe me. Smith will be arranging for arrests down there today."

"I don't believe a man named Torre is Manley any more than a man named Smith is Smith."

"Are you blind? Don't you see what went through Sugar Red's mind? Man, he thought. Give him the name of a man and I'll live. Any man. He was facing death and it almost brought out the truth: Manley. But in the seconds he had, he decided on the name that would throw you off, blast your faith in me, rip apart our alliance."

I renewed my grip on the suitcase handle, fearful that Mansfield would now take everything away from me.

"Do you actually think there is three million dollars' worth in that thing?" he said.

"I wouldn't know."

A buzzer sounded. He pressed the intercom.

"Don't bother me."

"It's urgent," a familiar voice replied.

"Not now." He snapped it off, irritated. "I'm glad I didn't

221

let you have it, Jon, the way you guarded it. We took out all the envelopes at the airport. All you were carrying was socks and underwear."

I kicked over the suitcase, unable to control my humiliation.

"Damn it, you are Torre!" I burst out, trying to bolster courage before doubt overwhelmed me completely.

"Part right," he said. "Steingut always dealt in parts, didn't he?"

Instantly I felt the chill of fear. I was right! It was exactly as I had thought. Yet now, with the truth so near, I did not want it. I wanted desperately to be wrong.

I watched Mansfield's hands near the revolver on the desk. It was time to test survival.

"That's the only part I need, Torre," I said. "I'll be going now."

I walked slowly toward the door, taking the final risk.

At the door I turned around. Mansfield's hands had not moved.

"I was Torre," he said.

"Yes, I know. Goodbye."

"For more than twenty years I was Torre. And for the past nine of them, you and I were a fair team. I could always count on you, Jon. You never missed."

"Yes, well, we just have some grand old memories, don't we?" I gave him a synthetic Lee Mansfield smile. "I'm leaving."

"Where to?" he said.

"Sugar Red used to ask me that question."

"You going to turn us in?"

"Maybe."

"Why not wait until you find the real Torre?"

"I have him now."

"No," he said. "I was Torre. I am no longer."

"That's convenient."

"I was Torre until last week."

"Make your fabrication fast. I haven't much time."

"How do I know you'll listen? You wouldn't hear my words coming in from the airport. I understood that. I knew what you were suffering. I went through it myself when it finally dawned on me that they'd taken this over. That sermon in the car, it wasn't for you, it was for me. I was talking to myself."

"Do you expect me to believe that? For all those twenty years, you were a government informer."

"No," he said. "Once again you've only proved to me my mistake. It took a great deal of figuring to discover that this network had been captured. But I made one error in arithmetic. I thought you'd help me. Stupid of me to hope. I should have known that you were too wrapped up in your own delusions. You didn't care about any cause except your own. And you knew I did care, that wasn't hard to sense. It's why you trusted and hated me at the same time, I saw that. If you'd thought beyond your own skin, you would have recognized that our cause was the same."

An informer's trick. Yet he was not smiling. I walked back.

"They were worried about us," he said. "After they killed Zuckerman and took over, we were the only ones who concerned them. But they needed you because you came from Bergère. They couldn't dispose of you. If Bergère ever became suspicious of Zuckerman's death and investigated, they were afraid he'd find a way to contact you. They wanted you alive, to report that all was well in the network, and if Bergère wasn't getting what he wanted, the trouble had to be further down the line."

"What about you?"

"My position. They couldn't afford to lose it. To keep the stuff flowing. Only, the stuff would be different. They fooled us both. It was only this month, four years after Zuckerman's death, that I began to link a number of peculiarities in this operation. Small things that had been bothering me, nothing conclusive. The places I went to drop the messages and parcels, they were always different, never twice to the same spot. I was given no chance to encounter the next man. And I was sure that more was coming in than going out. But I have you to thank for the first real evidence, Jon. You see, I wasn't certain what was in that suitcase until I saw it."

"You're a good actor."

"And you're not the first member of the audience. I also didn't know that Sugar Red was Steingut until you told me."

"I think you're acting right now," I said, acting, for I was beginning to believe him.

"Oh, I suspected he was in with the new crowd," Mansfield said, "but I actually didn't know. Last week I received a very strange message from Steingut. As of Friday I was relieved of my duties as Torre. I was to report to a bartender on the Bowery, a man named Sugar Red Fisher."

He was staring out the window, no longer talking to me. "That was a blow," he said, almost in a whisper. "What the hell did they have in mind for a man of my position, making martinis?"

His voice trailed off. I did not speak.

"They knew I was reliable," he said at last, addressing our tormentors. "I had a damn good war record, for us and for them. A Depression idealist in the OSS. Afterward I stayed with the government and I stayed with them. What more could they ask?"

I shrugged. He did not see me.

"No, I did not take that lightly. I decided to do some checking out. I waited until it was time for you to deliver a message at Penn Station. I spotted you at the Babylon rack, working on that schedule."

"You couldn't have been more obvious."

"All right," he said, "you're not bad, we know that. I'll admit it was a pleasure to see at last the man I'd been working with for nine years. You were fine. No one was paying a bit of attention to you, except me. And, I hoped, the new Torre. After you left, I waited more than an hour for him. No luck. Around noon, I stepped into the men's room for two minutes at the most. When I came out, I saw a man in a green hat pull a schedule from the Babylon rack and rush through a train gate. I ran after him. He was walking fast along the platform. I don't know if he saw me or not. The train was leaving. He may have been just another passenger hurrying to catch it. Probably was. I didn't bother chasing him onto the train. I had a feeling he was Torre, but what are feelings?"

He turned to look at me, as if I would have the answer.

"No, Jon," he said, "I am Torre no longer."

Yes, I believed him. Sugar Red was the key after all. I should have tortured him to the threshold of death. But I was so foolishly captivated by his revelation of Mansfield. Steingut, the master of deception. Now I would sit there, listening to Mansfield's confession, and it would take me nowhere. Tina was dead. Joe Hull was dead. Sugar Red would soon be dead, shot to silence in this office. And Mansfield and I were sitting there wondering if we were alive.

"So I went to see Sugar Red," he was saying, but it made little difference. "It was he, not the government, who gave me what information I have on you. He told me there was a key man upstairs he'd been watching. He had not been able to find out how much you knew about the network. He felt you were dangerous but he was not sure, just a feeling. He had reached the conclusion that it must be done directly. Direct questions by a law officer, scare you around a bit. Now, that was neat. Two pigeons with one stone. In that assignment they were testing both of us. After I talked with you in your loft, my hunch was that you didn't know what had happened to the network. But I guessed that as soon as you realized it, you would help me."

He was still looking at me, with more sadness than anger. "I don't owe you help," I said. "You've done far worse than scare me."

"I had to play it straight with them," he said. "Of course I did my job. Each day I reported to Sugar Red. I told him you'd moved to Jenny O'Leary's and then I told him you'd left her. I told him you had lunch with a man named Thaddeus. That, he knew. But I did not tell him you had taken up again with Katrina Athenasios. It was my own idea to have her arrested and bring you together. You'd find out what she knew and I'd get it all from you."

"She didn't know anything," I said.

Mansfield's fist slammed down on the desk. I was puzzled by his fury.

"That's the hell of it," he said. "I think she did. I'm convinced she was killed because they thought she was tipping us on this operation."

"You did it with that suitcase."

"I am sorry." He shifted his eyes to the carpet.

"You killed her."

"No," he said. "But I'll get him."

"You know who killed her."

Mansfield shook his head. "You're missing it, Jon, completely. There are links in this chain that are not hooked together. No one can afford to trust. Who's given in to the syndicate? Zuckerman obviously refused. They're wondering about the rest of us. You receive messages from Steingut. Torre receives them from you and from Steingut. But who sends them to Steingut? You don't know. I don't know." He picked the revolver off the desk and returned it to his holster. His smile, at last, returned. "You and I are just a couple of honest traitors who have been done in by thieves."

He pressed the intercom switch. "Did Russ go out on that job?"

"Right." It was the familiar voice again. "About this cable, Mr. Mansfield, it's very important."

"Oh, sure, everything's always important."

"I wouldn't have bothered you but — "

"Come in, then," Mansfield said.

There was a light rap on the door. Trusting, my friend from the airport, entered. He did not look so friendly now.

"It arrived a few minutes ago," he said. "Very sorry."

Mansfield glanced at the cable and threw it down. He rubbed his forehead with his fist.

"Check out the clothes in that suitcase. They're Turkish."

"Yessir."

"As for this matter," he said wearily, "I'll need the wife's first name, address, that sort of thing."

"Of course."

On his way out with the suitcase, trusting turned toward me with a look of contempt I shall never forget. It was the look I gave Joe Hull, the look reserved for a pigeon.

As the door latch clicked, Mansfield slumped down in his chair.

226

"Walk it off, Jon," he said. "I don't want you here when Sugar Red arrives. Take a walk and forget. There's nothing more you can do."

He tore up the cable and dropped the pieces in the wastebasket. "Should that concern me?" I said.

"Not unless you find grisly satisfaction in being right. You called it. Smitty was shot to death early this morning."

"Who?"

"Smith. His name really was Smith."

I stopped at a store to buy a sweater, then strolled up Amsterdam thinking about Lee Mansfield, American. Wasn't that the race I was sent here to destroy? What were they, these people, these peculiar revolutionaries who had deliberately mixed their blood with every frightened, hungry strain that would succumb to their bloodthirst. Did they actually believe the words of the slavers and bankers who wrote their documents?

They had energy, yes, enough to slaughter Indians, buffalo, a continent of ancient trees, enough to span and trap the mightiest rivers, to build violent cities on quiet islands and marshes and potato fields. They had guilt, about everything, which I had taken to mean there was some kind of vague humanity locked within them. Perhaps that heritage of conscience was the contribution of my countrymen. It was they who first corrupted the lovely forest isle of Manhattes, who decapitated the peaceful Wappingers and played ball with their heads. My father used to tell me that the beauty of Bali remained only because we Dutch arrived so late.

Americans. I had granted their shrewdness, their ingenuity, their generosity for all the wrong things. Was I now to believe they also had the courage of a Lee Mansfield? For years he had lived a fearful role to help destroy the system. Yet now he was even more enraged than I that the worst rot of the system had been using him. In the end, he was as much a chauvinist as the Commander. He could not separate his humanity from his nationality, a victim of his culture. My father would have understood.

"Walk it off. Take a walk and forget. There's nothing more you can do." And so I was walking. He had the key of Sugar Red. I had kept for myself the key of Amsterdam. Ultimately, he might find Torre. It was always, with Mansfield, a matter of devotion. He, therefore, refused to fail. Just as the cause had consumed him, so would his betrayal. They had made a fool of him, forced him to join his other enemy.

But I could not leave the game to him. With Tina's death, and now Smith's, his case had fallen apart. To protect himself, he would have to dispose of Sugar Red, throw away his last key. It could be years before he avenged the destruction of his own life. I had my own reasons to find out what had killed Tina. I was determined to find Torre first.

Yes, there were two networks in one, working together and despising each other, and perhaps a third, the men caught in between, some unsuspecting, as I had been, others confused and fearful. The men who questioned me in the backroom at Fisher's, which were they? Not Mansfield's men. Sugar Red was there, if I could believe him. Was one of them really Torre?

If I respected Mansfield's wishes, the war would go on without me. He would make it his own, working to salvage his career, killing those who knew his complicity, perhaps someday finding it necessary to kill me. I could not begrudge his motives for that. He was the only man I had met here who still believed. "You and I are alike," he said on our ride from the airport. "That's why I found you. No one else could have cracked this case." In that lie was truth.

I paused at the corner to watch the morning sun play on a brave patch of grass. The pressure was off. A turtleneck sweater hid the absurdity of my brace, my sins were forgiven by a government man, the menace of Sugar Red was dying at that moment. I recognized in slow reflection on sun and grass that there had been no betrayal. Time and again I had looked into Sugar Red's eyes and I chose not to suspect. There can never be betrayal, true surprise, or such a thing as coincidence.

As I turned the corner off Amsterdam, I was like the sleeping crowd, passing objects and faces already known. "Eyes will see,"

Thaddeus had said, "only what they are willed to see." And I had laughed at a blind man's longing. Now I willed to see everything, and so I could not miss, could not feel surprise to see my hand touch the fender of the car at the curb, its green stored in my memory, the Volkswagen that had been parked behind me on the highway when I opened the trunk to find Tina.

A few minutes later he came walking out of the brownstone, just as Sugar Red the night before, unaware of my presence. When he reached the sidewalk and turned toward the car, he saw me. I glimpsed only the beginning of fright on his face. Immediately, he ran off toward the park, then darted into the street and flagged down a taxi. I jimmied the door to the Volkswagen. By the time I had the engine turning, the taxi had disappeared around the corner.

It came into sight two lights ahead going south. A block later it turned west. I followed to Riverside Drive and circled, far behind, down to the marina. I jumped out of the car and ran out on the dock. A dinghy was halfway out to the blue cruiser.

"Crackjaw!" I yelled. He was rowing furiously.

The cruiser roared off and I walked back slowly to the car. Well, then, if all this were true, that I could know everything, what did I know? He was on his way to Fire Island, no doubt. He had kept Zuckerman's cottage after — after he had killed him? Yes, it must have been Crackjaw who gave in to the syndicate. Crackjaw, the trustworthy friend. He was still a commuter, dropping off and picking up hot cargo at the house off Amsterdam, and doing business with Flake as a cover. Or was Flake still buying? Could anyone but Zuckerman have been insane enough to consider Crackjaw the final arbiter of pornography? But he had yet another cover. I could not remember. "Press the buttons," Mansfield had said. So many useless memories would be dredged up sooner or later, why not the fact of Crackjaw's occupation? They were joking about it at the table, while I sat drinking the black rum, Zuckerman had made some joke about Crackjaw's true vocation. What was it? Damn me. It was as if I were planning all this, what to remember and when to remember, as if I were the master of my fate.

I drove onto the West Side Highway and nudged the car along the railing, watching the cruiser pass the midtown piers. Somewhere in the Twenties I stopped, allowing him to catch up. Behind me another car came to a halt. I watched carefully in the mirror. It was a bright red Falcon. That one was not stored. I had never seen it before.

When I moved on and stopped again, the shadow imitated me. It was not a professional. He was completely conspicuous. Yet he was not interested in overtaking me. Had Mansfield sent me his best, incompetent protection? Not likely. I was no longer his charge. Or did he think I could lead him somewhere? I made a halfhearted effort to shake him, forgetting for the moment about Crackjaw, speeding down the highway, through the Battery Tunnel and past the Brooklyn piers, glancing up at the promenade railing as if expecting once again to see Jenny smiling in the wind. Curving around the Brooklyn shoreline, I gradually slowed the car and finally pulled off on the grass near the Verrazano Bridge. The shadow was still with me. He stopped a safe distance behind.

I saw the holster then. It was stapled beneath the death seat, the butt of the revolver within easy reach of the right hand. I touched it and quickly withdrew my hand. There was no need to break precedent. He was clearly too unskilled to pose that much danger. I opened the door, stepped out unarmed, and walked back toward the shadow. As I approached, the driver ducked down in the seat and the car sped past me and on out of sight.

Returning to Crackjaw's car, I sat back and waited. It had been foolish of me to be diverted. He could have gone anywhere. Hoboken, Jersey City, Staten Island. I had probably lost him forever.

It must have been more than an hour later when a blue cruiser hove into view, closer to shore now, the bow smacking the whitecaps, the odd figure of Crackjaw bent over the wheel, his long hair flying in the wind. As soon as he had passed under the bridge, I started up and crept along the parkway, my eyes on the sea, until I lost him again as he rounded the point of Sea Gate.

The headwinds were strong. At this rate, he would not reach

Fire Island before sunset. Would he have to refuel? I turned in toward the marine gas pumps at Coney Island. The Saturday crowd was out. It took too long to park. When I reached the boardwalk, I saw the cruiser moored off the pier.

"Hit a hundred! Hit a hundred! Free ticket to the Fun House!" Barker! Barker!

The music was deafening. Bells, chimes, calliopes blared a confusion of waltzes and nursery rhymes.

"Hit a hundred!"

He was standing before a huge eye which formed the entrance to the Fun House, standing there cocksure that he had lost me, as sure as I had been when I sat waiting by the bridge.

I moved closer and watched a customer swing down the mallet. The pointer rose to fifty. The escort smiled nervously at his girl.

" 'At's all right, not bad at all," Crackjaw reassured him. "Try again. Just two bits for a second try."

The couple walked off quickly and three sailors took turns. I stood at the end of the line. The biggest of the sailors rang the bell. He accepted a Kewpie doll rather than brave the Fun House. His companions reached seventy.

"Hurry, hurry, hurry! Fun House closes in ten minutes!"

There remained two high school boys and a large Irish family, and then Crackjaw and I were standing face to face. His patter did not falter for an instant.

"Now, this gennelman here can do better than that, I can tell it from his eyes. He's the kind that always wins. Tell it just by looking at him. Watch it, watch it, here he goes, here he goes!" The best I could do was ninety. I turned to hand the mallet back to Crackjaw. He was gone.

I started to my right, turned back to my left. Then I saw him straight ahead, scrambling through the eye of the Cyclops into the Fun House. I followed, still clutching the mallet.

The hallway was narrow and pitch-black. The floor tilted at crazy angles. I heard a mechanical scream. A lighted jack-in-the-box, looking for all the world like Crackjaw, popped up in my path. As it vanished, the floorboards began sliding back and forth. I leaped over them, triggering a spray of steam designed for the ladies, and colliding with a luminous skeleton dangling from the ceiling. Colored mirrors streaked with kaleidoscopic light now stretched ahead of me. The hall seemed to run to infinity. I crouched against the wall and waited. There were footsteps down the hall. I strained to see but nothing appeared.

"Crackjaw!" My cry was taken up by echoes, resounding through what seemed to be other hallways and rooms. "All I want is to talk with you!"

There was silence. Then I heard the footsteps again.

They stopped suddenly.

"All right." It was Crackjaw's voice. "Talk about what?" He was trying to pinpoint me in the dark. I moved back and stood against the opposite wall.

"I'll be happy to talk," Crackjaw said. "Come out where I can see you." His voice was closer.

"Let's talk from here," I said, moving away. My foot hit a floorboard pedal. Another skeleton came whirling down from the ceiling. I dropped to my knees. There was a girl's scream far behind me. An innocent had been caught by the steam vent. The hissing subsided.

"We have company," Crackjaw said. It was impossible to identify the direction of his voice.

There was a flurry of footfalls. I crept forward along the wall, touching the boards gently. The feet seemed to be coming from behind me, running fast. I felt something brush by. Then I saw the shadow. I jumped. A high-pitched scream stabbed my ears.

"You and your damned curiosity!"

"I had to come," Jenny said.

"Get out!"

"Listen, I stole a car, do you realize that?"

"Now you're a hardened criminal."

"I mean, like, I borrowed it."

"Jenny, this isn't for you."

"Jesus! Is that my reward for finding you? I know you're in some kind of trouble, Jon, and I just love you so much I want to scream."

"For God's sake, don't!" I clamped my hand over her mouth. "I want you out of this, Jenny. Go find yourself a nice boy like what's-his-name. Ouch." I wrenched my hand from her teeth.

"Douglas," she said. "And stop talking nonsense."

"Go find him. Maybe you'll make that big moment next New Year's Eve."

Of all things, she clung to me and started to cry. I backed along the hallway toward the entrance, dragging her with me.

"Didn't you mean anything you said to me, Jon?"

"It's too late."

"It's not too late!"

"Get away from me, Jenny, or you'll end like Tina."

"Who's Tina? I keep asking you, who is she?"

"I can answer that." It was Crackjaw's voice, louder than before, but further away, as if it were amplified from a distant chamber.

"Who's that?" Jenny whispered, frightened for the first time.

"Your boyfriend is talking about my work," Crackjaw said. "But I missed on him. I wish they hadn't stopped me."

Jenny was trembling. I moved her further back, away from the voice.

"Don't move!" Crackjaw said. "I can see you. The crosshairs meet between the girl's eyes. It's a beautiful picture."

"You can stop the act," I said, none too confidently. "You left your cannon in the car."

"Believe me, I have another."

I pushed Jenny down and ran up ahead toward Crackjaw's voice. But she was incorrigible. I heard her footsteps behind me again.

"Go away, Jenny. For always." I knocked her against the wall. "Listen to me. You were just a piece. A wonderful piece, but that's all."

I don't remember which came first, the sound of her scream or the sharp pain as her hand struck my face with amazing force. I listened to her running back, tripping the skeleton, the steam vent, the jack-in-the-box, and then out through the eye of the Cyclops. But wasn't that the first principle of the movement? You must hurt them to save them.

"I'm coming to get you, Crackjaw." My voice was choked. It had all been to his advantage. I moved ahead recklessly, swinging the mallet at every shadow.

Machinery was whining. I heard the screech of clashing metal, then a slow, rhythmic thumping. The sounds grew louder as I moved. I saw a circle of light. It was at the far end of a long, revolving barrel. I stepped forward, taking care to walk against the roll. A figure crossed into the light. Crackjaw was standing on the floor beyond the barrel. I was correct. He had no weapon.

"Hit a hundred!" he said.

"What were you doing in that house?"

"Looking for a friend. He wasn't there. But why are you interested in me?" His voice passed through the barrel into the hallway and rebounded.

"For Tina," I said.

I kept losing my footing as the barrel alternately speeded and slowed, throwing me off each time I thought I had conquered the momentum.

"It's not me you want," Crackjaw said calmly. "Torre gave the order."

With each step, I seemed to be moving backward, away from Crackjaw. I dropped the mallet and tried to crawl forward. It caught between the slats of the barrel and rolled around over my head, falling back into my hands.

Then I saw that Crackjaw's hand was on a lever. He was controlling the barrel, tilting it, adjusting the speed, laughing at his prowess and my helplessness, which, I suppose, was justified. I must have looked an awful fool.

"Tell me where to find Torre," I said.

"But he was acting on orders, too," Crackjaw said.

"Then you will tell me everything, Crackjaw, before I'm through with you."

The barrel tilted sharply, knocking me onto my back, and then it ceased rolling. The circle of light blinked out.

"Why did you kill Tina?" I said.

"Because," he said, "Torre gave me the message about twelve trains to Babylon."

I was inching through the barrel on elbows and knees, my eyes fixed on the spot in the blackness where I knew Crackjaw was standing.

"Who is the man who gives the orders?" I said.

He did not reply. My elbow passed over the lip of the barrel. I lunged for him, bumping against the lever. The barrel began rolling again.

I heard footsteps in the distance.

"Crackjaw!" I pulled on the lever and the barrel stopped.

Screams broke the silence, far-off down the hallway. New customers were searching for fear.

"Crackjaw?"

I plunged ahead through the darkness.

"Crackjaw! Who was responsible? Tell me his name!"

Suddenly, the floor gave way beneath me. I landed in the center of the brightly lit room. It was a pentagon, with mirrors facing me from all five sides. Everywhere I turned, I saw that face devoid of expression, the blond hair of an American, a Swede, a Briton, a German, the pallid skin, the brown eyes. I stared in horror at that creature, through the eyes of the crowd, into the mirrors and from the mirrors. But the eyes changed as I watched them. I saw the eyes of Sugar Red glaring at me, filled with pain and loathing. I saw the hands moving high in the air, clutching the mallet, bringing it down, smashing each mirror in turn, aiming at the hair, the eyes, the mouth, until no one was left in the room but a pale reflection lying exhausted on a floor of broken glass.

"Two people cared about me. I killed one and I've just about killed the other."

"Women?"

"Yes."

"Good work," Thaddeus said.

He was tearing at his beef, angry at me for delaying his Sunday dinner.

"Five o'clock," he said in disgust. "You promised you wouldn't be late yesterday and you never showed at all. Well, no matter. This is the last supper."

"What do you mean?"

"I'm leaving tomorrow."

I felt as if my legs had been kicked out from under me, helpless in the rolling barrel. How could Thaddeus mean that much to me? I feared that this could mean only one thing: his work was done with me, his work for the network. Thaddeus, my trustworthy friend, as Zuckerman had trusted Crackjaw.

"I told you I would have the answer to that question," he said. "Which is it worse to be, a blind black man or a black blind man? Answer: a black blind man. So I return to Ghana and resume my old occupation of blind black man."

"You never told me where you came from."

"Did you tell me?"

"Then your name is not Thaddeus."

"No." He reached past his empty mug and commandeered my ale, not a mistake, an old trick of his, a chief advantage of his handicap.

"But I like that name, don't you?" he said. "Actually, it's Kwame. Which means nothing. Only that I was born on Saturday. And you. On what day were you born, if at all?"

"I don't know."

"Your memory again. It's very bad."

He put his hand on my arm. I tensed. Sugar Red had made that same gesture in Saint Patrick's.

"The shadow came back again," Thaddeus said. "Over in the corner. The shadow of a dead man."

I glanced at the corner. It was empty.

"Who?" I said.

"Who knows? You perhaps. Or me. It's all the same."

236

I ordered more ale, this time more for me than for him. He was beginning to frighten me.

"Apparently, you think it's you," Thaddeus said.

"Why do you say that?"

"Because suddenly you don't trust me. I felt it when I touched your arm. You're angry with me for leaving you in the lurch. Or something has happened. Why were you late?"

"I overslept."

"Where?"

"You won't believe it."

"Probably not.

"In a room with broken mirrors at Coney Island. I hadn't slept in days. It was very strange waking. Some children were shaking me. I thought it was a dream. It was hours before we found our way out. And the taxi ride back. Someone had stolen the car I had stolen."

"Is there no decency left?"

"You're not fooling me, Thaddeus. You know all this."

He sat in silence, gulping his ale. It was only a gamble. But if Sugar Red, if Mansfield, if perhaps even Tina, why not Thaddeus?

"You disappoint me," Thaddeus said. "Not much, but a little. I suppose you've never really trusted me. But I've enjoyed your pretending, for that is a friend."

"Who are you, Thaddeus?"

"What I seem. Your friend. An old sailor who drifted over here and now must drift back. A blind man who sits alone all day in the sawdust, spouting nonsense to himself and to anyone foolish enough to listen, which is only one man. But I've been no help to you, not in the end."

"Maybe you have."

"Is it so hard to believe I am only a friend? Whatever has happened to you, is it so hard to believe I have nothing to do with it?"

"Yes, I've wondered. I'm sorry."

"So am I. We've sat together in consolation, deceiving ourselves

237

that we were slowly approaching the truth, neither of us knowing who the other was. You have lied to me about your past, as I may have lied occasionally to you. And this is the way we part, with you wondering if I am your enemy. To hell with you, then. I have more important things on my mind. I need two hundred dollars for passage."

I pressed the money into his hand.

"Neither of us can see the future," Thaddeus said, with a gruff nod of gratitude. "But I can feel it. That's why you kept coming here, to sense my feeling. You asked me riddles and I replied in riddles. What is the train to Babylon? How should I know? Why must it mean more than it says? Why don't you just take the train to Babylon and find out?"

"Goodbye, Thaddeus."

As I started out, I heard the mug crash to the floor. Thaddeus covered his face in embarrassment. It was not like him. For all his vulgarity, he was a careful man, sure with the sight of fingers. A waiter rushed over and replaced the mug.

"Are you all right?" I asked.

"Get out of here," Thaddeus said.

"Don't say that. Not this time."

Thaddeus stuffed the money inside his coat.

"This time I mean it," he said.

On Fridays it was always Penn Station. And when I missed Friday, Torre expected me Sunday. That was the safeguard.

The crowd was coming in from Long Island. They rushed past me, sunburned and laughing, swinging knapsacks, beach bags, tennis rackets, flowers, fresh vegetables, a scene so healthy and joyous that I did not believe it. Was this what Jenny wanted? Surely, they were acting this scene because it was expected of them. Someone was watching them. It was for the benefit of me, the man standing by the glass information booth.

No, Jenny, try as I would, I could never be them. I would only be watching that man, wherever he stood, feeling for him, wondering at his thoughts, seeing myself in the crowd through his eyes.

That judgment was passed on me too long ago, to be alone, sun-burned only when the work required, laughing only in the bitterness of work, every minute working, never knowing what it was like truly to be at ease.

"Where is the 6:59 to Babylon?"

"Track Eighteen."

I saw it posted. It was my airport routine, placing trust to engender trust, asking what is already known. But now it was more. I wanted to speak to them, to take every risk. I had no need to hide. It was a relief, a joy, to ask that simple question, not fearing what my eyes might reveal. I looked at him and smiled.

"Thank you!" I said, and he stared after me as if I were the oddest duck he had encountered in thirty years of service with the Long Island Railroad.

"Beautiful weather today," I added, ambling toward the gate. Yes, I was talking to them, the most perilous game of all, talking of the weather, and what was the lesson? That could lead to talk of the day's events, personal feelings, life itself. The longer the conversation, the more difficult it is to extricate oneself without leaving an impression. But now I would cultivate impression, arouse him to tell his wife at the dinner table about that strange fellow who thanked him for doing his job. Damnedest thing happened at work today, Daisy.

"Where is that train going?"

The conductor at the gate pointed wearily at the sign.

"Babylon," he said.

"Thank you!"

Why not ask a few others? The man at the ticket counter, perhaps. No, I would buy the ticket on the train. I would go through the whole noticeable, dangerous transaction with the conductor, fumbling for change, delaying him, irritating him, making a worthless contact on a train ride without purpose.

I took a seat near the door, force of habit. The car was filling very slowly. Who would go out to Babylon on a Sunday night? The returnees, a small crowd into the city for a sunny, sweltering day better spent in Babylon. Or perhaps they were on that train for the same reason as I, for nothing, a lark, the luxury of riding a train with nothing waiting at the other end, not even a cover story. Would I have a seat-mate?

"And why are you going to Babylon, my good man?" I would open.

"I live there."

"Oh. Makes sense. But, you see, that's not why I'm going at all. I'm going because it doesn't make sense. A very long story, but the gist is that I am very tired. Of everything. Of codes, for example, do you know what I mean? Certainly, in your occupation, what are you? — a broker, how nice — well, there must be something analogous. My problem is that I have never been, up to this minute, a literal man. Like Mansfield, do you happen to know him? An American functionary of my acquaintance. What I want to know is, do you have that problem, too? Well, today, on the advice of a blind man I know, I am doing something completely, meaninglessly literal. I am looking into the actual train to Babylon. Why, you ask? Only because he suggested it. And I trust him. It is a matter of long experience, my friend. I have come to the conclusion that things are what they seem."

But no one sat next to me. The door closed and the lights in the car faded as the motor started up. It was stifling. The windows would not open. A fan overhead beat the air into hot gusts. On the adjacent track, another train's lights were flickering. The Long Island Railroad. It had never been the same since the government took it over. That was the way to talk. I would be invited to all the cocktail parties, a raving capitalist. Talk about the weather, money, children, the PTA, high taxes, the changing neighborhood, that's the way. In the window I smiled at myself with just the right touch of American arrogance.

We began to move. They read the Sunday papers while I stared through reflected eyes into the tunnel. The other train, most of its cars darkened, was pulling abreast of us, another crowd, another destination, I wondered who would move faster. For a time we rode side by side at the same pace. I peered at the windows, hoping to catch the other crowd unaware, dozing, munching, reading, playing cards, perhaps a pretty girl to remind me of Jenny, safely separated by two panes of glass.

In the window opposite was a silhouette, not, to my disappointment, that of a pretty girl. It was the ugly profile of a man, big, perhaps bald, holding up a magazine, staring at it in the darkness, patiently waiting for the lights to return. I felt a chill. My neck began to hurt again. The holiday mood vanished. I wanted that train to speed up or slow down.

But we were locked there together. The lights in the car across the way flicked on, then off, on again and off, so at first it was unreal, too eerie to believe, a trick of psychedelics. Then the lights froze on, and on, for a long moment of clarity.

There, alive, the eyes open, staring at the magazine, the breathing dead. "The shadow of a dead man," Thaddeus had said. Not a dream, no, it was the nightmare of reality. I could not be wrong about that face. It was Zuckerman. Zuckerman alive. I knew it was true, even as the lights flickered off and his train moved out ahead in darkness.

12.

In the racing mural on the tunnel wall, visions appeared, old or new, dream, memory, or desire, I could not separate the strands. From a spark off the third rail, a powerful streak of fire cut across the Eiffel Tower at twilight. The world was on the brink of ruin.

Then the window grew cooler, green and black, and Paris gave way to Amsterdam, always, always back to Amsterdam, where a boy was darting between the tables of a café in the square, running fast, as if his heart would break, slipping in the snow at the foot of Rembrandt's statue, then up and off again, over the Blauwbrug to safety. What was he shouting? The strike! It is the winter of the strike. Every dock shut down. He is running to spread the word, from shop to house, that no one should work today, lay down your tools, lock your doors, they have killed the Jews.

A girl in glasses stared back at me from the window. Blue beret, short white dress, a binocular case strapped to her neck. She seated herself and buried her face in a newspaper. Her hand reached toward me, passing a small brown envelope. Was I in Amsterdam dreaming of the future? Imagine dreaming that life would come to this, sitting next to a girl in white on a railroad car in New York.

I opened the envelope. It was my watch.

"Oh, no!"

Jenny turned the page, ignoring me.

"You are getting to be like a peripatetic taxi driver I once knew."

"Really? How interesting." It was always difficult for Jenny to affect boredom, but she was performing fairly well at the moment.

"Funny," I said, "I didn't know you wore glasses."

"Oh, really? Yes, it was difficult getting any reading done when you were around, wasn't it? Like now, for instance."

The pages were turning briskly. I realized, even while she mocked me, that Jenny had always been a little frightened of me.

"Well," she announced at last, smoothing out the paper and pushing her glasses down to the tip of her nose, "I did some heavy thinking about that little conversation we had in the Fun House."

"Some fun."

"I decided you were absolutely right. I am a nice piece. Thank you." She resumed her reading.

I erased my smile when she glanced over. But the second time she caught me.

"Also," Jenny said, somewhat encouraged, "I changed that bust of you again."

"Am I still up on that pedestal?"

"No. This time you came out shaped absolutely square."

Turning toward the window to muffle laughter, I saw the reflection of the conductor pausing at our seat. He walked away.

"Conductor!" I called after him.

"Yes?"

"I want a ticket to Babylon."

"The young lady gave me both your tickets."

Jenny was smiling into her paper. The conductor shrugged and moved on.

"How did you know my destination?" I said.

"The sign at the gate. Or aren't you going all the way?"

"Not with you."

"I suppose," Jenny said, "I could pop some corn, like, this time I won't take no for an answer. But that should be obvious."

"Jenny, if you come along with me, you're dead."

"Things couldn't be much worse."

She flipped to the obituary page. I was tempted to fling that newspaper across the aisle.

"My, they do die young these days," Jenny said. "Say, don't you think I'd make just a fabulous private eye? I followed you all the way from McSorley's with these." She patted the binoculars. "I used to think you were a master criminal, but I've changed my mind about that, too. You supplied me with the fatal clue, which is very ordinary. I've read all about it, don't you know, the compulsion to be captured and such. So here I am. Start atoning."

"I don't want you here, Jenny."

"Then why did you let it slip? I never knew where you lived, where you went, who you saw. Suddenly, you were telling me about having lunch at McSorley's."

"That was Friday. I didn't go there yesterday."

"Thought you'd never ask. How did I find you at Coney Island? Ask me."

"Jenny, this is not a game."

"Deny it. Go ahead and deny it was you standing outside my window yesterday morning at exactly 4:47."

"It was something like that."

"You rat. I had rabbit in the paella."

"I almost came up."

"But you'd run out of excuses."

"Do you really want to know why I was too late for dinner? I was torturing a man in the backroom of a bar."

"Beautiful. Try another, dear."

"If I had come up, we wouldn't be here now. I would have said to hell with it, Jenny, let's get away. That's how I felt. But I had an appointment to keep."

"Don't I know it. At the Customs office. It must have been terribly important. Did you cheat duty on a cashmere?"

"That was dangerous, following me."

"Oh, what a snap. Naturally, I've improved with experience. I drove far too close on the way to Coney Island. Otherwise, you would never have seen the car. So I bought these, ready for the new day. But you tricked me, Jon. After what you did to me, I was sure you'd come home to me last night. It wasn't nice."

"I never expected to see you again."

"All you had to do was apologize, for Chrissake."

"I couldn't begin. I owe you too many apologies."

"Two will do. For pushing me away in the Fun House. And for all these months of treating me like a common whore."

"I'm sorry."

244

"Say it again."

"I am sorry, Jenny."

"It's not convincing. Don't you realize how I worried? Don't I at least have a right to know what's wrong with your silly neck?"

"A bartender twisted it."

"Oh, balls."

"It was already hurt."

"Naturally. I wouldn't expect you to have something dull like an unbroken neck."

"It was the man in the Fun House."

"And you expected me to sleep last night, leaving you out there with that creepy voice. Well, maybe my worst fear should have been wishful thinking. I thought he had finished the job."

"No, he was just having fun. He had orders not to kill me. But he couldn't resist taunting me. He said he'd missed on your boyfriend. It happened Friday on a highway. I remember someone shouted at him. Someone stopped him."

"You've never shared any of this with me. I could have helped. I'm not exactly dumb, you know. I mean, it was, like, sheer brilliance to think of McSorley's this morning. And was that fun! I staked it out from a rooftop at high noon, awfully well done. Waited five hours, bless you, I was surer than ever you were dead. But patience is rule one. Now come my interrogation techniques. Don't tell me your troubles, I couldn't care less. All I want to know is, what are we doing on this train?"

The conductor walked by. I grabbed his sleeve.

"The train that passed us going out, where is it heading?"

"Same place. Babylon."

"Two trains to Babylon?"

He hesitated. I scrutinized his face. Good Lord! Did he know the codes, too?

"This is a local, more stops," he said. He reached into his pocket for a schedule. "That one goes further. On out to Patchogue."

Of course. The ferry from Patchogue to Davis Park. He was still living in the driftwood, running the empire from his island hideaway, why had I assumed otherwise? Only because four years ago

Steingut wrote that he was dead. The whole fiction, in the mind of the entire network, was based on that. His death had been in the papers. I had seen that item with my own eyes, but I would have questioned it if Steingut had not confirmed. Did Flake know? Had Tina known all along? "So weighted down the divers let him rot," Mansfield had said. It was not Zuckerman down there. It was someone else's corpse.

"Must I resort to torture?" Jenny said. "I am waiting for an answer. What are we doing on this godforsaken train?"

"Sweet Jenny, I don't know. You're here because I'm here. I'm here because someone suggested it."

"Who?"

"The man I met with at McSorley's. A blind man who called himself Thaddeus. But I know that I would have taken this train anyway. He was not the seer I had thought. He fears dying. He was forever talking about himself, not me. I deluded myself that my knowledge was his, that he had put himself in my dreams. In the end, I suspected him. I even suspected you, Jenny."

"Oh, good, I'm delighted. Do you still?"

"Not much."

"Then what are we after?"

"A face. Maybe just a vision. He may not even exist anymore. But I saw him through this window. How can I be sure? I'm going to find out."

"I'm game." She reached down and lifted a brown paper bag from the floor. "Have a hamburger. The national dish of Baltimore."

"No thanks."

"Well, don't mind me. While you were feasting in McSorley's, I was starving on the roof."

"When we reach Babylon, Jenny, you will take the next train back. Wait for me at your place."

"Are you kidding? This is dinner. I'm finished waiting for you."

"Please. This is for me."

"I've done enough for you, what about me? You said my apartment was dangerous. Thanks a lot."

"It's safe now. Two men know I was there. The one who found me there is a friend. The one who sent a letter there is in his custody."

"Then you go back," Jenny said.

"Would you like me to?"

She crumpled her paper napkin into a ball and was suddenly quiet.

"No," she said. "You're not free yet."

She reached over and squeezed my hand. It felt wonderful.

"Don't tell me that you love me, I might puke," Jenny said. "You're about to, I can always feel it coming. I've had quite enough of your nauseating pity and envy. Gratitude would be even worse."

"I do love you," I said.

She hid a smile behind her hand and leaned her head on my shoulder.

And it was, I had to concede, exciting next to her, with Jenny above all others, to face the most dangerous day. I wondered if that was love, to be so selfish that I no longer cared she was in danger. She had chosen to share the risks. I could argue with her no longer. I wanted to share them with her. It could be lonely at the end. I loved Jenny very much. It would be comforting to have such good company on the bier.

We sat in the Babylon station awaiting the next train to Patchogue. I set my watch. It would be more than an hour.

"It says something on the back," Jenny said.

"Thanks for getting it fixed."

"Is that German?"

"Dutch. And the laundry, good woman?"

"Ready tomorrow. If there is one."

"There was a handkerchief," I said.

"I didn't see it."

"No matter."

"Did someone give you this?"

"It was my father's. He had it engraved for me. He knew 'they were coming."

"What does it say?"

My neck was beginning to hurt again. I rubbed the engraving. It was badly faded.

"It says, 'To Jon, who will set the world aright. Papa.' "

For a moment I thought she was going to cry. I could not understand it.

"He thought I was going to be a prime minister or something," I said.

"What happened?"

"Or something."

"Then that's really your name? Jon?"

"Yes, I'm Jon. I'd tell you everything, Jenny, but right now I'm not sure of anything beyond my name."

"You're Jon. That's really all I need to know."

She sat smiling, in a strange contented silence, her hand in mine, until the train came in.

The heat was killing. It was one of the oldest trains, the kind that had turned commuters into revolutionaries. The sunset was barely visible through the grime-streaked window. But it would do for a revolutionary turned commuter.

"Do you skate, Jenny?"

"In this weather?"

"I'm curious to know. Do you?"

"Good God, no!"

The train jerked to a stop.

"Sayville! Next stop Patchogue!" the conductor called out.

"Come on," I said to Jenny.

We sprinted for the door.

"Is there a ferry from Sayville?" I asked the conductor.

"Where you going?"

"Like, out to the beach. Take my girl to dinner maybe."

"It's our first date, man," Jenny said.

He slammed the door closed. The train started up again.

"If you're going no place in particular," he said, "you better wait till Patchogue. See, I know this area. Fished it all. I'd be in hip-boots today if my wife hadn't put me in this monkey suit sixteen years ago."

"Yeah, well, that's interesting. I wonder if you could open that door."

"You must be new to this area," he said. "I just don't think you'd want to go out to Cherry Grove."

"We'll go there," I said. "That'll be fine."

He scratched his head and wandered off.

I opened the door. The train was rolling slowly out of the station. We jumped onto the platform.

"I don't ask much," Jenny whispered as we entered the taxi, "but let's at least know where we're going. First you're going to Babylon. Then you're going to Patchogue. Now you're going somewhere else."

"We're going out to Fire Island," I said to the driver.

"Positively great!" Jenny said. "I've never been there."

The taxi moved toward the docks. I looked at the driver in the mirror. Amazing. It was not Nathan P. Silver.

"Once upon a time, Jenny, I took a ferry to Patchogue from a place on the island called Davis Park. That's exactly where he'd expect me. I'm not taking that chance with you along. We're going to land far west of him."

I awaited her retort. It never came. She just smiled. I had expected something like "Stop bragging, will you? I mean, it's not like you just ushered in the age of chivalry." I expected such things from Jenny. I depended on her to save me with laughter, to giggle at the rust on my knight's armor before it spread to corrode my brain. But now she was silent. My God, what had I brought on myself! She was acting like someone who was beginning to fall in love.

The boat to Fire Island was nearly deserted. It traveled swiftly, high in the water. We looked up at the night, the same clear black sky that Tina and I had watched nine years before. Jenny stood at the railing on the top deck with the moonlight in her hair. It was too beautiful for a dream. I had no such beauty in me. I wanted her and she knew it. She was flirting with me as if our courtship had just begun. And as usual, she was right. I wanted her but not like before, not in her bed, taking her when I was lonely, banishing her from my mind until I needed her again. I wondered where we would go when we returned. The Waldorf or the Plaza? "The bridal suite," I would say, and watch the happiness in Jenny's eyes as the man at the desk summoned a parade of groveling bellboys.

"Would you like that?" I asked, as if she were sharing my thoughts.

"What would I like?"

She threw her arms around my neck. There was no pain. It seemed so faraway, far inside the sweater and the brace and the bandage. There could be no danger. It was not part of me.

Approaching the dock, we saw the weekend crowd waiting to return on the boat, deeply tanned young men, waving, embracing, throwing kisses.

"Just what in bejesus have you got me into?" Jenny said.

We struggled through a mass of bright shirts to the restaurant.

"Are you hungry?" I shouted above the din of shrieks and fare-wells.

"No!" Her eyes were too busy feasting. "I couldn't eat a thing."

We walked up the long boardwalk to the dunes and looked out to sea. The surf was low. Far out we saw the twinkle of shiplights. It was deathly quiet.

"I don't believe it!" Jenny stretched her arms toward the stars. "Isn't this too much?"

A young man with huge sunglasses and a sad, pockmarked face, was slowly climbing the wooden stairway from the beach. He was staring at Jenny. I did not like that, whatever his thoughts. Suddenly I felt very possessive. This damned American osmosis. Jenny broke away from me and ran down the dune and across the beach. When she reached the ocean, she turned and waved. The young man waved back and she dropped her hand in confusion.

"Can I help you?" I said to him.

"She's a joy," he said.

"Thank you," I said. "She's my wife."

He nodded and turned away. I felt sorry for him, sorry for everyone in the world who would never know Jenny, proud that she was mine, and bewildered by the entire sentiment. I walked down the steps. And we do engage ourselves, so far as in us lies . . . if either of you know any impediment why ye may not . . . love her, comfort her, honor her . . . to love and to cherish till death . . .

I reached her side.

"Do I know him?" Jenny said.

"No. He would like to know you."

"Why are you looking so sad all of a sudden?"

"I was saying the marriage vows."

"Is it that bad? The water's fine."

She was wading knee-high, allowing the surf to splash against her dress. I tied my shoes together and hung them around the brace. We set out walking east, hand in hand, through the ice-cold water. And then Jenny just stopped.

"Let's walk the other way," she said.

"This is east," I said.

"So?"

"This is the way we have to go."

"Let's not."

"Jenny, I have to."

"No. I want to go the other way."

"All right."

We turned back.

"You're testing me," I said as we walked west. A wave came in, higher than the others. I used it as a pretext to drop her hand. My feet were plowing through the water against my will.

"It's that girl," Jenny said. "This all has something to do with avenging, and I don't like it. She's dead. I'm sorry. I don't know who she was, I don't know who that voice in the Fun House belonged to, I don't know anything about this. All I know is that we love each other."

"Yes, that should be all." I looked at my watch under the moon. It was nearing midnight.

"Is it really so important what time it is?" Jenny said.

"I suppose not."

"If suddenly I said, all right, Jon, you win, let's walk east again, would you love me more?"

"Of course not."

"You're lying. And so was I. I came along to be your helpmate. But then I thought we might do something ridiculous like enjoy life for a change. C'mon!" She raced across the beach and up the dune. "Hey! Look!" She was pointing inland from the dune. "A forest! Out of all this sand!" It was impossible to join in her vacation spirit. But, then, life would always be like that with Jenny. We would be bankrupt, the house in flames, the kids taking LSD, and there would be Jenny shouting, "Hey! Look!"

I followed at a sad walk, smiling and loving her, wondering if perhaps, after all, she would make me forget in time.

"Fantastic!" Jenny said, as I joined her on the ridge of the dune. "We are standing above the treetops." We found a path into the forest, and then we were sinking, down the side of a sandy hill, while the trees climbed higher, growing taller as we descended, a sunken forest, the sky disappearing above thick foliage.

"Jon!" Jenny whispered through the darkness. "I'm scared. Where are you?"

"Stay right there." I moved down the path and found her. We walked deeper into the forest until we saw moonrays falling into a glen. Jenny sat down across from me and leaned back against a tree. We stared at each other, smiling, not touching, and so we might have remained for hours if I had not ruined it.

"The girl named Tina," I said. "I thought I loved her."

"Please don't."

"I thought you'd want to know."

"No girl with any sense wants to know. If you must talk, talk about me."

"I want you, Jenny."

"That's about you, not me."

"Can't you see I am asking for —" But I could not say it.

"For what, Jon?"

"I have to tell you."

"Who she was?"

"I don't know who she was. She was born on April Fool's Day. Maybe she was only a joke. Or maybe it was all an illusion. I thought I knew her very well. But then, you see, maybe I don't know you either, Jenny. You could be my enemy, leading me out here. I simply know that you are the only one I really trust, however foolish that may be."

Jenny put her hand on my cheek. "My, you do run on with the blarney."

"Help me, Jenny."

She picked up a pine cone and rolled it gently in her palms. It became the sole object of her concentration, as if she were distracting herself from whatever she was fighting, laughter or tears, I did not know which. That moment was agony before she spoke.

"It was hard to say, wasn't it, Jon."

"The hardest in my life."

"But you asked her for help, didn't you?"

"Yes. It was quite different."

"I know. You didn't love her. She's dead and you've turned to me, I don't hold it against you. I must say, I liked it better than all those easy apologies. My, they were sickening." She threw the cone hard at a tree trunk. It struck dead center. "I do want to help, Jon. It's all very selfish. It's my life, too."

"I work for an organization," I said.

"Chain letters."

"Not exactly. It's a system of safeguards. No one is allowed enough information to make him dangerous to the others. Except the inventor of the system."

"And that's who we're after."

"The papers said he died in an accident. A friend of mine on this case thought he was killed. Neither was true. I saw his face tonight."

"He has no name?"

"Zuckerman."

"And how did he supposedly die?"

"Drowned. Four years ago, off this island. The divers found a corpse imbedded in concrete. They never pulled it up."

"Whose corpse was it?"

"I don't know."

"Hmm. And where does this Mr. Zuckerman live?"

"In a cottage far east of here."

"Why did he choose to vanish?"

"Money. He changed the purpose of the organization and kept the channels. But he was responsible to a man in Europe."

"Name, please."

"Bergère. But for me, Zuckerman was his only contact here, and Bergère could not possibly find me. Zuckerman's obituary was chiefly for the benefit of Bergère. With Zuckerman's disappearance, Bergère lost his entire American network. I am sure he is convinced that all of us are dead or in prison."

"And was it Mr. Zuckerman who would send you the letters?"

"No. A bartender named Steingut."

"A bartender?"

"Sugar Red. That was his cover. He was also a narcotics dealer."

"But why would a man like that be in your organization?"

"What?"

"I said, why —"

"He wasn't! No, a man like that could not have been one of us. You have it, Jenny. Sugar Red was the syndicate's man. He was their agent in the takeover. He became Steingut. That's it. They persuaded Zuckerman, but Steingut was their stumbling block. He would not capitulate. He had to be replaced."

"Jon, I simply can't believe that Mr. Zuckerman could have lived out here without being seen."

She had me again. Fortunately, only for a moment. It dawned at last.

"Manley!"

"Who?"

"Alexander Manley. He lives in Puerto Rico, alone by the sea.

But he's here. He arrived last week. Mansfield believes he is Torre."

"Mansfield? Torre?"

"Jenny, you have done it. Mansfield said it was the same kind of chain that we have here. Zuckerman was assigned by his new benefactors to establish that operation. That's why they didn't kill him. They needed him. He taught Sugar Red the routines, just as he had taught Steingut, and then he went to Puerto Rico. But something has brought him back."

"Then who is Torre?"

"Once Mansfield, now Zuckerman. For some reason Zuckerman had to find me. He came looking for me at McSorley's, he gave Thaddeus the name Torre, but then, oddly enough, he ran away from me at the airport. I couldn't see his face. He was walking strangely, not like Zuckerman at all. He caught me off guard. The last person in the world I expected to be alive was Zuckerman."

"I don't understand what he was doing."

"Neither do I. That night I went to Tina's apartment. I thought she would know what was happening. But she didn't. I left a suitcase there. Zuckerman must have found it the next day. When he discovered it was empty, she was killed."

"My God, Jon, how did this all begin?"

"With a message about a traitor. I still don't know who sent it or who the traitor is."

"Please don't take this badly," Jenny said, "but I can't help wondering if it was that girl."

"No. I am convinced she knew nothing about the operation. She was always hiding something, but she did not lie. That was Tina's nature. Everything she told me was true. She knew that Zuckerman was alive, but she never said he was dead. She kept it from me to protect him, just as she protected me from him. I believe she knew only two facts that she would not tell me: Zuckerman's whereabouts and Steingut's identity. And she wrote me about Steingut in a poem."

I gave her the poem. She moved under the moon and read it very slowly. Her frown deepened from puzzlement to dismay. At the end, she folded the paper carefully and handed it back to me.

"You want another apology," I said.

"No. You said you'd been out here before."

"It wasn't real, Jenny."

"How do you get Steingut out of that, I'd like to know."

"It's a code she developed. This poem was in an envelope with a bookmark that Sugar Red had given me."

"Did she know him?"

"She was a junkie."

"Was she living with you, Jon?"

"No. She didn't know where I lived. She knew Sugar Red as a dealer, not a bartender. Wait. I only told her that the bookmark had come from a bartender in my building."

"There was a bar in your building?"

"I lived on the Bowery. Listen, Jenny. I was wrong. Tina could not have known the bartender was Steingut. She was returning the bookmark to me; it had nothing to do with Sugar Red. I trapped him, but not from her poem."

"If she was so innocent, what was she doing with a code?"

"She used it once in a note to me, just playing. The system began with the first and last three letters of the seventy-second word. In the poem, that's S-t-e-i-n-g."

"And?"

"I don't remember the rest of the system."

"Well, think, Jon, isn't this your business? How are you going to support me?"

"I don't have a pencil."

"Do you remember the note she wrote you?"

"Very well. It began like this: 'My love seeks you. It feels like a silent river — ' "

"Enough."

" '— cutting deeply into the soil. There are dry tears — ' "

"Jon! It may sound awfully cruel, but all I want to know is where's the *ut* in Steingut?"

"You have a pencil?"

"No."

"Then I can't do it. I have to keep too much in my head."

"You can do it."

I focused on the poem, trying in my mind to superimpose the note that had provided the message: "Honing the edge of fate." The only *ut* in the poem was in the sixteenth word, *but*. It had to correspond to *th* in the note because: Steingut
Honingth

The sixteenth word in the note was *There*. Initially, I was cheered by the discovery. But I soon recognized that with no hard clues on the poem's message, the trial and error would be infinite before I stumbled on the method by which the *b* might be dropped from *but*, making *ut* the equivalent first two letters.

"It's no use."

"Do you have it already?" Jenny said.

"This could take me all night."

"I have time," she said.

Fifteen minutes later, I had concluded that there was no possible way to draw together the *u* and *t* from the poem's forty-sixth word, *fourth*, to correspond to the note's forty-sixth word, *that*, and beyond. I looked up at Jenny. Her stare was mercilessly patient.

I decided to split the group, taking *u* as the first letter of the poem's thirty-ninth word, *under*, and relating it to *t* in the note's thirty-ninth, *The*. Eventually, however, the system fell apart. That setback struck me as very familiar. I realized that I had made the same error when I originally broke the code. Of course. It began with the seventy-second word, but after that, the word numbers were irrelevant. This was precisely how she had tricked it. The stanza slashes in the poem were also designed to confuse. By separating phrases, they reinforced preoccupation with the location of separate words. It was not the words at all, it was the letters. Mentally, I would have to squeeze the note and the poem to correlate positions. I would have to eke it out, letter by letter.

The process was painful, for I could retain only small groups at a time, but ultimately I flashed, bit by bit, the entire note over most of the poem:

```
myloveseeksyouitfeelslikeasilentrivercuttingde
wewalkedthatnightalongtheshorestarsdonotdieinp

eplyintothesoiltherearedrytearsjoyoustearschok
eaceisaidbutintheblazingagonytheyknewatbirthan

inginmyheartihavethisweirdfeelingthaticannotev
dsothisearthwillgoyousaidnowithascometopassund

enexpresstoyounowthetearsarecrystallizingintos
erafeverishsunswollenbythefourthangelsvialcour

parklingwallsthatkeepusinsidesafefromharmsotha
ageousairandseathatoncebattledthesuntobecannol

talllightismagnifiedandallthesearchinggraysaref
ongerresistnowintheblindingmistproudfleshscorc

ilterediithankyouforlovingmehonoringmeandtrusti
hedandsteamingburstsintoflameintheawfulheatoft

ngme
hatp
```

I searched again for the necessary correlatives to finish *Stein-gut* — *u* and *t* in the poem under *t* and *h* in the note — confident that they would appear deep in the code. As I neared the end, the odds narrowed and my confidence waned. They were not there.

Next, I moved to my hypothesis for the second word in the poem's message — *is* — assuming that she had been signaling who Steingut was. The occurrence of the *i* under *e* was at the one hundred and twenty-first letter but the *s* did not pan out.

Once again I began, this time changing the tense, and I hit them at 120-18-283, but it gave no key to a further pattern so I abandoned it. Soon thereafter, a decreasing progression began to develop +115, +91, +56, −243, rendering straight out 6-121-212 –268-25 — *k-i-l-l-e* — and there it broke down. It had been more than an hour's work and I had no idea how much time would be required to rediscover the next phase of the system. The message was not finished but I did not need to find the *r*. Tina had confirmed the name of her killer.

"It says —"

"Wait," Jenny said. "Let me guess."

"It's not a matter of guesswork," I said. "Steingut was the killer."

"Impossible. What do you think, she wrote the poem when she knew he was going to kill her?"

I went back to work.

"Please let me guess," Jenny said.

"Dammit, Jenny, you had better be wrong. I have just killed half my brain cells."

"Well, I hardly know anything about Mr. Steingut," she said. "But you did tell me he must have been replaced."

"It says: S-*t-e-i-n-g-u-t-k-i-l-l-e-*"

"I wonder what happened to the poor man," she sighed.

"No, it isn't. It's not an *r*. I have the *d*."

"And where do you think he is?" Jenny said softly.

"He's out there, Jenny! That had to be it. They gave him the cement burial. He was Zuckerman's stand-in. He —"

I saw the smile begin to form on her lips and then disappear. At least she made an effort to conceal her triumph.

"Don't get mad," she said. "I was only guessing."

She ran east along the shore, Jenny in the moonlight, no one had ever looked as beautiful to me.

"Move!" she shouted back. "You're acting like an old man."

"So this is it," I said to myself. "This is what it's all about." And Jenny heard me, skipping ahead in the surf, laughing over her shoulder, half-understanding, afraid to probe for fear that I meant not her but something in the mystery we were pursuing.

"You, Jenny! I mean you!"

She ran back and seized my hand, pulling me on, until I had caught her pace, and we were skipping together like schoolchildren, free of dread and choice, she with total ease, and I with an awkwardness less of age than of discomfort at this embarrassing resurgence of youth.

We saw the lights of Davis Park.

"Let's race!" Jenny said. She ran ahead but I was too winded to follow. The weight of the brace was bringing the neck back to life. Winded; the brace; but perhaps, really, it was only my fear that I could never catch her. An old man, yes, Jenny. Years are heavy, you will discover. But I wondered if she ever would.

And then I realized that this was the spot. There was the white tower where the lifeguard had waved at me, scared the hell out of me, as Mansfield would say, in that first moment when I came in from the sea. Here was the sand where my fellow Americans lay innocently under the sun as I floated into their midst. Over here was Tina in the golden pullover, with that smile of half-amusement. Here we had stood in the sea, watching the shooting star. And here, at the eastern edge of Davis Park, I had left her on that first night.

I looked up from the passing sand. Jenny was nowhere to be seen.

The chill returned. She had wanted to turn back. I had insisted. Had I pushed her into danger?

I tried to recall the distance. No, the driftwood cottage was far ahead, perhaps five, six miles. She would tire. I would reach her.

More than a mile of sand passed underfoot before I discovered, next to a pile of driftwood, a blue beret.

"Jenny!"

I ran blindly down the beach, crying out her name again and again, until I tripped and fell into the sand. I had stumbled over a binocular case. Beneath it was Jenny's white dress.

When I raised my eyes from the sand, I saw a naked little ghost standing in the surf, smiling in wonderment at soft patches of moonlight on her shoulders.

In relief, I could feel no anger. I just felt like a damned fool.

"I thought something terrible had happened to you."

"About time," she said.

"It wasn't funny."

"Really? What did you imagine?"

"Come here."

"No!"

"Stop acting like a little girl."

"Ooh!" A clump of seaweed landed in my eyes. The trajectory was perfect. "I'm on to you," she said. "You can't get away with it anymore."

"I said, come here!"

"No! Keep your damn distance! You just have a good look, Daddy. It might change your mind."

I watched her hands glide along the surface, those small, delicate child's hands, helpless and — wham! Streams of cold water shot up in a high arc and exploded in my face. My sweater was drenched. As I peeled it off, a second, massive attack pasted my shirt to my chest. I dropped my trousers to the sand. Jenny screamed and swam away.

Beyond the surf the water grew warmer with time but the brace was a heavy burden. Jenny was a powerful swimmer. She was moving further and further out to sea, rolling like a seal, side-stroking, back-stroking, breast-stroking, without pause.

"Jenny, come back!"

"Not until you promise, Daddy-o."

"All right."

"Promise to stop acting so goddamn superior."

"I promise."

"And no spanking!"

"No spanking."

She turned back toward shore. I floated on my back, waiting for her.

"I'm not even sure I want to be your wife," she called out.

"Don't talk, just swim."

"Why should I be your wife? Give me one good reason."

I began back-paddling toward the beach. Approaching the breakers, I glanced out toward Jenny. She was gone.

Again! How many deaths did I have to die with her?

But I was not really surprised to feel the pinch on my leg. A few seconds later, she surfaced in front of me.

"Thought I was a sandshark, didn't you?" she said.

No sandshark, just a winded, pouting Jenny. My pride was delighted that she was out of breath. I reached her at last and put my arm around her. We swam back together. As we neared shore, she said, "My God, we don't have towels!"

We carried our clothes into a hollow behind the dune. Jenny leaned against the rim of sand and shook the salt water from her hair. I lay near her, waiting. But she did not come. She was pouting at the stars.

"Come down here, Jenny."

"No thanks."

"Why?"

"I don't take orders."

"I'm sorry."

I jumped to my feet and held out my arms.

"You're doing an awful lot of apologizing today," she said.

"Sorry about that, too."

"Are you really? Or is it just a handy notion when you're lusting?"

"I want you to marry me, Jenny."

She stared at me in disbelief.

"Will you, Jenny?" I said.

"Will I what?"

"Will you marry me?"

"Of course, you idiot!" She leaped into my arms and squeezed her legs around my waist. We were laughing and crying and the throbbing pain under the brace didn't matter anymore.

There it was again, that frightening kiss, as if she would tear out my tongue by the roots. But then something clicked. For the first time the desperation was gone, the clinging infant was a woman. Jenny was giving, and I felt her gift would be endless, that I could never tire through all the years ahead of Jenny opening up more and more of herself to me. I wondered if I would lose the fear that I would never deserve it.

As I felt that rigid kiss relax, I let her feet down gently to the ground and pressed her back against the wall of the hollow, quickly, both of us wanting it so quickly, because we knew this was it, no dreams of miraculous skating, we were loving with our feet on cold sand, seeing each other clearly in the moonlight, feeling the damp grit of sand against our skin.

We lay down in the sand, staring up at the sky.

"Imagine that!" Jenny said.

It was nearly four o'clock by my watch when I felt her head go limp on my arm. The soothing rhythm of the waves began to fade and I fell asleep, wondering if this was why I came here, and which way we would walk tomorrow.

I awoke to find her dressed and sitting on the dune, her hair tied in a kerchief, peering through the binoculars out to sea.

"The damn fog," she complained. "Can't see a thing."

"It'll burn off."

"What nonsense! That's what they always say."

But it was a new smile I received, one she could not have shared before we came to that dune.

"It wasn't like New Year's Eve at all," Jenny said.

"No."

"What would my mother say? Standing up in a sand dune with a Dutchman in a neck brace."

"Ten points." I dressed. The clothes were still damp. As I emptied the sand out of my shoes, Jenny mumbled something from her observation post.

"What's that?" I asked.

"I said, when did you know you loved me?"

"Oh, that."

I tied my shoes. The right shoelace broke. I knotted the pieces together.

"Well?" Jenny turned and trained the binoculars on me.

"As I recall, it was about this time yesterday. When I woke up in a pile of broken glass."

"Peculiar."

"It was because I thought I'd never see you again."

"Fortunately," Jenny said, "I have these trusty binoculars. I can see you're just saying that in retrospect."

"Yes."

A bar of chocolate landed in the sand between my feet.

"What's this?"

"Breakfast," she said.

She stood up and brushed the sand off her dress with an efficient flourish, signaling the start of an organized day.

"Well," she said, "I don't want a church wedding. I'm still something of a believer, but I can do without the hocus-pocus."

I took the binoculars from her and swept the beach.

"Shall we get started?" Jenny said.

The surf was up. It crashed out of the fog, cold and furious. Through the glasses I followed a column of fat little sandpipers making quick tracks along the water's edge, retreating swiftly before each roaring wave, then darting back toward the sea to peck beneath the sand for breakfast.

Something startled the rearguard piper. He flew out above the crest of the wave, circling back to land farther up the beach. The others followed.

A boy came walking from the east. He was picking up shells and throwing them, wildly, in all directions, out to sea, at the dune, none of them traveling further than the short throw of a five-year-old.

"Do me a favor, Jenny," I said. "Go down and talk to that boy."

"Why?"

"Just do me the favor."

She nodded with a deference that surprised me, playing the good soldier, anxious to be my partner when the emergency was genuine.

I watched her scamper down the dune, hands and feet flying against the sea breeze, the white dress billowing as if to remind me that this was my bride. The boy spotted her coming. Through the glasses I saw the fear on his face. He turned and ran.

Jenny caught up with him. She picked up a shell and put it in his palm. He turned it over and threw it into the surf. She gave him another shell and this time he smiled at her. When I reached the beach, they were walking together in earnest conversation, his hand in hers.

The boy tensed when he saw me.

"What's his name?" I asked Jenny.

"He won't say."

"What's your name, boy?"

He stared at me with a frightened, stubborn expression, as if expecting me to torture the answer from him.

"You're not very talkative," I said.

"We were doing fine until you got here," Jenny said. Some of the old fire was back in her eyes.

"I know," I said. "That's why I asked you to go ahead."

"Then why not leave us alone?" she said. "We were having fun."

They walked off together, skipping every few steps, Jenny talking animatedly, the boy looking up at her as if she were some kind of sea goddess. I followed after them.

"Give him a shell," Jenny instructed me.

I found a blue and red shell chip. He inspected it carefully and threw it down.

"Another one," Jenny said.

"I'm afraid I'm not very good at this game," I said.

"You'd better learn," Jenny said.

A tiny starfish with one broken tip was protruding from the sand. I dug it out and gave it to him. He examined it from every conceivable angle and, at last, put it in the pocket of his shorts.

"Thank you," he said.

I took his hand and we walked east, the three of us together, dodging the surf like the sandpipers.

At one point, the boy stopped. He looked up at Jenny with a radiant smile.

"I love you," he said.

Jenny blushed.

"He lives near here," she said.

"Where are your parents?" I asked him.

"My father's having breakfast," he said. "I had mine. Poached eggs on toast. That's my favorite."

"And your mother?"

"Mommy's gone away for awhile."

"Where is she?"

"My father says she's not far away."

"Do you miss her?" Jenny asked.

"Oh, my father gave me some pictures of Mommy to keep in my new room. He says I shouldn't miss her, that it may not be too long."

"Who is your father?" I said.

"I don't really know him very well."

"What do you mean, you don't know him very well!"

Jenny stepped hard on my foot. I softened my voice.

"Your father must be a nice man," I said. "Who is he?"

"Mommy always told me he lived on an island somewhere way away. He came back and brought me new clothes and toys and everything."

"Did you come out here with him?" I said.

"He brought me and the boy-man brought Mommy. We played a game. Then the boy-man said that Mommy had to go and have her picture taken."

"Let's get him home," Jenny said. "Where do you live, dear?"

"There."

He pointed down the beach to the dune. I raised the binoculars. Swirls of fog were drifting out to sea past a sign driven deep into the dune, blocking it from full view, playing a game of missing letters. As the last wisp of fog snaked by, I could read the sign distinctly: Babylon. One of those pretentious names by which seaside cottages are known in America.

266

13.

There were three stacks on the horizon.

"Look in here," I said to the boy. "That's the Queen Mary."

"Where?"

"She's the one with the three smokestacks."

We had moved in behind the dune. We were crouched low, the binoculars propped on the ridge, like scouts, Indians, soldiers. Which would the boy prefer?

"Now look again without the glasses," I said. "You can't see it, can you? It is too far away. It is sailing across the sea to England. But look through the glasses again. Do you see it now?"

"I can't see it." He returned the binoculars.

"But I can see it," I said. "The water is climbing higher and the ship is sinking lower. Now all that is left are the tips of the smokestacks. And now I see only the waves. The ship has disappeared."

"That's because the world is round," Jenny said.

"I know that," the boy said.

I swung the binoculars toward the old secluded driftwood cottage. It was still there. But it looked like a tiny shack, a historic annex dwarfed by its modern attachments: telephone and electricity lines, television antenna, a kidney-shaped swimming pool, and a Bermuda-pink two-story house with sundecks, sliding doors, and a glass dome at the top. Redwood steps, guarded by a line of metal torches, paraded down to the beach.

"Now we're going to play a game," I said to the boy. "See that house over there?"

"That's my house."

"But let's pretend. We'll pretend it is the house where the railroad men live. And we are Indians. They have broken the treaty and put their tracks through our reservation."

"I'd rather be a cowboy," the boy said.

Jenny laughed at my ineptitude.

"Then I'll be your Indian comrade," I said. "In that tepee over there, my Apache brothers are having a powwow, making their plans to go on the warpath. How many are there?"

The boy was silent. I switched trails quickly. "We have to sneak into that tepee without being seen. How are we going to do that?"

"I know how." He jumped up, took Jenny's hand, and tiptoed ahead through the high grass behind the dune. Jenny winked back at me. "The fog is burning off," she said.

I looked across the marshland to the cove. The blue cruiser was sitting at anchor.

Monday morning. Mansfield's deadline. He had released me. But through the hours of those ten days, I had made it my own. Without thinking, I wound my watch. The stem barely turned. It did not need winding. I wondered why I had bothered.

"Shh!" the boy whispered. "Up these stairs."

We began climbing, very softly, a long procession of wooden steps leading to a high sundeck. Jenny and the boy were giggling at the pretense of danger in our game. They stopped abruptly at the sound of loud voices above us. We heard a door slide shut.

"Follow me," the boy said. "My secret place."

He led us back down the steps. Nearing the bottom, he jumped off onto the sand and crawled beneath the short stilts under the house. A startled rabbit scurried out and hopped off into the tall grass. I looked up and saw a man's back at the top of the stairs. He was oddly dressed for the beach. Black fedora, silk business suit, elevated shoes. Jenny and I scrambled after the boy.

The three of us knelt behind a water tank, listening to descending footsteps. Two men, then three, paused at the bottom of the steps. We peered out at them from our hiding place. Their chests and heads were cut off from our view by the bottom of the house.

"Who are they?" Jenny whispered.

I pressed her arm to silence her.

"We should get rid of him," the first man said. I had heard that voice before.

"He's a creep," another of the men said. It was a voice very rough around the edges. "We should have done it four years ago."

"No. We were right." A third voice, strikingly familiar, more pleasant than the other two, now dominated. "He's a genius at this. We needed him."

"We don't need him now." It was the rough voice again.

"I'm not sure," the third man said. "We're not going to make a move without checking."

"Then you check." The rough voice was growing angry. "You find out today and we'll come back."

"I will decide when to ask for that order and when you are to carry it out," the third man said quietly, secure in his status, ending the conversation, and it was then that I connected. That voice belonged to the man who claimed to be Torre in the back room at Fisher's. The other two were his accomplices that night. Yes, I was certain that those were the three, along with Sugar Red, who had sat there silently.

We listened to the clack of their shoes along the boardwalk past the house and over the marshland toward the cove. A sliding door slammed shut somewhere up in the house. Again there were footsteps coming down, these much quicker than the others.

"It's the boy-man," the boy whispered fearfully. "He can see!" He lay flat behind the water tank with his head on the sand. I pushed Jenny down with him and kept watch on the steps. Crackjaw stopped where the three men had stood. As he turned, I ducked down. I could hear his breathing.

"You in there, kid?"

The boy smiled mischievously, as if he had succeeded in eluding an ironhanded nursemaid. He began crawling backward toward the other side of the house. Jenny and I followed, staying low, until we reached the sunlight. We stood up and ran after the boy, around to the back of the house and through a driftwood door. It was a bedroom of the old shack.

"This is my new room," the boy said proudly. He pushed aside blue Mother Goose curtains to reveal the marshland and the bay. I raised the binoculars. Three men in black business suits were standing near the shore. I did not recognize their faces. They were talking heatedly, occasionally glancing up the boardwalk, obviously waiting for someone. They did not look happy, even when they saw Crackjaw moving down the boardwalk to join them.

"The boy-man is gone," I said.

"There's Mommy," the boy said, pointing at the pictures of Tina on the wall. They were magazine cutouts, all of them relatively tasteful. The wigged girl on the motorcycle was not there.

"She's beautiful," Jenny said.

"Who were those men?" I asked the boy.

"Friends of my father," he said. "C'mon!" He raced out the door and once again we followed the leader of our innocence to the front of the house, up the steps, and this time all the way onto the sundeck. I slid open the glass door to the kitchen.

"Not that way!" the boy whispered. But it was too late.

Emil Zuckerman was seated in a wicker chair pulled up to a glasstopped table. He was wearing leather sandals and a purple terrycloth bathrobe with a golden *M* emblazoned on the breast pocket. Spread before him on the table were poached eggs, toast, coffee, orange marmalade, a half-dozen magazines, and a green Alpine hat.

He looked up at me and smiled.

I heard a long, loud sigh.

"Hello, Jon," Zuckerman said.

The boy crawled between my legs into the room.

"We're cowboys after the Apaches," he said.

"Good work, son," Zuckerman said.

"Look what the man gave me!" The boy put the broken starfish in Zuckerman's hand.

"It's a beauty," Zuckerman said, returning it to him. "Why don't you go find another one?"

"He shouldn't be out there alone," Jenny said sternly.

Zuckerman turned slowly to examine his new assailant, very

carefully, from her ankles to her eyes. He rose from his chair.

"And who might you be?" he said.

Jenny's lower lip began to tremble.

"He was all alone on the beach," she said. "That's very dangerous so near the water."

"Well, I certainly wouldn't wish him harm," Zuckerman said.

"I want Aunt Jenny to go with me," the boy said.

"This is Aunt Jenny?" Zuckerman said. "Certainly, son. You run along with your Aunt Jenny." He looked over at me. "Nothing to fear," he said. "I'm the only one here. Crackjaw is boating my house guests to the mainland. He won't be back for an hour."

I nodded to Jenny. She took the boy's hand and they walked out the door.

"Don't be a stranger," Zuckerman said, sitting down. "Breakfast? No? Then, do you mind?" He bit into a piece of toast. "Starved. Really famished. You can't imagine what a week I've had. Or perhaps you can." He drained his coffee cup and pushed it aside. "Say, I really do fancy Aunt Jenny. A mite on the skinny side but a few injections can fix that. Poor old Flake could use some purity in his pages. The culture is changing, have you noticed? That came as quite a shock to me when I returned. The public has had enough of all this promiscuity, vile movies, violence on the campus, crime in the streets. Aunt Jenny has the eyes of a virgin. Is she? Law and order, that's what she conveys. But to the practiced eye, there's one hell of an animal lurking underneath, am I right again? She could serve a very important purpose for the magazines. I'm worried about poor old Flake, all alone there behind my desk, still mourning the death of his great teacher. Of course, due credit, he has endeavored his feeble best to keep pace with the times. Look at these two, now. Beautiful. Do you see what's happening here? He's integrating! Juxtaposition, that's the secret. Goes to show the importance of good training. But all the same, and just between us, Flake is a man of limited imagination. Try as he will, he can't transcend that. He would fail completely to capture Aunt Jenny. Were I still in this business, I'd show her with a lion cub on a leash. That's her law-and-order veneer. But get this twist. I'd have the lion all dressed up, mane to claw. And Aunt Jenny would be stripped —"

The empty cup, the magazines, the toast, the eggs, the marmalade splattered on the floor with a sweep of my hand, but I stopped short of touching him.

Zuckerman sat motionless, suppressing his rage.

"My apologies," he said. "I had no idea you were so sensitive." He knelt down to pick up the magazines.

"You want me to kill you, don't you?" I said.

Zuckerman looked up at me without fear.

"You can't," he said. "I'm already dead."

He abandoned the mess of yolk and pulp on the floor. I watched him move through an archway to an oak bar before a huge mirror.

"You're a little late, aren't you, Jon? We were up all night watching for you. Oh, but I believe I said that before, didn't I? Nine years ago. Interesting, how little you've changed. There always seems to be a pretty face interfering with our appointments, doesn't there? A shame. I truly had great hopes for you. Right to the end. That's why I gave you more than one last chance. Why, just think of the risk I took yesterday, going into Penn Station. I was pleased, of course, that you remembered to honor the safeguard. But why did you make such a fool of yourself, talking with all those strangers? Had you been alert, my friend, you would have followed me onto the correct train. What silly thoughts were beguiling you? Can it be that you did not even see me? Too bad. Three gentlemen were awaiting us here, just dying to meet you. Did you see them? What is it, Jon? Aren't you talking to me? You are Jon, aren't you? Bergère never sent me a description of you. Only the ink signal on the palm. I had to go on trust. But I'm a very trusting man." He poured out a glass of rum and toasted me. "You've come back because it's here that you came in. And now I think you want to go out. Well, I believe I can arrange that for you. Come here. I have something to show you." He was still with me. No lights would flicker out or trains move ahead or green hats vanish into the fog. "It's the message from

Bergère," he said, "the first message that you were coming."

The lure was effective. I walked to the bar and examined a piece of paper which bore a series of unintelligible curves and dots. Zuckerman pushed over the bottle of rum. It was the same black rotgut. I did not touch it.

"Do you read it?" he said.

"No."

"Don't despair. It's only half the message." He handed me a transparent air letter bearing similar nonsense. "Now do you understand?"

"I have no time for this."

"Time is your problem? When is your next engagement?" He placed the second sheet over the first. The markings coalesced and the message came clear:

Jon 33 coming by c 8–7 good worker well trained believer not killer watch B

"What do you get from it?" Zuckerman asked.

"It looks like a help wanted ad."

"And?"

"Simply that a trawler was coming to drop off a young man on a hot summer day. The rest is Bergère's assessment, which I would advise you not to believe."

"It's a little late for that, Jon." He poured out another glass of the black rum. "You've missed the meaning. You had it before, when you looked at the first message. It's meaningless. Both of them are without meaning. Until you put them together. Ah, you see the secret I taught Flake? Juxtaposition, that was the secret of my magazines. And of the network. But they must deal with far more than two's or even three's. That is why, as you know better than I, it is completely foolproof."

"No longer," I said, but he was gazing at me as if he did not for a moment believe in the possibility of my victory, as if he knew my every move in advance and controlled the game entirely. He took a long swallow of the rum. "I heard you died on that," I said.

"Oh? The papers can be so scurrilous."

"Sugar Red wrote me that. Four years ago. Yesterday he was arrested."

Zuckerman's glass slipped in his fingers. He quickly steadied it on the bar.

"Steingut is in custody and he's talking," I said.

"Steingut would never talk."

Mansfield can make anybody talk."

"Who is Mansfield?"

"The government man on your payroll."

"Never heard of him."

"You are lying."

"Correct," he said. "I am." He turned and walked out on the sundeck.

I joined him at the railing. "I still love this sea the best," Zuckerman said. He lit a cigarette, cupping the flame from the wind with a trembling hand. Down at the shore, Jenny and the boy were constructing an elaborate, many-layered sand castle. "May I?" Zuckerman said. I gave him the binoculars.

"I respect people who know when I'm lying," he said. "For such deserving men the most appropriate reward is the truth."

"Manley, I know the truth."

"Oh? That, too." He raised the binoculars to the horizon. "I wonder if you know how peaceful my village is. I'll wager not. There are more pigs and goats than people, which is a desirable state of affairs. Some would say the color of that sea is more beautiful, but I have missed this spot." He adjusted the binoculars and lowered them to the beach. "Have you ever been there, Jon? A few tourists come to a bay nearby to see the phosphorescent water. I can tell you that much because I won't be returning."

"You came back," I said.

"My, you are observant."

"Why are you here?"

"But that's what I asked you. Perhaps, after all, we have the same reason. I've been waiting for a man. I plan to kill him."

"It won't help you to kill me, Zuckerman. The whole thing is smashed."

"You're quite wrong, Jon. This network is perfect. Really, now, I should know. I built it. A few lost links like Sugar Red can't harm the chain." He put a hand on my shoulder. "You're bluffing, aren't you, Jon? Don't you know this? I have no secrets from you. Perhaps you have secrets from yourself."

I seized the lapels of his bathrobe. He smiled at the annoyance.

"Why hold me responsible?" he said. "Simply because I've made more money from it? But money means nothing to you. You could have done the same if you'd wanted to."

I released him. He leaned back against the wooden railing and turned to watching the building of the sand castle.

"The boy is Tina's," he said.

"I know."

"But have you any conception of his worth? Only while I'm alive, mind you. I will have nothing to leave him. During the next two decades I intend to spend everything. And the house in Puerto Rico, unfortunately, must be abandoned. A man named Smith discovered it, did you know him? Poor fellow. As for this tasteless pleasure dome, it's not mine, it's theirs. I gave them these acres of sand outright, which may have been the only mistake I ever made. They really have no appreciation, do they? I suppose it's been a rather useful meeting place for them."

"You betrayed us."

"Not at all. I didn't change a thing. Everything I have done has been for the single purpose of destroying the system that we both detest. Come, you don't really think I did it for money, do you? In the world of my village, I am the unseen gringo in the house on the hill, a man of great works. Name your favorite charity and I'll give it twenty percent of everything I have. Don't you see, Jon, I merely improved our operation. What earthly good was it to continue sending Bergère his little tidbits? You don't imagine that anyone can win a war these days. It must all be waged within. Don't stir up the enemy to revolution, lull him to passivity. Make of him not an activist but a voyeur and a junkie. Have pity on him. Give him his dreams."

"It won't wash. The money was everything."

"Just recompense for a just cause. But, really, Jon, all of this is quite academic. For what kind of truth did you come here? God's truth? Honest to God's truth? Will you settle for honest to Alexander Manley's truth? I really don't know what you have in mind."

"This." I pulled from my pocket the message from Steingut, the first message of those ten days. The twelve trains to Babylon.

Zuckerman glanced at it and turned back to the binoculars.

"You sent this," I said.

"No."

"You're not going to do this to me, Zuckerman. I know you sent it. Sugar Red swore he just passed it on."

"True."

"Dammit, Zuckerman, I know you're Torre."

"Of course. But it was you who passed that message to me on a schedule, remember? It was carried out like every other operation with Torre. All the baggage has come from you, Jon."

"I did not originate that message."

"But you know who did," he said.

"No. I do not."

"Then we should band together, Jon, for we are both in danger. Do you know what I'm talking about?"

"No."

"He didn't reach you? I wish I could believe you. Surely, you must know that the man I am waiting to kill is the one who sent the message."

"Are you speaking of suicide, Zuckerman?"

"It's neither you nor I, but you may know him. Do you see it?" He handed me the binoculars.

"What?"

"Look far out. At the edge of the fog."

When I had cleared the binoculars, I saw only high waves, remnants of the mist, and two small fishing boats bobbing in the sea.

"Do you see it?" Zuckerman said.

"See what?"

"The trawler."

"No."

"It's back, Jon. Bergère has sent another man."

He had arrived with the first rays of the sun exactly two weeks before, wet, hungry, exhausted, bearing the ink signal on his palm. Crackjaw, alone in the house, at first thought it a nightmare when the huge figure appeared in a pool of water at his bedside. "I am from Bergère," the man said. "You will take me to Jon."

As we strolled the beach, Zuckerman related the tale as a shared mystery. He was talking quite honestly, it appeared. What puzzled me initially was why. Gradually, it came clear, that neither of us could grasp the truth without the other. Zuckerman watched me carefully as he spoke, and I masked surprise at whatever information was new. My safety was assured by his fear that the man had, indeed, reached me. It was a brotherhood of foes, each aware of the other's threat, both joined to assess a common danger. The arrival of Bergère's man not only menaced the survival of Zuckerman's converted network. If I knew Bergère, he would be chiefly concerned that the American failure not be linked to him. The man had orders to find me, question me, and kill me.

Passing the sand castle, in what must have seemed cordial conversation, I nodded to Jenny to indicate that all was well. She looked thoroughly perplexed. About forty yards east, Zuckerman stopped and raised the binoculars again. We took turns, with no results.

"Have you yourself seen it?" I asked.

"I thought so. Yesterday."

"You're having hallucinations."

"That's where he is," Zuckerman said. "He's waiting."

"For what?"

"I wish I knew. For me perhaps, or you. He told Crackjaw he would return today. He did not stay long in the city. His clothes are wrong, he has a bad accent."

"What does he look like?"

"You know, Jon. You must have communicated with him."

"What was Crackjaw's description?"

"Very large. Not bright. Decidedly nasty."

We were both, however, wary of the description. To the waking Crackjaw, the man must have loomed as a fierce giant. It would also have been necessary to malign his intelligence, for his outwitting of Crackjaw had brought about the whole disaster.

Crackjaw, by Zuckerman's account, truthfully stated that he had no idea where to find me. The man was unimpressed. He insisted, citing Bergère's authority. Crackjaw, whom Zuckerman trusted as his liaison with Sugar Red, was in a panic. He could not allow Sugar Red to know of the man's presence nor the man to know of Zuckerman's good health. He attempted to send a cable to Puerto Rico but could not. The man was constantly at his side. For that entire day, the Monday before I received the message, Crackjaw was virtually held prisoner. The man demanded food, which he was served, and fresh clothes, which were not available in his size. Crackjaw dared complete only one telephone call, giving sick notice to his employer at Coney Island.

A meeting at the cottage to discuss a shipment had been scheduled for eleven o'clock Tuesday morning. Crackjaw knew that if the intruder were in the house when they arrived, it would all be over. In the dead of night he crept into the man's bedroom, prepared for an easy killing. His victim was sitting up, fully dressed, very much awake.

"I should acquaint you with two numbers," the man said. "The trawler sits exactly four miles out. They come in for me in seventy-two hours." He then lay down and closed his eyes. Crackjaw did not sleep that night.

Early the next morning, Crackjaw decided there was no recourse but to telephone Sugar Red, informing him, as obliquely as possible, that he must contact his superiors and cancel the meeting. The man listened to the conversation on an extension. At the end, he asked that he be taken to Sugar Red. Crackjaw refused, claiming that Sugar Red was a friend who knew nothing of the network. The man did not believe him. For the first time he hinted at Bergère's knowledge that the operation had changed.

The man had retained the telephone number from the operator's placement of the call. In the face of Crackjaw's intransigence, he called Sugar Red himself. It was arranged that Crackjaw would bring the man to Sugar Red's apartment on Thursday morning.

"So you want to reach Jon." Sugar Red, so Crackjaw told Zuckerman, appeared unperturbed, coolly determined to put the crisis to rest. "I believe there was a man named Jon," he said. "Unfortunately, my information was that he died shortly after Emil Zuckerman. Nearly all of us were killed. The network has been abandoned. I'm sorry."

The man wanted proof.

"Why don't we do this?" Sugar Red suggested. "Write him a message. I will transmit it through the old channels. If he is not dead, it will reach him."

While the man composed the message on Sugar Red's typewriter, Crackjaw and Sugar Red conferred in the kitchen. They came to agreement that the man could not be killed. It would only confirm Bergère's suspicion. But Crackjaw was angered by Sugar Red's concession of the message. He could not understand it. The conversation was interrupted by the man standing in the doorway, holding out the message.

"What is this about Babylon?" Sugar Red asked. "That is only a recent name for the house on Fire Island. Jon, if he is still alive, would not know it."

"Send it," the man said.

"Don't send it," Crackjaw whispered as he and the man departed.

"But he did, Jon," Zuckerman said. "He was keen to see what you would do. That, you may guess, was not a good reflection on me. I had assured them long before that the network was irrevocably cut off from Bergère."

"When did you learn all this?" I asked.

"It's not news to you, is it, Jon."

"When?" I repeated.

"Too late. Only that afternoon, after the man had left the island, promising to return today."

"Did the trawler come in?"

"No. He paddled out in a raft. The minute he disappeared, Crackjaw phoned me in Puerto Rico, a very dangerous procedure. 'What is Babylon?' I inquired. He explained that the fools had posted a name for their house, which the man had clearly seen. 'Stop the letter!' I said. But a half hour later, Crackjaw relayed Sugar Red's refusal. I left for New York immediately."

"I know. Did you see Sugar Red?"

"He met me in a car at the airport to reiterate his position. We reached a compromise. He would send a second special delivery letter, this one to Mansfield, changing his mission. I would become Torre and ascertain the difficulties. Sugar Red assented in a most surly manner. Unless the matter were cleared up, he said, his superiors would be convinced they had bought faulty merchandise. I was to look into the old network, tighten it, and return it in better form. That was his reason, but not mine. I intended to stop the letter."

"Mansfield doesn't know what it means," I said.

"Probably not. Unless you told him." He raised an eyebrow but accepted my silence. "Bergère sent me that code the month of your arrival, ultimately to be used, I am sure he anticipated, by one of us against the other. Over here, only you and I know it, Jon. Probably. The success of my network has not depended upon probabilities."

"Then it was all Sugar Red's stupidity."

"If he had known the code," Zuckerman said. "But he did not. I do not fault him. He took action by his lights to find how best to save the network. Do not underrate Sugar Red. He is, I believe they call them, a soldier. A brilliant soldier. Self-taught, of course, which leads to interesting speculations on the futility of formal education."

"You should not have let them kill Steingut," I said.

Zuckerman pulled out a heavy sigh from his bag of tricks.

"A dear friend. Honestly. As you well know, he was a clever and faithful man, too much so to make the switch in matériel without discovery and subsequent pangs of conscience. They guaranteed to me that he would go painlessly. But why be morbid, Jon, can't we at least share the laugh on Bergère? Soaring over the clouds, I could just see his face as he read my glowing obituary. I do pity him, of course."

If Bergère had suspected Zuckerman long ago, as had been my guess, he was right. The game, Zuckerman freely told me, was already afoot when I arrived. Only weeks before, Sugar Red had dropped into Zuckerman's office, sent to buy a piece of the magazines.

"There was no one but Steingut in whose ingenuity I could have complete faith," he said, "until I came to know Sugar Red. Just between us, I was at first aghast that such an apparently untutored man had been dispatched to negotiate with Zuckerman Enterprises."

"When did they take control?"

"Don't accuse, Jon, it's unseemly. I had little choice. I knew full well their intention to run me into the ground and then buy me out of bankruptcy. Muscling in, I believe it's called. Who, after all, would come to the aid of a man in my business? What would you have done? Gone to the police? Should I have compromised my principles for the pleasure of receiving a bullet in the head?"

He had found Sugar Red, he said, a "marvelously persuasive man." In the course of their transaction, they became interested in each other's true profession. "We stumbled upon a remarkable simpatico." Zuckerman hesitated a moment and then lowered his voice, as if he were imparting the first real confidence of our discussion. "I found that he could secure free models for the magazines. And rather superior models. It was a very neat juxtaposition of talents. He hooked them and I gained their services. An excellent enterprise."

He was watching my hands with amusement. They were foolishly clenched into fists.

"Really, Jon," he said sympathetically, "you shouldn't have worried about her. She was delightfully easy to convince. I merely stressed that you might be on the brink of liquidation. We had no trouble with her at all. And she protected you valiantly. Too bad she didn't protect me as well."

"I'm afraid she did."

"I wish I could believe that. But she told you I was alive."

"No," I said.

"Oh, that's rare. That would be my greatest triumph, knowing that she lied to you. But, of course, it's you who are lying."

The sudden shift in his tone made me stop and glance back over my shoulder. We had come too far. I could no longer see Jenny. The real menace of Zuckerman was revealed to me fully in that flash of fear. His old cover as pornographer was closer to the man than the operative underneath. He was his cover.

"Let's go back," I said.

"Your lies come too late," Zuckerman said softly. "Why waste them to protect a photograph?"

I turned around and began walking west.

He caught up with me, a little breathless, speaking more quickly now, sensing my concern, striving nervously to regain his credibility. "Well, my friend, she could not have told you a great deal else," he said, still probing. "Only that she and that little devil were under my wing. I told her nothing about the network. But for one error, right, Jon? That's how you found out about Steingut's demise, isn't it."

"How did she know?"

"Tears. Look! Look at me. Shall I shed them now? I am capable. I didn't know till that day. But when they told me my loyal friend must go, well, I knew they were right, but I could not help myself. Do you believe me? Bawling in front of her that night, what a terrible thing. I had to tell her the truth."

"Faster," I said. "Let's walk faster."

"But she smiled, can you guess why? Sugar Red was smart enough to know. I was too vain to see it. He understood that girl from the moment I introduced them. Tell me, Jon, would you have ever believed she would go on the needle? Sugar Red knew.

From the eyes, he said. She was a natural. I told him that she smiled at the prospect of my departure. It was a nasty crack he made, but true. She was delighted to get rid of me, he said. Why, do you know, she even selected my new name, Alexander Manley."

He had gone there because of difficulties with the shipments through Puerto Rico. He was to establish a twin system. As I had deduced, our network was acquired with Sugar Red trained and installed as Steingut. Sugar Red asked if the man to whom the messages were sent could be trusted not to know anything had changed. "Of course Jon is trustworthy," Zuckerman claimed as his reply. "I have succeeded in isolating him from knowledge of any other member of the network." Sugar Red was astute enough to know this could only mean that Zuckerman did not trust me.

"Now, really, Jon," Zuckerman said, "I saved your life. You could easily have been eliminated at that moment. It would have involved nothing more than breaking a promise to Tina. Yet you must know that I am a very sentimental man. I could not lie to Tina. The year before I left, every time I saw her she asked me if you were still in the country. Every time I saw her!"

He was suddenly angry. And, just as suddenly, he relaxed. "I could have disposed of you," he said gently, "and she would have never known. But I could not lie to her."

"Then she wouldn't go with you."

"They wouldn't let me take her!" Again he struggled angrily with himself. I wondered how many selves were at war in that creature. There were probably dangerously more than I had calculated.

It was the pleasant voice that resumed, the one I had heard when I first met Emil Zuckerman. "They said she was making too much money for the magazines. She was their property. And so I left, sad to leave, but sure in my mind that someday Tina and our boy would join me."

"But you came back," I said.

"That's the second time you've noticed that," he said. "It's very flattering."

As we approached the sand castle, I heard the boy crying. Jenny was standing strangely erect. Her face was contorted.

"Thank heavens," Zuckerman said. "He has returned."

Crackjaw, I then saw, was standing behind Jenny, holding her arm twisted high behind her back.

"This is Jon's girl. That son-of-a-bitch must be — " Crackjaw caught sight of me and stopped short.

"We're all acquainted," Zuckerman said.

"He's hurting Aunt Jenny!" the boy screamed. "He's hurting her!"

I started for Crackjaw. Zuckerman blocked the way.

"Let her alone, Crackjaw," he said.

Crackjaw released his grip.

"He hurt Aunt Jenny!" the boy insisted.

"Into the corner!" Zuckerman roared at the boy. "You will stand in the corner of your bedroom and face the wall!" The boy was terrified. He marched obediently up the steps to the house. Jenny watched helplessly, looking to me for a signal that did not come. Zuckerman smiled at her. "It's for his own good," he said. "I don't want him to hear this. He is too young to understand, but you, Aunt Jenny, should know what kind of company you've been keeping. Your friend Jon ordered the boy's mother killed."

"I told you!" Crackjaw gloated. "You wouldn't believe me at Coney, would you? I told you the order came from Torre to me."

"Don't believe any of this, Jenny," I said.

"I don't."

"But I think you do, Aunt Jenny," Zuckerman said.

"How long are you going to make him stand in that corner?" Jenny said.

"Now, Crackjaw," Zuckerman said, ignoring Jenny's plea, "exactly what did you tell these two at Coney Island?"

"I didn't touch them."

"What did you tell them?"

"You should have let me finish him in the first place. You shouldn't have stopped me."

"Did you tell him that? How much did you tell him?"

From Zuckerman's tone, it began to appear that Crackjaw would soon be sent to join the boy in the corner.

"I just told him that Torre gave the order on the girl."

"Well, Jon knows I'm Torre," Zuckerman said, "and I took my orders from him."

"I was right!" Crackjaw pointed a finger at me. "He's the one. He killed the girl."

Jenny's hand flew up to her forehead. I thought she might faint.

"They're lying," I said. "The man at Customs, Mansfield, has the whole story. His only mistake was thinking that Zuckerman had been killed."

Crackjaw laughed as if I had said something hilarious.

"Do you see what I mean?" Zuckerman said. "No one knows. Not even Steingut. Because he no longer exists."

Far from fainting, Jenny was beginning to smile.

"But I know where he went, Mr. Zuckerman," she said.

I tried to stop her but she was already pointing out to sea.

"Oh?" Zuckerman lit a cigarette. His hands were no longer shaking. "Have you ever had your picture in the magazines, Aunt Jenny?"

"No."

The smoke drifted up from his mouth. He sucked it into his nostrils. "We must do something about that," he said.

"She knows everything," Crackjaw said.

"But she is a lady," Zuckerman said, "and you are forgetting yourself. Tell her, Crackjaw, why I left you behind when I went to Puerto Rico."

"To guard the driftwood," Crackjaw said. "Listen, it wasn't my fault they built this thing. I tried — "

"That's not what I mean," Zuckerman snapped. "Tell them the other reason."

Crackjaw started to speak and then stopped.

"Tell them," Zuckerman said.

"To guard the girl."

"Yes, you see? To guard Tina from harm. You should know that, Jon, before you make rash judgments." He was playing it all for Jenny now, catching her smile, once again going to elaborate pains to isolate me. "I wonder, Aunt Jenny, if you would care to take a guess at something. While you were playing here with the boy, what was the nature of Jon's conversation with me? Care to try?"

"No."

"But it's simple. He offered your life for his. He has it well planned. He will take a boat far across the sea and leave you here with me. Of course, I have refused. Not that I didn't tolerate all that he had to say, but he hasn't convinced me. He has not, as I thought he had, been in contact with Bergère's man. In fact, despite his pretense, he knows nothing at all of use to me. It's been a very great disappointment. So, for now, you may join the boy, Aunt Jenny. Escort her, Crackjaw. And don't touch them!" It was then that he pulled the gun.

I sat across the room from the door, calculating the distance, looking down the gun-barrel, calculating the distance to the door, watching him rip the telephone cord from the wall. Surely, he was staging a melodrama for his old magazines. Any minute the photographers would be there to catch Jenny being flailed by a dwarf with a chain while I was held at bay by the fiendish Dr. Zuckerman. Beneath it all the caption would read: "Prepare yourself for the journey to hell." Oh, it had to be a game. That's the way they do it in America.

"Relax," he said. "There's nothing to fear from me. Crackjaw is the real expert on pictures."

"Please bring them up."

"You wouldn't want that, Jon. This room will not be safe for long."

"What will you do to them?"

"Nothing. I pledge it. My intention is that you should rest in peace."

"When?"

"The precise second that Bergère's man returns."

"He's not coming back," I said.

"You can't bluff it any longer, Jon. He gave Crackjaw his word."

"He won't keep his word."

"You don't know him."

"Oh, yes I do." Zuckerman nearly dropped his guard, but he recovered. "He would not take the chance," I said. "Before, he had surprise with him. Now, he knows that he might be ambushed."

"Don't jest. You haven't seen this man."

"I have seen him, Zuckerman. Years ago I spent time enough with him. He is the man whom Bergère would pick to find me."

"Who?"

"A man named Garneau."

"Large and nasty?"

"Indeed he is."

"Fine. And he will come back, Jon. He has to. My promise to Tina still lives. If you die, it must be Bergère's doing, not mine."

"Then put down the gun."

"Unless you force it to be mine. But I would much prefer what I have visualized ever since you walked in this morning and made a shambles of my breakfast. Watch now." He slid open the door opposite me and walked back into the room to a far window. "He will enter that door and see you immediately. Before you move an inch, he shoots you. Before he moves an inch, I shoot him. Perfect?"

"No. There would be men on the trawler waiting for him."

"Let them wait. I won't be here."

"But the other men," I said, "the three who were here this morning. They plan to kill you. I heard them."

"I won't be in Puerto Rico either. I will be a man they do not know in a place they cannot find."

The distance, I concluded, was twenty-seven feet. At that range, I did not choose to question the accuracy of Zuckerman's aim at a moving target, either Garneau or me.

"There's Mansfield," I said. "He'll find you."

"Try again. Mansfield believes I am dead."

"Smith reported to him."

"Are you trying to frighten me, Jon? It won't change your situation. Smith never saw me. He was really quite incompetent. His first brilliant success was also his last. Problems arose, didn't they, with a simple gray suitcase." A long cigarette ash dropped to the floor. Zuckerman spread it with the sole of his sandal. "Any more little theories, Jon? No? My thanks for your help. We now know that my plan is perfect. Whether Bergère's emissary arrives in one hour or five is of no consequence to me. It will be well worth the wait."

"Zuckerman, I know this man Garneau. I tell you, he would not chance coming back to this house."

"But suppose it is not Garneau."

"No one but a fool would chance it," I said.

"So perhaps Bergère has sent a fool. He did once before."

"Why is it so important to you that I be killed?"

"Simple justice. You nearly killed me with that suitcase. Don't you appreciate how very lucky I was to live through the night? I returned last night to meet with three of Sugar Red's more impatient friends. In this very room. Not very savory types. They were rather disappointed that I had failed to bring you along. They thought I had the suitcase. They actually threatened me with bodily harm."

"Mansfield has the suitcase," I said.

"Exactly what I told them. Unfortunately, they knew I was guessing."

The men informed him that, in view of the recent events, a decision had been reached to dispense with the services of several key people. Zuckerman maintained it was unnecessary, he only needed a little more time to straighten things out. "Again, Jon, do you see how I tried to save you?"

"I have met those men," I said. "One of them claimed his name was Torre."

"He would like to be. God, they are stupid. They think they know my business. I captured the drift of it, Jon. They would have disposed of us one by one. They are all liars. I am not responsible for their lies. They are not my kind of people."

The discussion had continued through the night. One of the

men, I assumed my interrogator, was fairly pleasant. "Were it not for him," Zuckerman conceded, "I would not be here." But he, too, was firm. He had his orders. He was to assume the duties of Torre and Zuckerman was to return to Puerto Rico. They did not dare risk touching Mansfield.

"I tell you this, Jon, so that there shall be no doubt in this room that I did everything I could to keep you alive. It was not only for Tina. I respected your own wishes. You have always placed an absurd priority on animated objects. I could tell it the day you arrived, when you scorned my photographs. You scorned them. I saw! You did!"

He took an angry step toward me.

"The message," I said quickly, trying to divert him.

"What's that?" His expression was more peculiar than ever. He seemed to be struggling against some schizoid demon, touching the borderline between roles and then pulling back, wondering, as I was, whether the man standing there was Zuckerman, Manley, Torre, or perhaps another being entirely.

"The twelve trains to Babylon," I said.

"But don't you see?" he said. "I thought you were working with Bergère's man. Put yourself in my shoes at that moment, as I had put myself into Torre's. You frightened me half to death. I reached into the schedule rack for Mansfield's Friday morning mail, fully aware of what it would be. But to see it, Jon, actually to see it! Well, now, you'd just have to call that a moment of terror, nothing short. I was sure that you had discovered my secret, that you knew everything. Who, after all, was the traitor?"

"But the other message," I said. "The second train, to liquidate."

"I sent it."

He lowered the gun and moved to the door, watching the sea. "I tried to reach you, Jon, and deal with it directly. It was a risky enterprise, my visit to McSorley's. And this man Thaddeus was most uncooperative. I did not like him one bit." He was silent. I wondered if he might actually have forgotten the gun in his hand. It was possible. For all his protestations, he could kill me or spare me with less interest in the choice than in selecting a photograph.

"You surprised me at the locker, oh, what a complete mess you made of that!" he said, as if the memory had suddenly assaulted him, wiping out for that instant everything else. "How could I have talked with you right out in the open? I waited for you in the Lady in the Skies chapel. But you never came. Didn't you have the sense to see it was the only possible hiding place? What did you think, I would jump in the pool? You made it very sticky for me. Some Customs men came in. Perhaps I should thank God that their superstitious upbringing prevailed over intelligence. They searched the pews thoroughly. They did not check the altar."

He turned and raised the gun. "I do wish you hadn't taken that suitcase, Jon."

"There was nothing of value in it."

"Yes, there was."

"Mansfield took it out," I said.

"No. Tina did. She must have. I was in love with that bitch and you made her the traitor."

He waited for me to erupt, his eyes beginning to focus on mine again. Mine shifted to the barrel of the gun.

"You see, Crackjaw is brighter than you credit him," Zuckerman said slowly. "You did kill Tina."

There was no need to contradict. I would let him have his lie. It was an easy trade for Jenny's life. If I misstepped and killed myself, she, too, would be gone. Zuckerman, little knowing, was allowing me to save Jenny. Because the price was ironic did not mean it was high. I had only to buy time by agreeing that I had killed Tina. And so I nodded.

Zuckerman betrayed his relief. "Ah, you did. For when you received the second message, instead of going to La Guardia, where Sugar Red's people were waiting to relieve you of the suitcase and your life, you sensed danger to Tina. You and she were working together. How I would have relished that moment! The two of you together, trapped with each other and the suitcase. What explanation could you have possibly devised, Jon, when you looked up to see me return from the grave? Tell me that. You would have been a jabbering, impotent idiot. Exactly as you viewed me when I first met you, oh, don't deny it, you could not conceal that from me. At last, my friend, she would have seen us together and known what you are!"

The glint in his eye was so special that I almost wished I had not deprived him of that moment.

"Yes, at last!" Zuckerman said. "I knew the real traitors."

"She wasn't."

"You can't protect her now," he said.

"That's not why she was killed."

"I know she told you everything."

"No, Emil," I said softly, "these things are in your mind. You have told me what you feared would happen, but it did not, just as you are waiting here for a man you know will not come back."

"You laughed at me together. She must have told you!"

"But you know she didn't. Someone else gave you that idea. You wanted her, Emil. You could not bear to see us together. You took her away when you heard me come in the building. How could you have killed her? She must have been killed by a lunatic."

"Yes. Yes, she must have been."

"A brilliant man, but he is sick. It was for no reason but his sickness. He is a man who does not know who he is. Once he was a very brave man but they took his bravery away from him. He could not bear the pressure of his corruption. Now he needs help. I came here to help him." I watched the gun. It did not drop. "Who gave you the idea, Emil?"

"Crackjaw. I should not have listened to him. The boy thought it was a game coming down the fire escape. She ran down after him, right into the car, what a fool she was. I don't know which she was after, the boy or the suitcase. I would not have harmed him. No. No, you can't make me believe that. Crackjaw was right."

"You ordered him, didn't you, Emil?"

"What could I say to him when he asked?" It was an apology. "Oh, it was right," he said. "The only way. Crackjaw asked to move her into his car. You must remember, he had guarded her from all harm."

"But you hesitated," I said.

"I asked him why. For the last photograph, he said. That's all he said. I take his judgment on these things. The boy was crying as we drove along behind them but he knew he was safe with me. Would I harm his mother? Yes, that was all it was, we were driving out to Patchogue, we were going to come over here for the last photograph. Only this time, don't you see, I was going to take it!"

I was safe. He no longer saw me.

"He stopped the car." Zuckerman's eyes were wild with the memory. "I pulled over in front of him. They got out. She was screaming for the boy. I took him back to Crackjaw's car, to be with his mother. Crackjaw said to me, why don't we take the picture right here? Yes! I said. Yes! Now! And I watched from his car, with my hand over the boy's eyes. It took just one pose. Just one! And then he came along."

"Who?"

"Jon! It was Jon braking his car and backing up."

"Yes, it was Jon."

"Crackjaw ran back and we watched Jon find the photograph! And then Crackjaw jumped out to take another picture. No! I said. He's one of us."

"You saved Jon," I said. "He's very grateful for that. Crackjaw didn't take a very good picture."

"Yes, I saved Jon."

"Then Crackjaw brought you and your boy out here and he went back with the suitcase to Sugar Red."

"She always wanted me to save Jon."

I lifted the gun from his hand. He did not struggle. He only smiled.

"Call Crackjaw," I said. "I want Jenny here." I pushed the barrel into his chest. He did not move.

"Crackjaw won't hear," he said quietly.

"Shout!"

"Crackjaw!" But the moment he started, I knew it was wrong. I clamped my hand over his mouth. I knew what he would shout. He would call for the final photograph.

I heard a door swing open down below and crash against the side of the house.

"Now back!" I said, but I saw that Zuckerman was too dazed to obey. I pulled him into the chair facing the sundeck and flattened myself against the wall near the door.

Jenny and the boy came in first. He was clutching the hem of her dress. Behind them was Crackjaw, idly swinging the bicycle chain.

"You may drop it," I said.

Crackjaw spun around, raised the chain in the air, looked over at Zuckerman, and stood frozen in the confusion of the moment.

"Drop it," I repeated.

Zuckerman sat staring ahead, smiling serenely, giving Crackjaw no clue.

The chain struck the floor. The boy jumped up into Jenny's arms.

"What else?" I said. Crackjaw shrugged. I slapped his pockets and found the revolver I had seen in his car. I had difficulty breaking it open. When it gave, I emptied out the cartridges and flung them through the doorway. They bounced off the steps down to the sand. Crackjaw shrugged again. I trained the first gun at his head and sent the second smashing into the mirror behind the bar. He was impressed.

"Is my father really an Indian?" the boy said. Jenny smiled and stroked his forehead. It was all over. We had won the game, captured the tepee from the Apaches.

First there was the slowness of time, then the speed, and then there was no time at all. I cannot remember the exact instant it disappeared. When it did, nothing remained but instincts. There was no time to fear they might be wrong.

Before that came the agony of long minutes inspecting the torn telephone cord. That much was a waste of time, perhaps shortening its existence. The repair was beyond my ken. I knew then exactly how Zuckerman had felt when he searched for me. He did not know what to do.

Now the burden was all on me. He sat in the chair at peace. Crackjaw lay face down on the floor, hands outstretched. His knees were oddly bent. He was ready to spring. I clicked the safety catch on and off again and he relaxed.

The boy was watching my clumsy attempt to splice the telephone wires.

"My father is a good Indian, isn't he?" he said.

"No," I said. "Most Indians are good but he is not." I looked to Jenny for approval of my paternal tone. Zuckerman's smile widened. Only Crackjaw, murderous in his humiliation, refused to join in the last game.

"Can't we go now?" Jenny said. "You're scaring the boy to death."

"No, no, this is fun!" the boy said, mistaking Zuckerman's smile. He squeezed tightly on my fingers. For all my uncertainty, I felt like the strongest man on earth, the savior of the innocents. I wondered what the boy would think if he saw me tie the telephone cord around his father's wrists. Would he hate me?

I pushed away his hand. Zuckerman was watching. It was crucial that he not sense affection. There was no escape left but to treat his son as hostage.

"All right, Jenny, I'll bring him. I want you to run." She moved down the steps. I picked up the boy and backed toward the door. There was no fear at all on Zuckerman's face. "I ask you to watch carefully, Zuckerman. You must see us go. You will wait here. Remember that we have your son."

My faith in his concern was not strong. I was not sure why. I hesitated at the door.

"Go ahead, Jon," Zuckerman said.

I stood on the sundeck, not daring to ask.

"He's not a good hostage, is he?" Zuckerman said.

"No."

"But go ahead. You have your son now."

"It's not true," I said. The boy was trembling. "He's yours."

"Oh, that's rare." Zuckerman laughed. "He may as well have been. I paid for him, every bit of him. Didn't I, Jonny? Tell him your name, Jonny, that name I would never allow spoken in my presence. You can say it now. Jonny! Tell him!"

The boy nodded fearfully.

"You knew it when you left her," Zuckerman accused me.

"No. I didn't know."

"But the boy knows," he said. "She told him."

I saw a flash of white. Jenny was standing on the bottom step.

"I told you to run, Jenny."

She stood silently, waiting. She had heard.

I fled down the steps and Jenny followed onto the beach. When I looked back, I saw Crackjaw coming down, the empty revolver already retrieved and in hand. He dropped to his knees and pawed at the sand, searching for the cartridges. Time was still dangerously slow. I was slogging through the sand, feeling the weight of the brace on my neck, holding the boy over my shoulder, enduring the painful slaps of the gun jouncing in my belt, tugging Jenny along by the hand, feeling the muscles strain in her arm, and we had covered less than fifty yards of the beach when I saw the burst of sand ahead of her feet. Then we heard the sound carried on the wind.

"What was that?" Jenny said. I pulled her down and we crawled flat on elbows and thighs until we reached the shelter of the dune.

The boy sat quietly in Jenny's arms, fondling the broken starfish.

"A traveling bullet, Jenny, which should make your vacation complete." She shuddered. I patted her hand. It was an absurd little gesture at such a time. Her smile was wan.

"Did you know, Jon?"

"This is no time."

"You must have known."

"What can I tell you, Jenny? Who can ever know? Does it matter?"

She held the boy tightly.

"Listen to me. Take this." I gave her my wallet. "Look along there, at the curves in the dune. You will run tight against them. He's not light but you can do it. I'm going up. You will start the minute you see me stand up, not before, not after."

"Where do I find the police?"

"You don't, unless you enjoy visiting day at the penitentiary."

"I'm staying."

"He can't stay, Jenny. Take the ferry from Davis Park. Wait for me at the apartment."

Jenny considered for a moment, and then she smiled for my benefit. I was not certain that she believed in my return.

"Goodbye, Jon," she said.

When I arrived at the crest of the dune, I could see the cross-rods of the television antenna reaching up into the sky. I pushed up slowly on my hands and the glass dome came into view. Kneeling, I saw the sundeck. Zuckerman was standing at the railing, holding Jenny's binoculars. Crackjaw was at his side. They were looking in the wrong direction, down toward the cruiser in the cove.

I stood up and ran inland. Crackjaw wheeled and fired. I saw leaves fluttering off a bayberry bush just before I fell into a deep hollow.

The rim of the hollow was nearly my height. I held the gun high over my head and slowly raised my eye to the sight. Crackjaw was scurrying down the steps to the sand. It worked. He had only found two cartridges. And there was Zuckerman at the end of the sight.

"You're doing fine, Jon!" Zuckerman shouted cheerfully.

I took very careful aim at his stomach. It was an expansive target. I could not miss. But I could not shoot.

"Shoot!" Zuckerman said. "You can do it. Just hold the camera a little higher. A little to the left. There you are. Hold it, hold it. Shoot!"

I jumped up out of the hollow. Crackjaw, kneeling on the sand, raised his revolver and jerked the trigger once, twice, three times, trying to locate the right chamber, but he had been correct the first time, and when he returned to it the hammer clicked harmlessly against a sandy cartridge. In a fury, he threw down the revolver and ran up the steps into the house.

Zuckerman had succeeded in focusing the binoculars on me. I slid back down the dune. Far along the beach I saw a tiny figure in white moving away fast. I set out crawling toward the house along the face of the dune.

"Ah, Aunt Jenny, where are you now?" Zuckerman said. "I can't see you, dear."

When I looked up, the house loomed directly above me. I had gone too far. The slats of the sundeck separated Zuckerman and me. I backed off. But there was no shelter.

Then I saw the sand castle. I ran for it.

It was no good. As I lay behind the castle, the waves lapping at my feet, I saw the binoculars trained directly at me. Crackjaw emerged from the house, holding the bicycle chain, and followed Zuckerman's gaze.

"Shoot!" Zuckerman called out. "Why are you so afraid to shoot, Jon? You can't do it, can you? You've never shot a man in your life."

Squeeze, don't pull, Bergère taught me. Watch for the kick. Aim a little low. Always squeeze, never pull. But as my finger squeezed slowly on the trigger, cold sweat broke out on my forehead, my vision was blurred, Zuckerman's maniacal face faded into green water, my hand holding the gun was disconnected from me, as if seeing it through a glass, and there beyond it was the Commander's face, the look of surprise as he saw he was about to die.

"You're afraid to shoot!" Zuckerman screamed. "You don't own a gun, I know that. I know all about you."

There was a shatter of glass. A red pool formed on the sundeck and tiny rivulets trickled through the slats with amazing speed. The bullet had smashed into the binoculars. Zuckerman was staggering, his hands over his eyes.

"I can't see!"

He stumbled on the top step. I expected to see him come tumbling down in a ghastly whirl of arms and legs. But he seized the railing, the bloodied binoculars still strapped to his neck, steadied himself with both hands, and began walking down, step by step. One eye was obscured by blood. The other looked from the distance like an empty socket.

Crackjaw, paralyzed by shock, looked on, unbelieving. It was not until he was three steps from the bottom that Zuckerman began to sway dangerously. One hand trailed off the railing, the other fumbled for its grip and lost, and then Zuckerman fell heavily, face down in the sand. Crackjaw ran down the steps, swinging the chain, and charged across the beach toward my sand castle, blind in his fury to the knowledge that he could yet save his friend, for I saw that Zuckerman was not dead. His fingers were clawing the sand. He was trying to raise his head. He was dying very slowly by suffocation.

Crackjaw was barely ten yards from me when I heard his shriek and saw him leap into the air. The chain flew over his head. He dropped to the sand, clutching his throat. His feet kicked twice, and then all was still.

The horror washed over me. I could not cleanse the sand of the blood. I could only drown the brutality I had intended. I swung my arm hard and winced at the jolt as the cold gun fled my fingers, sailing high over the waves, twirling and diving into the sea. I was mystified. I had fired neither shot.

"Mansfield!"

He raised himself up from behind the dune, smiling grimly, flicking the sand off his seersucker pants with infinite care. I could only laugh. Tears of relief would not do with Mansfield. I watched him make his way down to the beach, relaxed and victorious, his arms swinging as he walked.

"How did you find it?" I said.

"Sugar Red. After some rather intensive questioning." He winked. "Before he made the error of attempting to escape from custody. Russ shot him as he ran out the door."

"Zuckerman," I said. "He's still alive."

"Sugar told me."

"I mean right now! He is still alive!"

We rushed over. Zuckerman had succeeded in moving his head

a few precious inches so that a corner of his mouth was out of the sand. He was breathing in quick gasps. I bent down and dug my fingers under his chin. As I worked to free him, I felt an irresistible pressure. The chin grew heavier, slowly forcing my hand down into the sand until I felt my fingers would break.

Then I saw a black shoe, shined to glass, pressing upon the back of Zuckerman's head. I looked up at Mansfield. He was biting his lip with intense concentration, pushing down with all of his strength, as if he would not be satisfied until his foot was level with the sand. I heard a smothered cry. Zuckerman's legs rose stiffly in the air, his shoulders became rigid, his fingers twitched, then his hands turned palms up.

I stood up slowly to face Mansfield.

"Was it necessary?"

"Yes." He kicked at the sand near Zuckerman's feet, first aimlessly, then deliberately, as if to bury them from his sight. "Don't look at me as if I enjoyed it. I've never killed a man before."

He took off one shoe, the executioner's shoe, and shook the sand from it. Then he squinted up at the sun and breathed deeply. He was asking me to make it easier for him. I waited.

"We could not afford his talking," Mansfield said.

"He was insane. What jury would have believed him?"

"Enough innocence, Jon. I was an angel of mercy. I only administered the coup de grâce."

"You shot two men without warning."

"Is that the evidence you plan to turn?" he said. "You shot them."

"I saw you."

"And I saw you, Jon."

"But I didn't fire."

"Neither did I."

We stared at each other coldly, already in the courtroom vying for the judge's favor, each enraged at the obvious deceit of the other's alibi.

I am not sure at what exact moment Mansfield realized it, too, but I saw the proof in his eyes that neither one of us was lying.

A split second later, shards of glass sprinkled down upon us from the window of the house. I looked up in time to see the glass dome shatter. Then a small orange flame burst upon the sundeck.

As we fell to the sand behind Zuckerman's corpse, Mansfield rapped my arm and pointed across the beach. Jagged white puffs were floating in above the sea.

"Who?" Mansfield said.

Zuckerman's head would not move. I pulled on the binocular strap until it broke. Mansfield scooped out the sand and I yanked the glasses free. One cracked lens survived. Its focus cleared only after we had both applied our strength to the broken knob. More puffs appeared and the wooden stairway behind us splintered.

It came out of the mist, silently, eerily, moving slowly across the crack in the lens, but not, I knew, a trick played by flashes of sun on the waves. This was no ghost ship. I saw clearly five men standing on the bow, four of them in black fisherman's caps. Two held rifles with mounted sights. Another was loading a mortar. The fourth, and the biggest of the men, stood over a machine gun with his back toward shore. The fifth, wearing a stained, visored blue hat, was holding binoculars to his eyes. I recognized him. It was the captain, my friend. He saw me. I was tempted to wave at him. He had not wanted to leave me here that day.

"I can't let you off," he had said.

"But you must. It has to be there."

"Too risky."

"Don't worry," I said. "I'll find him."

Perhaps I should have listened to him.

But I did not wave, for at that moment the big man turned toward me. It was Garneau. He raised the machine gun and the beach erupted in a sandstorm. Mansfield cursed and pulled his revolver. He stood up and ran for the dune. I followed after him. Suddenly, my leg was on fire. It collapsed beneath me and I began to fall, stretching every muscle, straining my shoulders and arms until my fingers felt the sharp bone of Mansfield's ankle as I hit the sand.

Flames were everywhere. My ears rang with sounds so loud that I felt they alone could kill. My God, I was not in it. It was impossible. I was watching it, a spectator before a thundering stage littered with corpses, a bald head buried in the sand, a lifeless dwarf with its feet in the surf, a seersucker suit covered with muck.

A glint of sunlight struck my eyes before something hard came crashing down on the brace. I felt the sting of sand in my eyes and the raw pain of the metal band on my watch scraping off flesh. I looked up at the sun but I was struggling to see distant sparkles above blackness, looking through a dark glass that would not shatter.

Then it was cold. I knew I was conscious, that I must burst through and stay in the sun. Life was still my choice. I tried to see the dune. It seemed like a great mountain casting its shadow over all the earth. My eyes closed and dreams rushed by as I gasped for air.

Bright-colored leaves appeared. Jungle streams were everywhere converging. The cadence of the guns nurtured music, the calliope at Coney Island, the trumpets at Sammy's, until a sharp screech, the sound of the truck in Utrecht, flicked them off. I was lying in a vast silence of smiling masks.

An old man puffed on his pipe, his hair still blond, his cloak flapping in the wind. "Papa!" I tried to say. "I didn't kill her!" His lips moved silently in reply. I read them.

"How is your strength?" he asked.

"Fine."

"Lungs?"

"Excellent."

"How old are you now?"

"Thirty-three."

"A little old for this."

"We'll see."

He vanished and faces merged into faces, masks I could not read, the blood invisible beneath the skin, but I believed them now, even those I did not want to see, Thaddeus and Tina, Nathan P. Silver, the good Doctor Bernardi, Joe Hull, the Belgian girl tugging at my sleeve, and a little Dutch boy was skating backward on the pond.

"Jonny, Jonny, Jonny! I knew you were mine!"

It was my scream I heard, and with it, sound returned, tiny throbs inside. They were drowned out by a deafening rhythm outside, the unknown terror which gave birth to courage, nothing could ever frighten me so again. It was a booming thunder, the pulse of the ocean.

I opened my eyes. The tide was coming in. The waves were approaching the sand castle. It was still standing. I scanned the sea. The trawler was gone.

Mansfield was lying very still. I had come to accept his death before he said quietly, "Did they get you, Jon?"

He contained his irritation until we were well outside the clinic door.

"I knew it," he said. "No Blue Cross."

"I'll pay you back," I said.

"With what?"

Mansfield opened the car door for me, making sure to use the taped hand.

"Thanks, martyr," I said.

"And stay there!" He slammed the door and locked it. The inside handle had been removed.

I stretched my neck gratefully and rolled down my pant leg to cover the bandage. That much was a fair trade. The brace was gone.

"They're crazy," he said as we pulled away. "This will be a goddamn international incident."

"I don't see you running to call the Coast Guard."

"How could they miss it?"

"Mansfield, I crossed the ocean with that captain. He knows every line of the Coast Guard schedules. By now he is miles out, papers in order, not a weapon aboard. The whole thing could not have taken more than ten minutes."

"It seemed like a lifetime," he said.

"Yes."

The car bumped across the railroad tracks and moved past a block of tawdry storefronts.

"She's fast," Mansfield said.

"Who?"

"I saw her running along the beach. Who was the boy?"

"I don't know."

"Where were they going?"

"I don't know."

It was the last ride. I hoped it would go more quickly than the others. But he seemed to be in no great hurry.

"What will you do?" I asked him.

"About you?"

"About yourself."

"I'm not exactly sure, any brilliant suggestions? Shall I be a patriot and ruin my family? I suspect I will keep right on. I still have a job to do."

"We might have done better not to play possum," I said. "Some things are worse than death."

"Maybe. How many times have we killed you over here?"

"Seven or eight."

"That doesn't leave you much margin for error."

I would surprise him at the trial, I decided. When the moment came for my first appearance on the stand, a moment for which he had prepared every conceivable defense against my counter-accusations, I would say simply, "Mansfield? Is that his name? The one who was always whistling the 'Star Spangled Banner'? Well, I'm sure he's an extremely loyal and competent official, but I regret to say he arrested the wrong man." And Mansfield, long before he felt relief, would sit there boiling with anger, suffering the ultimate humiliation of being saved by the man he sought to doom. Yes, I would have him there, all right.

"What's the grin?" he asked.

"A plan I have."

"Please don't knock me out again. There's no point in escaping."

"It's better than that."

"Because I'm going to release you."

"What?"

"That's right. You're free."

"Damn you, Mansfield, don't you have the guts to get on that witness stand?"

"As you are so fond of reminding me, Jon, we made a bargain. You gave me Steingut and Torre, I am giving you your life, what's left of it. You're welcome."

I was, of course, thankful. But not for an instant grateful.

"Naturally, I will have to file a report," he said.

"When?"

"First thing in the morning. That gives you something like nineteen hours."

"I only need six."

The highway was clear but he stayed well below the limit. It was maddening.

"Will they go with you?" he asked.

"I don't know. I promised to make everything up to her, but I'll never be able."

"We'll be after you, Jon. So will Bergère. And, worse, so will our mutual enemies in the syndicate. How far can you go? It's a hell on earth you'd be offering."

"She'll have to decide," I said.

"Yes. I suppose you wouldn't be interested in knowing what Russ found in Sugar Red's cash register."

"Money, I assume."

"And this." He reached under the seat and pulled out the familiar manila envelope. A cold hand clutched my heart. "It's addressed to you, Jon."

"I know."

"Aren't you the least bit curious?"

"Those are instructions. Whatever they are, they're too late." I saw that the flap was open. "That's a federal offense," I said.

"It was unclaimed. But you're right. There's not much in it." He stuffed it in my pocket.

"You're really not going to read it?" he said a few minutes later.

"No."

When at last we pulled up to the curb on Schermerhorn Street, his smile was actually apologetic.

"It's the best I can do," he said. "Some day they will get you."

"Do you want to bet?"

He reached into his pocket for the quarter but it never came out.

"No," he said. "I don't."

I watched after the car as it turned the corner and disappeared. Then I pulled the letter from the envelope.

> *This is your last mission.*
> *You need not search for a*
> *code.*
> *Count to ten. Look up and*
> *you will see me. Pray.*
>   S

I did not count to ten before looking up. The man was standing on the corner, looking off in the distance, apparently satisfying himself that Mansfield's car was well gone. He was beefy and short-legged, making his black raincoat too long on the bottom but a size too small on top. When he turned back, a tentative smile crossed his pink, chubby face. He thrust his hands into his pockets and moved toward me with all the grace of a baby hippopotamus.

The waddle marked him for me. I remembered. He was the "tourist" who a week before had plumped down on the next stool in Fisher's Tavern and claimed to the boys that his wallet was empty. I had taken pity on him and suggested that he offer cigarettes to protect his money. He was the quintessence of innocence. I should have known better.

Six feet from me, he stopped, glanced around, then moved closer. I saw the fear in his eyes. It made him all the more menacing. A frightened man at that moment seemed far more dangerous to me than a confident one.

305

"Jon?" The whine in his voice made my identification positive. He searched my face, perhaps wondering if I recalled our first encounter. "I've been waiting for you," he said.

"So they didn't kill you after all," I said.

"No."

"Whose corpse was it?"

He seemed puzzled.

"Who are you?" I asked.

"Dougherty."

"Code name Steingut?"

"Code name Dougherty."

"What makes you think I am Jon?"

"The bartender called you that," he said.

"Do you know who he was?"

"No."

"He replaced you, Steingut, haven't you heard?"

"I haven't heard anything," he said. "That's why I've been looking for you."

"Well, he's finished. Zuckerman's gone, too. Killing me is hardly worth your while."

"Killing — but I'm Dougherty. I don't know those names. I know Torre. I'm the man Torre delivers to."

I looked again at the message.

"You didn't write this?" I asked him.

"What is it?"

"I'm not sure. Mansfield's last joke. Or Sugar Red's last piece of vanity." And my last error. I could not afford another. I was more than lucky to have survived this one. "Did anyone go in this building?"

"A girl with a small boy," he said. "Less than an hour ago."

"How long have you been waiting here for me?"

"Four hours. This time."

"You've been here before?"

"A week ago. Twice that Monday. The first time I followed Torre here."

"Torre was here?"

"That's right."

"What does he look like?"

"Don't joke with me," he said. "You know him."

"Describe him."

"A fairly big man. He smokes little cigars. These days he's wearing seersucker."

"Listen, Dougherty, did you see the man who just dropped me here?"

"No, I couldn't see him."

"Well, that's your Torre. You've lost him again."

"Oh, no!"

That was it. The links were torn apart and beginning to roll. The last people I wanted to see and suffer for now were those poor souls lost in ignorance. But I was to be spared nothing.

It was not Mansfield's doing. How could I have thought him that diabolical, when we had crossed the Styx together on the beach? All he had sought was the simple pleasure of hearing me sigh in relief when I read the message and saw how close I had come to dying at Sugar Red's hands. Poor Sugar. He missed his chance.

Sugar Red, Joe Hull, Crackjaw, Zuckerman, Tina, was I to blame for a million more? And now you, Dougherty, why must you haunt me? I am not responsible. You made your choice. This is the way it ended. There are no more questions to be asked, no more puzzles to be solved. You are only one man. Hundreds more are in it, wondering, just as you. The network is finished. Accept it. You will never know the reason. You will never find Torre. Don't bother to search. I have done it all for you.

I reached for my wallet. "Is it money, Dougherty?" The wallet was gone. I had given it to Jenny.

"Not for myself," he said. "Michaels is anxious."

"Who is he?"

"The next man. Torre would leave the money and I would pass on Michaels' share."

I pulled the two fifties from my belt. Dougherty raised his right hand in protest but his left managed to pocket the money.

"It's all the same," I said. "Torre and I were both paid by the same man."

"Do you know what's happened?" he asked.

"Yes. You're through." His shoulders began to tremble. "Not just you, Dougherty. We're all through."

"But why?"

"They've broken us, that's all."

"I knew it. I knew it, I knew it. Things haven't felt right for a long time. I was never sure why. Maybe I brought us bad luck. Just one day. I arrived early for a pickup to see if I could spot Torre. I spotted him, all right, but he left too fast. At least I found out what he looked like. I broke the rule. Bad luck."

"It's always a temptation," I said.

"Last Monday he came late. He left nothing for me. There was only one conclusion: he was working the same game. He was trying to spot me."

"Did he?"

"No, sir, not me. I followed him. And this is where he came."

"Yes, I remember. He and I had a bit of a conversation in there and then he drove away fast. Lost you again, eh? So when I came out, you followed me. You've been a busy fellow, Dougherty."

"You ate at McSorley's. Then you traveled up Sixth Avenue to make a phone call. It began to rain. You bought an umbrella and went down to Fisher's Tavern."

"Enter Dougherty."

"Then you came back here again and stood over there watching the building. You ran across and came out with an envelope, just like that one. I lost you in the subway."

"I went uptown to see a girl."

"Last Friday," he said. "Torre was supposed to make a drop. He never appeared. I returned yesterday. Sunday is our safeguard. And again, no Torre. So today I decided to stake this place out. He was here at least once, I saw you here twice. Now tell me what's in there."

"Nothing that concerns you."

"I have a right to know."

"Whatever it is, Dougherty, it won't be there long."

I turned to go in.

"Wait a minute," he said. "That message. Would it help me to know?"

"Dougherty, what's your job?"

"I can't say."

"With the government?"

"Yes."

"Listen to me now. Get back to work. Your cover is all you have left. And send word to Michaels that it's all off."

"Just like that."

"Forget everything. Clean slate. I say this for your own good. Don't try to follow me. Don't be seen anywhere near me. They're after me, and they are more numerous than you would ever guess. They'll be after you, too. You're next. All of us, one by one. I can't guarantee that any of us will escape. But you're not helping yourself this way."

I tore the message into shreds. While I was doing so, Dougherty did an amazing thing. He simply vanished. I had looked away from him for no more than ten seconds. There was no one passing on the sidewalk, no traffic on the street. All I saw was pavement and trees and then just a glimpse of a black raincoat flying around the corner.

That was all. Perhaps I should have heeded my own advice. Forget everything. Clean slate. But sometimes, still, when we watch the first shadows of nightfall from the kitchen window, or when I hear a sudden crackle of dry leaves at the edge of the woods, I think of Dougherty. I see him jumping at the sound of the doorbell, glancing over his shoulder on the street, standing in the corner at a cocktail party, careful to keep his back to the wall, his frightened eyes surveying the room.

Odd, but of all the faces I do not want to see, his remains the clearest. It keeps me from being afraid.